BATTLETECH:
A BONFIRE OF WORLDS

BY STEVEN MOHAN, JR.

BATTLETECH: A BONFIRE OF WORLDS
By Steven Mohan, Jr.
Cover art by Marco Mazzoni
Cover design by David Kerber
Proofreading by Trendane Sparks

Printed in USA.

Published by Catalyst Game Labs,
an imprint of InMediaRes Productions, LLC
7108 S. Pheasant Ridge Drive • Spokane, WA 99224

For my wife Jo Anne,
who makes all good things possible.

Lost in the Night

"Devlin Stone's Republic was supposed to be humanity's last, best hope to free itself from the scourge of never-ending warfare. But as soon as the going got tough what happened? The verdammt *Republic crawled down a rabbit hole and pulled the opening in after them."*

—Archon Melissa Steiner, TBC Interview, 14 March 3136

PROLOGUE

SCOUT-CLASS JUMPSHIP *BRIGIT*
INTERSTELLAR SPACE NEAR YORII
REPUBLIC OF THE SPHERE
18 AUGUST 3136

Of all the treasures in the universe, the only thing Dr. Elgin Sawyer really wanted was answers.

Nothing else mattered. He was pushing ninety, his chocolate skin wrinkled and cracked from a lifetime spent beneath the sun of Lyons. The passing years had long ago banked the fires of his passion, arthritis kept him from his garden, and a growing silence stole the voices of his few surviving friends. He was old and alone.

Answers were all that was left to him.

So Sawyer stood in the small, darkened wardroom of the little starship *Brigit,* foot tucked into a steel loop welded to the deck, looking out at the stars. At Yorii.

At ten trillion kilometers, Yorii's sun was a diamond chip, scarcely brighter than the other stars sprinkled across the dark tapestry of space. But it *was* different, yes it was. It was still part of The Republic.

Lyons was not.

Yorii lay behind an invisible wall, a wall erected by The Republic's Exarch, Jonah Levin. The building of walls had long been a human strategy, probably since the first Cro-Magnon realized you could stack one stone atop another. The Chinese had built the Great Wall to hold back the barbarian hordes.

Hadrian had bisected Britannia with *his* wall. Walls had been used to stem unwanted immigration and deter terrorists.

Sometimes they even worked

If you didn't think about what happened to the people trapped on the other side.

A bitter smile twisted Sawyer's lips. Who would have ever thought Lyons would be jealous of Yorii? Yorii had been ravaged during the Jihad, and her wounds were still healing. Much of the planet's soil was cracked and poisoned, her riverbeds parched and clicking with radiation.

But Yorii's people were safe behind the wall.

"Why, Exarch?" he whispered. "Why did you leave us outside?"

It was the first of the questions he wanted answered.

He heard the distant sound of a hatch open and a pair of reflections appeared in the ferroglass. Sawyer touched his hearing aid, turning up reality's volume. "Yes?"

"*Hope*'s drive and battery are charged," said the young man. "We can go as soon as you give the word." Derrick Carter was twenty-seven and handsome: black hair cut short, eyes blue, strong jaw, a bright smile. He wore gray slacks and a dark blue polo shirt emblazoned with the Carter crest.

The woman standing next to him rolled her eyes.

"Cassandra?" said Sawyer softly.

Cassandra Holliman, *Brigit*'s captain, was a pretty woman in her forties, her auburn hair cut spacer short. She wore green coveralls. "The whole point in hanging out here was to monitor Yorii's broadcasts, learn something about Levin's wall. But we haven't learned a damned thing. We still don't know if—"

"And we'll never know," said Carter hotly, "if we never jump."

"Beware of brave nobles," Holliman shot back, "they're great for getting commoners killed."

"Enough," said Sawyer softly. It was his expedition, and that made it his headache. He sighed. Why had he let Nancy Carter put him in charge? College professors shouldn't be part of the grand sweep of history—they should *read* about the grand sweep of history. He was a damn fool to be out here. Becka would've talked him out of coming.

But Becka was dead.

And Felicia. And Trevor. And *their* kids. All killed in the last Falcon raid.

Sawyer turned back to look at Yorii.

As he watched, the JumpShip *Orphan's Hope* occulted the star. Sawyer could see the rounded bulb of *Hope*'s bow and her long, narrow body finally ending in a radial display of fins. Unlike little *Brigit, Hope* was a giant, a massive *Monolith,* her outline distended by DropShips: *Union*s and *Overlord*s and *Leopard CV*s.

Sawyer didn't expect his expedition to make planetfall, but every contingency had been planned for. A great host was embarked aboard the *Monolith* and her daughters: aerospace fighters and battlesuit infantry, armor and BattleMechs. Lyons had questions.

And they were going to insist on answers.

And yet, Sawyer still couldn't shake a feeling of doom. Since Levin had raised his terrible wall, no one who'd jumped into a Republic system had ever managed to jump back out again. Holliman's people crewed both JumpShips. She begged him with her eyes not to send them in.

Sawyer had no desire to send these people to their deaths. "Maybe—" he began.

"Malvina Hazen isn't going to stop," said Carter, his voice hard.

Malvina Hazen. Clan Jade Falcon. Sawyer saw the face of his dear Becka, the kids, his *grandbabies* for God's sake, all killed when a *Jagatai* had come down during the last Falcon raid, their deaths collateral to a monster's ambition. Someone had to make Levin explain why he'd abandoned the worlds outside the wall.

Someone had to make the man live up to his responsibilities.

"One hour." There was steel in Sawyer's voice. "And not a second longer."

One second *Orphan's Hope* was there, and the next she just—wasn't. A timer in the lower left corner of the *Brigit's* main viewscreen started counting down from one hour. Sawyer waited, strapped into a jump seat, staring at the flickering green numbers set against the background of stars.

For the entire hour, Sawyer and the bridge crew waited in silence, sweating, and staring at that screen. Until the numbers hit 0:00:00.0 and flickered from green to red. And started to count up. When the timer hit plus three minutes, Holliman cleared her throat. "Young Master Carter seems to be a bit tardy."

"Knew that kid couldn't tell time," said the navigator, and a titter of nervous laughter made its way around the bridge.

Sawyer said nothing.

The timer hit plus five minutes. Six. *Seven.*

"What are we going to do?" said the captain in a low voice.

"Whatever happened to the *Hope,*" murmured Sawyer, "we owe Lyons answers."

"What does that mean exactly?" asked the navigator.

"What is the distance to the pirate point?" asked Sawyer.

"The pirate point is the second gas giant's L4. It's four hundred forty-seven light hours from our present—" Holliman stopped. "Wait." Her voice was suddenly arctic. "You're not proposing we jump after them?"

"No," said Sawyer sadly. "I'm proposing we wait. For four hundred forty-seven hours."

6 SEPTEMBER 3136

Eighteen point six days had passed since *Hope* had jumped into the Yorii system, and Sawyer knew she wasn't coming back. It had seemed like such a simple plan. Jump into the outer system, gather intel on the wall, broadcast his world's plea for help, and then jump out again before they could be attacked.

What possibly could have gone wrong?

Lyons had to know. *He* had to know.

So he found himself again on *Brigit*'s bridge, watching numbers flicker and dance as they chased their way down to zero.

At minus two minutes, Holliman leaned towards him. "The timer accounts for the light speed lag between *Hope*'s theoretical insertion point and our position. There is always some jump variation so the true distance could vary by as much as—"

"It's fine," said Sawyer softly.

Time drained away to nothing and again, the numbers flashed red. Everyone turned to the communications officer, a narrow-faced man named Hill, with a shaved head and dark eyes. He shrugged, shook his head.

"Maybe *Hope* met with some kind of jump accident," said Holliman. "Pirate points can be..." Her voice trailed off.

The counter hit plus one.

Sawyer just stared at the diamond chip centered on the viewscreen.

"How long do we wait?" asked Hill quietly, dragging a hand over his smooth skull.

"As long as it takes," said Sawyer coldly.

"Sir," said Holliman gently. "If we haven't heard anything after an hour—"

"*No*," said Sawyer sharply. "We have to report to Lyons."

"*Hope* is lost," she shot back. "Isn't *that* worth reporting?"

"Listen—"Sawyer snarled, but he was interrupted by the crackle of static.

"Incoming message," shouted Hill. He looked up. "*Hope*'s call sign."

The image of Yorii was gone from the viewscreen, replaced by an electronic blizzard. Still, the picture was clear enough for Sawyer to see that something was horribly, horribly wrong.

Through the static he made out a bridge, *Hope*'s bridge. The right side had been smashed; chairs crushed flat, panels twisted into bizarre geometries, a shower of blue sparks spitting from a naked power coupling. Someone had splashed scarlet paint across the bridge, except Sawyer knew at once that it wasn't paint, it wasn't paint at all.

Despite all the damage done to the starboard half of the bridge, the port side was pristine. Untouched. It was as if some terrible line had cut through the *Hope*'s bridge, separating life from death.

And Derrick Carter had been standing in the bridge's center when it had hit.

Both sides of him looked fine, looked whole. But his two halves weren't quite...*aligned.* The right side of his face, it was *lower,* a centimeter *lower* than the left. His eyes were offset, his mouth a pair of gashes not quite touching, *there was a jog in his skull.*

"Derrick," Sawyer whispered, though of course the boy couldn't hear him.

"Doh not," croaked Carter with his two half-mouths, struggling to form the words, his grotesque face twisting with the effort. "Fall. Oh. Do *not.* Follow." He shook his funhouse-mirror head. "Don't. Know. How. But." He closed his mismatched eyes.

"Is. Hell."

And then the message cut out, replaced by a serene star field, Yorii at its center.

The shocked silence on the bridge of *Brigit* was absolutely complete.

In that moment, Dr. Elgin Sawyer realized that The Republic was simply *gone,* as surely as if God Himself had reached down and plucked it from the Inner Sphere.

And there would be no answers.

PART ONE

A Distant Howl

"Yesterday, AFNN received ComStar's First Quarter results. The communications giant reported its twenty-sixth consecutive quarter of red ink. Even more troubling, the company reported a seventy-eight percent spike in non-operating income from the sale of capital assets. The markets interpreted this fire sale as a sign that ComStar can't fix the HPG blackout. Our analysts predict stock prices will plummet across the Inner Sphere as the news radiates outward."

—Atreus Financial News Network, 25 April 3139

CHAPTER 1

Tucker Harwell worked alone in the small laboratory that was both his home and his cell. There wasn't much to the room: work bench, cot, a small, enclosed bathroom. The far wall was a mirror—so his captors could look in on him whenever they wanted. He didn't even have a light switch. For Tucker, it was always day.

His captors hadn't told him much about Luyten, the mysterious world that had become his prison, but it was clear that ComStar had once maintained a base here.

ComStar...or Word of Blake.

There had been some kind of battle, a battle that had scarred the world's face and smashed the network of satellites and habitats in low planetary orbit. No one had told Tucker this—but he'd surmised it. Adepts kept bringing him damaged devices—recorders, circuit boards, data cubes—a distressing percentage of them radioactive. The radiac on his workbench clicked merrily to itself as he worked, this time on an old, battered memory core.

ComStar had grown desperate, desperate enough to look for answers from its violent past.

The core was a small box, its black paint peeling, the screws holding the casing to the base plate rusted solid. He plugged the core into a power supply and inserted a probe in the dataport. He worked quickly and without hope. Whatever data the core had once held, it likely had been washed clean by decades of radiation exposure. He glanced at his noteputer and sighed. More wasted effort.

Unaccountably, the 'puter beeped.

Startled, Tucker glanced at the characters scrolling across the small screen:

CLARION C&+% PROTOX)MS WILL BE GNT+IATED ONLY ON 4#W #FCXERS OF GFD PRYK%NTOR MX*TIAL. MA@ T!E PR5CE OF %*AKE BE WITH YOU.

He blinked. Clarion? What the hell was Clarion? The first sentence was cryptic, but the second was clear enough. *May the peace of Blake be with you.* He shuddered.

"Problem, Tuck?"

Tucker jumped and wheeled around.

His sister leaned against the frame of his open door, arms folded across her chest. Her words were cheery, but there was no hint of good will on her face. There was nothing on her face. She wore the frozen expression of a mannequin.

Like Tucker, Patricia Harwell was slender, and she had the same black hair, though hers was straight and shoulder-length, while his was unruly and short. She was a couple centimeters shorter than he and more attractive, but the resemblance was unmistakable.

And they wore identical white uniforms.

But for all that, they weren't the same. Patricia was an advocate of old ComStar, what Tucker had come to think of as fundamentalist ComStar, the branch of the organization that had once metastasized into Word of Blake.

The Blakists believed the technical workings of interstellar communications were infused with mystical meaning and they worshiped ComStar's founder, Jerome Blake, as if he were a god. It was crazy—and scary. Scary because the Blakists believed so fervently in their cause that in its service they were willing to undertake any measure to spread their beliefs.

Any measure.

Most of the Inner Sphere believed the Blakists had been wiped out during the Jihad. Tucker had learned to his sorrow that this was not the case.

Tucker met Patricia's steady gaze. *Is this same girl I played freeze tag with in the back yard, the same girl who cried when Pepper the cat ran away, the same girl who taught her five-year-old brother to ride a two-wheeler?*

Where did the fanaticism come from? he thought. *The hatred?*

"Buhl wants to see you," she said.

"I'm working." He jerked his head at the core.

She stared at him, her face blank. And then she smiled, a bright smile that was somehow all the more disturbing for its warmth. She walked over to him and tousled his hair. "Don't worry, Tuck. You won't need that research. Because today's your big day."

Tucker frowned. "I don't understand."

She just laughed softly and walked out of the little room.

Tucker hurried to follow before the door closed and locked him in, knowing his sister wouldn't come back for him.

Patricia led him through a warren of hallways, up an elevator, through yet more hallways until they reached a pair of sliding glass doors that looked out on an open-air balcony. Tucker saw Precentor Malcolm Buhl sitting at a table splashed in sunlight, eating breakfast.

Patricia pushed through the doors and Tucker followed her out.

Where he could see the sky.

Luyten's sky was a shock of bright blue, a broad red sun crouched low on the horizon. A slash of silver cleaved the sky like a knife. So the world had a ring of debris in near orbit. How unusual.

Tucker suddenly felt cold. *They had let him see the sky.* They'd never let him see the sky before. A sky could be remembered, a sky could be used to ID a world's location, and Luyten's location was a secret.

His mouth tasted dry. There were only two kinds of people you shared secrets with. Those you trusted. And those who had short life expectancies.

"Please," said Buhl, "sit. Would you like something to eat?"

Tucker glanced at Buhl's breakfast: greasy bacon and hash browns swimming in egg yolk and curry. A wave of nausea washed over him. He swallowed hard and sat down. "No, thank you."

Patricia didn't sit, she leaned against the wall behind him, arms folded.

Buhl shrugged. He was a heavy man, bald on top, thin brown hair shadowing the sides of his skull. He sopped up curry with a piece of toast.

"So," said Buhl, "today we will test a new idea."

It was Tucker's turn to shrug.

"You don't seem excited," said Buhl, washing down his breakfast with iced coffee. "Let me explain the importance of this test. ComStar—" Buhl took another bite of toast. "—is a communications company. At least we were before Gray Monday."

Gray Monday. There wasn't a man or woman who served ComStar who didn't know what that term meant, and Tucker was no exception. Gray Monday. August 1, 3132. The day *someone* (no one knew who) used a computer virus and multiple terrorist attacks to take down more than eighty percent of the interstellar communications network. It was a disaster.

Until ComStar realized the virus prevented them from restoring the hyperpulse generators that were the backbone of the network.

Then it looked more like the end of civilization.

As system after system slipped into darkness, humanity turned into an unruly mob: scared, angry. Ready to kill.

"Naturally," said Buhl, "our revenue has dropped since the blackout began. We've hung on for seven long years." He shook his head. "But we cannot hold on forever. What the markets know is that we've sold holdings not related to our core communications business. What the markets do *not* know is that we've also been borrowing. In the next few years those loans are going to begin coming due."

"And you can't pay them back," guessed Tucker.

"We used voting rights as collateral," said Buhl softly. "If we default on these loans, we will start to lose control over ComStar itself."

Patricia's hard gaze was an itch in the back of Tucker's neck.

Buhl leaned forward. "But you, my boy, are our salvation. You're a genius."

Tucker said nothing. It occurred to him his life would have been simpler if he were *not* a genius. Certainly Buhl's faction wouldn't have kidnapped him if he'd been just another adept.

Buhl was still talking: "—child prodigy. First in your class at the DeBurke Institute. That's why I assigned you to the Wyatt HPG. And you didn't disappoint, my boy. You brought Wyatt up. You are the only person in the whole of the Inner Sphere who's managed to repair an infected HPG."

"Unfortunate that he hasn't been able to duplicate that effort," said Patricia coldly.

"Yes," said Buhl softly. "Unfortunate."

"So why didn't you bring up the Millungera HPG, Tuck?" Patricia smiled sweetly.

"T-the same approach on Wyatt—I mean the same *frequency,* um, it didn't work. I don't know why." He really didn't. And nothing made Tucker more uncomfortable than things he didn't understand. "If I could just have—"

"No need to worry," Buhl said smoothly. "Because we've found another approach. We haven't been able to eradicate the virus that caused the blackout. So we've come to the Polar Network solution, two brand new hyperpulse generators, one here and one on Mars, both of them built from scratch, every bolt, every capacitor, every circuit board assembled in brand new facilities. It cost billions of C-Bills, but we have allowed no vector for the contagion to infect this new network."

Buhl pushed his plate aside. "We must succeed *this* time. We are running out of chances." He peered at Tucker. "That's why you're going to bring up our new network."

"I'm ready to do whatever you wish, sir," said Tucker steadily.

"Are you, my boy?" asked Buhl softly. "I wonder. You see, I know you've been fighting us."

"Sir, I—"

The precentor held up his hand, and Tucker fell instantly silent.

Because what Buhl said was true. For four long years, Tucker Harwell had been playing a desperate game of delay and obfuscation. He inserted subtle errors in his notes. He dropped a word here, a phrase there, sending ComStar technicians scurrying down blind alleys, plumbing useless, esoteric theories. He told small, carefully crafted lies. Sometimes, when he was sure his captors wouldn't believe him, he told the truth.

And now that they knew, what else could he say?

"So," said Buhl. "If the Polar Network fails..." He smiled faintly and shook his head.

Tucker felt Patricia's hand on his shoulder, and he stood. And why not? There was nothing else Buhl needed to say.

His meaning had been perfectly clear.

Patricia stopped in front of the entrance to Tucker's lab. His *cell.* He expected her to open the door, but she didn't. Instead, she said, "I have one more thing for you to think about, brother. Yes, Buhl will have your head if the Polar Network fails. But consider, what will happen if the test *succeeds?*"

"ComStar will have the template for restoring the HPG network."

"That's right." She flashed him a tight smile. A triumphant smile. "And then, all of a sudden, we'll have no need for boy geniuses."

Tucker blinked. He'd always known Patricia would hurt him if her duty required it, but he suddenly saw she was just willing to. *She wanted to.* At that moment, something inside him broke.

"Patricia," he whispered.

She laughed and it sounded brittle. "So, the genius finally understands."

Tucker stared at her for a long moment and then he drew a deep, shuddery breath. "You are my sister. I love you. I *love* you. Whatever—" He swallowed had. "Whatever you do to me. I want you to know. I want you to *remember.* I forgive you."

Her face softened and the cold gleam in her eyes seemed to fade away. "Oh, Tucker," she whispered. "Oh, Tuck." She smiled sadly and shook her head. "But I don't forgive *you.*"

Tucker's jaw sagged open.

Her eyes narrowed. "It's always came so easily for you," she snarled. "*You.* Who are a heretic. Your sins stain me, brother. *Me,* who has always faithfully walked the path set out by the great Blake."

"Patricia, I never meant—"

"It's too late, Tucker," she said coldly, opening the door with an electronic key. "You'll get no absolution from me."

And then she shoved him into his little prison and closed the door.

Tucker was so upset by his sister's words that it was full minute before he realized the battered memory core was missing.

The HPG's control room was a study in understated elegance. The space was fifteen meters in diameter reaching up to a domed ceiling. Consoles and computer equipment ringed the room. Executive chairs fashioned from hand-tooled brown leather sat in front of the consoles, each occupied by a technician in a dazzling white uniform. The floor was black granite, polished to a high sheen. Tucker glanced down and saw himself looking back up.

It was like looking in a dark mirror.

In the center of the room was the HPG core, a stem that passed through the domed ceiling and opened into a flower fifty meters across, the business end of the hyperpulse generator. It was the antenna that would rip a hole in spacetime and broadcast a message that would be instantly received by a station orbiting *another star.* Beneath the floor, a dedicated fusion reactor provided the tremendous power the process required.

But none of it was possible without the core. Inside the steel cylinder, the core was a maze of branching circuits linking germanium processors to shielded magnetic coils. It was the most sophisticated piece of technology in human space.

And like everything else in the room, it was brand new.

Tucker crossed the dark floor to the core. He wore gloves that prevented any electrostatic discharge that might damage the core's intricate circuits. For a moment he considered taking the gloves off—but, no, Buhl's people were watching his every move.

He reached out and touched the core's metallic surface. He remembered how it had felt to touch the core on Wyatt: like he was touching the beating heart of interstellar civilization. But that's not how it felt today.

Today it just felt cold.

Tucker let out a deep breath and turned. Six meters from the core, centered on a dais, there was a chair.

Like a man going to the gallows, Tucker marched to the chair and sat down.

He reached up and rubbed his neck. To his watchers it must've looked like Tucker was trying to relieve the tension in his muscles. But what he was really doing was brushing the tips of his fingers against a tiny dot of metal hidden on the inside of his high collar.

What he was really doing was taking strength from wherever he could find it.

The little piece of jewelry was a Knight Errant's rank pip, given to him by Alexi Holt on Wyatt, a parting gift as Patricia and the Com Guards took Tucker away. He thought of it as a promise, a promise that Alexi and The Republic hadn't forgotten him.

It had been four years, and so far that promise hadn't turned out to be worth much. But Tucker hadn't abandoned the tiny sliver of hope the pip represented. It was foolish to hope The Republic would come for him.

But sometimes a foolish hope was better than none at all.

"Preparing initiation sequence," someone said.

Tucker glanced at the master control board, watching the HPG come to life.

"Eighty-two percent," said the adept at the secondary control station. What was her name? *Wharton.* She frowned. "I'm getting flux in the primary hyperspace coil. Variance of three percent. Five. Six."

It was a little high, but Tucker wasn't worried. This core was free from the virus that infected the rest of the network. Which was why he'd finally run out of options. Even if he committed some last desperate act of sabotage, it wouldn't matter. They'd just kill him and try again. Either way, the Polar Network was going to work.

Despite Tucker's best efforts, Buhl's technicians had hit upon a strategy that would certainly defeat the persistent virus everyone knew was causing the blackout. Instead of trying to fix the existing network, they would rebuild it. The strategy was horrifically expensive—but that scarcely mattered. If ComStar was to survive as an organization it had to bring the network back up, no matter the cost.

Buhl would become Primus. No doubt an accomplishment of this magnitude would give him the power to push aside Primus Koenigs-Cober. He would rule ComStar, returning the organization to its techno-religious roots. Which way would First Precentor Brian May jump? Did it even matter? He would either adopt the new order or he would be swept aside. Word of Blake would be reborn.

The last time the Blakists had been unleashed, they'd plunged the Inner Sphere into an unholy jihad that had killed billions. Whole worlds had been sterilized. Realms shattered. Death and destruction on a scale never seen before or since.

And this time, the heirs to the Blakist tradition were rising in a universe where The Republic had disappeared. Tucker saw a tide of darkness washing over humanity.

And it would begin in this room.

"Adjust beta coil plus-five megajoules," Tucker ordered, trying to balance the primary coil, at once protecting the core...and the wicked future struggling to be born.

He glanced at Buhl who was sitting, watching him, his face a fat mask of pinched concern. Patricia stood next to him, arms folded across her chest, nothing, absolutely *nothing,* on her face.

"Flux level, holding at seven," reported secondary control. "We're in the pipe."

Tucker listened to all the controllers run through their statuses, all of them reporting go. So he had no choice.

How did I let it come to this?

He swallowed in a dry mouth and said, "Begin sequence alpha one. Engage."

To his left, Buhl leaned forward.

"Test Packet Release," called out the woman at secondary control. They had pinged the other pole of the new network. Buhl smiled.

Suddenly an indicator flickered from green to yellow. Flux was climbing in the primary coil.

Again. Tucker stood, his hands balled into fists. *I've seen this before,* he thought. *But it's impossible.*

There is no virus here.

Flux was climbing faster. *Eight nine ten.*

"Shut it down," Tucker croaked.

"Do not obey that order!" Buhl roared, launching to his feet.

Twelve fifteen nineteen.

Tucker's eyes were locked on the flux indicator. It flickered yellow to red. "We're going to lose the—"

"Adept Harwell is relieved," Buhl shouted. He pointed at the woman at secondary control. "Adept Wharton, take over and—"

"Cascade!" she shouted. "Generation rate is thousands— no, *millions* per second!"

Buhl's eyes were wide. "Shut it down. *Shut it—*"

But it was too late. All the screens went dark, and the *hum* of the core suddenly dropped out. The room settled into a terrible, terrible silence.

Tucker stood, staring at the blank displays. The Polar Network had failed.

But that is impossible.

CHAPTER 2

KEFALCZYK HUNTING PRESERVE, NEW GREENLAND
REPUBLIC OF KASNOV-GREENLAND
NEW OLYMPIA
FREE WORLDS LEAGUE
23 SEPTEMBER 3139

The sheer savagery of Clan Wolf's attack made the raging inferno look like sanctuary. Like all MechWarriors, General Dmitar Todorov of the New Olympia Home Guard feared heat, but the Wolves were cutting his people to pieces. So to escape the blizzard of jeweled beams before him, he had to embrace the conflagration behind.

He backstepped into fire.

Todorov felt the control sticks of his *Patriot* grow sluggish in his hands as he cleared the Central Island Highway. For a moment, just a moment, he saw a brown *Ryoken* framed in angry orange fire. He dropped his reticle over the Wolf machine and pulled into his main trigger.

A jagged shard of azure lightning tore into the fire and a wave of terrible heat blasted through Todorov's cockpit, searing his lungs and flash-drying the sweat that sheened his skin. What damage, if any, he'd done to the *Ryoken* he did not know.

But he was willing to spend the heat on the shot anyway, if only to encourage the Wolves to join him in the burning forest.

Most MechWarriors would think twice about charging an enemy who was shooting at them from the heart of hell. Not the Wolves, though.

They'd look on it as an invitation.

Todorov staggered back through the conflagration, surrounded by the sharp *pop* of exploding trees, pines and firs going up like Roman candles, hungry yellow flames racing through the underbrush. He heard the freight train roar of the fire even through his sound-insulated cockpit. He'd ordered his troops to fire the forest as they withdrew, and they'd followed his orders to the letter.

His *Patriot* moved slowly, burdened by the terrible heat load, but as soon as his heavy particle projection cannon recycled he fired again, aiming blindly into the inferno ahead.

Just to remind the Wolves he was still there.

He glanced down at his rear-view strip and saw daylight through the blaze. He gritted his teeth. *Almost there.*

And still no sign of the Wolves.

He stepped his machine back and finally found himself clear of the inferno. His *Patriot* stood in a blackened no-man's land between the fire and the forest's green heart, a hundred meters of felled timber and cut brush, all of it burned to charcoal. The Home Guard Medusas who'd survived the brutal Wolf assault waited for him there. Their machines were painted like his: forest camo marked with a snake-headed Gorgon.

There's too few of them, Todorov thought. A battalion whittled down to four bloodied lances.

He caught movement in the trees behind him and saw a *Warhammer IIC* move out of the forest, the great machine shouldering aside a Scotch pine as it stepped out into the open. The tree, which barely overtopped the 'Mech, cracked and fell as the *Warhammer* pushed it aside.

The assault machine was a humanoid design, its arms ending in a pair of PPCs, the cockpit where the head should be, a pair of box launchers perched on its broad shoulders, a fusion reactor as its beating heart.

BattleMechs were the lords of the Thirty-Second century battlefield. Reaching heights of ten meters or more, heavily armed and armored, nothing could challenge a BattleMech—except another BattleMech. The *Warhammer* was a particularly lethal example of the breed—eighty tons of destruction waiting, *begging,* to be unleashed.

"Soon enough," Todorov whispered.

Like the Medusas, the *Warhammer* was turned out in forest camo—but the emblem painted on its chest was different. The great machine bore a purple Marik eagle, its head wreathed by five silver stars—one for each of the planets of the Covenant worlds when the tiny nation had been taken into the League.

The *Warhammer* belonged to the First Covenant Guards.

As Todorov watched, more machines emerged from hiding: an *Ostroc,* a *Hatchetman,* two *Spiders*, an SM1 Destroyer. A reinforced battalion of the best troops the Free Worlds League could put on the battlefield. Enough raw power to wipe the Second Wolf Assault Cluster right out of existence.

New Olympia was a little world, a stepping-stone to grander places. There was no reason for the Wolves to expect there'd be anything here other than planetary militia. And so far, that's all they'd seen.

That was about to change.

Warden-General Thaddeus Marik stepped his *Warhammer* into the clearing, waiting for the Wolves to come.

The no-man's land had been rapidly cleared by a corps of civilian workers when the Wolf DropShips were still racing in from the zenith jump point, so the retreating Marik force would be able to fire the forest without burning the whole of it down. And so now the First Covenant Guards stood clear of the fire, fresh and unburdened by heat load. The Clanners would emerge sluggish and hot, slow and bewildered, and the Free Worlders would pick them off one by one.

Jessica had been against allowing her Warden-General— and incidentally, her husband—from leading this mission, but as a former paladin of the Republic, Thaddeus was used to using either diplomacy or force of arms to solve problems—

sometimes both at the same time. That wasn't the argument that had won Jessica over, of course. Nothing moved Captain-General Jessica Halas-Hughes Marik save for the cold logic of need.

And right now the League's need could be summed up in precisely two words.

Alaric Wolf.

The first Alaric history remembered had been the barbarian king of the Visigoths and an enemy of Rome. *That* Alaric had sundered a mighty empire.

It was an uncomfortable parallel.

The Free Worlds League looked like a tipped-over "C." The bowl of the "c" was a thin bridge that connected the League's two main bodies. If the Wolf advance continued, they'd cut the League in two *and* threaten Atreus.

Alaric *had* to be stopped.

Unfortunately, that was easier said than done. He'd crushed every commander Jessica had sent against him. (And all of Anson Marik's commanders before that.) Which was why Thaddeus was here now. Because Jessica needed a victory more than she needed a husband.

In the privacy of his cockpit, Thaddeus allowed himself a sardonic smile. Well, if something *did* happen to him, at least he'd left Jessica his name.

He centered his targeting cross hairs over the burning forest, waiting for the Wolves to emerge.

Except they didn't.

It's been too long. He glanced down. The fire was playing hell with his thermal sensors, but his MAD gear showed the Wolves moving north along the highway, angling to cut the militia off before they could reach their base near the aerospace academy.

The Wolves had neatly side-stepped the trap.

Thaddeus watched the blips on his screen racing north and clenched his jaw. And then he saw it.

Racing.

The Wolves were running.

Which meant they'd left their slower units behind.

He pulled up a map. The Wolf DropShip had set down to the west, along the coast. Alaric would be south of the forest and of the Captive River, moving his wounded and his slow units, his assaults and heavies, back to the *Overlord.* He'd hop north and link up with his fast movers to crush the militia he expected to find emerging from the forest's northern edge. It was a beautiful plan.

Except Thaddeus saw what was coming.

A cool breeze rippled across thigh-high grass shading the crest of a low hill. Generous spring rains had nourished the grass; it was lush and dark. *Thick.* It was nearly impossible to see the man hidden in that grass, lying prone, binoculars pressed to his face. The man's coveralls, his face paint, even the binoculars, exactly matched the color of the grass. He had to be careful.

If the Wolves caught him, it would mean his life.

The man called himself Samuel Bone, but the name was like the camo—a means to remain hidden, and nothing more.

Bone's vantage afforded him a beautiful view of the muddy brown Captive River and the forest to the north, but right now he had his binoculars turned to the east where he could see part of the Wolf force moving south of the river, heading west, toward their waiting DropShip.

He set the binoculars down and slowly exhaled. Glanced at the forest.

And caught the glint of sunlight on glass.

Bone jerked his binoculars up, flashing on something hidden in the darkness between the trees. It faded back into the shadows before he could ID it, but one thing was certain.

It was big.

Thaddeus watched twenty-two Clan BattleMechs and vehicles slog across the riparian grassland south of the river. His force wasn't any faster than the Wolf heavy hitters, but he had angled through the forest.

Giving him time to set a trap.

The Clan machines were painted the dark brown of a wild wolf's coat, but with molten orange highlights, to remind their enemies that these Wolves breathed fire. The colors of the Wolves' Beta Galaxy.

Best of all, a *Mad Cat IV* led the long column of machines.

Alaric.

At 75 tons, the *Mad Cat* massed nearly as much as Thaddeus's *Warhammer. Mad Cat* was an Inner Sphere designation. The Clans had another name for this fearsome machine.

Timber Wolf.

Although this *Timber Wolf* was of the *Savage* variety. The pilot sat in a sleek, rounded cockpit perched atop two back-bent legs. A pair of lasers extended from the cockpit like arms and missile pods sat above the pilot, right and left. The *Mad Cat* looked like it was crouching, eager for a fight.

Which made it the perfect machine for Alaric Wolf.

Thaddeus would never get a better chance to defeat the commander of Clan Wolf's Beta Galaxy.

The Wolf forces were divided, giving Thaddeus a decisive advantage. The Wolves had brought four Trinaries to New Olympia, but Alaric only had his command Trinary with him, plus whichever machines were too slow or too hurt to run north. Thaddeus had a full battalion, plus the surviving Medusas in reserve. He had Alaric better than two-to-one, and he had surprise.

Would it be enough?

The ferocity of Alaric Wolf was legendary. Even outnumbered, the Wolves were dangerous prey. He needed another advantage.

The Warden-General's eyes marked the terrain. *The river.* The Captive River was a broad, slow meander colored brown by tannins and mud. Some said it got its name from its languid, swirling current that captured small boats and spun them around. Others said the name came from the colony's earliest days, when prisoners were transported on the river.

If they could fight their way to the Captive, it would serve as a massive heat sink, improving his units' heat loads. Thaddeus nodded.

It would be enough.

Bone felt the movement before he saw it, a deep bass rumble transmitted through the earth, a heavy vibration he felt in his chest and his legs. A massive 'Mech stepped out of the woods, a *Warhammer,* marked in— Shock wrenched a gasp from his chest. *That's Thaddeus Marik's 'Mech.*

This planet was supposed to be guarded by militia only. Where the hell had the First Covenant Guards come from?

He pressed a red button on the binoculars, setting the digital device to *RECORD.*

The *'Hammer* fired an alpha strike. The sizzle of the paired PPC beams missed the Clan *Mad Cat* close right, but the advanced tactical missiles smashed into Alaric's rounded cockpit, rocking his machine and starring his canopy.

Bone's grip on his binoculars tightened.

Marik machines were boiling out of the forest: an *Ostroc,* an *Albatross,* a *Cougar,* two *Spiders,* SM1s, conventional armor.

Bone saw the danger right away. The Free Worlders outnumbered the Wolves and they'd just gotten the first punch in for free. If they could gain the river, they'd add heat to their list of advantages. Next to enemy fire, nothing was more dangerous to a BattleMech than heat. Heat could slow you down or lock you up. Heat could roast a pilot alive in his cockpit. So the river was a key tactical advantage.

And the Wolves were giving ground.

Paired shards of blue lightning slashed past Alaric's right side and then it was raining missiles. Orange fire sheeted across his canopy as the ATMs rippled across the sheet of feroglass shielding him. Multiple concussions shook his cockpit, slamming him back in his command couch, the straps of his five-point safety harness biting into his flesh. He tasted blood. For a moment, the world was tinged with gray. Alaric took an unsteady step forward.

Neg.

I will NOT *yield.*

Clenching his teeth, Alaric side-stepped right, loosing a one-two missile strike at the *Warhammer* and then splitting his shot, slicing into the *Ostroc* coming up on the *Warhammer*'s left with emerald fire, melting composite armor across the heavy 'Mech's broad chest.

The *Ostroc* quickly backstepped out of Alaric's field of fire.

In the brutal heat of his cockpit, a smile flickered across Alaric's handsome face.

He pivoted and stalked left, firing at the *Warhammer* on the move.

It was then he saw the emblem on the assault machine's chest. On a planet that was supposed to offer no more serious opposition than local militia, his troops faced the First Covenant Guards.

It is a trap.

They have sent Thaddeus Marik against me, Alaric thought. *The finest warrior in all the Free Worlds League.*

It was at once a dishonorable trick and a gesture of respect.

And Alaric would make the Free Worlds League pay for both the trick *and* the gesture.

His radio crackled and Verena's calm voice filled his cockpit. "Galaxy Commander, Shadow Two. They are pressing on our left."

Pressing on our left.

Verena had once been a mere bondsman, a captured enemy taken as one of the spoils of war. But in the last few months she had grown into something more, proving her mettle as a Wolf warrior. She would not be calling for help unless her side of the line was nearly ready to snap under the weight of superior enemy numbers.

The two forces faced each other in two long lines abreast, the Free Worlders north of the river and the Wolves south. Outnumbered and outgunned, most commanders would have formed their troops up in a column, set a rear guard, and ordered a fighting withdrawal.

Alaric was not most commanders.

He toggled the all-unit frequency. "All Wolves, fall back fifty meters and reform your lines."

As he backstepped, Alaric traded blows with the *Warhammer*, tearing into the Marik machine with his lasers, scorching the machine's camouflage paint and melting the armor underneath.

The *Warhammer* answered with its own mix of lightning and thunder, melting and smashing armor along Alaric's left leg. His wireframe schematic flickered green to yellow to red.

You will not beat me, Thaddeus Marik, Alaric thought fiercely. *You will not.*

His Wolves fell back.

Strapped into the cockpit of his *Savage Wolf,* Alaric looked little different than the average Clanner. His shoulder-length blond hair was tucked beneath his neurohelmet, the muscles and scars won by a lifetime of fighting hidden beneath his cooling vest.

Only the terrible intensity of his glacial blue eyes hinted that he might be something more.

If others did not know him, did not see his true nature, this did not bother Alaric. In fact, he worked hard to make it so. It was always easier to strike an enemy down from the shadows.

And there was no aspect of Alaric's life not governed by the love of combat.

So Spheroids saw him as brutal and dull—not knowing he had taken his political training from the most powerful despot the Inner Sphere had ever known. His fellow Clanners saw him as enigmatic; talented, yes, but unable to win a Bloodname—not knowing that Alaric was biding his time, waiting for the perfect moment to step forward and claim his true legacy. The leadership of Clan Wolf saw him as a distasteful genetic experiment masquerading as a son of House Ward, an experiment that one day might have to be put down.

Not knowing that the experiment had already proven successful

No living human being, *no one,* knew all that Alaric was. Those who *had* taken his full measure had paid for that knowledge with their lives.

And today it would be Thaddeus Marik's turn to discover the true Alaric Wolf.

Alaric gritted his teeth, fighting to hold his reformed skirmish line. The Spheroids were pushing his people back, manhandling the Wolves by shear dint of numbers, driving for the river and the heat advantage it offered. There was just no way to stop them.

As Alaric watched, the great *Warhammer* waddled into the muddy water. Steam rose, carrying away the assault 'Mech's heat load.

His command Trinary was doomed.

A grim smile touched the lips of Alaric Wolf.

Just as he had planned.

Thaddeus dropped his cross-hairs over the *Mad Cat*'s cockpit and fired. A double flight of missiles scoured the Clan machine, followed by the whipcrack of his PPCs.

Almost instantly, the river carried away the heat spike.

"It's finally over," Thaddeus whispered. The Wolf offensive was going to die on this world. *Right now.* All along the river his troops tore into the retreating Wolves.

Suddenly the Wolves stopped. And then they surged forward, charging into the teeth of the Free Worlders' withering fire.

It was a desperate maneuver, one for which the Clanners would dearly pay.

Thaddeus's crosshairs blinked gold over the *Mad Cat.*

He pulled into his trigger—

Just as the death rattle of an autocannon joined the fray, shells smashing into his back, carving away armor and throwing his PPC strike wide of the *Mad Cat.*

He glanced down at his rearview strip and his guts turned to ice.

A brown SM1 Destroyer tore into his weak rear armor with its Ultra AC/20. It was flanked by a *Raven,* an *Ocelot,* and Elementals boiled out from between the tree like armored ants. The Wolf fast-movers were emerging from the forest.

The move to the north had only been a feint. *They'd circled back through the forest.*

It's a trap.

Alaric's surge had pinned the Free Worlders in place so the balance of the Wolf force could hit them from behind.

Thaddeus staggered right, fighting the mud that swirled around his 'Hammer's legs, trying to get clear of the SM1's fire while beating back the *Mad Cat*, but the water kept him from really *moving.* The Destroyer kept on his back, hammering away chunks of armor.

Thaddeus's wireframe flashed yellow to red.

"Covenant Actual, Covenant Two. Can't hold, can't hold."

"Stand your ground," snarled Thaddeus from between clenched teeth.

Captain Ramirez would have none of it. "Lost Jones, Palenti, and Nguyen. They're cutting us to rib—"

"*Hold your position!*" Thaddeus roared. He didn't have anything better to tell Two Company's commander.

There weren't any other options.

His eyes flickered right, looking for help. He flashed on a Covenant *Spider* staggering left, just as an Elemental's missile smashed into its back. The light 'Mech shuddered, a sure sign of gyroscope damage.

No help there.

He put a flight of missiles into the *Mad Cat* and followed with a PPC strike. "Damn it, back off," he whispered between clenched teeth, "*Back off.*"

He shrugged left, buying a second's respite. Glanced down. *There.* Had to pull Three Company together with the Medusas, concentrate fire and punch through the Wolf line. If they could break out, maybe they could wheel and hit the—

Thaddeus suddenly heard the deep *crump* of Wolf artillery, the shrill whistle of a deadly rain. He glanced right in time to see the *Spider* with the damaged gyroscope stagger clear of the harassing infantry.

Then go down *hard.*

The BattleMech crashed to the earth with the terrible shriek of rending metal. The aftershock of the *Spider*'s death reverberated through the earth's flesh, shook Thaddeus's *Warhammer,* buzzed in his bones.

There had been a shadow, the merest blink of a falling *something,* and then it was like an invisible hand had smashed the BattleMech.

Thaddeus had grown up hunting deer on his father's lands. Once, when he'd been nine, he'd seen a five-point white-tail buck charging cross a grassy clearing at full gallop, the rhythm of its hoof-beats rising up into a blue, blue autumn sky.

Then Thaddeus had pulled the trigger.

The sharp *crack* of the rifle had filled the world and the buck had just *collapsed,* so fast it seemed like the two events happened at exactly the same time.

Just like the *Spider.*

It had just *dropped.*

Thaddeus turned his eyes front, his mouth suddenly dry. Shells punched holes in the muddy river, sending fountains of angry white water geysering into the air. Shells slammed into the riverbank, gouging craters out of the soft earth and kicking up brown clouds of debris. Thaddeus couldn't see. His machines, the Wolves, they were all barely visible shadows hidden behind a screen of dust, shells exploding all around him again and again, shaking his 'Mech, his whole world that brutal sound. League machines slogged desperately through water and mud, trying to scramble free of the thunder hammering down all around them.

The Wolves had turned the wide, slow river into a killing field.

Out of the corner of his eye Thaddeus saw the shape of General Todorov's *Patriot* stop and *jerk,* its arms flying wide like a man shot in the back. The great machine toppled forward. For just a moment it looked like a corpse floating face down in the river, and then it sank out of sight.

Alaric had rushed forward to pin the League machines, and so the barrage was falling among the Wolves too, but it didn't seem to matter. The Wolf *Uller* to the *Mad Cat's* left was suddenly battered to the ground by the horror of falling shells.

Alaric didn't even *flinch*.

He just stood there, pouring hellish energies into Thaddeus's chest armor. Molten metal ran down the *Warhammer*'s chassis, sizzling and popping as it hit the water.

A militia *Cougar* broke first, bolting for the forest. A dozen emerald and ruby beams impaled the fleeing 'Mech. One moment the *Cougar* was a war machine of the New Olympia Home Guard.

The next it was a sphere of golden light and the roar of terrible, catastrophic destruction.

Thaddeus blinked away red after-images. The *Cougar* was just *gone*.

Nothing to mark the fact that it had ever existed except for a blackened crater.

And at that moment, Thaddeus Marik realized the Captain-General would have neither her victory nor her husband.

Bone watched Alaric cut into the *Warhammer*'s cockpit with the emerald fire of his lasers, burning the Warden-General of the Free Worlds League down to atoms. All along the length of the Captive River, trapped Free Worlders were dying as the Wolves fell upon them.

Only seconds before, the Wolves had faced certain defeat. And then Alaric had turned defeat into brutal victory. What Bone had just seen confirmed what he'd already believed.

Galaxy Commander Alaric Wolf could not be stopped.

That's when Samuel Bone put away his binoculars.

He'd seen all he needed to see.

CHAPTER 3

The first thing Tucker Harwell thought was, *I don't want to die in Buhl's office.*

The Precentor's desk was antique cherry wood backed by a matching credenza. A black leather sofa in front of the desk sat across from two steel-frame chairs. But the office's most impressive feature was its ferroglass walls. Since Buhl's office sat atop the planet's highest tower, it felt like they were meeting in the sky.

The *sky.* Tucker hadn't seen it once in four years, and now he'd seen it twice in a week.

It was a beautiful office, to be sure, he just didn't want it to be the last place he ever saw.

The next thing Tucker thought was, *they'll never execute me here. You just can't get blood out. They'd have to replace the carpet.* And then: *I'm in trouble if the next meeting's in a room with tile.*

Or if Buhl's thinking of redecorating.

And then he thought, *none of this is funny. They're going to kill me. They're really going to kill me. So why does it all seem so hilarious?*

Fortunately, Buhl didn't *look* like he was thinking of redecorating. Buhl looked like he was thinking of having a stroke. The Precentor's head was an unhealthy shade of pink sheened with sweat, and he didn't seem to be blinking. He paced back and forth between the sofa and the chairs.

Patricia, on the other hand, looked perfectly calm. She sat next to Tucker on the sofa, her legs daintily crossed, her hands resting neatly in her lap.

Buhl jabbed a meaty finger in Tucker's face. "*You destroyed my core.*"

"I tried to save your core," said Tucker reasonably. "You were the one who insisted on keeping it on line."

"You *sabotaged* it!" Buhl roared. "When we weren't watching, you *sabotaged* it!"

And right then Tucker realized he had the power to save the entire Inner Sphere. It was like a bucket of ice water in the face. No longer was he a ludicrous character in a cruel farce. Suddenly he had a *choice.* And that made it, all of it, *real.*

He started to sweat.

He could save humanity with a single word. And that word was "yes." "Yes," he could say, "I *did* sabotage your core." Buhl would have him executed, and that would leave ComStar with no one with the gifts needed to unravel the mystery of the blackout—at least not in the time the organization had left to it. The company would collapse and would be taken over by its creditors, and Buhl and the last vestiges of Word of Blake would be buried beneath the wreckage.

All he had to do was say "yes."

Except he suddenly found he couldn't do it. It wasn't because he feared death—oh, he did—but if he could save billions of lives by sacrificing himself, he'd do it. It wasn't the prospect of oblivion that stopped him.

It was the puzzle. There was a puzzle here, and the failure of the Polar Network was a crucial clue. Tucker just couldn't leave a puzzle unsolved.

He just couldn't.

He would just untangle this last knot for himself. Yes, that's what he'd do. He wouldn't tell anyone the answer. Certainly not *Buhl.* It would be his last gift to himself before they killed him. Just this one last puzzle.

So he cleared his throat and said, "You know that's not true. I had no chance to sabotage your core—and if you think I'm lying, go back and look at the security tapes."

Buhl stopped and gave Tucker a long, hard look. Then he started pacing again. "We've been poring over data for a week, and we still don't understand." He glared at Tucker. "I suppose *you* think you know what happened."

Patricia looked up at him curiously.

Tucker licked his lips. "I know what *didn't* happen," he said slowly.

Buhl folded his arms across his chest and narrowed his eyes.

"Look, you took extraordinary efforts to keep the Polar Network clear of the virus. Any chance they didn't work?"

"No," said Buhl coldly.

"Then it can't be the virus."

Buhl and Patricia stared at him blankly.

"Think," said Tucker, "We've scrubbed millions of lines of code looking for the virus, we've spent hundreds of man-years checking and rechecking the network, and then you gave up and rebuilt everything from scratch. *And it still doesn't work.*"

"Wow," said Patricia flatly, "you really *are* a genius."

"Don't you see?" said Tucker. "We've spent so much time investigating the signal and we've found *nothing.* Maybe it's not the wave, but the *water.*"

"I don't follow," said Buhl slowly.

"I'm talking about the *medium.* If nothing's wrong with the signal, there must be something wrong with the *medium.*"

Buhl's face contorted into a question. "You think there's something wrong with...*hyperspace?* What kind of phenomenon could possibly affect hyperspace?"

"I don't know," said Tucker, "but—"

"And JumpShips travel through hyperspace," said Patricia. "If it had been altered somehow, why would they still be able to travel between the stars?"

Tucker licked his lips. "I—" He shook his head. "I don't know.

Buhl and Patricia stared at him stonily and Tucker suddenly realized it hadn't mattered what he'd said, after all. Because this was one puzzle he was never going to get the chance to solve.

UNION-CLASS DROPSHIP ARCHON'S GLORY
ZENITH JUMP POINT, AUTUMN WIND
WOLF OCCUPATION ZONE
7 OCTOBER 3139

Alaric Wolf reached for the handhold mounted in the overhead and flung his body forward, grunting with the effort, his teeth bared. He shot down the passageway, well ahead of his Elemental escort.

Most flatlanders had difficulty with weightlessness. Not Alaric. He applied the same intensity to the exercise of moving through zero gee that he brought to every challenge he faced.

He made a savage grab for the next handhold. Keeping his body straight so he did not careen into the overhead, he threw himself forward, gaining still more speed.

Speed speed speed.

All he wanted was speed.

There was a starboard turn up ahead. Alaric reached for the next handhold, this time using the strength in his arms to roll his body over and send it hurtling down the side passageway. Pain lanced through his arms as they took the force of the turn. He snarled at the pain.

But he gave up not a particle of speed.

The Elementals followed behind him without a sound.

The woman stood in the wardroom looking out at the vastness of space, her polished white boots tucked beneath a steel rod set ten centimeters above the deck. She wore white coveralls, a concession to practicality. Her hair was the color of straw and it reached nearly to her waist. She had braided it, weaving white silk ribbons into the braid every few centimeters. In space, long hair was impractical, and in some circumstances, actually dangerous.

Alaric realized the ribbons were not mere decoration—they were tethers that anchored her long braid to her coveralls, so it seemed to hang naturally. That was the essence of Katrina Steiner.

Pragmatism and vanity woven together into a dangerous whole.

"I read your report on New Olympia's conquest," she said softly, not turning. "It is an important world."

Alaric studied his reflection in the viewport's ferroglass surface. Like Katrina, he was slender. And he was not especially tall. (*That* had come from his father's genetic heritage, he was sure.) Strong jaw, cheeks blooming red with exertion, a helmet of lank blond hair that hung down even with his chin. (He did not share Katrina's vanity.) His body bore the marks of violence, scarred knuckles, a knotted rope of tissue along his right arm, a small crescent scar shadowing his left orbit.

Intense blue eyes.

He realized he was not smiling. Alaric rarely smiled, but it was a mistake to sulk in Katrina Steiner's presence. He quirked his lips into a grin. Maybe she had missed his lapse.

She turned, her blue eyes locked on his face. Her face was lined with the passage of many years, but she still possessed a trace of her former beauty.

And she was still dangerous.

"New Olympia *must* be important—considering what you risked to win it."

"I destroyed Thaddeus Marik." said Alaric carefully. "That defeat will break the League's spirit. Is not such a victory worth the risk?"

Katrina stared at him for a long moment. "I am sorry. Here I am lecturing you about trifles when clearly you are angry."

"I am not angry," said Alaric evenly.

"I am not angry—" said Katrina, imitating him perfectly, but drawing out the last word to indicate that something should come after.

"I am not angry." Alaric drew a breath. "Mother."

Katrina smiled at her little victory. "But you are, my son. I see it in the blood in your face, in the beads of sweat at your hairline. I saw it when you failed to smile at me."

Alaric said nothing. In his whole life he had never given ground to anyone. But no one had ever defeated him half so much as this woman.

"You are angry because at the very moment Atreus lies within your grasp, you are called away to confer with Khan Ward. And worse yet. *His Spheroid allies.* Glory awaits and instead of rushing to meet it, you must submit yourself to the whim of the *Archon.*" She shook her head. "But there is value in this delay, my son."

Alaric was wary. It was not uncommon for Katrina to set traps of logic for him. She would invite him to analyze a situation in which the facts pointed to a single conclusion. Then she would offer another consideration that shattered Alaric's entire analysis. Katrina considered it educational. Alaric found it unsettling.

But she had told him what he was thinking, so he returned the favor: "You believe we must consolidate our gains. And the reformation of the Free Worlds League means we will have to reconsider our offensive. Troops will have to be shifted along the border to address these new realities."

Katrina waved his words away with an impatient hand. "*Aff, aff.* All true—and all irrelevant."

Alaric stared at his mother for a long moment. What would she consider important? Ever since she had been toppled from her Lyran throne, Katrina had learned to despise her former countrymen.

"The transport of our civilian population." He peered at her, but Katrina's face betrayed nothing. "Our people travel through Lyran space. And the Lyrans augment our lift capability. They hold a knife to our throat. Every moment we delay is a moment closer to the end of our migration and thus our vulnerability."

A small smile curled across Katrina's weathered face.

"But why should that be a concern?" asked Alaric. "The Lyrans brought us here. We fight by their side." Alaric did not say that the Lyrans were allies. Wolves did not have *allies.* Wolves were not domesticated.

She raised a pale eyebrow. "You trust them?"

He shook his head. "They are Spheroids, and so they are treacherous by their very nature. It is better to say I understand what they want. They need us as a bulwark against House Marik. It would not serve their purposes to delay our move."

"Of course," said Katrina. "You are right."

Alaric stared at her. Katrina's mind was as sharp and dangerous as a laser's emerald kiss. She had not brought up this issue just to say, "You are right." Did she see something he had missed? Or was her concern just a product of her bitterness and paranoia?

It was a dangerous assumption—the Inner Sphere was littered with the bodies of people who had thought they were smarter than Katrina Steiner—and yet Alaric could see no realistic Lyran threat.

"It does not matter," said Katrina easily. "I called you here for another reason. I do not think you understand the danger that faces you at this conference."

Alaric shook his head. "No danger awaits me on Cavanaugh II. The possibility of advantage, perhaps. The chance to bid for the next phase of the offensive, certainly. But danger...?" He shook his head.

Katrina studied him for a long moment, her face blank, her blue eyes glittering. "How do you believe you are regarded by Seth Ward?" she finally asked.

Alaric met his mother's steady gaze, searching for the meaning behind her words. He wanted to say: *I am worthy. I developed the plan that allowed Clan Wolf to move safely into Lyran space. I was struck down by Anastasia Kerensky, and yet I rose back up. I killed Thaddeus Marik. Exploits worthy of a Khan.*

A Khan.

"You suggest he fears me," said Alaric.

"The conservatives do not like you because you have a mother and because of your peculiar relationship with the woman Verena. But most of all because you are the most successful product of the Ironborn Sibko."

"I am of House Ward, *quiaff*?" said Alaric mildly.

Katrina snorted. "Publicly, *aff.* But there are those who see through Vlad's little trick. Those who do not like the thought of Steiner-Davion genes pretending to be something they are not."

"But the experiment has been a success," Alaric pressed.

"Opinions vary," said Katrina softly.

For a moment silence hung over the space.

"You spoke of the Khan," said Alaric.

"The Khan," said Katrina. "Seth Ward wishes to *remain* Khan."

Alaric frowned.

Katrina speared him with her gaze. "A great battle will be waged during the conference on Cavanaugh II. It carries with it the same element of danger you faced on New Olympia. The same possibility of glory."

"You speak of politics." Alaric could not keep the disdain out of his voice. Katrina Steiner was a master of politics. She wielded intrigue like a stiletto, slipping it between the ribs of her enemies. It was this skill that had made her the ruler of the Federated Commonwealth when that privilege had rightfully belonged to her brother.

It was this same skill that had been her ultimate undoing.

"You disdain the thrust and parry of politics," she said evenly.

"We are not treacherous Spheroids," said Alaric indignantly.

A small smile graced Katrina's face. "Honorable warriors," she agreed, "ruled by the best among them, with no appeal save for that of the sword."

There was no sarcasm in her voice, but Alaric sensed it anyway—not in her voice, but in the pattern of the conversation. These sessions with his mother had taught him to read human interactions like he might read a map. He had learned to look past the masks people wore.

So he was not at all surprised when his mother said: "Politics is present in all human endeavors, Alaric. Clan Wolf is not immune. You will find that politics is present whenever two people want the same thing."

TIME AND LOCATION UNKNOWN

Tucker's face pressed against...something hard. His right cheek tingled with pins and needles. *How...long?* he thought groggily. *Where...?*

He slowly opened his eyes and immediately shut them again. Burning, *burning.* He breathed heavily for long minutes, eyes screwed shut against the terrible light.

After awhile he opened one eye carefully, squinting at his surroundings. Black. His surroundings were *black.* A long stretch of black.

Work...bench, he realized. And then: *lab.*

He was in his lab. On...where? Somewhere. But...

Don't look at the sky, warned some distant part of his mind. He didn't understand the thought and let it flit away.

Cold. The workbench was cold on his cheek. *Had he fallen asleep while he was working?* Move...head. He tilted it—

Thermonuclear pain blossomed in his head, a pain so cruel it was like he'd never felt pain before. Darkness swept over—

Woke up. On floor. Felt tile beneath his hands. *Tile. Mygodohmygod, tile.* His cheeks were wet with tears, his breathing a hoarse rattle, his head ringing with the bright echo of the terror that had filled his skull when he'd moved it a fraction of a millimeter.

He tried opening his eyes again. World was blurry: gray blob. Looking up. At blob. He drew a shuddery breath. After a moment, the gray blob resolved itself into something he finally understood.

Patricia.

She sat on his bunk, wearing her gray uniform, her *military* uniform, hands folded in her lap, a faint smile on her lips.

She'd— She'd. *Watched.* Him. Watched him suffer. Patricia.

"Good morning, sunshine," she said happily.

"Trish-uh," he croaked.

"DNI," she said.

"Wha?"

"I'm sorry, Tuck. I know you're not at your best. Direct Neural Interface. It's a nifty little tool developed to achieve a better man-machine interface."

A sudden chill wriggled up Tucker's spine. "By...who?"

Patricia flashed him a dazzling smile. "Manei Domini."

Tucker's breath caught. *The Master's Hands.* Word of Blake's most brutal and fanatical faction. The Manei Domini were cyborgs, their bodies altered in terrible ways to better serve the will of Blake. They had been the shock troops of the Jihad that had rippled across the Inner Sphere.

"The Manei Domini used DNI to jack into their vehicles and BattleMechs," said Patricia. "But I've always thought if a human mind could look *out* through the link, maybe a human mind could also look *in.*"

Tucker stared at her blankly for a long moment and then his stomach shriveled into a tight knot as he finally decoded her words. He reached up with a trembling hand and touched his skull.

His bare skull.

He dragged his hand across his head, feeling the stitches, the jagged cuts, the violation of his very mind.

"We've made a few useful alterations," said Patricia cheerfully.

"Buhl," croaked Tucker. "Buhl...won't..."

"Buhl doesn't know," said Patricia. "He's still deciding what to do with you. I don't suffer from that level of indecision."

"Buhl *won't,*" Tucker insisted.

She snorted. "If I bring him the answers he wants, he won't care how I got them. And believe me, I will. Because you won't be able to *not* tell me what I want to know."

Incandescent pain suddenly filled Tucker's head, a pain so terrible that it eclipsed the agony he'd felt only a few moments before.

And then Tucker Harwell was lost to screaming.

WESTERN COAST OF HALL ISLAND
AUTUMN WIND
CLAN WOLF OCCUPATION ZONE
15 OCTOBER 3139

Alaric loved the roar of the ocean as it crashed into the rocks. The ocean's fury was gray-green water churned into foam, the taste of brine in the cold snap of sea air, and that *sound*, always that sound: the rush of water, the boom of terrible power, the sloshing, hissing retreat as the sea gathered itself for another blow.

The shore was a battlefield, the beach a prize in the ocean's never ending battle against the land. *That* was what Alaric loved about the sound of the ocean.

He and Verena picked their way across the narrow strip of bronze sand. They climbed over black edifices of rock rising out of the sand; their irregular shapes softened and hollowed out by time and surf, forming little pockets of ocean that were home to small fish and mollusks.

The sea bends everything to its purpose, thought Alaric.

"You never did tell me why Katrina Steiner summoned you," said Verena.

She glanced back at him. Verena's golden blond hair was cut short and her face was full, lending her an air of innocence and purity. She had just returned from a training exercise and she still wore MechWarrior togs: black leather boots, tight brown shorts and nothing but a cooling vest and a sweat-soaked t-shirt covering her bare chest. "What did she want?"

Alaric frowned at the sea. That was always a good question. What Katrina wanted was not always obvious. *She is like Anastasia Kerensky in that way*, Alaric thought.

"She came to warn me," he said.

Verena's laughter was a rich, musical trill. "Warn you about what?"

He thought a moment before answering, scrambling up the side of a jagged rock. It was an unseasonably warm day and after the frustration of his summons to Cavanaugh II and his conversation with his mother, it felt good to work his muscles.

"About the treachery of the Clans."

Verena snorted. "The Clans are many things, but they are not treacherous."

"Which is most likely why she felt the need to warn me. Because I might believe as you do."

She peered at him, her head tilted, a breeze playing with her short, blond hair, her cerulean eyes on his face. His eyes went to her wrist, her bare wrist, where only a few months before she had worn the three cords he had given her when he had taken her as his bondsman.

"The conservatives look upon me with disgust," said Alaric carefully. "Because of her. Not everyone appreciates Katrina Steiner's exalted place in our Clan—or that she styles herself a mother."

Verena's blue eyes burned into him for a moment and then she looked away, turning her face to the angry ocean. "Or could it be—" She stopped and swallowed. "That you style yourself a, a *husband*." Her voice broke on the last word.

Husband. It was a Spheroid word. It had no place in the Clans. The Trueborn were not actually born at all; they were children of the iron wombs. To be a Clanner was to be the product of a ruthless eugenics program. The genes of the weak were winnowed; only the best warriors won the honor of passing on their genetic legacy.

So sex between Clanners did not carry the same emotional weight that it did for Spheroids. Sex was no act of procreation for Trueborns, no act of union. The physical act of love was a joy freely given between warriors. It was pleasure, it was release.

Nothing more.

But sometime during her long captivity, Verena had grown to be more than a bondsman to Alaric, more than a fellow warrior. He had been with no other woman since Verena and he first coupled—and he knew she had been with no other man.

"Well, there is one sure way to address the conservatives' suspicions." Verena's voice was stiff, tightly under control. She still was not looking at him. "Take one of them into your bed."

She was right. It was the logical solution, and it would cost him so little. *A joy freely given.*

Then why was he not going to do it?

He reached out and took her wrist, her bare wrist, touching it gently with his hand, feeling smooth skin, the tendons flexing beneath, the throb of her pulse.

Unlike Verena, he had not lived among Spheroids, had not served them. How little he truly understood them.

She turned. Tears traced down her face.

He hesitated. Then he leaned in and kissed them away.

She crushed his mouth to hers. He reached hungrily beneath her cooling vest. They coupled like Clanners, enthusiastically and without shame, making love right there on the beach, not caring about the sand or the sea or who might see.

Afterward, Alaric watched her sleep, stretched out on her stomach, her head pillowed on her bare arm, her blond hair in her face.

All his life Alaric had prized the ethic of Clan Wolf, modeling himself after Vlad Ward. He had once even hoped that he carried Vlad's genes. It had turned out not to be true, but he still looked to the example of the former Khan. Alaric was the very embodiment of the Clan warrior. And that was the face Alaric presented to the world.

But there was more to him. There was the cold, calculating influence of his mother, Katrina Steiner. And maybe...a part of himself that he owed to his true father.

Victor Steiner-Davion.

He remembered the delicate feel of Verena's wrist under his hands, the miraculous articulation of the joint. How could he feel such wonder at such a small thing? *What is this?* Alaric thought.

Whatever it was it could not have come from Vlad Ward, Vlad who had loved only war. Nor could it have come from Katrina Steiner, Katrina who loved only herself.

It could only have come from Victor. *His father.*

He leaned forward and brushed the hair out of Verena's face. She stirred and looked up at him. A broad smile curled across her pretty face.

Suddenly his heart was pounding. Alaric was startled by his own feelings.

What IS this?

EXCALIBUR-CLASS POCKET WARSHIP ARCHON'S FIST
ZENITH JUMP POINT
BOLAN, BOLAN MILITARY PROVINCE,
LYRAN COMMONWEALTH

Trillian Steiner sat back in the darkened situation room that served as the Archon's mobile command post and listened to the smooth, self-satisfied voice of Leutnant-General Maurer fill the space. "The Lyran thrust continues to advance. When the assault resumes we expect to swallow the Protectorate Coalition."

As he spoke, the map on the bulkhead screen shifted. A Steiner blue arrow slashed into the swarm of lavender stars that made up the Free Worlds League.

"And the Covenant Worlds?" Archon Melissa Steiner asked coolly.

"The Covenant Worlds are under the personal protection of Thaddeus Marik," said Maurer. "Beyond them lies the Clan Protectorate. We know our offensive must end somewhere. And though Duke Vedet has advanced steadily, it hasn't been against Clan warriors—or a former Paladin of the Republic."

The general's voice was heavy with contempt. Despite the successes of Operation Hammerfall, the Lyran Army still resented having to take orders from Vedet Brewer.

Melissa's lips quirked ever so slightly. Trillian was quite sure she was the only one who'd seen the tiny smile. The Archon glanced at her. "Trillian, you will manage the campaign's conclusion."

By which she meant that Trillian would maneuver Vedet into a final defeat that would undercut the prestige he'd gained in leading the Lyran half of the operation. Trillian tasted something sour at the back of her throat. How many soldiers' lives would be spent to serve Melissa's political needs? But she bowed her head and said: "Of course, Highness."

With a quick glance at Gunter Duiven, the nondescript head of Loki, Melissa turned back to Maurer. "What of the Wolves, General?"

"The Wolf thrust is anti-spinward of ours." A brown arrow slashed through the narrow bridge that joined the League's two halves. "As you can see, Highness, the Wolves are driving rimward, their ultimate aim to break the spine of the Free Worlds League."

Trillian felt a light flutter in her stomach. She doubted very much that Maurer had any idea what Clan Wolf's ultimate aim was.

The Wolves were carving a nice little occupation zone out of the Free Worlds League. In what Melissa no doubt considered a clever move, she'd brought the Wolves rimward to help fight her war. She'd done what any major company did when courting a highly valued employee—she'd offered to pay for their move. Even now Lyran JumpShips were moving Wolf civilians to their new worlds on the Commonwealth border.

It was typical Melissa. Buy the Wolves' allegiance with new planets, and force House Marik to pay the bill.

The Archon's ambition was breathtaking. Aside from her Wolf gambit, something else was going on. Lately Trillian had become aware of huge sums flowing out of the Commonwealth, billions of kroner finding their way to ComStar holdings outside Fortress Republic. So far Trillian's cousin hadn't seen fit to explain that particular operation, and Trillian hadn't pressed. She was more concerned about the Wolves.

Looking at the map, Trillian wondered if Melissa had been too clever by half. The Wolf OZ stretched from Stewart to Kirkenlaard. And there was no sign the Clanners' advance would stop. Ever.

"If I may, Highness," said Duiven, "Loki has intelligence on the Wolf advance."

Melissa nodded.

"Archon, this vidclip comes from a highly placed asset, codenamed Bluebird. I must caution you, I cannot answer any questions regarding sources or methods."

Trillian sat up a little straighter in her chair. Bluebird was a prized intelligence source operating within the Free Worlds League. To protect the operative's identity, only four people in the entire Lyran Commonwealth knew his (or her) name. Duiven was one of the four. No one else in the room was. Not even Melissa.

"Very well," said the Archon.

A video began rolling. Trillian watched a camouflaged *Warhammer* settle into what looked like a mud-bath. The 'Mech wore a Marik eagle over its left breast.

Melissa gasped. Trillian turned to look at her.

The Archon leaned forward. "That's— Is that—"

"Thaddeus Marik, yes," said Duiven. "You have an excellent eye, Highness. I am at liberty to tell you that this footage was taken on New Olympia three weeks ago, before the pause in the fighting."

Trillian watched a dark brown *Mad Cat* with brilliant orange accents stalk forward to challenge Thaddeus Marik. *Alaric Wolf,* she suddenly realized. *That's Alaric Wolf.*

The two machines lashed each other with their energy weapons, traded missile blows. But the Wolf 'Mech was backstepping, giving ground. *Were the Wolves losing?*

The *Warhammer* lurched clumsily, taking an unsteady step forward. The view drifted back to the treeline and— *There.* An SM1 Destroyer painted in Clan colors. And a *Raven.* And—

It was a trap. Alaric Wolf had lured Thaddeus Marik into a trap.

The view expanded. Free Worlders were breaking under the two-sided assault.

"Note," said Duiven softly, "Alaric has maneuvered the planet's defenders into an untenable position. At this point, it is likely he will win the battle. But for Alaric Wolf, winning the battle isn't enough."

On the screen artillery began to fall, shells plunging into the midst of the battle. It was a brutal assault. The fire was concentrated on the Free Worlds line, but stray shells were landing among the Wolves, too. Marik machines were bolting like stampeding cattle, but the Wolves stood in there, ignoring the deadly rain falling all around them.

The *Uller* beside Alaric fell. But the *Mad Cat* didn't move, didn't step away, didn't react at all. Alaric Wolf was totally focused on the *Warhammer,* tearing into it.

Thaddeus Marik's 'Mech stumbled like a punch-drunk fighter, and then it crumpled to the ground.

And then the view zoomed in on the *Warhammer*'s mangled cockpit, its contents reduced to carbon ash, the *Mad Cat* standing triumphantly over its kill. The image froze.

There was a moment of absolute silence, as if the terrible images they'd just witnessed had drained the universe of sound.

"I think," said Duiven softly, "that perhaps we can contemplate an attack on the Covenant Worlds, after all."

"So the Wolves have taken New Olympia," said Maurer hopefully. "They are still moving rimward. As we've directed."

"It seems so," said Duiven.

"It's the word *seems* that concerns me," said Melissa dryly.

Around the room her aides shifted in their seats.

"Empty Cupboard?" asked Maurer, raising an inquiring eyebrow.

Trillian shook her head. "Empty Cupboard is a dangerous move. It'll infuriate the Wolves."

"It will remind the Wolves who holds the leash," said Maurer stiffly.

"Take it from a diplomat, General," said Trillian, "the goal isn't to remind the Wolves who holds the leash. The goal is to pretend there *is* no leash. If we're not careful we'll—"

"Empty Cupboard was set in motion two weeks ago." The Archon's voice was cold, firm.

Shocked silence filled the room for a heartbeat. Trillian realized her mouth was hanging open and shut it. "Yes, of course, Highness," she said softly.

"I trust you were speaking of something other than Empty Cupboard, Archon," said Duiven.

Melissa leaned forward in her chair. "There is a practice as old as hunting itself. It's called baiting. Hunters would set out meat for a bear—or a wolf."

"And the animal would be led to its death," said Maurer.

"We have reason to work with the Wolves," said Melissa. "Nevertheless, we will take precautions." Her eyes found the frozen image of the *Mad Cat*. "Just in case."

CHAPTER 4

OVERLORD-CLASS DROPSHIP *BEC DE CORBIN*
LOW ORBIT, ROMULUS
CLAN HELL'S HORSES OCCUPATION ZONE
17 NOVEMBER 3139

Beckett Malthus stepped on to the DropShip's bridge and shut the spacetight hatch behind him. *Bec de Corbin*—Beak of the Crow—was accelerating as she maneuvered for orbital insertion. For a few moments at least, Beckett enjoyed the luxury of weight.

No one looked up as he entered.

A viewscreen dominated the bridge, watchstanders arrayed before it. Beckett went to the bridge's aft bulkhead and leaned against a console designed to pull up any tactical display, link with any ground command. This had once been his station.

Not any more.

The vessel bore Beckett's name, but that was just another lie. Like the lie that he was the Khan of Clan Jade Falcon. In reality, the ship, the Clan, even Beckett himself served a single master: Malvina Hazen, who called herself *Chingis Khan.*

Emperor of all Mankind.

Beckett was a big man, saturnine and watchful, his body clothed in a black and green Falcon uniform. A gray beard framed his broad, calculating face. He looked out on the universe with eyes the color of a pond skimmed with green algae.

A world turned on the bridge's giant screen. The planet possessed blue seas, but what really caught the eye were the fecund greens and golds of the continents, the colors of spring, of plenty. Of life.

Malvina planned to conquer this world. Although she had yet to issue challenge, she had already laid out her strategy. It was intricate, but simple at its heart. The only part of the plan Beckett failed to understand was why they were here at all.

Clan Jade Falcon was already overextended. The Falcons clung to a perch in the Skye region, giving them a second hostile frontier with the Lyrans. And now that the Wolves had abandoned their coreward holdings, the Falcons were rushing to fill the vacuum before the Horses and the Ghost Bears swallowed the former Wolf worlds. Worst of all, the Falcon *touman* had still not recovered from the vicious rending that had brought Malvina Hazen to power three years before.

So why attack a backwater like Romulus? No one would dispute that Malvina Hazen was mad—but Beckett had never known her to be stupid.

The hatch opened and Malvina Hazen stepped on to the bridge with her pet, the Spheroid girl Cynthy.

Beckett felt a little shiver of disquiet looking upon the girl. She wore a bright pink blouse and denim pants, her blond hair tied back in a ponytail with a pink ribbon. Beckett judged her age at nine years. She was eating a chocolate bar. *Was there no indulgence Malvina would refuse her?* he wondered. The girl's small hand was sticky with half-melted candy, and a smear of chocolate marked her chin.

Cynthy turned her blue eyes on Beckett and gave him a long, frank look that knew neither respect nor fear.

Wrong.

The woman standing next to the girl was tiny, herself barely larger than a child. She wore a uniform of her own design: black with green and yellow details. The slight color mismatch of her pale blue eyes and the black plastic fist that emerged from her left sleeve hinted at the presence of prosthetics. She had fine, elfin features and full lips. Her ice white hair fell to her shoulders like a frozen waterfall.

She would have been beautiful except for two things. One was the scar that started at her left eyebrow and curled down toward her rosebud mouth.

The other was the casual cruelty that marked the lines of her face.

"We have shaped orbit about the planet," said the tech on the nav console, reporting the fact just as Beckett felt weight leave his body.

"Very well," said Malvina in an even tone. "Signal the Horses."

"Yes, Chingis Khan," said the technician on the communications console. He was a lean man with short, black hair, his face alight with a worshipful glow. Cynthy had drifted over to where the man was seated, studying his panel with evident interest.

His fingers flew over the board and there was an audio crackle. "I am Galaxy Commander Rose DeLaurel of Clan Hell's Horses, Zeta Galaxy, Heaven's Wrath."

"This is Chingis Khan Malvina Hazen, and I challenge you to a Trial of Possession for the world of Romulus. With what forces will you defend, Rose DeLaurel?"

There was a slight pause as the distant Horse considered. "I defend with a Trinary of vehicles and a Trinary of ProtoMechs. With what will you challenge?"

"I will match your vehicles," answered Malvina. "I have no ProtoMechs, so I bid two Stars of Elementals and a Star of BattleMechs. And I will choose the ground."

Beckett blinked, surprised. The Horses' expertise in armor gave them the edge in vehicles, and since ProtoMechs outmatched infantry, they held a slight edge with the second Trinary, as well.

"Bargained well and done," the Horseman replied, and then broke the connection.

Malvina turned and saw Beckett watching her. She kicked off and drifted over to him.

"You do not approve of my *batchall*, Khan Beckett?" she asked in a low voice.

Malvina was mercurial and deadly, ready to kill any who challenged her. But if he offered advice he was not challenging her, he was aiding her.

If he did it carefully.

"In this case, I do not understand the advantage of choosing the ground." He pitched his voice low, so no one else on the bridge would hear them. Often privacy was the difference between advice and challenge. "That is why you bid as you did, is it not, Chingis Khan, so you could choose the location of the trial?"

A small smile curled Malvina's lips. She glanced back at the world on the viewscreen. "The land is everything."

Beckett's eyes followed hers. "Why this world, Malvina? Why not return to Skye and continue the *desant?* Or take more of the Wolves' former holdings?"

Malvina turned back to look at him. She opened her mouth to speak, but her eyes flickered down to the console. She suddenly went white with fury. Beckett looked down.

An emerald light glowed on the console. The light indicated the station console was broadcasting to the entire ship.

Malvina braced herself against the console and pushed off, gliding forward. "Communications," she barked, "Report status of my station."

The dark-haired tech glanced at his board and then started. "T-the station is set to shipwide b-broadcast, Chingis Khan." He rose to his feet, arms at his sides, hands open in supplication, turning to face her as she tumbled toward him. "I d-didn't—"

In one fluid motion, Malvina pulled a curved blade from her hip and slashed down. His words were lost in a terrible gurgle as her knife severed his windpipe and the carotid artery. He grasped his neck with his hands, trying to stanch the spray of blood, but red droplets floated between his fingers, his life drifting away in a fine crimson mist.

The tech's error had transformed Beckett's advice into a challenge—and Chingis Khan would tolerate no challenge to her authority. Beckett knew he was lucky the tech had paid for the transgression—and not he.

"Clear the bridge!" Malvina shrieked.

Obediently, the crew rose and abandoned their stations.

Beckett glanced at the girl, Cynthy, wondering if the sudden display of violence had frightened her. The girl reached for the hatch, and then she turned to look back, her blue eyes on the dying tech, her chocolate-stained face totally blank, save for a little quirk at the corner of her mouth. *A smile.*

Cynthy was *smiling.*

In a flash, Beckett understood. He remembered the girl's interest in the comms board. *She* had set the station to broadcast.

The girl had manipulated Malvina into killing the technician.

Monster.

Beckett opened his mouth to tell Malvina what he'd seen, just as he saw her glance down at the board. She scraped something off the panel with an index finger, something dark. She popped the finger in her mouth, tasting the substance.

Chocolate, thought Beckett with sudden insight. *She knows.*

Malvina looked at the hatch through which Cynthy had departed.

And Beckett saw something on her face he'd never seen before.

Shock.

MAMMOTH-CLASS DROPSHIP *WAYFARER*
ZENITH JUMP POINT, VECKHOLM
DONEGAL MILITARY PROVINCE
LYRAN COMMONWEALTH

In the dim light of pseudo-night, Captain Jonas Krick stepped over the young woman sleeping on the elevated catwalk. He glanced down at the small, huddled form and debated calling the master-at-arms. Technically, no one was supposed to be sleeping up on the catwalks. She was young, maybe early twenties, though the short black hair curled around her pale face made her look younger, and she was slender. A smudge of dirt on the left side of her chin told him she hadn't been through the wash bays recently. She didn't even have a blanket, she'd wrapped herself in a small, brown windbreaker.

That's when he noticed the toddler snuggled up against her, his blond head peeking out from beneath the light jacket.

Krick swallowed hard and turned away. *I'll let this one go*, he thought. *Just this once.*

*Mammoth*s were gigantic cargo ships, able to haul north of forty thousand tons of cargo, which, just to put it into perspective, was something like seven *battalions* worth of BattleMechs. But Krick's vessel wasn't carrying a single 'Mech on this journey. Nor did she carry even a pallet of cargo. *Wayfarer* had been impressed by the Transport Division to carry Wolf civilians, and that's what she'd done month-in and month-out for the last two years.

It was hard, cruel duty.

Krick looked out over the *Wayfarer*'s Number Four Cargo Bay and saw a vast refugee camp. Each civilian inhabited a two-meter by four spot on the deck (four by six for a family of five). Minimal privacy was provided by free-standing canvas sections bolted to the deck. And the *smell*. All those unwashed bodies created a terrible miasma that rose out of the cargo bay and made Krick's eyes water. He imagined what it must be like to live down there and shuddered.

People in pens. Like some kind of obscene zoo.

One of the *Wayfarer's* cargo decks was dedicated to feeding the refugees (not that there was ever enough food), another dedicated to washing them down (not that there was ever enough water), and a third dedicated to disposing of their waste (*that* there was plenty of.)

Once when he had owned a smaller ship, a *Mule*, Krick had transported a herd of cattle from one world to another. He glanced at the young woman sleeping with her child on the catwalk. This was a lot like that.

It was night watch now, and twelve thousand souls slept aboard Krick's vessel. Sometimes he felt like he had all of the Inner Sphere crammed into *Wayfarer*, though in reality his present cargo was only a tiny drop of all the refugees that would need to be moved. Clan worlds typically had smaller populations than normal worlds, and the Wolves had only selected the cream of their citizens to move—typically young, able-bodied farmers or factory workers and their families.

Make all the qualifications you wanted, the refugees still numbered in the *billions.* The bulk of the population of the former Wolf Occupation was scattered in crowded camps from Ginestra to Amity. People were hard to move—and it took sixteen jumps to travel from one end of the pipe to the other.

The expanded metal that made up the catwalk's decking shook in its steel frame as someone approached. The power of the footsteps told him exactly who it was. Krick didn't turn.

"There is another delay." The voice was a powerful alto. It rumbled out of a broad chest that somehow belonged to a human being. Somehow belonged to a *woman.*

"I am aware of that, Star Commander Amy," said Krick without turning.

"This is not acceptable," said the giant Elemental steadily, as if her will could change the situation.

Krick closed his eyes and bit back a sarcastic reply. He counted to ten and turned.

She towered over him. Krick was not a small man, but Amy was a meter taller. She wore camo fatigue pants and a black tank top stretched across her most impressive chest. (Her breasts were about at his eye level.) White-blond hair fell to her shoulders.

She stood uncomfortably close to him—whether because she was trying to intimidate him or because she was clueless about the Inner Sphere concept of personal space, Krick didn't know.

"Look," he said as calmly as he could. "Every ag world in this stretch of space has been struck with a virulent strain of rust. We think it's genetically modified, maybe a latent holdover from the Jihad suddenly catching fire."

"I have heard this before," said Amy. "And I do not care. Our people must be moved to the Occupation Zone."

"But they still must be *fed*, right? Even Clanners have to eat."

"So feed them."

"By stealing it from worlds facing food shortages? Not a chance."

Amy clenched her massive fists. It would only take a single blow from one of those giant hands to smash his skull in.

"You will resolve this situation. *Now.*"

"Are you offering to have your civilians help us sort the suspect grain?" asked Krick archly. "That *will* speed up resolution of the issue. Though I can't guarantee any of your people will be alive when we reach the Wolf OZ."

"You are *not* amusing," Amy breathed.

Krick drew himself up to his full height. "Nothing's going to move until we get this sorted out, got it?"

Amy leaned down so only a few millimeters separated her face from his. "*Not* acceptable," she growled. And then she turned and stalked off, shaking the catwalk as she went.

Krick watched her go. Then he turned to look at all the people sleeping fretfully below, prisoners in his cargo hold. Krick didn't mind lying to the Elemental, but he *did* mind holding these miserable people, delaying a jump that would take them one step closer to a real life under an open sky.

"Devil take Melissa Steiner," he muttered darkly.

And then *he* stalked off, departing along the same route Amy had taken.

After his departure, it was quiet up on the catwalk for several long minutes. And then the young woman under the windbreaker stirred. She stood, not sparing even a glance for the stray toddler who was not, in fact, her child.

She followed the catwalk five, ten meters until she reached the far bulkhead. Then she crouched down and pulled out a communication device that would automatically encrypt her words, raising the device to her lips.

"This is Caroline," she said softly. "Of the Watch."

CANDERON AGRICULTURAL DISTRICT
ROMULUS
CLAN HELL'S HORSES OCCUPATION ZONE
22 NOVEMBER 3139

Beckett stood in a field of winter wheat that reached up to his chest. A gentle breeze rippled through the grain. It was like standing in a shallow, golden sea. All of Canderon was like this, a great expanse of cropland stretching across the heart of a continent.

A hundred meters from Beckett's position, a Tyr infantry support tank and a point of Elementals waited, hidden behind a low hill. Beckett had elected to observe on foot. He raised binoculars to his face.

Right now he was looking east at a ribbon of blue. A dust devil moved along the river, the Horses transiting Rural Route Four. The enemy was moving quickly, pursuing the smaller Jade Falcon force of armor and infantry cutting west across the golden wheat.

It was a trap.

Malvina's command Star was hidden in the river. When the Horses moved past her position, her BattleMechs would rise from the water and strike from behind. Malvina would fall upon the Horses' hindquarters, raking them with her sharp talons. It would be enough to bring them down.

It always was.

A clutch of seconds died. Then another. Beckett felt his breath tighten in his chest. He was certain the bulk of the Horse armor was south of the ambush point—what was Malvina waiting for?

A spark of ruby light was his answer.

He raised a pair of binoculars. Infantry in Elemental power armor were rising from the broad expanse of wheat. The left arm of each soldier ended in a wicked claw, the right arm in a laser. A pair of missiles were mounted over their shoulders, right and left.

Looked like...both Stars. Fifty troopers.

A flurry of ruby beams sliced into the enemy's lead tank—a Scimitar Mark II painted in Zeta Galaxy black. There was a moment of pregnant silence and then the Scimitar erupted into an orange fireball, the victim of a secondary explosion.

Missiles streaked in toward the column of armor as the Elementals fired their SRMs, leaving behind gray lines of smoke hanging in the air.

Pointing back to their positions.

A black Enyo strike tank rotated its turret, tearing into an exposed Elemental with its pulse laser. Ruby darts of energy blew apart the unfortunate trooper, and then set fire to a patch of wheat.

Black *Orc* ProtoMechs stalked forward, sending flights of SRMs into the Falcon infantry. A Falcon Heimdall tried to move forward to give the retreating infantry cover, only to take a laser strike from the Enyo.

The Falcon force was drawing the Horses away from the river, but they were paying a fearsome price to do it. The shriek of lasers and the death rattle of autocannons filled the air. *And still the BattleMechs are nowhere to be seen.* The Falcon infantry was dying point by point, men and women toppling to the ground under the terrible weight of a coordinated, overpowering assault.

Beckett slowly lowered the binoculars. How had Malvina's plan gone so badly wrong?

Water cascaded off the monstrous *Shrike* as it rose from the river. The thirteen-meter assault 'Mech was painted black with green highlights, its silver cockpit molded into the hook-beaked shape of a falcon's head. A pair of wings, painted buff and gold, extended from its broad shoulders. Its right arm ended in a terrible claw, its left in a pair of PPCs. *Black Rose* stalked out of the river on backward-bent legs.

The *Shrike*'s right thigh was marked with the emblem of its name: a dark flower in bloom. Soulless blue eyes stared out from its chest.

Through the water sheeting off her canopy, Malvina watched the Horse line pulling away from the river. She dropped her crosshairs over the rear armor of an *Orc*. The dot at the center of the crosshairs blinked gold and she pulled into her main trigger.

Twin lightning strikes tore into the ProtoMech's ebony back. The lightly armored *Orc* staggered and went down.

Malvina turned, looking for another target. She found a Scimitar and ripple fired her Longbow ten-rack. Missiles tore into the tank and sent it careening into the earth.

All around her, her BattleMechs rising from the river: a *Turkina* to her right, a *Phoenix Hawk IIC* to her left, an *Eyrie* farther down the line.

She dropped her reticle over a black SM1 and pulled into her triggers.

The Horses had been transformed from hunters into prey. A klick to the west, Malvina's armor stopped its fighting withdrawal, hitting the Horse tanks at point blank range, refusing to allow Zeta Galaxy to punch through their lines and escape the 'Mechs marching on them from behind.

Malvina's Elementals did not join in the brave stand of the Falcon force.

There were none left.

She worked her way forward, ripping through the Horse line, mopping up. She had already won the Trial of Possession for this world, even if the Horses had yet to realize it. She stalked her machine through a charred landscape. All around her the golden wheat was gone, burned away by stray weapons fire. The conflagration had left nothing behind but bare earth dotted with glowing orange embers.

And the wreckage of war.

She stalked past a point of fallen Elementals, their armor burned and blackened. Saw a Falcon VV1 Ranger, its smashed launchers putting her in mind of a broken neck.

She crested a hill and came across Bec Malthus's Tyr. Her radio crackled, and the deep, sonorous voice of the Crow rose from their personal channel. "Chingis Khan, why did you delay your attack?"

"I did not delay the attack, Khan Malthus. All has unfolded as I envisioned it."

"But Malvina, our infantry has been slaughtered. Our armor is in tatters."

She looked to the horizon where the fire was still burning, hungry flames racing through the breadbasket of a world. Malvina's laughter was joyous. "Why, Bec, you surprise me. How little you understand of what is truly important."

To the north, billowing, black smoke poured into the world's blue sky.

TIME AND LOCATION UKNOWN

Tucker awoke to the gentle beeps and whirs of machines. He was swaddled in softness. A diffuse light the color of cream filtered through the room.

Hospital...

Am in... Hospital...

He closed his eyes and shuddered.

He...remembered. Patricia's mind. In his. Somehow. *Taunting him.*

From inside his skull.

He tried to swallow and jagged pain tore his throat.

"Your throat will be tender for a few days," said a voice, a woman's voice. *(Not Patricia!)* They had you on a respirator before you started breathing on your own."

"Wha—?" Tucker croaked. He made out a woman standing by his bed. She wore a gray uniform like Patricia's military uniform, but the rho on her collar marked her as ROM. Auburn hair cascaded to her shoulders. Her eyes were hazel, her skin pale and sprayed with a mist of delicate freckles. She was beautiful.

But she wasn't smiling.

She held out a gray plastic cup with a straw. *Water.* He suddenly realized he was thirsty. *So thirsty.* He'd sell his soul for a drink of water.

He reached for the cup. Just as his fingers closed around it, something jerked his hand back. He was *chained to the bed.*

He looked up at the woman.

"That's the first lesson, Adept. You're not a pet, and you're not a special project, and you're sure as hell not a boy genius. You are a prisoner. *My* prisoner."

She held the cup out of his reach for a moment longer to emphasize the point.

Tucker nodded, and she handed him the cup. He sucked greedily on the straw. The cool water was the most wonderful thing he'd ever tasted, even though the cold cut into his tender throat.

What the hell's going on? The thing with Patricia...Had that really happened? Where was Buhl? And who *was* this? He managed to croak: "Who...?"

"My name is Demi-Precentor Sandra Whitfield. I am going to be your—" her lips quirked, "—minder."

"Where is—"

"Patricia will not be joining us. Precentor Buhl has decided that her interest in you is too...personal."

"What...I?"

She raised an eyebrow. "What do we have planned for you?"

Tucker hesitated, and then nodded.

She smiled coldly and brushed back a strand of red hair. "It's quite simple, really. You're going to end the games and tell us everything we need to know. All of it."

Tucker wanted to say something, to answer, to *protest,* but somehow he couldn't make himself speak.

"Oh, I know you're somewhat challenged. Demi-Precentor Harwell's treatments have done some damage. You've been in a coma for quite some time. And it's likely there are some parts of you that will never wake up."

Tucker felt panic surge through him. *Some parts of you that will never wake up.* Brain damage. She was saying he had *brain damage.*

"Still, I know you'll do your best."

She leaned down so her face was only centimeters from his, her breath warm on his skin. "You may think the pain Patricia caused you was terrible. You may think the indignity of mind-rape is as bad as it gets." Her voice dropped to a whisper, a lover's whisper, soft and intimate. "But I assure you, the terrors have only begun."

Her breath was hot on his face, and he tried to jerk away, but—

He couldn't move his head.

What? He tried to lift his arm— *It wouldn't respond.*

A shrill beeping filled the room.

"I see by your heart rate that you have begun to understand your situation," said Whitfield calmly. She held up the gray plastic cup. "The water you just drank was laced with tetrodotoxin. TTX is a drug from a small island called Haiti. It induces total paralysis. The followers of certain... *exotic* religions refer to it as the Waking Death."

Whitfield reached down and swept aside the bed sheets. "Your mind is awake," she said conversationally. She pushed his hospital gown up above his knees, looked frankly at his bare legs. "And believe me—" She touched his inner thigh, dimpling the skin with her nails as she drew her fingers down his leg. "You will feel every last bit of whatever indignity I choose to subject you to."

Tucker would have shivered if he could.

She looked up, met his helpless gaze. "So you *will* tell me the truth. Always."

She stepped away from the bed and out of his field of vision. "Oh, sorry." She stepped back to and turned his head to the side, so he was looking a small, steel wardrobe painted institutional gray. She stepped to the wardrobe and opened the door. Tucker saw a white ComStar uniform hanging there. *His?*

"And just so we're clear—" She reached up and did something to the collar. She came away with a small, metal dot. *Alexi Holt's rank pip.*

"There's no hope for you." She dropped the pip on the floor and smashed it beneath the heel of her boot.

"None at all."

CHAPTER 5

The ballroom was exactly as Alaric imagined it; opulent, decadent, and wholly unnecessary. Crystal chandeliers splashed golden light across the immense room. The lower half of the walls were paneled in a rich, lustrous mahogany; The upper half painted dark red, giving the room a warm, cozy feel.

A bar constructed from the same dark wood as the room's wainscoting (Was that the right word?) occupied the east wall, though there were no guests at the bar. Instead, tuxedoed servants bearing silver trays circulated through the room, ready to instantly satisfy any guest's needs.

Not my *needs*, Alaric thought.

The only part of the decor that truly mattered were the twin banners hanging from the rafters at the north end of the ball room, one blood red and bearing a wolf's head, the other a mailed fist centered on a field of Steiner blue.

The two banners hung side by side.

But the Archon's guests put the lie to the banners' symbolism. Wolves and Lyrans stood in two groups on the parquet dance floor, the Clanners in gray leathers, the Spheroids in dress blue uniforms or formal attire.

It took all of Alaric's considerable will not to turn around and leave.

Certainly the delay in the migration of the Wolf civilians would add a pall on the Wolf side of the reception. Reports were coming in from Watch operatives salted in the civilian population that their transports had been delayed because of an ugly shortage of food.

Alaric could not help wondering if it might be something more.

If the Lyrans abandoned the move, Clan Wolf did not have the lift capacity to finish the migration. Much of the Wolf population would be stranded along the spinward border of the Commonwealth.

Knowing the magnitude of such a disaster, Alaric had not settled for reading the Watch's summaries, but had spent hours sifting through the raw intelligence. He had found a troubling piece of information. The captain of one of the waiting DropShips was overheard cursing Melissa Steiner for the delay. Now how could the Archon be held responsible for an agricultural pandemic?

Unless the reason for the delay was really something else.

Alaric wondered if any of his fellow Wolves had bothered to dig out that tiny morsel of information.

He walked forward, seeking out Khan Seth Ward. He glanced at the Khan on the other side of room. Seth was a man of slender build, the pale skin of his face pock-marked by acne scars, his dark brown hair thinning on top. He did not look formidable.

Until you looked at his eyes.

Seth Ward's intense eyes were dark brown and deep-set, lending him the appearance of a skull stripped of its flesh. One only had to look into those eyes once to realize they would never let you go.

Standing next to the Khan was the Wolf Loremaster, Liam Ward. Liam was tall and lean. Light brown hair rising from a widow's peak shadowed his head. His pale face was set into grim lines of rectitude. As Loremaster, it was Liam's task to keep the ways of Clan Wolf, to ensure his people kept to the truth of Nicholas Kerensky's path.

Liam's eyes flickered to Alaric and then he leaned over to Seth. The Khan looked at Alaric, and then turned to say something to his Loremaster.

A great battle will be waged during the conference on Cavanaugh II.

Without his mother's coaching, he doubted he would have even noticed the exchange between Loremaster and Khan. Now it was all but transparent.

Liam met his eyes and offered a tight smile, a smile that hinted at hidden triumph. For a moment Alaric stared back, his expression blank. And then he allowed a broad, cold smile to stretch across his face. *Be careful who you choose as an enemy, Loremaster.* He turned his back on Liam Ward and walked to the Lyran side of the room.

Although he did not really have anything to say to the Spheroids either. Gathered around the Archon was a gaggle of Lyran generals, gray-haired and *elderly,* well past the age where they were truly warriors. They did not deserve his attention.

He saw Trillian Steiner talking with Colonel Roderick Steiner of the First Steiner Strikers. Alaric approached the pair.

Roderick offered a small nod. He was of average height, maybe a centimeter taller than Alaric, with short blond hair and *green* eyes—unusual for a Steiner. "We are honored to see you, Galaxy Commander."

"Believe it or not, he really means it," Trillian interjected. She looked like a younger version of the Archon, blond with sapphire eyes and a mischievous smile. She wore a short black dress that hugged her body. She shook her pretty head. "Look, no one's talking. It's like a *Mittelschule* dance. Everyone's afraid to mingle."

"We are not *afraid,*" said Alaric stiffly.

"No no, of course not," said Trillian quickly. "I didn't, excuse me, did *not* mean it like that. I am quite sure you would wrestle an *Atlas* barehanded, if your honor required it. I just meant Clanners are not so big on small talk."

"Is it not more efficient to plainly say what is on your mind?" asked Alaric.

Trillian smiled sweetly. "No, as a matter of fact, it is not."

Alaric frowned.

Trillian shook her head. "Clear communication is efficient, uh, *quiaff*?"

"*Aff*," said Alaric slowly.

"Ideas are communicated more *clearly* when people are comfortable with each other."

Alaric just looked at her.

A waiter came around with Champagne. Roderick handed a flute to Trillian, another to Alaric, and took one for himself.

Alaric took the glass and sipped. The wine was sweet and bubbly. It was like much that came from the Inner Sphere— at once pleasant and frivolous. It was not the kind of thing Alaric would have chosen to drink, but if the Wolves were to survive this strange new relationship with House Steiner, they would have to learn something about Spheroid ways. He forced himself to take another drink.

Trillian sighed and brushed a strand of golden hair out of her eyes. "Okay, let's try an exercise." She indicated Roderick. "Say something nice about Rod, here."

"Trillian," said Roderick in a low, warning voice.

"Anything, really," said Trillian, "as long as it is a small thing and plausibly true."

Alaric looked at Roderick for a long moment. "You are an adequate leader," he finally said. "And I have never observed you behaving dishonorably."

"Wow," muttered Roderick, "thanks."

Trillian clapped her hands together and laughed merrily. "Okay, apparently we still have some work to do."

"You think Clanners are incapable of understanding Spheroid social dynamics?" said Alaric coldly.

"Not incapable," said Roderick. "Just out of practice, that's all."

Trillian offered him an impish smile.

They are of Steiner blood, Alaric thought. *As am I. In a way, we are sibkin.* Suddenly he did not like this woman making sport of him. Alaric looked around the room, calling on the skills Katrina Steiner had spent years teaching him, seeing the people with his mother's eyes.

Alaric pointed at Duke Vedet Brewer. The Duke wore a white cotton suit that set off his ebony skin nicely. He was very tall and his head was shorn. Duke Vedet stood near a clutch of generals, a drink in his hand. The Duke appeared to be listening to their conversation, but he stood half a pace outside their circle and none of the general officers met his gaze as they talked.

"Vedet is not well liked," said Alaric. "Or perhaps it is worse than that. Perhaps it is that the Duke is *out of favor.*"

He turned back to Trillian and Roderick. They were both watching him closely. He met Trillian's gaze. "And what of you, Lady Steiner? Not once during our time together has your—cousin? Is that the proper word? Not once has your cousin the Archon looked at you, nor you at her."

"Melissa is busy attending to her guests," said Trillian primly, "as am I."

Alaric shook his head. "No. There is some disagreement between you. I feel it like the crackle in the air that precedes a PPC strike."

"I serve the Archon in all things," said Trillian tightly.

"One out of two," said Roderick. "Not bad."

"Sure," said Alaric. "One out of two."

Trillian bowed her head. "It seems I underestimated you, Galaxy Commander."

"As I did you, once, Lady Steiner." Alaric gestured with the hand holding the Champagne. "I am sure it is a mistake neither of us will make again."

Trillian opened her mouth to answer, but right then a hush fell over the crowd and Melissa Steiner's voice rang out. "We welcome our guests who have come so far to visit us." The Archon was dressed in a dress of aqua satin that complemented her golden hair and picked up the blue in her eyes. A pearl choker was her only ornament.

"I propose a toast." She raised a white-gloved hand holding a flute of Champagne. "To a lasting partnership between Clan Wolf and the Lyran Commonwealth."

"*To partnership,*" said Trillian and Roderick, who clinked their glasses together.

Alaric said nothing. He just sipped his Champagne.

6 DECEMBER 3139

A bonfire of worlds hung above the great holotable, their combined light illuminating the darkened command center. The planets were divided into three colors: a delicate shade of purple for the Free Worlds League, Steiner blue for the Lyran Commonwealth, brown for Clan Wolf.

Melissa leaned forward. "The Lyran thrust will pass through the Protectorate Coalition, continue through the Covenant Worlds, and then hit the Clan Protectorate."

Over the holotable a blue arrow arced through the spinward half of the Free Worlds League, inscribing a backward "C" on the map.

Alaric looked at the schematic and then at Melissa. *She is lying,* he thought suddenly. He did not question how he knew it. He just *knew. Why is she lying to us?*

The Archon was not looking at Vedet, though it was he who would carry out her orders. Alaric looked at Trillian, who sat next to Vedet. She was not looking at him either. His breath caught. *Maybe this lie is not meant for the Wolves.*

The Duke is a danger to Melissa's position, Alaric suddenly realized, *but he is too powerful to destroy outright. The offensive will stop prematurely, and Vedet will be blamed for its failure.*

Alaric glanced at Seth Ward. *Is this what you are planning for me, my Khan?*

A Lyran supply general of some sort was talking about the logistics required to support the offensive.

"Excuse me, Archon," said Alaric, cutting the man off. "You are planning to attack the Spirit Cats *and* Clan Sea Fox? That is most ambitious."

Melissa Steiner looked at him as if she had just noticed him for the first time. "We have tremendous respect for the Clans," she said evenly. "But we do not fear them."

An answer that is not an answer, Alaric thought. *So the offensive will be halted before you ever reach Marik.*

This *was* a battle. And he had just seen an opening in the Archon's line.

Alaric turned to Seth Ward. "Perhaps there is an opportunity here, my Khan. Once we take Atreus, surely the

Captain General will retreat to her Oriente Protectorate. By attacking spinward, we can draw Marik reinforcements away from the Lyran thrust and ensure the Spirit Cats have to divide their forces to protect both their borders."

And, he did not say, *we will be well positioned to thrust into The Republic's weak underbelly, carrying us ever closer to Fortress Republic.*

And Terra.

Seth Ward met Alaric's gaze. Then he turned to Melissa. "The idea has merit, Archon Steiner."

Melissa Steiner shifted in her chair. "You can best help us by moving anti-spinward and cutting off the possibility of reinforcements from Tamarind-Abbey and the Rim Commonality."

She cannot allow us to support Vedet's drive, Alaric thought. *She cannot risk the possibility that it will succeed.*

Khan Ward sat back in his chair, his dark eyes on the Archon.

I wonder if he understands why she cannot accede to my plan, thought Alaric. He decided it did not matter. Seth Ward was Wolf. No doubt he smelled blood, even if he did not know its source.

"Once we pierce the bridge that joins the League's halves, I doubt the anti-spinward Free Worlders will fight through our holdings to reach your lines." The Wolf Khan bared his teeth in a fearsome smile. "If they try, they will receive a most determined reception. I believe Galaxy Commander Alaric's plan will best support your offensive."

Melissa glanced at the supply general Alaric had interrupted, and then back at Seth Ward.

"Unfortunately, we are hindered by transport," said the general. "We just cannot provide the logistic effort needed to support the current Wolf and Lyran drives and also an added Wolf thrust."

"Especially," said Melissa softly, "since most of the excess jump capability in Bolan Province has already been consumed."

Moving Wolf civilians, she did not say. And there it was. Every Wolf farmer still needed to grow food, every Wolf laborer still needed to manufacture spare parts was a hostage against the Wolves' good behavior. *Just as Katrina had predicted.*

So Melissa *had* orchestrated the delay.

Melissa Steiner would never say it aloud, but until the Wolves completed their move from their coreward holdings, she held the upper hand.

And everyone in the room knew it.

"I see your point," said Seth Ward, his voice flat.

"Excellent," said Melissa. "I am glad to hear it." She looked around the room, catching each person's gaze in turn. "Because I believe in the alliance between Lyrans and Wolves. Such an alliance promises to be most...profitable."

Profitable? Alaric thought. *Freebirth! Does she think Wolves fight for profit?*

But then her eyes alighted on him and Alaric smiled—a warm, charming smile that would have made his mother proud.

UNION-CLASS POCKET WARSHIP *SNARLING LEAP*

A troubled council of Wolves met in the *Snarling Leap*'s wardroom, contemplating the battle plans the Archon had just laid before them. The *Leap* was the personal transport of a Khan and so, by Clan standards, it was opulent—though it boasted nothing compared to the luxury Lyran nobles claimed for themselves as a matter of course.

Red carpet covered the deck and select passages from the Wolf Remembrance were carved into crystal and set into alcoves inset in the room's bulkheads. A map of the Inner Sphere hung on the far wall, Terra in gold, Wolf holdings detailed in bright scarlet. The map was a message: a pack's success was measured by the size of its hunting ground.

Alaric did not doubt the map was perfectly up to date.

Khan Seth Ward leaned back in his chair and steepled his hands, touching his fingertips to his lips. "She threatened us," he murmured.

"She did not," said Khan Patrik Fetladral of the Exiles. His voice was a rumble from deep within his broad chest.

Alaric glanced from one man to the other. The room's steel table was circular, implying equality, but Alaric understood the implication was false. Seth and Patrik were the two most powerful men in the room. It was they who would make the decision.

Interesting that they do not agree.

Seth leaned forward. "She made it clear that if we did not do her bidding, she would withdraw Lyran logistical support for the move of our civilians."

"She merely brought the logistical difficulties to our attention, *quiaff?*" said Patrik. He was a head taller than Seth, a big, muscular man who looked like he might have a hint of Elemental in his genetic make-up.

"*Aff,*" snapped Seth, "to remind us of our vulnerability. Thus she makes the threat without ever having to utter the words. Is that not how it is done in the Inner Sphere?"

"Just because you hear the threat, Khan Ward, does not mean it has been leveled against you," said Patrik.

Alaric knew Seth had the right of it, but now was not the time to speak. There would be a better moment coming.

The Exile's saKhan, Selvina Woods, leaned in. "Does it matter whether she thinks to threaten us? The movement of civilians is well underway, but it will not be complete for a good year, especially with the recent delay. Why should we not feast on the worlds of the Free Worlds League while we consolidate our new holdings?"

Alaric saw the answer to that question written on the faces of the men and women around the room.

Liam Ward put their sentiment into words: "It is unworthy for a Clan to bow to the threats of Spheroids," said the Loremaster in a low, aggrieved voice.

That brought silence to the room.

Patrik glanced at Liam. "The Exiles have long benefited from our partnership with the Lyrans. The price for such a relationship is *compromise.*"

He will never turn against House Steiner, Alaric realized. *The Exiles are more Lyran than Wolf. Many things will have to be concealed from them.*

"We have yet to hear from our *ristar,* the commander of the invasion," said Liam Ward. The Loremaster turned to gaze at him. "What say you, Galaxy Commander Alaric?"

Alaric saw at once that the question was a trap. He had gained position and prestige from the Marik conflict, and Liam expected him to press for continuing the invasion. But even if he did not, what could Alaric say? Melissa Steiner had left them without alternatives. So Liam thought.

Because that was what Alaric wanted him to think.

Liam, like the Lyrans, did not understand that a great warrior would never trade away his honor, not for a civilian life, not for a *billion* civilian lives.

Alaric looked at the gathered Wolves and allowed a charming smile to grow on his face, showing his brothers and sisters the same face he had shown to Melissa Steiner. "Why, we should continue the invasion, of course."

Liam leaned back, the hint of that triumphant smile again quirking his lips.

"Really, we have no choice," said Alaric. "For are we not Melissa Steiner's tame wolves? Are we not her *dogs*?"

The room lapsed into stunned silence.

Until Khan Seth Ward threw his head back and laughed.

Right then, Alaric knew he had won. And then he was back among the bonfire of worlds Melissa had shown them, remembering three perfect gems colored Steiner blue.

Where his victory would begin.

**COMSTAR SECRET RESEARCH FACILITY OMEGA ONE
LUYTEN 68-28 (EXACT COORDINATES UNKNOWN)
PREFECTURE X
9 JANUARY 3140**

Tucker Harwell found himself in the most surprising place he'd ever been in his life—Sandra Whitfield's personal quarters. There wasn't much to the place—it looked like a hotel suite. And like a hotel, it was anonymous. Tucker didn't see any personal touches.

She's new here, he thought.

He stepped into a living room: sofa opposite the wall screen. Behind a half-open door, Tucker flashed a scrap of shimmering white silk cast aside over rumpled covers.

Whitfield followed his glance and arched a delicate, red eyebrow. "Really, Tucker? My bedroom? Surely you don't think you've earned *that* kind of incentive?"

Suddenly, Tucker was tripping over his tongue. "No, I just—I mean, the door was open and I just glanced—"

"Sit down," she said coldly. Tucker dropped onto the sofa.

Whitfield paced back and forth for a moment as if considering something, then she settled on the low-slung coffee table opposite the sofa, her knees nearly touching his. She leaned forward, her hazel eyes catching his gaze.

"I am afraid you're not quite living up to expectations, Tucker," she murmured.

Tucker swallowed.

"Here you were supposed to be our best hope to undo the blackout, and I have to say, you haven't come up with any new leads since—"

"Since Patricia damaged my mind," he croaked.

"Really," said Whitfield, "aren't we past the my-sister-did-it stage?"

Tucker shrugged. He was tired. *So* tired. He no longer cared if Whitfield shot him or not. A part of him just wanted it all to be over.

Tucker Harwell no longer knew who he was. Huge parts of himself, huge *swaths* were gone, stolen by the terrible things Patricia had done to his mind. Everything was harder. *Walking* was harder. *Thinking* was harder. He no longer could do single-order differential equations in his head. *He had to write them down.* And his hands shook when he jotted down the equations, the terrible tremors a reminder of just how much he'd lost.

At night he dreamed of a cat. He couldn't remember what the cat looked like or even its name, but he *did* remember its soft fur under his hand, the rattle of its contented purr. It was like someone had tried to erase all cat memories from his mind, but had only managed to find the boxes marked: "Cat Names" and "Cat Pictures."

Sometimes he fell asleep at night, sobbing desperately into his pillow for a lost cat whose name he couldn't remember and whose face he couldn't see.

Everything was harder.

So yeah, she might execute him. But he no longer cared. Hell, he wasn't even sure who'd she'd be killing. The *real* Tucker Harwell, well, Tucker wasn't sure that guy was even really around. He shared the man's face, but he didn't feel like *that* guy.

Maybe Tucker Harwell was already dead.

Unaccountably she reached forward and patted his knee. "Don't worry, *Tuck,*" she bit the name out, "Buhl turned to me because I'm in the solution business." She flashed him a cold smile. "And I haven't quite given up on you yet."

She reached into her pants pocket and pulled out a thumb-sized device fashioned from translucent green plastic. She tossed it to him.

Tucker reached for it with shaking hands, but it tumbled it from his grasp and bounced off the brown and gold carpet.

Whitfield clicked her tongue as she bent to retrieve it. For a second, her hand brushed against his as she pressed the little piece of plastic into his palm.

"What is it?"

"It's a key. It will give you access to Omega One's network. Apparently, you can no longer get by on what's in your head. So we're going to augment your effort."

She is giving me network access. For the first time Tucker was glad the damage to his mind had turned his face into a wooden mask, so she did not see the hope that surged through him.

He closed a fist around the small piece of plastic and said, "Okay."

There was a knock at the door and then a brute with a laser rifle slung over his shoulder pushed it open. "Is the prisoner ready to go, ma'am?"

Whitfield nodded, and Tucker climbed shakily to his feet.

She stood as well, all slender grace. Tucker turned from her and plodded to the door and the waiting guards.

"Oh, and Tucker."

He turned, found her peering at the carpet, hand pressed against her forehead as if she were trying to remember something. She dropped her hand and looked up. "Remember, here on Omega One, someone is always watching. So don't try anything naughty—or there will be consequences."

Their eyes locked and Tucker was unable to suppress a shudder.

A little smile of triumph curled across Whitfield's lips. It was enough to make Tucker angry. "Even you?" he snapped.

"*Oh, yes,*" Whitfield whispered fervently, a cold smile blossoming on her pretty face. "*Especially* me."

THE FERTILE STEPPE
HARVEST
JADE FALCON OCCUPATION ZONE
15 JANUARY 3140

Death lay across the land like a black shroud. A gentle breeze was enough to lift a swirling cloud of ash into the air. Beckett Malthus tasted soot.

It was not just that the land was charred, burned to blackness, but that it had been despoiled. There was worse here than the mere work of fire. There was the stink of petrochem and diesel, the electric taste of ozone, the terrible heat still roiling off mounds of burning metal slag, the invisible caress of radiation.

The smell of rotting flesh.

Khan Gottfried Amirault of Clan Hell's Horses stood looking out at the land that had been his before his warriors had lost yet another Trial of Possession.

"This land will never grow again," Gottfried said in a low, deep voice. Beckett almost he imagined he could hear grief in that voice.

Gottfried was a big man, tall but lean in a khaki tunic trimmed with dark brown and matching trousers. His skull was shaved, except for a queue of luxuriously thick brown hair that curled down from the back of his head.

He had turned his back on Malvina Hazen.

Beckett had known her to kill for less. Maybe it would be better if she killed Gottfried and shattered any possible alliance with the Horses. Better for all humanity.

But for once, Malvina Hazen did not succumb to the narcotic of violence. Instead she said: "Such are the wages of war, my Khan."

My Khan. Beckett thought that was a particularly nice touch. That was why he was here, Beckett realized, to show Gottfried there was still room for khans in Malvina's new Mongol order.

Gottfried turned to face her with a raised eyebrow. "You have attacked our agricultural worlds. Why have you done this, Malvina Hazen?"

"We are Clanners. Need there be any reason other than the right of the strong to take from the weak?"

Gottfried's handsome face twisted with rage. His black eyes marked her face. "You have slashed open the Horse's belly. Hunger stalks our worlds. Is this what you intended, Malvina Hazen?" The sweep of his arm took in the ruined land. "The Clans have always engaged in civilized war. But this, *this*, is wanton destruction. Is this what your perversion of the Mongol Doctrine has come to?"

"I will thank you to reconsider your words," said Malvina, her voice arctic cold.

Gottfried took a step toward her.

Something flashed in her right hand. It was not the knife Beckett expected.

It was a data crystal.

"Here is the answer to your question, Gottfried Amirault." She tossed the crystal down. It landed at his feet.

The Horse Khan looked down. "What is it?"

"BattleROM footage," said Malvina. "From our recent battles. It is uncut and unedited. It shows that the destruction of the croplands was incidental to the battles."

Gottfried frowned, but after a moment he leaned down and picked the crystal up. He held it front of his face, peering at it.

"We Jade Falcons are not fools, my Khan," said Malvina. "We fight for what we want. We do not then destroy it."

And then it all clicked in place for Beckett. The reason for the strange battle on Romulus. *Malvina had to make her scorched earth policy look like an accident.* All those lives sacrificed so she could offer Gottfried plausible deniability.

The Horse Khan's eyes flickered from the crystal to Malvina's face. "What do you want?"

"I want Terra," she said simply.

Terra. The cradle of humanity. What Khan did not dream of taking Terra and raising his Clan above all others? Whichever Clan claimed Terra would become the ilClan. They would rule all Clans and bring humanity to heel.

Beckett *was* Jade Falcon, but he was also skilled in the use of political machinations, so he was able to suppress the shudder of dread he felt at the thought of Malvina Hazen set above all humanity. *This cannot be.*

Gottfried did not bother to ask her how she planned to penetrate Fortress Republic. Perhaps he knew, as Beckett did, that Malvina would throw her body against the very gates of Heaven if her goal lay within.

"But," said Malvina, "I know Clan Jade Falcon cannot complete this glorious quest on its own."

Gottfried froze. "You propose an alliance, *quiaff*?"

"*Aff*," she easily.

Gottfried stared off into the distance, considering his options. Beckett suspected the Khan had placed a member of the watch inside the Fire Horse Galaxy Malvina had adopted into her Golden Ordun. Surely he knew Malvina was mad, mad enough to use chemical weapons against civilians, mad enough to murder Manas Amirault.

Mad enough to plunge a WarShip into Clan Jade Falcon's heart.

Still, the Horses would gain much by joining with the Falcons. The Horses were surrounded, on one side by the

Falcons and on the other by the Ghost Bear's Rasalhague Dominion. Alone, they had no path to Terra.

But to follow a monster...

Do not make the same mistake I did, Beckett thought.

"And if I refuse?" said Gottfried finally.

A slow, frightening smile slipped across Malvina's pretty face. "Then you should remember that you would not be the first Khan I have destroyed."

CHAPTER 6

**COMSTAR SECRET RESEARCH FACILITY OMEGA ONE
LUYTEN 68-28 (EXACT COORDINATES UNKNOWN)
PREFECTURE X
23 MARCH 3140**

Tucker Harwell lifted his trembling gaze to the radioactive disposal bin on his workbench. The radiac built into the wall chattered steadily, each *click* proof that an energetic photon or a lumbering alpha particle or a sleek, dangerous neutron had passed through the device's detector. Proof that invisible poison was sleeting through the room.

He glanced down at the noteputer in his hand.

And looked back up at the pile of debris sitting in the bin. The radiation level wasn't high enough to kill a human being. Oh, it would probably elevate Tucker's cancer risk later in life—always assuming he was granted a "later in life"—but it wouldn't kill him.

He was fairly certain it would kill a hard drive, though.

He thought sometimes when he was sleeping they came and took his 'puter. He'd find settings changed, like someone had used it. No doubt Whitfield was downloading his hard drive and tracking his keystrokes with a key logger. The first time he accessed something dangerous, like a map of the facility, or a JumpShip schedule, they'd know.

For two months he had been the model prisoner. He'd told himself he was biding his time, but the truth was he was afraid.

He clenched his fist, drew a savage breath. *No security is infallible, Tucker.* Whitfield is brilliant and ruthless and terrifying. *But not infallible.*

He was leaving.

Tucker could no longer wait for the Republic. He remembered the sound of Alexi Holt's pip crushing under Whitfield's heel. Alexi still hadn't come for him. It was time to put away childish things.

If he were to escape, he was going to have to do it himself.

He glanced down at the 'puter and swallowed. And then he began to type.

When he was done, he casually placed the device next to the radioactive disposal bin and laid down on his rack.

Someone was opening his door. Tucker woke up just as *she* stepped through the door. She was tall and strong. She wore MechWarrior togs: cooling vest, shorts, boots. A needler rested on one slim hip. Her blond hair was cut short and spiked on top. Her green eyes settled on him, and she broke into a huge smile.

"Tucker."

He tried to swallow in a dry mouth. "Alexi," he whispered. "I thought you had forgotten me. I didn't think you were ever coming."

"I could never forget you, Tuck." She leaned over him, gently touching his cheek with her hand. Then she pulled her hand back—

And slapped him.

The sting jerked him out of his sleep. His eyes fluttered open and he saw—

Whitfield.

"Don't worry, Tuck," she said, her voice mocking, "I'll never forget you."

Tucker sat up, gasping for air, his heart racing, his eyes locked on Whitfield. *She held his noteputer in her left hand.*

Whitfield wagged her finger at him and made a *tut-tut* sound with her tongue. "Tucker, I am afraid you have been very careless." She held up his 'puter. "You destroyed a very expensive piece of equipment."

"I'm sorry," said Tucker desperately.

"Oh, I'm afraid sorry won't do it this time, champ." She brushed a strand of red hair out of her eyes. "I've brought along someone to help you understand the importance of treating other people's property with respect."

The door opened again. Tucker instantly recognized the person who stepped through.

"Patricia," he whispered.

"Hello, Tuck," said his sister. "How are you doing?" She smiled, and it made her look beautiful. "I've missed you."

**MERLIN-CLASS DROPSHIP *FWLS MARATHON*
NEAR THE NADIR JUMP POINT, ATREUS
FREE WORLDS LEAGUE
12 MAY 3140**

As *Marathon*'s commanding officer, Marion Helm could have been asleep in her rack, but there was something about the midwatch that appealed to her. Her vessel was designed to watch.

And the dead of night was the time when watching was most important.

The *Merlin*-class DropShip certainly could defend herself in a fight, but she hadn't been placed on station to do battle. She was a command and control platform. To that end, two of her extended range large lasers had been removed to make room for an extra-large telescope and the digital processing power to crunch any image or signal she might detect.

Helm sipped a bulb of coffee as she stared out at a black viewscreen. The jump point was as quiet as it had been yesterday, and the day before and the day before *that.*

The coffee, on the other hand, tasted especially terrible. She would've had to add sugar and perhaps a little cream to make it taste merely *bad.* She smiled. Somehow she couldn't bring herself to drink anything else. What was it about naval officers and bad coffee? That was one tradition that stretched back to the days of sail.

"Sweep is clear, Captain," called out Junior Lieutenant Jerome Carter.

"Very well, OOD." The boy was good, but he was young. *Earnest.* Carter probably thought Clan Wolf was going to come pounding out of hyperspace any second. If he wasn't careful, he was going to have a stroke. Then she'd have to train a whole new bridge officer.

Helm sighed. "Listen up, everyone," she said calmly. "We're a picket. That means we wait, and watch. Of course, I expect, I *demand*, absolute devotion to duty. But it has been more than four months since our brave soldiers halted the advance of the Wolves and Lyrans. Do not be spooked by the silence. Every day of that four months, every *second,* is a victory for the League."

"Yes, ma'am," said her people slowly, nodding thoughtfully, absorbing her words.

Helm smiled into her coffee bulb. *There, that ought to do it.* Now if they could just have a nice, quiet mid-watch to think about—

Something flashed bright against the darkness of space.

"Jump," sang out the petty officer at navigation. "I have EMP. She bears zero six three relative, one zero eight thousand klicks."

Helm pointed at her Boatswain Mate. "Boats. GQ."

Petty Officer Xia yanked the GQ alarm lever down and a panicked gonging filled the bridge. He reached for the 1MC and put the mike to his lips. Xia's deep voice filled the ship. "General Quarters, General Quarters. All hands to battle stations. Set condition Zebra throughout the ship."

Even before he had finished, Helm raised her voice and said: "This is the Captain, I have the deck and the con." She glanced at tactical. "Get me a firing solution, *now.*" She kicked off against a bulkhead, zipping neatly over to nav, where she grabbed a handhold and pulled herself down next to the quartermaster. "I want an ID on that bird as soon as she clears jump."

"Aye, aye, captain." Beads of sweat lined the quartermaster's upper lip.

For a moment, the bridge was a tumult of noise as GQ watchstanders relieved their mid-watch counterparts. Then the bridge was totally silent.

The silence was worse.

"She's clear," sang out the tactical action officer. Helm looked up at the screen. What she saw was a *Scout* carrying no DropShips, her white hull marked with a Marik eagle.

Helm's mouth tasted like sand.

Painted on the *Scout*'s bow was the name *Pericles*.

So she wasn't surprised when the GQ navigator reported, "I've verified her IFF." He looked up and his young face was chalk. "She's transmitting the proword 'canary.'"

"World," Helm barked.

The navigator glanced down at his board. "Aitutaki."

"Radioman to the bridge," Helm barked. She didn't trust herself to speak. *It was me who needed the pep talk,* she thought bitterly, *not my crew.*

After the death of Thaddeus Marik, the Free Worlds Navy had set up a network of JumpShips in the systems surrounding Atreus. These canaries were supposed to jump to Atreus if their home system was attacked. It wasn't as fast or detailed as an HPG transmission, but the appearance of a canary carried a message nonetheless.

In this case, that Clan Wolf was assaulting the world of Aitutaki.

The radio chief poked his head into the bridge. "Yes, Captain."

Helm swallowed. Her palms were sweating and her legs were trembling, but somehow when her voice came out, it was steel. "I have flash message traffic for the Captain-General."

The radio chief swallowed, but nodded.

"Jump," called out the TAO. "Two one seven at one six two thousand klicks."

Helm turned to stare at him, her mouth hanging slackly open. *Another* jump? "Are you—" She almost said, "Are you *sure?*" but she was cut off by her GQ OOD.

"I've got another one at three five five."

"*Four!*" shouted the navigator. "Zero four six at two five four thousand klicks."

Marion Helm reached down with a trembling hand to steady herself against the nav console. When she had been a young woman, her husband had been killed in a hoverjeep accident. She still remembered the deputy sheriff standing at her door, the sick lurch of unreality as she listened to his words, the terrible heaviness in her stomach, her skin hot, her guts ice.

That's exactly how she felt now.

My God, she thought. *How many systems are the Wolves attacking?*

THE HOUSE OF GOVERNMENT
ATREUS CITY
ATREUS
FREE WORLDS LEAGUE

"Six, Your Grace," said Torrian Dolcat grimly, "including Atreus."

"Six," whispered Captain-General Jessica Marik. "*Six?*"

Philip reached out and touched her elbow, steadying her. It was all happening so fast. The phone had rung at two o'clock in the morning, jerking her out of sleep. She remembered the crisp voice of the watch officer: *The Wolves are attacking.*

A little shiver wriggled down her spine. That voice, those words would stay with her the rest of her life.

However long that might be.

And now she was standing here in the sitting room of the family quarters in her dressing gown with her husband, her *real* husband beside her, discussing the destruction of the Free Worlds League.

"Ionus, Aitutaki, Manihiki, Escobas, Loyalty, and of course, Atreus," said the head of SAFE.

Dolcat's sweating, thought Jessica. *My God, I've* never *seen him sweat before.*

The young man was still talking: "—starting to come in as our second-line pickets jump. In the other systems,

Elementals have secured the jump point charging stations. Their DropShips are racing in at standard combat acceleration. They are not answering hails. They are not bargaining."

No bargaining, Jessica thought. *Just conquest.* She shook her head. "Six worlds."

The Wolves' first wave was no doubt intended to decapitate the League by capturing the seat of government. Worse, it would snap the spine of her realm, separating its spinward and anti-spinward halves.

Six worlds.

Could the Wolves really sustain a half-dozen separate offensives? Jessica had moved forces spinward from Tamarind-Abbey and the Rim Commonality, but she had not expected to defend six worlds at a time.

Dolcat cleared his throat. Jessica looked up. *There's more.*

The head of SAFE swallowed. "This is a coordinated strike, Your Grace."

"Obviously," said Jessica dryly.

"No, Your Grace. I mean this strike is coordinated with a new Lyran offensive. We've just received word they've hit three worlds in the Protectorate Coalition."

"Jessica," said Philip gently. "It's time to consider Chronos."

"We have your DropShip standing by," said Dolcat. "The ready JumpShip is prepped at the Atreus-Wendigo L4."

"Chronos," Jessica whispered. Had it really come to that?

In ancient mythology, Chronos had been the king of the Titans. Fearing that his children would overthrow him, he swallowed them whole. But Zeus escaped. Eventually he was able to cut his father's belly open, and his brothers and sisters emerged whole and unharmed.

Thus the Olympian Gods were reborn from the body of a tyrant.

The two men were silent, looking at her. Waiting for her to give the order. They were talking about abandoning Atreus. Relocating the capital.

Jessica raised her head, straightened her back. *I am the Captain-General of the Free Worlds League.* "No."

"Atreus is exposed, Jessica," said Philip reasonably. "We can't hope to hold it from a determined Wolf assault."

A dark chuckle escaped from Jessica. *A determined Wolf assault*. Was there any other kind?

"Oriente is well back from the front lines—" began Dolcat.

"I said no," said Jessica mildly.

The head of SAFE drew a deep breath. "Your Grace. The Atreus assault force." He shook his head. "It's led by a *Congress*-class WarShip, the *Rogue*. We count three pocket WarShips, one belonging to the Wolf Khan himself. Enough 'Mech carriers to account for an entire galaxy."

"Jessica," said Philip. There was a note of pleading in his voice.

She had worked so hard to reform the League. Her false marriage to Thaddeus to gain the Marik name and the legitimacy it conferred. Using the Lyran war as a rallying point to bring her people together. The intense diplomacy, the many compromises.

And Atreus was the symbol of all that. If she fled Atreus, the League would splinter—and this time there would be no putting it back together.

She shook her head. "We can't flee Atreus in the middle of the night. We can't let that be the story of the Wolf assault."

"But—" began Dolcat.

"Oh, we'll leave," said Jessica coldly. "But first we need to change the narrative."

CLEARWATER NATURE PRESERVE
OUTSIDE ATREUS CITY

It was a cool spring day, the trill of a red-wing blackbird singing counterpoint to the soft gurgle of a brook. Fluffy white cotton from a stand of cottonwoods floated down through the air like lazy snow.

Samuel Bone had Clearwater all to himself. Most people were desperately trying to secure passage off the planet. Bone watched trails of fire and smoke mar the pretty blue sky as DropShip after DropShip filled with fleeing citizens lifted for space and the nearest JumpShip with an empty docking collar. The Wolves were coming, and no matter what brave noises Jessica made, Atreus *was* going to fall.

Bone wasn't worried about it. He'd already secured his method of transportation. His ride was willing to hold out quite a bit later than most commercial traffic. Bone had paid them well for their patience, and they were used to unusual business requirements. They were the kind of people for whom the term "pirate point" wasn't just a euphemism.

He put his binoculars to his face, studying the wide cut in the earth where the little brook flowed. He wondered if a 'Mech could get through there.

If the news reports could be believed, the Halas bitch wasn't running. Bone hoped it was true. Clan Wolf would put a proper end to Jessica Halas-Hughes *Marik.* There wasn't a trick, a negotiation, *an intrigue* that would work on the Wolves.

Before coming here, Bone had met with his LIC handler face-to-face and had passed on everything he knew about the current situation, which was quite a lot. It was a dangerous move, but now was the time for dangerous moves. Besides, he was willing to bet that SAFE was so busy looking *outside,* they might miss a thing or two *inside.*

Bone's report would be carried out of the system via a commercial JumpShip traveling to Lyran space. When the courier reached his destination, a special command circuit would bring it to the Archon. At least that's how Bone would have done it. LIC didn't really tell him anything. It was bad tradecraft to share any more information than was absolutely necessary with any one person in the chain.

Bone studied the trees and the brook through his binoculars. This little park was where the Wolves would come through. There was a civilian drop pad not twenty klicks to the south, and the forest would cover their approach.

This was it.

Of course if he were wrong, he had his hoverbike. He'd make it to the action one way or the other. But he was almost never wrong.

The Lyran handler had offered to get him out, a reward for faithful service, but Bone had demurred. Jessica and the Wolves promised to be one helluva show.

And he had a front row seat.

ZDENEKOVA ESTATE, OUTSIDE MOLFETTA
CARRABESTO, GIENAH
BOLAN MILITARY PROVINCE
LYRAN COMMONWEALTH

Melissa Steiner cradled a glass of white wine in her hand as she leaned over a stone balcony that looked out over the leviathan called Molfetta. After a long space journey, it would have been nice to stand outside on a beautiful summer day and enjoy the sun on her face, cool tendrils of wind toying with her hair, the smell of pine clean and sharp on the air.

But whatever pleasure she would have taken from that, Molfetta stole it away.

Molfetta was a monster. It was glass and steel thrust into the blue sky. It was ribbons of ferrocrete draped over the fertile land. It was noise and motion, the *speed* of hovercars and the steady clank of factories. It was pollution and production, corruption and cooperation, decadence and determination.

It was profit.

Which was what made the world a problem for Melissa.

She turned to Duke Stanislav Zdenekova. Duke Stan was a small, round man, not more than one meter seventy in height. His face was the color of cinnamon, and he was smiling faintly. Melissa couldn't ever remember him not smiling.

"I am sorry, Archon, but there are concerns about the new situation."

The new situation. A euphemism for her conquest of huge chunks of the Free Worlds League. "Once the new worlds are assimilated, business will double," said Melissa evenly.

"Business was fine here before the new situation," said Duke Stan.

And there it is, thought Melissa. In a province that feared and hated the Mariks, Gienah had cultivated commercial relationships with the Free Worlds League.

It was conversations like this that were the reason for Melissa's tour of the Bolan Military Province. Bringing new worlds into the Commonwealth was a great victory, but someone still had to make the adopted kids feel welcome, and let the older kids know they hadn't lost their place in the family.

Melissa decided now was the time to bring out her big gun. "Because of your expertise in dealing with League corporations, I've decided to administer the integration effort through Gienah." She smiled.

Duke Stan frowned—*frowned*—and looked away.

Melissa opened her mouth, surprised. That wasn't the reaction she'd expected. Billions and billions of kroner would flow into the province to bring the new worlds into the fold, and Gienah would be in position to skim a healthy cut off the top.

"Stan?" She shook her head. "This will preserve your commercial relationships with the former League worlds."

Duke Stan snorted. "What about our commercial relationships with Gannett? And Helm? And *Stewart*?"

She blinked. "Over time, the Wolves are sure to see the benefit of working closer with us."

"Oh, I'm sure the Wolves want to be *closer*," said Duke Stan bitterly.

Melissa straightened and set her glass down with a *clink.* When she spoke her voice was cold. "If you have something to say, Duke Zdenekova, why don't you say it?"

He turned to her, anger twisting the lines of his soft, friendly face. "You've brought the Wolves to our doorstep, Archon. What if they turn on us?"

"We are watching them closely," said Melissa placidly, "to ensure their attention remains focused rimward."

"They could turn easily enough," he snapped. "Attack Ideyld, Sheridan, or Amity."

She frowned. "Why those three worlds?"

"*I can read a map!*" he nearly shouted.

"And you think I cannot," said Melissa softly. For a moment the question hung in the air.

Duke Stan drew a deep breath, and Melissa could see by the look on his face he realized he'd gone too far. "Archon, I didn't mean to—"

Melissa cut him off with a look. She held him silent for a long moment with those blue eyes. *Well,* she thought, *I did come out here to consolidate my rule.*

She leaned in to him. "What I am about to tell you will mean your life if it is ever repeated to another living soul," she whispered.

Duke Stan was suddenly very still.

"I have stationed tripwire units on Ideyld and Sheridan and Amity. Yes, the Wolves *could* turn and attack us." She turned to look out at the squalid wealth of Molfetta. "But it is a poor master indeed who does not plan for her pets' misbehavior."

THE GRAND RESORT
BROTHERHOOD ISLAND
AMITY
BOLAN MILITARY PROVINCE
LYRAN COMMONWEALTH

The beach was a sun-drenched arc of white sand wrapped around a small bay. A coral reef shielded the bay, so its waters were calm and blue. Perfect for snorkeling or swimming or horsing around. On the beach, guests sprawled face down on towels, their bodies shiny with oil, the smell of coconut heavy in the air. Or they reclined in cabana chairs beneath giant beach umbrellas, clutching tall glasses of gin that sweated more than they did.

Beyond the beach there was a hotel, a silver tower of steel and glass that reached thirty stories into the perfect blue sky. There were pools, three of them, and tennis courts and bike paths and an English garden and a hundred meters away, IndustrialMechs were putting in a world-class golf course.

A man stood on the white sand beach and studied everything carefully. He was a tall, powerful man with bronze skin, a square jaw, and a face that made women look twice. But in the end it wasn't his face that won them over—it was his *eyes,* a dark, stormy blue that sent women searching for words like *indigo* and *cobalt* and *pelagic.*

Yes, he would have done just fine on the beach.

If he hadn't been wearing a crisp dress-gray uniform and polished black boots.

Landgrave Jasek Kelswa-Steiner turned his attention to the resort's vast parking lot. He raised a communicator to his lips and clicked the SEND button. "Execute."

There was a distant rumble, somewhere below the ground. Jasek felt the vibration in his legs. The lot's blacktop began to crumble as if a sinkhole were opening. A *Storm Raider* BattleMech painted in jagged gray and black urban camouflage emerged from the hole. Jasek knew it was walking up a ramp, but it still looked a demon arising from hell.

None of the guests standing in the bay, or drinking their gin, or browning in the sun, looked at the BattleMech. Not one. It was as if Jasek was the only one who could see it. Of course, the "guests" were not really guests at all. They were members of Jasek's Stormhammers.

Jasek nodded and clicked the communicator. "Excellent." Looked like the deployment plan would work.

Besides the lance of BattleMechs hidden beneath the parking lot, there were a pair of Condors, a Demon, and a hoverbike squad hidden in the hollowed out shell masquerading as a hotel. A few blocks away, a parking garage hid a short battalion of light vehicles. And the IndustrialMechs working the golf course were all armed and armored beneath their bright yellow paint jobs.

Clanners sneered at hedonistic pursuits and overlooked the frivolous. If the Wolves came to Amity, Jasek was counting on them overlooking this resort.

The faux hotel was eighty klicks south of Imstar Aerospace and fifty-three kilometers south-southwest of a ferrocrete pad built for emergency DropShip landings. If the Wolves turned on the Commonwealth, they would attack

Amity. And if they attacked Amity, they would land here. They would drive for the planetary militia protecting Imstar. And once they'd taken the bait, the Stormhammers would hit them from behind.

A look of dark determination flickered across his face. If the Wolves came to Amity, Jasek would crush them. He had already lost one world to Clanners.

He wasn't about to lose another.

CHAPTER 7

Deep beneath the surface of the world, the Captain-General of the Free Worlds League waited for the Wolves to come.

The command center lay a good three hundred meters beyond the touch of the sun's light. It was encased in a reinforced ferrocrete shell that was hardened against nuclear attack, its dedicated comms lines shielded from EMP. Aside from the Captain-General's secret exit, the only way in or out of the command center was a two-meter-thick steel door.

That door had been shut and locked.

A platoon of infantry in Purifier armor guarded that door in the hopes their deaths would allow their Captain-General a few extra minutes to escape.

Jessica thought of them and had trouble swallowing past the tightness in her throat. *Maybe it will not come to that.* And then: *Don't lie to yourself, Jessica. There is no room for self-delusion here.*

She wore a white uniform tunic with the Marik crest in gold over her heart. The tunic was trimmed in gold with flared purple sleeves and was paired with a matching skirt. She wore a sword at her hip. This was a day of war, and she had dressed for it.

She drew a deep breath and tucked a wayward strand of gray hair behind her ear. She stood in the center of the immense room, stood at attention.

Waiting.

Jessica had no illusions as to how this day would end. *The Wolves would have Atreus.* Neither she nor her advisors could see any way to stop that. But she would bloody their noses so badly they could go no further.

The Wolf assault would end here.

"*Distant Howl* has achieved low orbit," called out one of the many officers hunched over consoles that were arranged in rows behind her. "Your Grace," said the man. "She is positioned directly overhead."

"Very well," said Jessica calmly. She allowed herself a small backward glance. Philip stood behind her, leaning against the wall, out of the way. He flashed her a smile that was somehow both sad and encouraging at the same time. Jessica had ordered him to go to Oriente. Philip had refused.

And here, at the end of things, she just didn't have the heart to arrest him.

"Your Grace," said her Aerospace Commander, "the Eagle's Wings request permission to—"

"Denied," snapped Jessica. "Stand by your guns."

"Yes, Your Grace," said the admiral, his voice tight.

Jessica hadn't contested the Wolf armada's transit in-system. She refused to throw her aerospace forces away in a fruitless battle against that WarShip and her retinue.

No, she'd spend her aerospace forces targeting the DropShips that would fall from the sky like leaves in autumn. (And to fight her way into orbit, of course.) She would give her ground forces every chance she could.

Even if she already knew it wouldn't be enough.

"Incoming message," said a force commander at communications. She looked up. "From the *Congress.*"

Jessica swallowed and took a defiant step toward the giant screen that covered the wall she faced. "Go ahead."

There was a moment of static and then a man appeared. He looked like a giant on the huge screen. He wore a simple gray jumpsuit without rank or ornament. He was thin, his face pale, the deep-set eyes burning with intensity.

Khan Seth Ward of Clan Wolf.

The Khan's dark eyes glittered as he looked down on her. There was the slightest twitch at the corner of his lips, as if he were amused by some private joke. He inclined his head.

This was a key moment. If the League were to survive the fall of Atreus, it would have to be a mythic fight. They were planning a desperate, bloody battle in which the Captain-General was lost, and then—miraculously—found.

But for now, she had had to strike a defiant tone.

Jessica took another step toward the screen, squared her shoulders. "I am Captain-General Jessica Halas-Hughes Marik of the Free Worlds League. As I stand here on Atreus, I stand on Ionus and Aitutaki, on Manihiki and Escobas. I stand on Loyalty. Across these six worlds I have sent orders. No mercy shall be given to Wolves, nor shall any be asked for. The hand of every man, woman, and child in the Free Worlds League is raised against the Wolves. Blood will be met with blood, savagery will be met with savagery."

Her voice rose to a roar. "I am Captain-General Jessica Halas-Hughes Marik, and *this is my vow*!" Jessica looked up, a snarl pulled across her face, her hands balled into fists.

Khan Ward looked down at her gravely for a long moment, his dark eyes meeting her gaze and then he threw his head back and laughed.

Jessica blinked.

"It is a most impressive bid, Captain-General," said Khan Ward, a smile curling across his pale face. "But before you choose to die, perhaps you should hear *my* bid."

CLEARWATER NATURE CENTER
OUTSIDE ATREUS CITY

Samuel Bone lay on his stomach, hidden in the grass, looking up at the sky. A new star had appeared, a diamond pinprick against heaven's blue bowl. Bone knew what it was even before he raised the binoculars to his face.

His powerful binos resolved the tiny jewel into a vessel, no bigger than a child's toy in his glasses, but unmistakable for all that. The vessel's engines held her in orbit over this precise spot. A row of tiny spheres ran along the vessel's spine, seeds, they looked like seed. Seeds of the League's destruction.

Bone smiled to himself, he just couldn't help it.

Now that the Wolves were here, it was finally and completely over. Oh, there might be the ridiculous bidding process if the Wolves hadn't gotten that over with on the run in. *Hi, I'm the Halas bitch and I'm defending this world with blah, blah, blah. Hi, I am Khan Ward and defend with whatever you want, because I am going to destroy you.* Sure. Great. But once that formality was over, there was nothing, *nothing* Jessica could do to save herself.

So Bone watched the sky. Any moment now, the Wolves would launch their armada, aerospace fighters plunging into the atmosphere, their sleek bodies limned in fire, DropShips riding down on pillars of golden plasma, BattleMechs with jump packs falling like giant paratroopers in a classic vertical envelopment.

Any moment now.

Bone stared into the beautiful blue sky at that beautiful Warship until his wrists ached from the weight of the binoculars.

What's taking them so long?

He kept his eyes trained on the heavens for another five minutes before he glanced at his watch.

It was only then that he felt the first stirrings of alarm.

COMSTAR SECRET RESEARCH FACILITY OMEGA ONE
LUYTEN 68-28 (EXACT COORDINATES UNKNOWN)
PREFECTURE X

Tucker worked on one of the relics his guards had brought him, this one a little noteputer that had been badly weathered by sand and time. The radiac clicked noisily to itself, so Tucker took the doubtful precaution of wearing rubber gloves as he worked. At least the gloves would stop alpha radiation, if not gamma or neutron. His own 'puter registered nothing, of course. The old noteputer was probably fried, but from time to time he'd found things on these old devices, so he kept working.

He grabbed a Phillips head with his trembling hand. It took him three tries to line up the screwdriver with the screw. He bit his lip, sweat sheening his face, *concentrating.* After what seemed like forever, he managed to pop the 'puter's case.

He tested the power supply and found that it was dead. So maybe the chip was still good. He reached for the device. His traitor hand spasmed, spilling parts everywhere, screws and plastic keys scattering across the bench and bouncing off the floor.

Tucker took a deep shuddery breath, fighting down the urge to sob.

He bent down to pick up the fallen parts, a maddening task with his damaged fine motor skills. He was down on his hands and knees when he found the chip. It was a black plastic wafer attached to a bright green circuit board, the whole thing the size of his thumb down to the first knuckle. It was dusty, and at least slightly radioactive.

But it might be good.

Tucker stared at it for a long moment. Without thinking, he snatched it up and popped it in his mouth.

It tasted bitter and metallic. Tucker imagined he could feel the radiation sheeting through his jaw, irradiating the calcium in his teeth, spawning horrific cancers in the soft tissue beneath his tongue.

He heaved himself to his feet and dumped the parts he'd collected into the disposal bin. He was breathing hard, sweating freely. His heart was racing. He shuffled toward the bathroom. As soon as the door was shut behind him, he spat the board out.

He peered at it. It might work. *It might really work.* It would take months. He'd have to build his computer from parts salvaged from the debris the ROM adepts brought him and carefully hide it from the people behind the one-way glass, but with patience and luck it might work. He might build a device on which he could hack the network, a device with no signature that could be tied back to him.

Tucker knelt down and hid the board with its precious chip behind the toilet's base and as he did he realized a strange and wondrous thing.

His hands weren't shaking.

INVADER-CLASS JUMPSHIP *LOPE*
ZENITH JUMP POINT, HELM
WOLF OCCUPATION ZONE
21 MAY 3140

Verena was intensely aware of Jacob's maleness, the way he *smelled,* like soap and light aftershave and something more primal underneath. He was tall with ash blond hair cut short, but long enough on top for a stray lock to fall playfully into his cerulean eyes. Whenever he looked at her, he flashed her a lopsided smile.

They stood at the rear of the *Lope's* bridge, on a narrow catwalk a meter above the main bridge, their feet tucked beneath a low rail, their hands resting on a waist-high railing, awaiting the jump to Bainsville.

Tension was thick on the bridge as naval personnel ran through intricate jump calculations. Alaric stood next to the vessel's captain near the holotank in the bridge's center discussing something in a hushed tone. Like the naval techs, Alaric was worried about something, she could see it in the hunch of his shoulders.

Jacob was the only relaxed person on the bridge. He had drifted just a little too close, his body brushing against her right shoulder. Verena edged a few centimeters left.

As a former Exile herself, she had been assigned to escort the Exile exchange officer, Star Colonel Jacob Carns. It was important for her to work effectively with him to support Clan Wolf's goal of reunification with their estranged cousins.

What made the situation even more complicated was that she and Jacob had grown up in the same crèche. They were sibkin, that strange Clan relationship that was part sibling, part competitor, and part lover.

"Jump detection," called out a technician. Alaric turned to the holotank, a scowl on his face, his blue eyes locked on the icon that hovered there. His helmet of golden hair bowed as he listened to something the JumpShip's captain was saying.

Alaric was not making it any easier. Over the last few months he had grown distant. Secretive. He was keeping something from her.

She tried to tell herself that he was just unhappy Beta Galaxy had not been selected to lead the attack on the Free Worlds League. After Alaric's brilliant assault on world after world in Marik space, it was a strange and bitter decision. A *shameful* decision.

But in her darker moments, she wondered if he had decided to take Katrina Steiner's advice and abandon her. Perhaps he had seen their relationship was a political liability he could no longer afford. *Yes, that sounded exactly like Katrina.* Was this how it would begin? Had he already been with another woman? Was his...*love, be honest with yourself,* she thought, *the word was love*—was his love for her a shallow thing he could afford to discard?

These were all very unnatural thoughts, un*clan* thoughts, and yet when she thought such things, her heart throbbed painfully in her chest and she tasted bitterness on her tongue.

What have I become?

"JumpShip confirmed as Wolf vessel," called out the tactical officer.

"Batteries are charged," reported the deck engineer.

"Incoming message for Galaxy Commander Alaric," sang out the tech on communications. Alaric drifted over to her station.

Jacob's shoulder bumped against Verena's, and she looked up at him. He smiled at her, that beautiful lopsided smile. "It is most pleasant to see you again, Verena."

"And you, Jacob," she said, edging another few centimeters to her left.

Somewhere in the background she heard the boatswain mate pass the word, "Ready Force, lay to the bridge."

He reached out and touched her face. "Would you like to couple after the jump?"

She looked up at him and then she turned away, breaking his touch. "Jacob, I—" There were no words for a Clanner to explain what she was feeling. To not couple with an old friend, a man who was *sibkin*, it was like a Spheroid refusing to come to a family dinner.

She could not explain, so she just looked up at him and said, "*Neg.*"

He did not look hurt, only puzzled. He stared at her for a long moment, and then a knowing smile curled across his face. "Verena," he whispered. "You are in *love.*"

She recoiled as if slapped.

"Who is the man?"

Without meaning to, her eyes flickered to Alaric.

Jacob saw her glance and smiled. "Alaric?"

"H-how did you—"

"Station-keeping drive engaged," one of the techs called and Verena felt weight return. Terrible, terrible weight.

"How did I know? The Exiles live and work among the Steiners. You are not the first Clanner to fall in love. Though it is surprising you had to come all the way to Clan Wolf for it to happen."

"Excuse me." Suddenly Alaric was standing on the other side of the railing. His eyes were on Jacob, and his face was stiff. Was he...*jealous?* Verena did not believe it was possible, but Alaric's face was cold, hard.

The space tight hatch behind her opened and a pair of Elementals stepped onto the bridge. The genetically engineered soldiers were huge, pushing three meters tall.

Alaric met Jacob's eyes. "Star Colonel Jacob Carns, I take you prisoner."

Jacob's eyes went wide with surprise. His body tensed, but before he could move the Elementals tackled him from behind. They hauled him to his feet.

"You *stravag* dog," Jacob snarled. "I challenge you to a Trial of Refusal."

Alaric shook his head. "There will be no trial. But I offer you a choice. You can choose to become my bondsman. Or

Clan Wolf will grant you the Right of Return and turn you over to the Exiles."

Jacob struggled against his captors, but the massive Elementals held him fast. "You are *mad*, Alaric." He glanced at Verena. "Is this because—"

Alaric chuckled. "No."

"Then why? What are you doing?"

"We are not jumping to Bainsville, Jacob. We are preparing to attack the Lyran Commonwealth."

Jacob gasped. "*What?*"

Verena found her mouth was hanging slackly open.

Alaric smiled faintly and nodded. "It is true."

"But—" Jacob shook his head. "Wait. Is this about your civilians? Why do you not negotiate with the Archon for more lift capacity to speed the migration?"

"We tried," said Alaric flatly. "For two months. We asked her to provide additional JumpShips from other military provinces, but she refused." He raised his voice. "The Archon enjoys holding *our leash* too much to ever let it go."

"And *that* is worth turning on the Lyrans, *quineg*?"

"*Aff,*" said Alaric. "That and the Archon blocks our thrust into the Republic toward Terra. But there is even a greater reason for fighting the Archon: *you.*"

"*Us?*" Jacob rasped.

Alaric nodded. "You Exiles have grown accustomed to the collar. Melissa brought us to her realm thinking she was getting another obedient pack of dogs. But we, *we* will never grow accustomed to the collar."

Alaric's voice rang out. "*We are wolves.*"

"*Seyla!*" shouted the Wolves on his bridge as one.

Jacob swallowed.

"Bondsman or Exile," said Alaric. "Think on it well, Jacob. You could slink back to Arc-Royal. Or you could become a true Wolf." He nodded and the Elementals dragged Jacob away.

Alaric raised his voice. "Captain Paul, secure station-keeping drive and recalculate jump for Amity."

"As ordered, Galaxy Commander," answered *Lope's* captain.

Alaric pulled himself up the short ladder that led up to the catwalk. He took up station next to Verena, where Jacob had stood a few moments before.

"I do not understand," she said softly. "How can we launch attacks against two great houses at once?"

Alaric shook his head. "We cannot. The attack against the Free Worlds League was a feint. The JumpShips we sent into their systems carried few troops. Instead our forces have been massing on the coreward side of our occupation zone."

"A trick to fool House Steiner."

"And House Marik. We showed Captain-General Jessica a glimpse of what we could do: annihilate her nation, annihilate her *line*. When faced with that, is it not obvious she would agree to anything to stave off those horrors?"

"You thought of this," said Verena with wonder in her voice.

Alaric simply smiled.

"Is it not dishonorable to resort to trickery?" asked Verena.

"We are not hidebound Jade Falcons, after all. Although—" Alaric rolled his eyes, "—hidebound Jade Falcons are not what they once were, either. We are now denizens of the Inner Sphere. And when in Rome..." For a moment, she thought he sounded like Katrina.

"So Khan Ward negotiated a truce with the Mariks."

"More than that. They recognized our borders, we even won favorable trade terms."

"To make up for the civilians we will lose when we turn against the Lyrans."

Again, Alaric smiled.

"Incredible," Verena whispered.

The shrill call of an alarm sounded throughout the bridge. *Lope*'s commander picked up the 1MC mike. "This is the captain. All hands, prepare for jump."

Alaric stared at the viewscreen and Helm's dim orange primary. "There is only one thing I regret," he said in a low voice.

Verena turned away, not daring to look at him. She, too, stared at the screen.

"Because of our close association with the Lyrans and the Exiles, this operation had to be planned in absolute secrecy. My orders came from Khan Ward himself." His voice dropped to a whisper. "I would have liked to tell you."

Then he reached down, and without turning to look at her, he squeezed her hand.

Lope jumped. And right then reality twisted into a terrible, impossible shape and there was nothing in the universe but Alaric standing there, holding her hand until—

—they were on the other side and she was trembling with the affects of the jump, ashamed that this man who meant so much to her could feel her weakness. He said nothing, did not turn to look at her.

But he squeezed her hand harder.

Verena drew a deep breath, steadying herself. Her eyes were still locked on the viewscreen, this time centered on Amity's brilliant red sun. She swallowed. "If you forgive me, Galaxy Commander," she said softly, "there is a problem with your plan."

Alaric turned to her and raised a blond eyebrow. "Oh?" he said, a faint smile touching his lips.

"Whatever else they may be, the Lyrans are not fools. They will have staged tripwire units on the worlds most likely to be attacked."

"You think so?" asked Alaric.

"It is what you would have done," said Verena.

She expected him to answer, but he said nothing. After a moment, she opened her mouth to speak— But the cry of the jump alarm cut her off.

"This is the captain. All hands, prepare for jump."

This time when they jumped, Alaric's laughter filled all space and time.

MONOLITH-CLASS JUMPSHIP *ARCHON'S REACH*
ZENITH JUMP POINT, DAR-ES-SALAAM
BOLAN MILITARY PROVINCE
LYRAN COMMONWEALTH
23 MAY 3140

Archon Melissa Steiner stood on the bridge of her JumpShip and looked out on the stars. *Her* stars, not to put too fine a point on it.

Again and always.

Trillian drifted up to the Archon and handed her a noteputer. "Your Highness, an update on that matter we discussed."

Melissa took the device and clicked through a number of screens. What she saw was a logistics report. Everything a military needed to operate: parts, munitions, fuel, even *paint* was flowing coreward to units on the Jade Falcon border.

And away from Vedet.

Trillian had done a masterful job. Every item of material was tied to a specific requisition. And in order to cover the hit on Vedet, supplies were being pulled from Bolan militias, too. Even some front-line units would lose some support to preserve the illusion that it was a widespread need for supplies that was causing the shift, not a political vendetta.

Vedet's offensive would bleed from a thousand cuts, and Melissa's fingerprints would be nowhere to be found.

Melissa handed the 'puter back to Trillian. "This will play."

Trillian's mouth hardened into a thin line. She looked away.

Melissa drew a deep breath. "Do you have a concern?"

Trillian glanced around the bridge, carefully gauging what she could say in an open setting. "LIC is reporting that something is going on between the Falcons and the Horses. And I read Von Texeira's analysis."

The diplomat's report had warned that Malvina Hazen had made an overture to the Horse's during the Falcon's civil war. If the two Clans were to join forces...

"You think we focus our attention on the wrong border," said Melissa softly.

Trillian said nothing. She would not criticize Melissa in public, however obliquely.

"There was no avoiding this trip, Trillian."

Trillian nodded, acknowledging the point.

There really was no substitute for face-to-face meetings. The attitude of Melissa's lords confounded her. She had expanded their reach in this region and had beaten back House Marik, a perennial enemy of Bolan Province. And to top it off, they would grow wealthy as they assimilated the new worlds *she* had conquered. And if she could pull off her little plan for ComStar, the Commonwealth might very well become the most powerful realm in all the Inner Sphere.

And still some of her lords could do nothing but wring their hands.

Well. Now she understood which ones could be brought along into the new world her vision had provided, and which would have to be left behind.

Another benefit of face-to-face meetings.

"In any event," said Melissa, "there may be troops to move coreward soon enough, since the Wolves should keep House Marik off-balance for some time."

"I hope so, Highness," said Trillian softly, and it was Melissa's turn to purse her lips. *Later, we shall have a discussion about your attitude, cousin. However bright and useful you are, you are* not *Archon.*

Melissa raised her voice. "How soon will be jumping, *Kommodore?*"

"First run jump calculations have been completed, Highness," said *Leutnant-Kommodore* Derrick Kohl. "I expect to complete the check set shortly. Assuming we obtain a match, we will jump within ten minutes."

"Very well," said Melissa.

Melissa's security detail required that all calculations be duplicated to minimize the chance the Archon would be lost in a jump accident. It was tedious, but there were limits to even her authority, and the Diplomatic Guard took their jobs *very* seriously. They had even cleared the Dar-es Salaam's zenith jump point of all traffic to prevent a terrorist from destroying her vessel with a close jump.

She glanced at the screen. In time to see it flash with light.

"Jump detection," sang out the tactical action officer. "Zero Eight Nine at seven two thousand kilometers."

"Scheiße!" exploded Kohl. *"Action stations!* Herr Bern, direct all DropShips to launch, save *Archon's Fist.* Put them between us and that *verdammt* ship, *now!"*

Reach's holotank suddenly filled with blue icons as DropShip after DropShip launched, racing to protect their Archon from the new intruder.

Kohl jabbed a finger at his navigator. "Load first set of calculations and standby for emergency jump."

"Jawohl, herr Kommodore," sang out the navigator.

Then he snatched the handset from the red bridge-to-bridge phone perched in the overhead and dialed a new frequency. *"Fist* Actual, this is *Reach* Actual. *I have Alpha Lima Charlie embarked."*

Alpha Lima Charlie. Archon of the Lyran Commonwealth.

"I am prepped for emergency jump." He listened to something, barked out a *"Jawohl,"* and turned, still holding the phone. "Highness, we will wait for the intruder to clear jump. In the event we are facing an overwhelming threat, we will risk an emergency jump. If the threat is small, we will transfer you to *Archon's Fist."*

Melissa nodded. "Very well."

"She has cleared jump, *Kommodore,"* reported the TAO. *"Merchant-*class, Lyran colors, two *Mules,* IFF confirmed."

One of the guards from Melissa's security detail grabbed her arm. "Highness, please, this way."

"Wait," she commanded. It earned her a second of hesitation. She pulled her arm away from the guard and drifted to the railing.

Kohl snatched up the red phone and dialed up another frequency. "Contact off my starboard beam, this is Lyran Naval Vessel One One Eight Six. You are in restricted space. Power down all systems immediately, or you will be fired upon."

He pointed at his comms station. "Put this channel up on speaker."

A bridge speaker crackled and suddenly Melissa heard a panicked voice say: "This is *Kaptain* Robert Ditch of the

Hessian Fortune. I'm relaying a report from an LIC agent. I report Contagion Outbreak. Quarantine is not set. I say again, Quarantine *is not set.*"

Melissa felt an icy hand suddenly close around her heart.

Contagion Outbreak. Enemy forces had crossed the Commonwealth's rimward border.

Quarantine is not set. The Enemy had bypassed her string of tripwire worlds.

She clutched the railing, her knuckles white.

"Is the Archon embarked?" asked the shaky voice from the speaker. "I have amplifying information."

Melissa's body suddenly felt strange, like it didn't belong to her. *This isn't real. This* can't *be real.* "This is the Archon," she said firmly.

"We just— They hit everything at the jump point— We barely got out. An LIC officer on the charging station ordered me to relay a message before he was shot. He said they're in Uhuru and...Nestor, Concord and Togwotee and...McAffe.

"*Who?*" snapped Archon.

"It's the Wolves, Archon. The Wolves. *They're attacking everywhere.*"

PART TWO

The Scent of Prey

"Woe be to those who ignite the inferno of war, for the flame cares not who it burns."

—Captain-General Jessica Marik,
Address to the Nation, 27 May 3140

CHAPTER 8

**COMSTAR SECRET RESEARCH FACILITY OMEGA ONE
LUYTEN 68-28 (EXACT COORDINATES UNKNOWN)
PREFECTURE X
22 JUNE 3140**

No one had ever accused Adept Peter Frazier of being especially smart, but he *was* loyal, and so ROM had found a way for him to serve the Will of Blake. So what if that meant carrying pieces of radioactive garbage to the Prisoner? The way Frazier figured it, he was ushering in the glorious future just like anybody else.

The Prisoner, on the other hand, *was* especially smart, in fact he was supposed to be a *genius,* and where exactly had it gotten him? The Prisoner had been tortured and beaten, by his *own sister,* no less. (And didn't that just make you think about the messed-up way things turned out?) And while Frazier had to carry radioactive crap around, the Prisoner had to take it apart and try to make it work.

Maybe being smart wasn't such a good deal, after all.

Frazier unlocked the Prisoner's room and stepped inside. The man was sprawled out on his workbench, eyes screwed shut, head pillowed on his left arm, his right hand hanging down beneath the bench. The Prisoner, the *smart* Prisoner was obviously sliding into despair. For one thing, he smelled rank, and his hair was greasy and matted. Frazier didn't think he'd showered lately. Also his bed was still made; the Prisoner never slept in his bed anymore.

And there was an ugly yellow bruise along his jaw. Frazier happened to know there were more bruises like that one, on the Prisoner's body, on his face.

In places he didn't want to think about.

For all his supposed brains, the Prisoner had resisted the Will of Blake, and it was destroying him. Even a regular guy like Frazier could see that Prisoner had lost the thing that prisoners needed above all else.

Hope.

Frazier set the tray filled with recovered memory cards on the edge of the workbench so the radiation wouldn't scramble the Prisoner's brains any more than the beatings already had.

Then he paused. He really didn't want to wake the Prisoner, but he was supposed to tell him that he had to work. Also, he wasn't sure about how radiation worked, but he didn't think the guy should be sleeping so close to crap from the wasteland.

For a full minute, these twin impulses warred within Peter Frazier's slow mind. In the end, he leaned over the sleeping man to gently shake him awake.

It was the last mistake he ever made.

Tucker's heart was racing in his chest, his breathing shallow as the big adept stepped into the room. The thug slammed something onto the workbench, and Tucker almost screamed. *Hold it together, Tuck. Hold it together.*

There was an impossibly long pause during which the adept neither moved nor spoke. *He's deciding whether or not to kill me,* thought Tucker.

The adept leaned over him. Tucker couldn't see him, but he could feel the big man's gravity, like a gas giant pulling a fleck of stone into a decaying orbit. Tucker's nerves sang with tension and the urgent need for release.

The adept touched his shoulder—

Tucker jumped, his right arm swinging up in a fast, unsteady arc, his hand clutching a weird device that was half-shiv and half-gizmo. He plunged the razor-sharp blade into the adept's thigh, narrowly missing the femoral artery. It didn't matter.

Because the capacitor built into the device instantly discharged, sending an eighty-two-milliamp current sizzling through the adept's groin, shocking his heart into arrhythmia.

The man's eyes widened, and he toppled over. Tucker only had a moment to smell burning flesh and the electric odor of ozone before he jerked the adept's slug thrower out of its holster, turned, and fired into the mirror.

The weapon *roared,* a sharp punch of thunder followed by the tinkling rain of falling glass. The recoil wrenched Tucker's arm up. The echo of the weapon's voice rang in his ears.

The observer on the other side of the glass was a woman, mid-thirties, not especially pretty, but still somebody's daughter. She wore a gray ROM uniform.

For a second they both froze, staring wide-eyed at each other.

Then Tucker remembered the things Patricia had done to him and jerked his weapon back down, his gunsight on the woman's body. The observer dove for an alarm.

But she was not faster than a bullet.

The first shot caught her high in the neck, releasing a red spray of arterial blood and spinning her around. The second shot caught her in the torso, smashing her to the ground. It only took him a few seconds to scramble up over the jagged shards of glass in the window's frame, but by the time he checked for a pulse, she was already dead.

Tucker went to her computer console and plugged in the little device in his pocket. Hands shaking, he typed a command into the terminal's keyboard, executing a program.

The little drive and the program it contained represented months of his life. Every night he would go into the bathroom and build his little 'puter from cobbled-together parts, stealing moments to write careful code.

Now he was going to see if it worked.

Sweat crawled down his sides as he waited. Each second was a pulse of blood in his ears. *Doesn't matter,* he told himself. He clutched the weapon so tight his knuckles hurt.

Doesn't matter, doesn't matter. Either way, I won't go back. I don't care if it works.

(Please please please work.)

Suddenly alarms wailed, loud shrieking sirens. Tucker looked wildly around.

But no one came.

His eyes found the computer screen over the console. A schematic of the facility came up below flashing red words: SECURITY BREACH. SAVAGE DEFENDER PROTOCOL. Red "X"-icons blinked over all the doors on the schematic, indicating they were locked down tight.

All except for nine doors that traced the most direct route from his cell to the base's vehicle bay where a hoverjeep waited. The line of freedom cut south through the building.

Tucker went to the room's half-open door, peering out at the bright hallway through the small hinge-side opening between the door and its frame. The shriek of the alarms made him want to jump out of his skin, but he forced himself to wait. *Wait.*

He counted ten Zebebelgenubi, then darted into the hallway, turning right. *North.*

He sprinted ten meters to the locked door at the hall's end. Breathing hard, he leaned against the door, his right hand resting on its stainless steel handle, watching the glowing red light embedded in the doorplate.

It flashed green.

Tucker jerked the handle down and shouldered the door open. A ROM operative stood with his back to him, trying to punch a code into the far door's keypad. The man wheeled as soon as Tucker's door clicked open. This time there was no hesitation.

Tucker shot him down.

He hurried down the hallway, stepping over the operative's prone body, and waiting for the door's light to blink from red to green.

For the first time since he'd attacked Frazier, Tucker began to believe he might just make it out. The code he'd written would hide the random door openings from security. Even if *that* ruse were somehow defeated, the doors only opened for five seconds—difficult to notice unless you were looking for it. Besides, Buhl would look for him moving south. His troops would be trying to get to the vehicle bay.

And in two minutes, a hoverjeep was going to blink off the bay's vehicle list. If he were very lucky, they would continue the search in the desert.

The doorplate blinked green, and Tucker pushed through. Moving one door at a time, he made his way to the hangar where a *Leopard* waited. He'd hide in one of the engineering bilges. Hangar to DropShip, DropShip to JumpShip, JumpShip to *freedom*.

It was going to work.

Tucker opened the last door and heard the roar of high-velocity engines and the low diesel growl of service vehicles. He stepped through.

The hangar's retractable roof arched high overhead. Right now it was closed, but the giant doors were open, revealing blue sky over black tarmac. The hangar was a cavernous space, big enough to accommodate three DropShips side-by-side.

Right now there was only one.

Tucker's eyes skipped over an eclectic collection of smaller craft—a Mark VII torn apart for maintenance, a hot dog-shaped S-7A, a couple of sleek *Shivas*—and settled on the *Leopard*. The aerodyne DropShip was painted ComStar white.

A wide smile spread across Tucker's face. *It was really working.*

He would have to be careful. There were maintenance techs spread throughout the building. Red emergency lights mounted on the walls were turning, but someone had muted the siren. OK, he thought, the trick is to be calm. Make it look like you *belong*.

He drew a steadying breath and quietly shut the door he'd come through. And *jumped*.

Whitfield stood there, a laser pistol pointed at his chest.

Tucker jerked his gun up. "Put the laser down," he said from between clenched teeth. The gun shook in his hand.

Whitfield frowned. "We don't have time for this. They're going to see through your little tricks any minute."

"*Put it down.*"

She took a step toward him. *"Tucker,"* she whispered. "*Please.*"

"*Put. It. Down.*"

She hesitated. Then she knelt and gently set the weapon on the ferrocrete deck. "Tucker," she said softly. "Don't you know me?"

Tucker's voice was harsh. "Oh, I know you."

Whitfield shook her head. She reached up with her left hand and brushed back a strand of red hair. "I—I don't think so." A shy smile came to her face. Hesitantly, she reached out and touched his face with her left hand.

Just like the dream.

"Tucker, I've come to rescue you. *I'm Alexi Holt.*"

PRADESH HOTEL, SAKUNTALEM
LYRAN-OCCUPIED KALIDASA
PROTECTORATE COALITION
FREE WORLDS LEAGUE

The western horizon glowed orange-gold as the sun slipped from the world, but Duke Vedet Brewer saw patches of purple that bordered the sunset, waiting to claim the sky for night. Sakuntalem's lights winked on, like the stars coming out. And just like that, the ballet of color and form was gone.

Replaced by darkness.

Duke Vedet, who followed the Skye tradition of attaching his noble title to his given name, stood on the hotel's penthouse balcony, looking out at the city, a tumbler of scotch cradled in his right hand, a scrap of paper crushed in his left.

He ignored the man who'd brought him the message, *Leutnant-Colonel* Thomas Kirk of the First Hesperus Guards.

The "balcony" was more like a small plaza. Vedet felt not stone under his feet, but grass. He smelled saffron and jasmine, orchids and lemon grass. He heard the playful bubble of a fountain behind him, felt its cool mist on his skin. Marble benches were sprinkled throughout the balcony, though neither man sat. They both leaned against the balustrade that kept people from falling the twenty stories to their deaths.

The scotch had started as scotch on the rocks, but the ice had melted while he watched the sun set. Now it was just a slurry of alcohol and tap water.

"This could have been the beginning of something great," said Vedet, his voice rough. "Kalidasa has always been a place where commerce tied together House Marik and House Steiner. It could have been that again. *But for us.*"

Kirk said nothing, which was a healthy indication of his intelligence.

Suddenly Vedet winged his glass out into the night. He didn't hear the tumbler smash, which was vaguely disappointing. "When do the New Hope Raiders arrive?"

"Four days," said Kirk softly. "Looks like they're taking a nice slow run in."

"Why not," said Vedet bitterly. "They have us, and they know it."

Somewhere in the near darkness, Kirk shifted.

Go ahead and disapprove, thought Vedet savagely. *I don't need your approval.*

His Guards were battered and bloody, and his supply lines were extended nearly to the point of breaking—not that anything was coming through them, anyway. He had fought at Melissa's behest, taking world after world for that bitch, and this, *this* was how she repaid him.

She had stripped him of parts and munitions. Oh, it had been cleverly done, of course. The subtlety with which his equipment and consumables had been shifted coreward to the Falcon border suggested the treacherous hand of Trillian Steiner. Melissa had organized this whole war to destroy him.

And it had worked.

Vedet would be the man who lost Kalidasa, the man who fumbled away the whole Free Worlds offensive. He felt the paper crumpled in his left hand.

The man who couldn't restrain the Wolves.

The message had been brought to him via JumpShip only an hour ago. It was short and to the point. He unfolded it and read it again:

Z 231443MAY40
FROM: ARCHON LYRANCOM
TO: COMBOLANMILPROV
ALLPLANMILITIAS BOLANMILPROV
ALLFORCES LCAF
COMFIRSTHESPERUSGUARDS
COMFIRSTSTEINERSTRIKERS
COMSTORMHAMMERS
TOP SECRET//N06788//
SUBJ: ATTACK ON LYRAN COMMONWEALTH

1. ON 21 MAY 3040 GAL CDR ALARIC WOLF STRUCK ACROSS LYRAN BORDER, ATTACKING FIVE WORLDS IN BOLAN MILPROV. FIRST-WAVE TARGETS ARE UHURU, NESTOR, CONCORD, TOGWOTEE, AND MCAFFE. HIGH COMMAND ANALYSIS INDICATES THIS IS A FULL-SCALE ASSAULT.
2. THE LYRAN COMMONWEALTH IS AT WAR WITH CLAN WOLF.
3. LIC REPORTS NON-AGGRESSION PACT BETWEEN FWL AND CLAN WOLF.
4. ALL OPERATIONAL COMMANDERS ARE TO IMMEDIATELY CEASE HOSTILITIES WITH FWL. HOLD CURRENT POSITION AGAINST ATTACK BUT DO NOT ADVANCE.
5. STORMHAMMERS WILL IMMEDIATELY REDEPLOY TO UHURU.
6. FIRST STEINER STRIKERS WILL IMMEDIATELY REDEPLOY TO HYDE TO AWAIT FURTHER TASKING.
7. FIRST HESPERUS GUARDS WILL HOLD KALIDASA UNTIL FURTHER NOTICE.
8. IMMEDIATELY CANX ALL LEAVES FOR LCAF PERSONNEL. INITIATE FULL MOBILIZATION.

ARCHON MELISSA STEINER SENDS
BT

This was a disaster of unimaginable proportions. It might very well drag down Melissa, but Vedet would certainly fall with her. He was tied politically to her Free Worlds adventure. If the nobles and the shopkeepers and soldiers decided this war had been a mistake, she would get most of the blame.

But there would be plenty left over for him.

Especially since his First Hesperus Guards would not be part of the desperate, heroic defense of the Bolan Military Province. While the Stormhammers rushed to Uhuru to blunt the tip of the Wolf spear, and the Strikers were prepped to defend a second-wave world, the First Hesperus Guards were assigned garrison duty.

He snorted. If the New Hope Raiders had their way, *that* would be over soon enough.

"I bet now you're sorry you shipped all our supplies coreward, eh, Melissa," muttered Vedet. Then he froze. *That's it...*

His mind raced, working through the possibilities, the angles. *It might just work.* He'd have to write a message that infuriated Melissa, but that should be easy enough. His very existence seemed to infuriate Melissa.

"What did you say, Duke?" asked Kirk.

Vedet peered at the message again. It ordered the First Hesperus Guards to remain on Kalidasa, not the *Commander,* First Hesperus Guards.

"I said..." said the Duke slowly, "that I am turning operational command of the First Hesperus Guards to you."

The man blinked. "Sir, I don't—"

"I am departing Kalidasa immediately."

Kirk goggled at him. "Sir, you can't— I mean— What about the Raiders?"

Vedet placed a hand on the man's shoulder. "I would not leave, Colonel, but I have a service I must render to the Commonwealth. A service no one else can provide."

"But, sir. What am I supposed to do?"

"Why, hold, of course," said Vedet, managing to sound surprised. "For as long as you can."

COMSTAR SECRET RESEARCH FACILITY OMEGA ONE
LUYTEN 68-28 (EXACT COORDINATES UNKNOWN)
PREFECTURE X

Tucker stared at her. This woman who had tormented him, who had mocked him, *who had loosed Patricia on him.* This was— He shook his head. "You don't look like—"

"Of course not. Do you think I could've infiltrated ComStar if I looked like the Alexi Holt you knew?"

"Infiltrated?"

"I was ordered to by Paladin Sorenson to find you. To *rescue* you."

Tucker shook his head. "No," he whispered. *"No..."*

"Do you remember the last thing I said to you? When I gave you my rank pip."

Tucker swallowed.

She reached out and enfolded him in an embrace. "I'll miss you, Tucker," she whispered. "But at least you'll be safe."

He broke the hug, looking sharply at her. "Y-You took that from my—" He shook his head. *"Patricia* took that from my mind. "

"No, " she said sternly. "I was *there*. It's *me*."

"But—"

"No," she said firmly. "No, there's no more time for doubts. We have to get out of here. This way." She picked up her laser and started moving right.

Tucker glanced left at the *Leopard.* "But—"

"Adept," she barked, "*this way.*"

A technician looked up at them and Tucker turned and walked briskly toward Whitfield. *Or Holt? Could this* really *be Alexi Holt?* He fell in step with her. They strode toward the S-7A.

"But I was going to hide on the—"

She dropped her voice to a whisper. "We won't get out of here by hiding. ComStar's only hope for survival is to find you. If they think you're still here, they'll take that DropShip apart bolt by bolt. If we're going to get clear, we'll have to do it ourselves."

And then, pointing her laser up in a two-handed grip, she stepped onto the shuttle.

S-7A IN HIGH ORBIT
LUYTEN 68-28 (EXACT COORDINATES UNKNOWN)
PREFECTURE X

Tucker saw the aerospace fighter flash by, painted ghost white, sleek and deadly. It arced around in a slow, graceful orbit, reminding him very much of a great white shark circling, circling. As the fighter reached the apogee of its turn, it arced into a climb and then tipped over, slicing down toward the helpless shuttle like a javelin.

Ruby fire cut into the shuttle, rattling the vessel, and throwing Tucker against his safety restraints. Pain slashed through his chest, and for a moment reality grayed out.

"Good thing they're going easy on us," said Whitfield.

"You think this is *easy*?" asked Tucker incredulously.

"Those are two SHV-O *Shivas* out there," snapped Whitfield. "The only reason they haven't already blown us out of the sky is that ComStar wants you alive."

"Great," said Tucker, "well, let's keep it that way."

Whitfield shook her head and threw the shuttle into a hard port bank just as another shark flashed by.

Was this all part of some elaborate ruse to win his trust? Tucker wondered. *How could this be Alexi Holt?*

His thoughts were interrupted by a staccato pounding on the shuttle's hull. It sounded a little like gunfire, only less regular, less *certain*. As if whatever it was might kill them, but only if it got around to it. "What's *that?*"

"Debris," Whitfield bit the word out. "We're crossing the plane of the ring."

Tucker craned his neck, looking out the shuttle's ferroglass canopy. A bright swath of silver climbed up at right angles to his field of vision. He could just see the structure starting to arc. *The ring.*

Unlike the rings of gas giants, this ring wasn't made up of ice crystals and dust motes, no it was constructed of garbage, everything from metal particles all the way up to dead spacecraft. No wonder it sounded like bullets hitting the ship.

Luyten had been home to orbital factories and massive space stations, all of which had been destroyed during the Jihad.

Another one of the *Shivas* flashed by and the shuttle shook hard as it took another hit. Pain lanced through Tucker's ribs.

"Shuttle," said the radio, "this is Demon Flight One. Return to planet or we will be forced to destroy you. This is your final warning."

"So much for taking me alive," muttered Tucker.

"Oh, they're bluffing," said Whitfield.

"Good to know."

"They'll just wait for us to run out of fuel and tow us in," said Whitfield.

"Oh," said Tucker. He swallowed. Felt the bulk of the slug thrower shoved into his pants pocket. "They can kill me." He shook his head. "But I'm not going back."

Whitfield glanced back into the compartment. Tucker followed her gaze to a locker containing five or six space suits. He turned to look at her.

"No one's asking you to," she said.

Adept Miguel Costa brought his bird around in a tight arc, his crosshairs settled comfortably on the ungainly midsection of the odd-looking S-7A. The reticle, the targeting pip in the center of the cross-hairs, glowed a deep gold, signaling target lock.

Costa's gloved thumb caressed the red button on his stick that pilots called a pickle. He felt the hard plastic through his Nomex glove. Just a few newtons of pressure—

But those were not his orders. His orders were to bring the shuttle back.

Costa didn't have anything against the people in the shuttle—indeed, he had no idea who they were—nor did he have any problem following orders, but he was the pilot of an aerospace fighter, and aerospace fighters were not designed to bring back prisoners alive.

In its nose the *Shiva* carried missiles, a small laser, and an LB 20-X, to say nothing of the quartet of large pulse lasers spread across its two swept back wings. Simply put, the *Shiva* was beautifully designed to kill. To do anything else just seemed wrong.

He felt the pickle through his glove like an itch.

Somehow, he managed to resist the temptation. He swept his aircraft up and over in another plunging attack, dialing down his laser's power. As he dove toward the shuttle, he stitched underpower ruby beams across her hull, just to remind them Demon Flight was still here.

Suddenly the shuttle did the last thing in the universe he expected. It swung nose up, aiming straight for him.

Startled, Costa had only an instant to react, and did just what his combat-honed instincts demanded. He jammed his thumb down on the pickle, trying to blow apart the obstacle before he smashed into it.

He didn't have time to dial up his laser power or tie his other weapons into his primary trigger. Weak ruby light washed off the shuttle's hull, burning paint and opening rents in the craft's thin metal skin.

But hardly blowing it apart.

Costa had only an instant to realize his error, and then Demon One smashed into the shuttle at a thousand kph, igniting fuel and warheads and releasing the nuclear fire that burned in the *Shiva*'s guts. In a fraction of a second, raging energies transformed the shuttle, the fighter, and Miguel Costa into a thin gruel of superheated plasma that arced across a hundred kilometers, adding yet more debris to the planet's glittering silver ring.

Tucker's magnetic boots glued him to the shuttle's steel hull while the entirety of the universe passed overhead. Whitfield stood next to him, a couple steps away, a silent figure in a snow white space suit occulting the stars. They were tethered together by a three-meter line. Tucker wasn't sure what was going to happen next.

But he had a bad feeling he wasn't going to like it.

He keyed his LOS transmitter. "Hey, what's the plan here?"

Whitfield turned and slashed an angry hand across her neck. Her meaning was clear enough. *Kill the chatter.*

She stepped over to him using the peculiar step-lock-unlock-step gait unique to spacers. She bumped her head against his. "Radio silence," she yelled. Her voice sounded small and tinny. "Got that, Tucker? *Radio silence.*"

"Yes," he said sheepishly, "but—" She had already stepped away.

She looked back at the fighters and then at the ring. Fighters and ring. Fighters...Ring. High above them (though there was really no "above" in space) one of the *Shivas* climbed towards the height of its arc.

She bumped her helmet against his. "Listen. When I count three, jump."

"*Jump!*" squeaked Tucker.

"Yes, jump. When—"

"C-can't we just stay with the shuttle?"

"*No.* I've programmed the shuttle to do something very bad. *On three.* And do *not* hesitate, or you'll kill us both."

"But—"

She crouched down and glanced back. She held up her hand, balled into a fist. Then she counted off with her fingers.

And leaped.

Tucker swallowed and jumped after her, remembering only just in time that he had to unlock his magboots as he leaped. He tumbled through the void, small particles of debris scoring his faceplate with a sharp rattle that set his teeth on edge.

Whitfield kept her body wrapped into a ball. She didn't turn to look back at Tucker, she just kept looking straight ahead, as if she were searching for something.

Something flashed bright in Tucker's peripheral vision, brilliant white but totally silent, like distant lightning on a hot summer evening. He glanced back.

The shuttle was gone, just *gone.* In its place was a cloud of glowing white gas and a string of debris traveling along the steep angle of the fighter's fatal plunge.

He felt a tug on the line that connected him to Whitfield and looked back. She pointed at something: a star, an *irregular star*, because Tucker could see the pool of light wasn't spherical, but...cylindrical.

Whitfield fired the small jets in her pack, vectoring her toward the strange light. Their relative velocities changed, and the tether pulled tight. She scowled back at him. He hurried to fire his own jets.

Slowly they drifted toward the cylinder, making tiny course corrections with their jets, never firing more than a second or a two.

As they drew nearer, Tucker realized the structure was *big*, maybe eighty meters along its major axis and twenty in diameter. Its surface was pocked with craters. A thin rime of ice crystals shadowed holes shaded from the kiss of sunlight. The station had once possessed a pair of gold-filmed wings, solar cells. One of the arrays had been snapped cruelly in half, but the other appeared to be undamaged.

Whitfield fired her jets and landed on the derelict's hull in a graceful crouch, anchoring herself with her magboots.

Tucker swung around and hit the hull with his shoulder. For a second he panicked as he felt himself spin away, nothing below him but vastness. Only Whitfield's purchase and the tether's pull saved him.

The line jerked him back toward the hull. He bounced again, sending a lance of pain through his ribs, but this time he managed to grab a handhold on the way out. The force nearly wrenched his arm off, but somehow he held on.

He lay there for a moment, breathing hard and clinging to the shattered station as if it were salvation.

COMSTAR SECRET RESEARCH FACILITY OMEGA ONE

Patricia Harwell stared up into the blue sky, wondering how everything had managed to go so suddenly and totally wrong. As usual there was one word that served to explain every facet of the disaster.

Tucker.

Buhl stood next to her, his body rigid, his breathing heavy, his round face turned to the sky. He had at least as much to lose as she did—probably more.

"Demon Flight has isolated the shuttle," reported Demi-Precentor Dakota Hansen, the senior aerospace officer on-planet. Hansen was a tall, fiftyish man of European stock. He wore a headset in his thinning brown hair that connected him to the base's control nexus. He pointed up at the world's silver ring. "I think you can see laser fire."

Yes. Patricia saw red sparks dance in the sky, like embers leaping from a campfire on a cool fall night.

"*We want them alive!*" Buhl bellowed. He was flushed. He did not look well.

"Y-yes sir," stammered Hansen. "The *Shiva*s' lasers are set to low power, warning shots only."

Buhl's poisonous gaze rested on the man for another ten seconds before he turned to look back up at the sky without a word.

He's like a reactor that's about to lose containment, thought Patricia. *Whoever is standing near him is going to vanish in a flash of light. But not me.*

Oh, no. Not me.

Suddenly a pinprick of white light, nova bright, flashed in the world's sky.

"What is that?" snapped Buhl. "What the *hell* is that?"

For a moment Hansen's mouth worked, but no sound came out. He licked his lips. "Demon Two reports that Demon One collided with the shuttle."

"*What?*" snarled Buhl. "What about survivors?"

Hansen swallowed and shook his head.

Buhl rounded on Patricia. "How could you have let this happen?" he asked in a low, menacing voice.

Patricia's smile was cold. "Don't even try, Precentor. It wasn't me who assigned Tucker to the care of Sandra Whitfield. And you should know I have collected every order regarding my brother's security arrangements, all backed up in several locations."

If Buhl was going to save himself by sacrificing someone to Brian May, it would have to be someone else, because it was *not* going to be her.

Buhl stared at her, a muscle in his cheek pulsing as he worked his jaw. Then he turned and stalked off. There was nothing he could say or do to her, and he knew it.

Patricia looked up at the sky, where the nova of her brother's death had already faded to nothing. She shook her head. "Too easy," she whispered.

"It must be hard—" started Hansen, a note of maudlin sympathy in his voice.

"It's not that," Patricia snarled. Her eyes found the silver arc of debris bisecting the blue sky. "It's just that Luyten is a world where the garbage tends to hang around."

CHAPTER 9

EXCALIBUR-CLASS DROPSHIP HIMMELSTOR
WOLF-OCCUPIED UHURU
BOLAN MILITARY PROVINCE
LYRAN COMMONWEALTH
2 JULY 3140

The DropShip bucked and shuddered as Uhuru fought her descent. The air itself tore at *Himmelstor*'s thick hide, shaking the mighty vessel, buffeting her with gale-force winds, and finally shrieking in frustration as the DropShip slipped away.

Wreathed in fire, *Himmelstor* fell.

Even deep in the heart of Heaven's Gate, it was a rough ride down. Jasek Kelswa-Steiner sat in the DropShip's Combat Information Center, strapped in as securely as if he'd been in his *Templar*. He had one of the eight seats with an unobstructed view of Combat's massive holotank.

He knew he didn't rate it: during this phase of the assault, Leutnant Kommodore Deborah Becker, the spaceborne commander was the task force's final authority. Still, Jasek's people were fighting and dying out there.

He couldn't not watch.

The holotank was a 3-D realtime schematic of the desperate battle being waged outside *Himmelstor*'s hull. Jasek's blue DropShips dove for the hard deck, while Wolf fighters marked in crimson harried them, screaming in for an attack, then turning swallow-quick and screaming away. Golden lines of weapons fire slashed between the combatants. Ground fire rose from the earth and battered the task force like upside-down rain.

Jasek glanced at Becker, a small, fiftyish woman who wore her brown hair long and didn't bother hiding the fact that it was streaked with gray. He marveled that anyone could follow the chaos spilling through holotank.

"Adler Flight, target the Visigoths, I'll get—"

"This is Eclipse. I hold Wolf Union at One One Six, five eight klicks, moving in fast."

"This is Sierra Charlie," said Becker. "Desig *Union*, Bogie Four Seven. Adler Four and Five break from fur ball and harass the *Union*. Let her know we see her."

"Wilco," barked the pilot in Adler Four.

Jasek grunted as a pocket of wicked turbulence suddenly slammed him against his five-point safety restraint, the quick-release digging into his sternum. Then just as quickly the ship smashed him against his seat, punching the air out of his lungs. For a moment the sound of the naval chatter was knocked right out of his brain.

Then it was back again.

"*Himmelstor*, I hold two *Jagatai* full throttle climb toward your belly, four o'clock low."

Somewhere below him Jasek heard the shriek of lasers as *Himmelstor*'s gunners desperately tried to hold the marauders off for just a few seconds longer.

Just a few seconds longer.

After four days of hell.

Jasek's task force had jumped into a deep pirate point four days out, hoping for surprise.

It hadn't quite worked out that way.

Wolf aerospace had been ready. They had staked out seven key pirate points—leaving the zenith and nadir jump points unguarded. Outnumbered and outgunned, the Wolves still managed to launch a savage attack against Jasek's JumpShip just as she cleared hyperspace, trying to kill the invasion aborning.

They'd rammed a Mark VII into the *Invader* and sent a Star of Elementals bounding into space, ripping into the JumpShip's hull with their terrible claws.

The *Himmelstor*'s guns had picked off about half the toads as they leaped toward the JumpShip, sending their broken bodies spinning off into infinity. The *Invader*'s small contingent of marines got a good chunk of the rest, targeting the exposed Clan infantry from the partial cover of an open airlock.

In all, only six Elementals made it aboard the JumpShip, slightly better than a Point. All the Clanner shock troops were killed, but not before they'd slaughtered half of the *Invader*'s crew and sown panic throughout Jasek's command.

Meanwhile, the Wolf forces stationed at the other pirate points raced toward Jasek's DropShips. The Wolves fought the task force all the way to the planet, contesting every millimeter of space and sky between the jump point and the LZ, fighting with everything they had.

Alaric's aerospace forces were true Wolves, concentrating their attacks on the weakest member of the herd, the *Eisenhimmel*, hitting the little *Leopard CV* again and again on the long run in, worrying armor and silencing her guns one after another. The *Iron Sky* carried a healthy chunk of Jasek's VTOL force.

Jasek had to get his force *down* before the Wolves crushed his assault in the sky.

"This is Sierra Charlie. Hand-off Bogie Four Seven to *Star Chaser*. Adler One, vector fighters along Three Four Nine. Target Four Seven's forward armor and lead her into *Star Chaser*'s guns."

"*Jawohl*, Sierra Charlie," barked Adler Flight's commander.

Jasek touched the little screen at his arm, tapped through a few commands and called up video from *Himmelstor*'s external cameras. What he saw was unbroken blue sky. Occasionally something small and gray zipped into the picture and then out again. It was like watching flies on a summer's day.

Then he saw it. A black dot growing bigger. The *Union*.

A bright orange flower opened against the sky. Jasek turned his head back to the holotank just in time to see the icon for Adler Two go dark.

The Wolf DropShip turned and plunged into the swarm of *Eisensturm*s, smashing through Adler Flight like an angry lion charging into a pack of hyenas.

Jasek's mouth went dry. "Becker—"

"I see it," Becker snapped. "*Eisenhimmel*, Four Seven is closing, fall back, best speed. *Chaser*, get on that DropShip *now*."

Lights danced in the holotank in a delicate ballet of death. Golden lines joined the three DropShips: The *Union* tearing into the defenseless *Eisenhimmel*, with *Chaser* desperately trying to save her sister.

He turned back to the screen in time to see the sky suddenly swallowed by molten orange flame. He didn't have to check the holotank to know which ship had just died.

Jasek's knuckles whitened as he gripped the arms of his chair.

Have to get down NOW.

THE RED DESERT
WOLF-OCCUPIED UHURU
BOLAN MILITARY PROVINCE
LYRAN COMMONWEALTH
9 JULY 3140

Heat ruled Jasek's world. It shimmered off the long, flat stretch of hardpan held by the Wolves, roiling the air and transforming Elementals into blurry, phantasmal figures. It baked the red rocks that littered the ground at Jasek's back, radiating off buttes and mesas, boiling out of the broken landscape that was the Red Desert.

A white scale of dried salt caked Jasek's skin. Sweat stung his eyes. His cockpit was a hellish sauna, an *oven*. Heat ruled Jasek's world—and it was a cruel master.

Still, he stalked his *Templar* forward and lashed into a pair of Wolf Demons harrying a Stormhammer *Pack Hunter* with their lasers. Heat spiked another five scalding degrees in his cockpit. But the two fast tanks turned and raced for the safety of their lines.

Jasek gritted his teeth and hit them again.

This battle would not be won by half-measures.

He glanced at his tactical display. Red and blue icons littered the schematic. The front was a long, shallow "U." The Stormhammers were giving everything they had.

But they were bending.

The moment was coming soon when their courage would not be enough, and they would break.

Right now the Wolves were prevailing through sheer numerical superiority. Alaric Wolf was playing to his strengths.

That was okay. Jasek had strengths, too.

By leap-frogging Amity, Alaric had won the opportunity to defend rather than attack. That was a significant tactical advantage. And Alaric's force was bolstered by the garrison units needed to hold the worlds he conquered. So he had numbers.

What he did not have was time.

Except for the Stormhammers and a scattering of planetary militias, nothing stood between Alaric and a long march coreward. So how many worlds could he take before the redeployment orders already flashing through Lyran space brought more front-line units to contest his advance? Alaric couldn't afford a long war of attrition.

For the first week of the battle for Uhuru, Jasek had taunted the Wolf commander with hit-and-run tactics, using the Red Desert as a hidden base. What made the insurgent strategy viable was the total absence of air cover.

Both Wolf and Lyran aerospace forces had been destroyed in the brutally contested landing. Other than their DropShips, neither side could put anything in the sky. Which meant there was no way to pin down an enemy force that didn't want to be found.

Which was why Alaric was here now with all his front-line troops and a good chunk of his reserves. Given the chance to finally crush the Stormhammers, he was going to take it.

Unfortunately for Clan Wolf, that was exactly what Jasek had expected.

He toggled his common frequency. "Toy Surprise, Storm One. Target Grids One Six through Two Eight and *fire for effect*. Stormhammers, let's invite the Wolves inside."

There was a second's hesitation and then Jasek's artillery, hidden in the wasteland behind him, opened up. The barrage started with the whistle of shells, but soon their shrill cry was swallowed by the terrible, rolling concussion of explosions.

"So you like to play with artillery, do you, Alaric?" Jasek whispered. He had seen the New Olympia footage. "Well, I'll give you all the artillery you want."

Taking advantage of the covering fire, the Stormhammers turned and raced for the cover of the Red Desert, disappearing into hidden passages mapped before the battle.

Most commanders, faced with the tactical situation Jasek had presented Alaric, would have withdrawn, happy with a draw. Why charge through artillery fire only to find yourself in the Red Desert?

The desert was winding box canyons and blistering heat. Time and the blazing sun had carved weird towers and arches of hard rock out of the softer sandstone. There was little room to maneuver, and no room to hold a formation. The shattered rock sliced into the max speed of 'Mechs and tracked vehicles. Sheer walls made line-of-sight comms impossible. The heavy concentration of iron ore screwed up magscan, while noontime temperatures pushing forty degrees Celsius turned thermal pictures into a degraded blur.

Superior numbers counted for little in the Red Desert.

Faced with this tactical situation, most commanders would have withdrawn. But Alaric Wolf wasn't most commanders. That was something Jasek had learned from the New Olympia footage.

Alaric would bare his teeth and charge forward.

Even unto his destruction.

STORMHAMMER LZ
UHURU AUTOBAHN

Kaptain Eduard Goran of the *Himmelstor* walked around his massive DropShip, his sharp eyes marking damage and monitoring the work his DC teams had done to repair it. There was no telling when *Heaven's Gate* would be called into battle again.

It was late morning, a blush of heat just starting to burn off dawn's residual coolness. Birdsong mingled with the *snap-hiss* of welding arcs, the whine of hydraulics. All things being equal, Goran preferred the sounds of repair to the sounds of nature.

Landgrave Kelswa-Steiner had ordered his DropShips down in the middle of the largest road on Uhuru's surface, a twelve-lane ribbon of reinforced ferrocrete that stretched from coast-to-coast. It looked strange seeing the three surviving DropShips lined up along the road, but it was a good choice.

It was easier to operate on ferrocrete, and the network of arterials branching off from the autobahn gave the Stormhammer BattleMechs and vehicles fast access to huge swaths of the continent.

The only thing Goran didn't like was the forest on either side of the highway, a collection of spruce and fir and some native thing that looked like a spiny palm. Fortunately, the landgrave didn't like having forest at his back any more than Goran did. Kelswa-Steiner had set aside an infantry platoon to patrol the LZ.

Goran had gone a step further and put together a work detail to cut down trees. So far they had cleared the vegetation north of *Himmelstor* out to fifty meters.

Goran still didn't like it.

He sighed. Somehow the landgrave was always getting him to do things he didn't like. That was just the price of—

The communicator on his belt crackled.

He pulled the device from his belt. "Goran."

The *kaptain* was greeted by static. He could tell someone was trying to speak, but he couldn't make out any of the words.

"This is *Kaptain* Goran. Say again."

"Crunts—par—hour—osing—shun." A roar of static, and then: "—eing—ammed."

Bemused, Goran stared at the device. And then his brain put it together. *Being jammed.*

Suddenly his heart was pounding.

He shifted frequency. "Deck Officer, this is the *kaptain*. Sound general quarters. Issue immediate recall, and prep for emergency lift."

He didn't wait for the officer to acknowledge his report before shifting frequencies again. He heard the panicked gonging of the GQ alarm carrying through the still morning air as he sprinted toward the nearest ramp.

Goran's mind raced through the possibilities. Alaric Wolf was supposed to have hit the landgrave with the majority of his force. But what if that had been a feint? What if he were really after the DropShips?

"Goran," snapped Becker from his communicator. "What the devil is going on?"

"I think—" he began. He never got the chance to finish. A flight of advanced tactical missiles rose from the forest, slashing forward in flat trajectories. They zeroed in on his ship (*his ship*) smashing into a repaired section of the hull, the new armor still pea-green with primer, shattering it all to hell.

Suddenly the forest blossomed with missiles.

Himmelstor's guns answered back first, tearing into the forest with lasers and autocannon. *But they couldn't see who they were firing at.*

DropShips boasted massive firepower, enough to put even BattleMechs to shame. But they were not invincible. What if Alaric had sent his reserves in second-line machines to hit the Stormhammer DropShips? Soften them up so the Wolf DropShips could finish them later. Was that the kind of trade Alaric Wolf might make?

Ja. After the brutal fight down, it sounded *exactly* like the kind of trade Alaric Wolf might make.

Goran made the ramp, stepping into a cavernous bay. A deck hand hurriedly raised the ramp behind him. He raised the communicator. "Recommend emergency lift, *Kommodore*."

"The landgrave's orders—" she began.

"The landgrave's out of comms," answered Goran. "Lifting clears the threat area and preserves tactical flexibility. When the landgrave leaves the Red Desert, we will be able to link up with him."

Decker made her decision quickly. "Do it."

"*Jawohl, Kommodore,*" snapped Goran. All around him his hull echoed with the unsettling sound of a hard, punishing rain.

THE RED DESERT

Jasek edged his massive *Templar* along a wall of sandstone tinted red by iron oxides. The fight in the Red Desert had turned into a deadly game of slow-motion hide-and-seek. Jasek guided his great machine carefully, slowly over uneven rock. His 85-ton *Templar* was a big, bulky machine, barely capable of an earth-shattering 65 kph even under the best of conditions. But boy, could it hit.

He reached the cliff's edge and leaned forward to see—
Nothing.

His maps showed this was a box canyon that curled away from its mouth. Something could be hiding behind the wall of red stone. If he went in, he might catch a Wolf napping—or someone could slip in behind *him,* and he'd be trapped with his back to a wall while being hammered by a superior force.

But if he walked past the canyon's mouth, he might be leaving an enemy at his back. Jasek stepped into the canyon, moving slowly to keep to the low side of his heat curve.

"Are you back there, Alaric Wolf?" he whispered, careful not to trigger his voice-activated mic. "Want to come out and play?"

Jasek had fought Alaric before. He had engaged in an honor match that pitted Julian Davion, Calamity Kell, and himself against Alaric, Yori Kurita, and Kisho Nova Cat. The match had been a replay of the War of 3039, fought in a Republic simulator.

But what Jasek had learned about Alaric had been real enough.

The Clanner had given Jasek all he could handle, using his superior speed to rush in and hit Jasek's *Atlases* and *Behemoths*, darting away before Jasek's assault machines could tear apart the lighter, faster enemy. When Jasek held a position, the Wolves harried him with hit-and-run tactics. When Jasek tried to exploit an opening in the Wolves' line, his probing unit was cut off and killed.

Tricking an *Atlas* into overpursuit was quite a feat.

The fact his side had lost the honor match didn't bother Jasek in the slightest. He had learned how to beat Alaric Wolf, and it hadn't cost the life of a single private to do it.

Jasek reached the end of wall, again looking for prey. He flashed on a Condor hover tank painted in Wolf colors of brown and fiery orange.

Jasek fired a snapshot, slicing into the little tank with the particle cannon built into his left arm.

The Condor struck back with LRMs, but the missiles shot wide left, corkscrewing past the *Templar*'s hip and impacting on the rock wall behind the assault 'Mech.

Jasek stepped out from behind the wall and hit the tank with the one-two punch of his paired PPCs, holding off on his medium lasers to preserve his heat load, and saving his TharHes four pack for a more dangerous target.

The Condor hit back with its LRM fifteen-pack chewing armor away from Jasek's high left shoulder while it walked its autocannon across his low-slung cockpit. Jasek rode out the attack and then answered with a mix of PPCs and medium lasers, tearing into the hovercraft's skirt and spilling air. The Condor slammed into the ground, the shriek of a lift fan tearing itself apart shrill in the thin, dry air.

Suddenly the Condor had been transformed from hover tank to gun emplacement.

Jasek stalked forward to finish it.

He laid into the tank with both his PPCs, ripping through its armor and igniting the Condor's missile load-out. One second the tank was there and the next it was *raining* tank, a column of fire and acrid black smoke clawing its way into the blameless blue sky.

Well, they'll know I'm here now, Jasek thought.

He turned his *Templar* around and lumbered forward, not wanting to be caught in the box canyon as the Condor had.

It was not only Alaric's prowess as a warrior that worried Jasek. It was the young man's evident political skill.

Alaric had accepted the quick surrender of the Uhuru's overmatched militia, even granting them *hegira*, allowing them to take a third of their equipment and keeping the rest as *isorla*. He had made feeding civilian refugees a priority and moved quickly to restore civil order. The Galaxy Commander had even pledged to honor commercial contracts, thus establishing a truce with what was always the most powerful class in Steiner space: the merchants.

Perhaps his greatest triumph was how he'd dealt with Uhuru's unpopular governor. The Wolves had stopped his limousine on the way to a spaceport, interrupting his flight from the planet. Rather than simply letting him go or shooting him at the side of the road—both acceptable solutions from a Clan point of view—Alaric had accused the governor of betraying the people of Uhuru by failing to protect them, and turned him over local authorities for *trial.*

It was a deft political move. Not only did it show the Wolves' respect for local customs, it gave the populace a focus for their anger other than Alaric.

LIC gave Seth Ward credit for the unorthodox move of signing a non-aggression pact with Jessica Marik, but Jasek was beginning to wonder. He'd seen plenty of outside-the-box thinking from Alaric, almost as if he was being counseled by a genius in Lyran politics.

The young Wolf had grown since Jasek had met him on Terra. Alaric fought with all the savagery and brilliance of Malvina Hazen, but there was something else there, a subtle political genius. The combination might make Alaric Wolf the most dangerous man in the universe.

And so the key to beating Alaric Wolf was *beating Alaric Wolf.* If he could catch the Galaxy Commander in the right match-up, he could take out the Alpha Wolf—and Jasek doubted any of the Betas would live up to Alaric's legacy.

He moved through the Red Desert, searching every box canyon, every snaking passageway, looking for his opposite number.

And the end to the Wolf invasion.

Jasek Kelswa-Steiner had engineered his own defeat.

This Alaric saw as clearly as he saw the red rock he stalked his *Savage Wolf* past. Only the foolish believed battles were fought on battlefields. *Neg.* Battles were fought in the minds of commanders before the first 'Mech stepped onto the field.

It was true an enemy could shatter your most carefully considered plans, that weather or terrain or even blind chance could turn against you. But Alaric believed none of that mattered in the end.

If you had already won the battle inside your opponent's mind.

As he had won the battle within Jasek Kelswa-Steiner.

He had once faced the Lyran in a silly game on Terra. During that match, Alaric had torn apart Jasek's simulated command. No doubt Jasek believed that gave him some insight into Alaric, into his fighting *style.* Maybe he believed Alaric favored slashing attacks, savage hit-and-run tactics, and Jasek had chosen this land to take those attacks away from him.

Jasek was badly mistaken.

The truth was Alaric favored no particular fighting style. He adapted his tactics to the conditions at hand, and more importantly, *to the commander he faced.* He was happy to mount slashing attacks, *aff,* but he was just as happy to mount a stolid defense and allow his enemy to throw themselves against his heavy guns.

There was no constant save victory.

Here Jasek had "lured" Alaric into a trap, their forces separated and out of communications, fighting desperate duels, neither side able to use their crippled aerospace forces to spot for them. Alaric had a numerical advantage, but the more forces he poured into the desert meat grinder, the better for the Lyrans. It would only leave him fewer warriors and less material to press his invasion. Alaric would bleed time in the desert, time he could ill afford to lose, while the next target world and the one after that went unconquered.

That was the lay of the land in the battleground that was the set of Jasek's assumptions. Alaric smiled. What the Lyran noble did not realize was that he was about to be flanked in his own mind.

EXCALIBUR-CLASS DROPSHIP *HIMMELSTOR*
HIGH ATMOSPHERE

Goran watched five red icons race toward the Stormhammer formation: an *Overlord*, a *Leopard*, two *Mules*, and an *Intruder*. Even without fighter support, the five vessels represented a lot of firepower.

Becker had ordered her little fleet to maintain a healthy distance. If the Wolves wanted a fight, they were going to have to make the first run in.

"Looks like you were right," she said. "The ground attack was to soften us up so their big boys could finish us off."

Goran nodded absently.

"Looking for the *Union*?" she asked softly.

Goran snorted. "That vessel is captained by the devil himself."

"She was badly damaged during the spaceborne assault," said Becker. "They probably have her grounded for repairs."

"*Ja*, probably," Goran admitted. "But I think I'll keep looking for her." A chill wriggled down his spine. "We can't afford any surprises."

THE RED DESERT

Jasek turned a corner and found the *Puma* trapped in a narrow draw, its back to him. The light 'Mech had tried running from his *Templar*—a good move—until it stumbled into a passage that dead-ended.

Jasek tore into its back with a flight of short-range missiles, followed by twin lashes from his PPCs. He'd linked up with a pair of VV1 Rangers and a Joust and they added their fire to his.

The *Puma* didn't stand a chance.

Jasek didn't have comms with most of his command, but based on the damaged and destroyed Wolf equipment he'd seen, he judged the battle was going well. Alaric had blundered into his trap: a battle where the Clanners' aggressive style was a disadvantage, and where pure numbers conferred little advantage.

He smiled tightly. He'd gotten his war of attrition.

He tore into the *Puma* again as it tried to turn. He cut deeply into the machine's back, carving through the armor and into the critical mechanisms underneath. The *Puma* shuddered briefly, a sure sign it had suffered a gyroscope hit.

It was then he heard the roll of massive thunder. At first Jasek thought the deep, bass roar was the sound of Wolf artillery.

Then he looked up.

A mountain of steel was falling out of the blue sky, balancing on four pillars of golden plasma. A *Union*-class DropShip.

Painted in Wolf colors.

For a second, just a second, he didn't understand what he was seeing. His DropShips were supposed to monitor the air picture and run interference for the ground forces. How had this vessel slipped through?

Realizing he wasn't going to get an answer, Jasek keyed his unit frequency. "All Stormhammers, Storm One, Omega Violet. Execute."

He raised his 'Mech's right arm, which had been fitted with a special strap-on mod, and slammed his fist into a button on his console. A single missile arced high into the sky, exploding into a brilliant purple starburst.

The signal to retreat for those Stormhammers outside radio range. Not a fighting withdrawal—a desperate headlong flight, every warrior for himself.

The Rangers and the Joust made a run for it, sprinting down the draw.

Fire lashed out from the hovering *Union.* The Joust died by the strobed light of a PPC. One of the Rangers was crippled by a twenty-missile flight of LRMs and finished by the DropShip's AC/5s.

The third Ranger made it out.

One out of three. Jasek had a bad feeling that number might just hold up.

And the *Union* was engaging other targets, too. Jasek saw ruby lasers stab down from the DropShip, aimed at some target a couple hundred meters to the north.

There was no question of fighting on. The second the *Union* had appeared in the sky, the battle for Uhuru was lost.

Now Jasek's only goal was to save as many of his people as he could.

CHAPTER 10

DERELICT ORBITAL STATION IN HIGH ORBIT
LUYTEN 68-28 (EXACT COORDINATES UNKNOWN)
PREFECTURE X
22 JUNE 3140

Tucker's gaze followed the ragged line of the station's broken hull. His stomach sat heavy in his gut. This was not a place of hope. This was where hope came to die.

Whitfield led him to a hatch marked EMERGENCY AIRLOCK. She knelt on one knee and turned a stainless steel hand wheel counterclockwise.

Tucker frowned. The hatch was probably jammed—and even if by some miracle it wasn't, what were the odds there was any atmosphere down there? So he was surprised when the hatch popped open and a little puff of white gas rushed out.

Whitfield didn't even look at him, she just climbed down into the lock. Tucker peered after her. It was dark down there, the only illumination Whitfield's helmet light. Weird shadows danced off the lock's cramped walls. Tucker swallowed.

And dropped down into the hole.

Whitfield reached up behind him and closed the hatch again, sealing them in semi-darkness, without even the stars for company.

"There," she said. "Now we can talk. But keep it line-of-sight only, OK?" Her voice sounded distant over the radio.

"Uh, sure," said Tucker. "Where are we exactly?"

"Here. I'll show you." She spun a wheel set in a second hatch, opening it. She made an after-you gesture and Tucker lowered himself down.

Into a world of cold and shadow. "What *is* this?"

"There's a lot of junk up here, and some of it's still useful."

"Oh, yes," said Tucker sarcastically. "This is great."

"It's better than being dead," said Whitfield. She drifted over to a viewport that was clouded with scratches, and tapped on the ferroglass. "Luyten's right down there." She pointed at the airlock they'd just come through. "And there's the door."

"It's not that I don't appreciate the effort," said Tucker "It's just that—" He glanced around. Their suit lights painted dim swaths of gray in the blackness. Debris floated everywhere casting crazy, scuttling shadows against the feeble light: batteries and a stapler and half-used drink-bulbs and—

Tucker's breath caught.

His helmet light caught a face, half-hidden by shadow, the skin gray and mottled and pulled tight against the skull. The mouth hanging open in a silent scream, the eyes wide and unseeing.

"Yes," said Whitfield turning so her helmet lamp played light across the mummified corpse, "we're hiding in a graveyard."

The man—or woman, he couldn't tell—wore white coveralls, Word of Blake's sword on the sleeve, but otherwise the uniform was just like his.

When Tucker spoke, his voice was hoarse. "This is not right."

"What do you think is going on here, Tucker?" said Whitfield angrily. "You're at ground zero of a war for humanity's future. For humanity's *soul*. The choices are Devlin Stone's Republic—or the Master's Jihad. You don't like *that*—" She jerked her head at the corpse, the flicker of her light making the face look like it shifted in the darkness, like it *winked* at him. "Well, neither do I. *That's* what we're fighting against."

"Y-you're really Alexi Holt?"

She shrugged. "If I tell you one more time, *then* will you believe me?" She shook her head. "You're just going to have decide for yourself."

Tucker was silent for a long moment. Then he drew a deep breath. "Tell me the plan. I mean, is there a way off? A lifeboat or something?"

She shook her head. "No. In order to escape, we'll have to call for help."

Tucker looked around. "Uh—"

"Luyten used to be an important Blakist base," said Whitfield. "During the Jihad, most of their orbital stations were blown to hell. But not all of them. This should be right up your alley, Tucker. This station was once an orbiting HPG. The antenna and reactor were lost, but a good chunk of the station itself survived."

"I think you're using the word 'survived' loosely," said Tucker dryly.

"We'll need to make repairs. Priorities are CO_2 scrubbers, water, power, comms."

Tucker shook his head. "You can't get the HPG up again. There's just no—"

"Not the HPG. All I need is one high-gain RF antenna."

Tucker frowned. "For what?"

"You're going to write a very special program. A virus that embeds a message in ComStar communication protocols. We'll broadcast it to a ComStar JumpShip, and—"

"And when it jumps back to Terra, it'll tell the Republic where we are." Tucker nodded, considering. "That...just might work." He shook his head. "How did you know about all this?" He waved his arm to take in the station.

"I spent a lot of time preparing your extraction, Tucker," she said softly.

Tucker nodded uneasily.

"Anyway, I'll go find the scrubbers." She unzipped a pouch on her suit and tossed him a noteputer. "In the meantime, you get started on that program, OK?"

She turned to go, but Tucker stopped her with a word: "A-Alexi."

She turned and looked at him.

"If you're really Alexi Holt. Why d-did you do the things you did to me?"

She looked at him for a long moment, her hazel eyes marking his face. So different than Alexi Holt's soft, green gaze. "The practical answer is that I *had* to do it so I didn't blow my cover. But that's not really what you're asking. What you're asking is if I'm really Alexi Holt, *how* could I do the things I did to you?"

He saw her swallow hard, straighten her shoulders.

"I'm not a fairy book knight, Tucker. We don't all get to live happily ever after. I thought you understood that on Wyatt. I thought you wanted to help people."

"I did." He shook his head. "I *do*. But what you did to me..."

She touched her gloved hand to the chest of her suit. "You'll never know—" Her voice broke, and Tucker could hear the grief and anguish twist her words. "—what it cost me to hurt you." She was crying. "But I am a soldier." She punched the words out, trying to maintain control. "Being a soldier means sacrifice. Sometimes your own life. Sometimes even the lives of people—" She swallowed again. "You care about."

Then she turned and pushed off, leaving Tucker alone with the specter of death.

THE ROYAL PALACE
THARKAD CITY, THARKAD
DONEGAL MILITARY PROVINCE
LYRAN COMMONWEALTH
1 AUGUST 3140

Trillian Steiner had grown up a cousin to the Archon, raised more like Melissa's younger sister than her subject. Trillian was no stranger to power, nor to the privilege her Christian name commanded. She was the Archon's most trusted advisor, a brilliant diplomat and politician.

But all that melted away when she stepped into the throne room.

Melissa Steiner possessed the most formidable home court advantage in the entire Inner Sphere.

A long ribbon of carpet (not red, but Steiner blue) led through a forest of immense columns, until the throne room expanded into a space that dwarfed every cathedral in human space. And cathedral was not the wrong word, for this was a place of worship—of House Steiner and everything it had achieved. The galleries in the wings of the throne room were like pews for the faithful; the murals depicting great moments of Lyran history were paintings, but they might as well have been fashioned from stained glass. The blue carpet traveled up the steps to the royal dais, right up to the high-backed throne, where Melissa sat beneath the shimmering blue Steiner fist.

But the most impressive feature of the room was the two BattleMechs on either side of the Archon's throne. The 'Mech on Melissa's left was a 75-ton DFN-3S *Defiance* outfitted in the colors of the First Royal Guards: a base of Steiner blue with a gold stripe down each side and matching highlights. It bristled with weapons, not the least of which were the two 1001 extended range PPCs that were its arms.

At Melissa's right hand was a true monster, a 100-ton *Fafnir* painted in the distinctive half-blue, half blue-and-white checkerboard of the First Skye Jaegers.

Both machines were a visible reminder that although the Lyrans were known for their business acumen, they weren't bad at war either.

Trillian reached the foot of the dais, went down on one knee, and bowed her head. "Archon," she murmured.

She heard Melissa rise. "Come, Trillian. Walk with me."

Trillian rose, following her Archon away from her advisors and her galleries, leaving behind all the pomp of her office. The Archon's gesture would be interpreted as a sign of Trillian's favor at court, but Trillian herself knew better.

An arctic coldness had grown between the two women since Alaric Wolf's invasion. Trillian knew Melissa blamed her for the ugly break with the Wolves. Trillian blamed herself, too, whether because she had failed to anticipate the Wolves' treachery or because she failed to persuade her cousin of the danger, she did not know.

Either way, it was her fault.

Melissa studied something scrawling across her noteputer. "It's a message from Vedet," she said coldly. "Listen to this. *'Your Highness, our forces suffer from inadequate supply. Please allow me to take this duty from you, so you will not be distracted as you turn back the Wolf onslaught that threatens our Commonwealth.'*"

Melissa's lips tightened into a thin, angry line. "He *dares* to tell me my duty even as he whines about his lack of supplies."

Trillian felt her stomach tighten. There was something dangerous hidden in Vedet's message, though she could not say what it was. "I think a measured response might be called for, Highness."

"Nonsense," snapped Melissa. "Vedet has forgotten his place, and if I don't remind him, he won't be the last."

"Highness..." said Trillian slowly.

Melissa turned to look at her.

"You recall the incident on Helm? When Alaric slaughtered Silver Hawk Irregular troops as they tried to surrender to Vedet? I suppressed the story by telling the Duke if he went public we'd portray him as a coward, accepting a fake surrender while Alaric—"

"—fought on. You cast Alaric as the hero."

"Obviously that threat will no longer work."

"Obviously."

"Anyway, someone has leaked the battleROM footage from the Helmdown Massacre. At least three different versions, all showing Vedet bravely trying to protect his prisoners against Clanner brutality."

"*Someone*," sneered Melissa.

"Yes, well, it's obviously Vedet's agents who leaked the recordings. The point is the footage makes him look sympathetic. Even...heroic."

"A moment ago," said Melissa, "I informed you how I would handle Vedet. Was my meaning unclear to you?"

"No, Highness, I just—"

Melissa's voice was cold. "Perhaps, then, you are having difficulty separating the role of cousin from that of *subject*."

Trillian's breath caught. "*Nein*, Archon. I serve you in all things."

Melissa stared at Trillian a moment longer to press the point. "In any case," she said, her voice not a degree warmer, "I did not call you here to discuss Vedet."

"Yes, Highness."

"The Wolves have taken all the first-wave worlds. Now they attack Launam, Gienah, Ford, and Megrez. Alaric has already taken Rahne, and has moved on to Fianna."

Trillian drew a deep breath. Jasek Kelswa-Steiner's defeat at Uhuru was bitter news. Maybe... "Our tripwire forces—"

"Rush to confront the Wolves and leave only militia to defend the front-line worlds," said Melissa grimly. She stared at Trillian for a long moment.

Trillian finally understood. "Oh, no," she whispered.

"We received word an hour ago. Wolf reserves have launched a new assault. It looks like they're sweeping up everything they bypassed in the first wave, from Amity to Shasta." She stopped and turned to face Trillian. "I want to know how this could happen. Why did the Exiles not warn us?"

"I think Khan Fetladral is just as shocked as we were. In fact, if you were to move them in the Wolves' path, I think—"

"*No,*" said Melissa firmly. "I have had enough dealings with Wolves. For now we will leave Khan Fetladral on the Jade Falcon border so his hot-blooded countrymen are not subjected to...temptation."

"Do you really believe the Exiles might turn on us?"

"Let us just say this situation has caused me to reevaluate who I can trust."

Trillian did not miss the double meaning. "Of course, Highness."

"I wish you to journey to New Avalon and request aid from your cousin, First Prince Caleb Davion."

Trillian blinked. She and Caleb were both descended from Hanse Davion and the original Melissa Steiner, but the Commonwealth and the Federated Suns had undergone a rather messy divorce in the generation after *that* union. Long gone were the days when the Commonwealth could count on the aid of its cousins in the Suns.

"I'm sorry, Highness. I am unclear on your expectations."

"I *expect* a regiment of troops to fight the Wolves. As a fallback position, I will accept Suns troops stationed on the Jade Falcon border so we may move forces rimward. But if this is all you achieve, I shall be most disappointed."

Trillian opened her mouth and shut it again. "Highness." She swallowed. "The Suns skirmish with the Capellans and the Combine. And relations between our realms have been chilly at best. Why would Caleb help us?"

Melissa's cheeks were flushed. "Surely he must see that the Wolves threaten not only my realm."

No, Trillian thought, *surely he sees you brought the Wolves to the heart of the Inner Sphere to threaten us all.* "I don't think—"

"To whom should we turn then, *Trillian*?" snapped Melissa, rounding on her. "Daoshen Liao? Or do you think *Jessica Marik* might help us?"

"Highness, I—"

Melissa's voice was low and venomous. "I ask you to execute a simple diplomatic initiative. I once knew a Trillian Steiner who would not shrink from such a challenge. Now I wonder if she is gone. So tell me simply, *Trillian,* will you or will you not do your Archon's bidding?"

Trillian felt like she'd been punched in the gut. She bowed low. "I serve at the Archon's pleasure."

"Yes," said Melissa coldly, "you do."

After dismissing Trillian, Melissa stepped into a small anteroom. The young woman waiting for her there rose as the Archon entered, bowing deeply. "Highness." The woman's doe-brown eyes were grave as they met Melissa's. For once there was no outrageous color streaking the tangle of hazelnut hair that framed the woman's lovely face, and she wore a Kell Hound dress uniform rather than brightly colored riding leathers.

Melissa appreciated the show of respect. Callandre Kell didn't dress up for anyone.

"I have a mission for you," said the Archon. "A service you can perform for the Lyran people."

"You can count on me," said Kell.

"Good," said Melissa. "It will be good to have someone to count on for once."

DERELICT ORBITAL STATION IN HIGH ORBIT
LUYTEN 68-28 (EXACT COORDINATES UNKNOWN)
PREFECTURE X
24 JUNE 3140

Tucker stuck the noteputer to the console and pressed his palms against his eyes. He'd been struggling with the program for six hours, and somehow he didn't seem any closer to the end. He sighed, puffing out a cloud of steam. He rubbed his arms, trying to force some warmth back into them.

He knew he had no right to complain. The Aux Communications Nexus was the most comfortable spot on the station. There was a cracked-leather chair, electrical power to two of three main consoles, and all the oxygen he could breathe. Hell, Alexi (Alexi!) had even moved the three mummified corpses out of the nexus for him. Really, who could ask for more? For the life of him, he couldn't imagine why he couldn't concentrate.

He sighed. Self pity. Sure. *That* would solve the problem.

The key to this particular jumble of code was to write something that wouldn't be detected by a JumpShip's virus software, something that wouldn't be detected even after it broadcast its message. Tucker knew a lot about ComStar communications protocols and system security, enough to guess. But not enough to be *sure.*

And he didn't want to gamble his life on a guess.

Time was running out. They weren't sure when the next JumpShip would come. And they still had to fix the high-gain RF antenna before then.

Alexi had managed to bring the CO_2 scrubbers up and she'd sort of fixed the water recycler, enough so they wouldn't quite die of thirst, but they wouldn't exactly be taking Hollywood showers either. She'd fixed the heat, too, but they had to be careful with heat. Make the station too cozy, and someone might see them on IR.

Anyway, Alexi was good at fixing things, but she was going to need his help on the antenna. And he couldn't do that and write code, too.

So no self-pity. But maybe it *was* time for a break.

Not that there was a lot of recreational opportunities on the station. He dug out a tube of sweetened bean sprout paste, thinking *spacer rations really ought to be against the Ares Conventions,* and dug through a filing cabinet, looking for something to do.

He was hoping for a novel, or maybe a blank logbook, somewhere to document his confused thoughts, but all he found were some personal belongings—rings and a watch and family pictures—and a tray of data cubes. He didn't go through the personal stuff—that felt too creepy. Instead he took the cubes.

He plugged the first one into the main console and something came up on the screen. It was...a duty roster. A Blakist duty roster. Tucker shook his head. Great. Jerome Blake has foreordained that you will work Third Shift in reclamation. *Right.* He detached the cube and tossed it away. It bounced against a bulkhead and settled in mid-air, slowly drifting toward the overhead.

The next two didn't work at all. They either had been shock-damaged or wiped by radiation. He almost didn't try the fourth cube.

But he was bored out of his skull, and he wasn't ready to tackle the program again. So he slid the fourth cube into the slot. What came up on the screen was a title page:

CLARION NOTE
EMERGENCY PROTOCOLS

Clarion Note? Now where had he heard that before? Frowning he scrolled to the next page, the table of contents. A phrase jumped out at him: *Super Hyperpulse Generator.*

Super Hyperpulse Generator?

He feverishly poured through the text. Apparently SHPGs had been a Blakist innovation that allowed communication over the entire Inner Sphere, rather than just the fifty light years of a standard HPG.

But what really stopped him, what set his heart to pounding in his chest and bathed his face in sweat was the introductory paragraph under the heading of *Emergency Protocols*:

"The use of an SHPG shall be considered deployment of a weapon of mass destruction. As such, CLARION NOTE protocols will be initiated only on the orders of the Precentor Martial. May the Peace of Blake be with you."

He *had* seen this before.

He skimmed the text, trying to pick out what exactly Clarion Note was. When he found the answer, his breath caught and he heard the roar of blood in his ears.

Clarion Note was the use of an SHPG to cause a complete communications blackout.

DEFIANCE INDUSTRIES, MARIA'S ELEGY
HESPERUS II
BOLAN MILITARY PROVINCE
LYRAN COMMONWEALTH
2 SEPTEMBER 3140

Duke Vedet Brewer stepped to the dais, jeweled sunlight gleaming on his dark face. Normally he favored light colors to complement his complexion, but today he wore a dress uniform of Steiner blue to remind the Commonwealth's people of his recent history fighting on their behalf.

And for those who chose to see it, there was a more subtle message as well.

He waited for a moment, looking out over the crowd, smiling, holding up his hands to accept the factory workers' cheers even as he gestured for silence. After a few minutes, the crowd quieted.

Just as planned.

Vedet didn't want them to stop cheering immediately. He wanted the citizens of the Commonwealth to see him basking in the love of his people as he stood before the gaping maw of an open door at the end of the Defiance production line. Two 'Mechs stood behind Vedet, an *Atlas* on his right and a *Zeus* on his left, both painted in the colors of the First Hesperus Guards, graphic reminders of the importance of Hesperus II.

And if it happened to echo the symbolism of the Archon's throne room, well, that was just a coincidence.

Vedet raised his hands again, and finally the people stopped cheering.

"My fellow citizens," he said, "it is troubling times that bring me before you today. In the midst of a great victory over the Free Worlds League, we have suffered a treacherous blow. The Wolves have turned on us."

He shook his head. "Now is not the time to assign blame for entering into this troubled alliance with Clan Wolf."

So he got credit for being a statesman during wartime while *still* reminding people that it was Melissa's disastrous plan that had opened them up to the Wolves' predations.

"Now we must pull together to *win this war.*"

The crowd broke into three minutes and twenty seconds of spontaneous applause. Vedet had to fight the urge to look at his watch to see how well they hit their mark.

"Here at Defiance Industries, our workers have been fighting this war as valiantly as any of us on the front lines." In truth, Vedet had been fighting House Marik, not Clan Wolf. He hadn't so much as slugged a Wolf infantryman, but most people wouldn't make that distinction. "These brave people you see before you have been working double shifts, building the equipment needed to support the war effort." He raised his right hand, palm flat, gesturing at the *Atlas.*

"But my friends," he said, his voice grave, like the family doctor forced to deliver terrible, terrible news, "this equipment will not do a bit of good if it is not delivered to the men and women on the front lines."

He looked straight into the holorecorders. "Through some terrible miscalculation, supplies that our brave troops need to beat back Clan Wolf have been moving coreward to our quiet border with Clan Jade Falcon."

He swallowed hard and looked down. Drew a deep breath. Steeled himself to go on. Looked up. "In fact, it was a lack of supplies that allowed House Marik to defeat our own First Hesperus Guards on Kalidasa."

He shook his head. "Ten weeks ago, I sent the Archon a message requesting no more than the opportunity to assist in unsnarling this logistics disaster." His voice grew cold. "Today I received her response."

He drew a slip of paper from a pocket and glanced down. "'*I find our logistics effort to be adequate*,' writes the Archon. '*Your help is neither desired or needed.*'"

Vedet lifted his face to the cameras, a look of incredulity stamped on his features. "Adequate? Our logistics efforts are *adequate*?" His voice rose with indignation. "Tell that to the dead soldiers on Kalidasa!" he thundered. "Tell that to the people of Uhuru, new subjects of Clan Wolf!" He slammed his fist into the podium. "Tell that to the citizens of the Lyran Commonwealth as all of Bolan burns!"

"We have the will and the might to win this war." He raised his hand to the *Zeus* on his left as he looked directly into the recorder. "Archon Steiner, I beg you, please let us place swords in the hands of our brave soldiers."

The crowd rose in thunderous applause.

Vedet graciously accepted the factory workers' acclamation, knowing that the recording of his speech was already in post-production, and in an hour a JumpShip would carry it to the contested planet of Bondurant, the nearest world with a working HPG.

And from there it would spread throughout the Commonwealth.

DERELICT ORBITAL STATION IN HIGH ORBIT
LUYTEN 68-28 (EXACT COORDINATES UNKNOWN)
PREFECTURE X
25 JUNE 3140

In a sea of cold, Tucker and Alexi huddled together for warmth. Tucker lay next to the heating element, clipped to the deck so he wouldn't float away. The little resistive heater glowed cherry red in the darkened space, like a fire burning down to its embers. Alexi lay next to him, her head near the heater, her face centimeters from his.

"We really can't turn up the heat?" he murmured.

"Not unless you want to signal Buhl that we're here," she said sleepily. Her eyes were closed, her head pillowed on her hands.

Tucker studied her beautiful face. That strange, alien face. *Was this really Alexi Holt?*

She *smelled* like the Alexi he remembered. Sweaty, yes— Alexi had never been afraid to get her hands dirty—but there was something underneath, vanilla maybe, or lavender. Something delicate and feminine.

And then he remembered the last time their faces were this close: when she'd roused him from his coma and had drugged him with TTX.

It was a weird and unsettling juxtaposition. Tucker almost believed they were two different people: the vicious and cruel Sandra Whitfield, and the brave and beautiful Alexi Holt who just happened to be disguised as Sandra Whitfield.

"What did you find again?" Alexi murmured.

"Something called Clarion Note. It was a Blakist plan to cause a communications blackout."

"What?" Alexi opened her eyes and sat up. Her sudden motion propelled her up a few centimeters until her tethers pulled taut, and jerked her back down.

"The Blakists were able to use something called an SHPG to bend and twist high frequency hyperspace."

Alexi frowned. "High frequency?"

"We transmit messages through high freq. JumpShips travel through low freq."

"So that's why JumpShip travel is unaffected. This...SHPG doesn't affect low frequency hyperspace?"

Tucker shook his head. "No, there's an effect in low freq, too. It's just that the lower energy states means the change is smaller. If you could plot average jump error before and after the blackout, I suspect you'd see a mean shift. It's just not big enough for anyone to notice."

Alexi chewed on that for a moment, staring off into the distance. "All right, I still don't understand," she finally said.

"But never mind. What I really want to know is why you were able to fix Wyatt's HPG, but not any others."

Tucker nodded. "The topology of hyperspace is affected by local gravity wells—the mass, kinetic energy, and angular momentum of stars and planets. Every star system is different. I found the right frequency for Wyatt, but that same shift won't work for any other system."

"You need to finish your program. We've got to get out of here."

"Really?" He looked around the battered, rusted room. "Because I was thinking of settling down here."

She scowled. "No, I mean, we can't afford to let ComStar stumble upon this information. We can't let them get hold of SHPGs again."

Tucker frowned.

"What is it?"

He met her pretty hazel eyes. "Clarion Note was a Word of Blake protocol. A plan of last resort. But the Blakists never triggered their ultimate weapon. Gray Monday took place more than a half-century after the Jihad. *So who triggered the blackout?*"

"Don't you see?" said Alexi. "Word of Blake never died. It's like a cancer. ComStar's in remission, but it's not cured. The true believers still live. And one of them must have sounded this Clarion Note."

BLUE MOUNTAINS
RONEL (FORMERLY PREFECTURE IV)
THE REPUBLIC OF THE SPHERE
20 NOVEMBER 3140

Julian Davion hunched into his parka as he watched fat, wet flakes of snow drift down from a leaden sky. The snow seemed to swallow all sound, which was one of the reasons he was out here.

He needed peace.

And the Republic liaison had told him he had a visitor choppering in to the Richmond drop port. That was another good reason to disappear into the mountains. The last thing he needed was another meeting with some slick politician eager to enlist the First Davion Guards in a new post-Republic alliance.

He stood at the top of a snow-covered ridge that plunged down at a steep 45 angle, his back to an evergreen forest, dark pines and firs blanketed in white. The ridge defined a narrow pass that curled around a low-slung mountain, just wide enough to let a 'Mech through.

Julian was muscular and good-looking, still thin, still strong, his Davion green AFFS uniform still crisp. Even his red-gold hair was cut short in accordance with regulations. He would not break faith with his nation—even while he was in exile.

Especially while he was in exile.

Julian sighed. He was supposed to be scouting the location for the next set of war games. Had to keep the First Davion Guards sharp. And how did you keep an army with nothing to do sharp, except to drill, drill, drill, and drill some more?

He shook his head.

When did this world begin to feel like a prison?

When I lost the ability to do anything meaningful, he thought, answering his own question. Like Caesar in Gaul, he was forbidden to return home. Caesar had crossed the Rubicon anyway, but Julian would not. He thought about the two data wafers locked in his classified safe back on the *Markeson Pride.* Data that suggested what Caleb *was.* Data given to him by Gavin Marik-Davion.

He shook his head. Whatever Caleb was, whatever he had *done,* Julian would not bring dissension to the Suns.

Would not bring *war.*

This wasn't really about Caleb *or* him. It was about what best served the people of the Suns. Caleb was a weak and dangerous prince, but civil war was a cure worse than the disease. Julian would look after his people first. He thought Harrison Davion, the last Prince of the Suns, would have approved.

If only Harrison had lived...

If only Caleb hadn't been ill...

If only Harrison had acknowledged Julian as his heir...

Julian had never wanted to be First Prince, never expected to be anything more than the Prince's Champion. Had never seen the signs that Harrison was grooming him to lead one of the Successor States.

If only.

"Turn and face me, Davion dog!" cried a muffled voice.

Julian started. He'd thought he was alone. He wheeled, his hand going down to his sidearm.

And took a stinging snowball right to the face.

He stumbled backward, tripped, and suddenly found himself sliding down the ridge slope. Cold snow pushed its way down his parka as he fell down the mountain. For a moment, Julian was cold, wet, and disoriented.

Blinking snow out of his eyes, he saw a figure bounding towards him in the thick snow.

"Hey, Jules," said a familiar voice. "Looks like you've lost a step."

The figure pulled down her black, fur-lined parka and Julian gasped. He instantly recognized the lovely face, the lopsided smile, the doe brown eyes, the tangle of hazelnut hair.

It was Calamity Kell.

She reached down and offered him a hand. Julian grunted as she pulled him up. "You know you could've just dropped by the office like a regular person, Callandre."

Her brown eyes twinkled. "I *tried* that. The folks on the *Pride* told me you were ducking me."

They walked up the hill, slogging through the snow. She wasn't dressed in one of her usual outfits. It looked like regulation Kell Hounds uniform pants beneath the parka. When they reached the top, she leaned against a pine tree, her arms folded across her chest.

"I wasn't ducking *you* exactly," said Julian, brushing snow off himself. "I thought you were some tedious politician."

She snorted.

Callandre Kell was many things, but the last thing she was, was a politician.

She was a warrior and a phenomenon. She was the best Destroyer pilot in human space. No one could drive an SM1 like her. And if there was a way to buck authority, "Calamity" Kell would find it.

Julian had known her since she was the Nagelring's "darling rogue," from the class of 3129 (and 3130 thanks to her suspension—and she'd managed to tangle Julian up in that little adventure as well.) They had dated briefly—very briefly—but that part of their relationship just hadn't worked out. Still, she knew him better than anyone ever had. She was the best and truest friend Julian had ever had.

Even if every time she appeared, she tore through his life like a tornado.

And then, right *then,* he understood why she was here.

Julian swallowed, his heart breaking. He plastered a smile on his face. "That uniform looks good on you. And what, no color in your hair? Keep this up, and people will talk."

She snorted a little laugh as forced as his smile. "Look, Julian, I—"

"No," he said softly. He swallowed hard against the tightness in his throat. "I'm sorry, Callandre, but the answer is no."

She stood there for a moment, her face white, looking like he had just slapped her. Julian had never felt so wretched in all his life.

Her mouth worked for a second before any words came out. "How did you—?"

He shook his head. "When you were recalled by the Kell Hounds, I figured you'd be fighting the Wolves on the front line. But here you are. And I can only think of one service you could provide to Melissa Steiner more valuable than your crazy driving."

She swallowed. "The Archon asked—"

"I don't serve the Archon," said Julian softly, and then, even though it tasted filthy in his mouth, "I serve the First Prince."

"Alaric Wolf," said Callandre. "You remember him from Victor Steiner-Davion's funeral. He killed Thaddeus Marik and crushed Jasek Kelswa-Steiner. No one can stop him. *No one.* But *you,* you and I, we could stop him. And if we stop Alaric, this whole terrible war could be over."

"Please don't," said Julian. "I don't disagree with you, Callandre. I just...can't."

"Jules." She was pleading now. "I fought with you against the Senatorial Revolt. That wasn't my war either, but I stood with you."

"If it were just me, my life, my 'Mech, you would have it, you know you would. But I can't commit the First Guards."

"Why can't you—?"

"Caleb has explicitly ordered me to remain on Ronel." He shook his head. "If I took the First Guards to fight the Wolves, I'd be committing treason."

"Then come *without* the Guards. Take a leave of absence. I'd take just you," she said fiercely.

A leave of absence.

It sounded so easy. Except...Caleb would use a leave of absence to drum him out of the Armed Forces of the Federated Suns. Maybe he could live with that.

Against his will, he remembered the data wafers locked up in his safe.

Except he owed it to the people of the Suns to deliver them from madness. And he owed it to Harrison Davion to repay the trust the man had placed in him. If he walked away now, he would carry those debts the rest of his life.

"No," Julian said softly.

He saw how deeply that word wounded her. She stared at him like she'd never seen him before. "Why?"

He opened his mouth. Wanting to tell her everything. Callandre Kell was his best friend. But there were some secrets a prince could not share. Some terrible duties a prince must bear alone.

He had learned that from Harrison.

And so, knowing she wouldn't understand, knowing it would only hurt her more, he drew a deep breath and shook his head.

"But—"

"*No*," Julian's voice was steel. "I will not betray the people of the Federated Suns."

"Every moment you serve Caleb you are betraying the people of the Federated Suns, *and you know it*." Callandre's doe-brown eyes flashed with anger. And then she turned and stalked through the trees, disappearing into the white fall of snow.

Julian laid a trembling hand flat on the bark of a pine tree, bowed his head. And closed his eyes.

DERELICT ORBITAL STATION IN HIGH ORBIT
LUYTEN 68-28 (EXACT COORDINATES UNKNOWN)
PREFECTURE X
22 JULY 3140

Tucker drifted down the darkened passageway, his helmet light sending shadows skittering like spiders across the bulkheads. "There are no bodies here," he said nervously.

"Just yours and mine," said Alexi. Her voice sounded different over the radio.

"Well, that's good luck," Tucker muttered. He felt the comforting weight of his slug thrower in his right leg pouch. He knew it was irrational to fear mummified corpses drifting through a dark and silent world. Still he was glad he had the gun.

Alexi snorted. "There was no luck involved. The mess decks are right below the access hatch—I put them in there."

"You put them in with the food?"

"Don't worry, Tucker. They've been dead for fifty, sixty years. I don't they'll take any of your sweetened bean sprout paste."

Tucker made a gagging noise. "Alexi! That stuff's hard enough to eat as it is."

She laughed. "Sorry. Look, this is a fifteen-minute procedure. We'll dump your program into the buffer, manually align the antenna, set the timer, and then we're done. We can curl up in aux control with bean sprout paste until the cavalry gets here."

"I hope the cavalry brings cheeseburgers," Tucker muttered.

Alexi snorted.

They reached the access hatch. This part of the station was depressurized, so they wouldn't have to bother with an airlock.

"Here, I'll go first," she said.

"I'll do it," said Tucker, a little stung that she'd been laughing at him.

"All right, all right. Just make sure you anchor as soon as you get topside. Don't drift away on me."

"I *know,*" said Tucker indignantly.

The hatch was set into the bulkhead at waist level. He unbolted it and set it aside, letting it drift slowly through the passageway. Then he stuck his head through the hole. There was a moment of disorientation as "sideways" suddenly became "up." Of course there was really no such thing as either "sideways" *or* "up", but tell that to a hominid brain designed for life on Terra.

He climbed out onto the station's surface. The deck plating was puckered and warped, whole sections peeled back by the force of a terrible battle waged before Tucker was born.

He picked out the antenna, twenty meters away along the main axis of the station. He started walking, careful to always keep one boot locked down.

Out of the corner of his eye he saw a flicker of motion. Alexi? He glanced back to check. No, she was behind him, half-kneeling as she unpacked the tools they'd need.

Nerves, Tucker. There's a million particles of debris orbiting the station, caught in its microgravity. That's all you saw. He resumed walking. Step-Lock. Unlock-Step. But he unzipped his pocket and slid the slug thrower out. The one he'd taken from the adept who brought him the radioactive junk.

The one he'd killed with.

He moved more carefully from feature to feature, crouching behind a mangled upwelling of metal *here* and wondering how much cover that crater would provide *there.*

Tucker snorted. Like Blakist ghosts would give a damn about cover.

He stepped out behind jagged metal and flashed on three space-suited figures. The suits were snow white and all bore the familiar two-rayed star emblem of ComStar. And floating just beyond the station's hull was a Mark VII landing craft.

Tucker didn't even think. His hand jerked up and he *fired.*

The recoil knocked him backward, but his feet were anchored to the deck. For a second he looked like a limbo contestant.

Ruby light sliced past his head, missing him cleanly right.

The astronaut he'd hit had his hand over his starred faceplate, a red mist freezing into ice on the desperate man's gloves.

Tucker shot him again and then stepped behind his tortured metal shield. "Alexi!"

"Tucker, what did I tell you about radio silence?"

"Um, I don't think it matters anymore. We've got company."

"What?"

Ruby light sparked off the jagged metal a few centimeters from his head. "And they're *shooting* at me."

"Do you have a defensible position? Can you hold them off?"

Tucker edged around the makeshift shield's other side and fired. Both astronauts ducked. He didn't think he hit either of them, but at least they'd think twice about charging him. The third astronaut stood motionless, his boots still locked to the deck, arms floating limply, his face mask coated with red-tinged ice.

He ducked back behind his shield. "Yeah, I can hold them off—*until you get up here.* Where are you anyway?"

"How many are there?"

"Uh, two, now. Looks like I, uh, killed one of them."

"Hold on, Tucker. I have to get a few things."

"What?" he snapped. "What are you talking about?" But the line was dead.

A red dot glowed on the metal shield, metal glowing red to yellow then *white.* A fist-sized hole punched through his shield. Tucker glanced at the watch built into the inside of the suit's left wrist. *Where was Alexi?*

Only one way to hold them off. Tucker ducked out to take another shot and ruby light sparked off his helmet. The helmet didn't breach, but it wouldn't take much more.

Still no Alexi.

He looked at the watch again. Where *is* she?

And then the radio crackled. His heart leaped. *She's coming back for me.*

But the voice on the other radio wasn't Alexi Holt.

It was the *devil*.

THE FOX'S DEN, OUTSIDE THE NEW CITY
NEW AVALON
CRUCIS MARCH
FEDERATED SUNS
14 DECEMBER 3140

First Prince Caleb Hasek-Sandoval-Davion stood in a room full of stars, the whole of the Inner Sphere laid out before him. He loved holding tactical briefings in the Den's huge command center.

The real Fox's Den, the *first* Fox's Den, was entombed beneath the shattered ruins of Mount Davion. Still, the new command center possessed the spirit of the old—even if it wasn't *exactly* same room where his ancestor, Jackson Davion, had orchestrated the magnificent resistance to Word of Blake's monstrous occupation of New Avalon. After the Blakist withdrawal, Davion patriots had dug out much of the original Den's wreckage. This center had been constructed of the same steel as the first.

Caleb could *feel* it.

This is who I am, he thought. *If only my father had lived to see. If only Julian had not tried to steal my father's love. My place.*

Belatedly, Caleb realized Sandoval was speaking. "—reconsider Trillian Steiner's request."

Caleb blinked and peered at his Prince's Champion. Lord Erik Sandoval-Groell was a young man, his dark hair arranged in a traditional Sandoval topknot, the sides of his head shaved clean. He wore an immaculate dress-green AFFS uniform.

"You think I *should* send troops to support Melissa Steiner."

"No, Highness. But I do think you should not *refuse* to send troops to support Melissa Steiner. That's not at all the same thing."

Caleb stared at him.

Sandoval stepped over to the map projector's controls. The map ballooned in scale, replacing the entire Inner Sphere with a smaller slice of stars. Starting at the Republic's Prefecture I, the diagram reached as far rimward into the purple Free Worlds League as Oriente.

Fortress Republic was a silver spray of stars sequestered behind a bright red border. The Suns and the Capellan Confederation were yellow and green fingers reaching into the gray Republic worlds caught on the wrong side of Exarch Levin's wall. The Jade Falcon Occupation Zone in Skye was an emerald cancer. Anti-spinward of the Republic was the Steiner blue Lyran Commonwealth, albeit with a large, brown Wolf bite out of its flank.

Yellow note boxes tied to individual worlds indicated DMI or MIIO reports on military unit locations. A flashing red star indicated fighting.

A string of red stars decorated the Lyran-Wolf border.

"The Lyrans are the wealthiest state in the Inner Sphere, and we do much trade with them. An outright refusal will have consequences," said Sandoval.

"We have problems of our own. And *we* did not invite the Wolves rimward."

"Agreed, Highness." Sandoval still worked the controls, focusing in on the former Republic. "So do not say 'yes.' But that doesn't mean you have to say 'no.' You can give Trillian Steiner the impression you are thinking seriously about her proposal, that you *might* say 'yes' in the future. But always delay, never make a firm commitment."

Caleb nodded slowly, beginning to understand.

"And when the Lyran cause is surely lost, you can order a very special unit to aid Melissa Steiner."

The map came to rest on the Republic world of Ronel. The yellow note box read: *First Davion Guards.*

"You get the political credit for trying to help House Steiner. Julian Davion gets the blame for the debacle that is sure to follow." Sandoval smiled.

Caleb gazed down at the map. "And if we are very lucky indeed, the Wolves might just take care of our little problem for us."

DERELICT ORBITAL STATION IN HIGH ORBIT
LUYTEN 68-28 (EXACT COORDINATES UNKNOWN)
PREFECTURE X
22 JULY 3140

Patricia dodged right using Henderson's body, still maglocked to the hull, as partial cover. Stupid Henderson. He always did have the knack for being in the wrong place at the wrong time.

"You know she's not coming back for you, don't you Tucker?"

"Right. And I should listen to you because up to now you've had such a good handle on things."

She saw him duck beyond his little shield and chased him back behind cover with a well-placed shot that just missed his right sleeve. Normally a glancing blow to a limb was not fatal, but then normally you didn't carry your air in your clothes.

She pointed at Adept Sally Yu and made a circling gesture with her index finger. Yu's single nod was enough to convey that she understood Patricia's order.

Patricia laughed. "Good to see you picked up a little spunk, Tuck. Has she told you she's Alexi Holt yet?"

"No," said Tucker, but there was the tiniest trace of doubt in his voice.

"Well, I shall have to rebuke her when we get back to Omega One. Her orders were to try to gain your trust."

Tucker popped out from behind his cover. Patricia was ready for him, delivering another glancing shot to his helmet.

She mentioned Alexi Holt and he took a shot at her. He couldn't help it. So predictable.

Meanwhile, Yu was almost around to the other side of the barrier.

"You're lying."

"Think, Tuck. If she weren't working for us, how else would I know she was pretending to be Holt?"

Yu had disappeared from Patricia's view. It wouldn't be long now.

"Who else would rescue me?"

Tucker was a fool. If he thought about it, he'd realize her orders were to take him alive. She had to keep him talking for another few moments, keep that ginormous brain of his from really thinking through the situation.

"So you still believe she's here to rescue you. Sandra Whitfield is the brave knight. What does that make you, Tuck? The damsel in distress?"

She didn't hear the gunshot, so she had no warning of what had happened until she saw Yu's suit drift up into the black. There was just enough light to see several crimson holes scattered across her suit.

Patricia swore under her breath. Apparently Tucker hadn't been as distracted as she'd thought. This markedly changed the tactical situation. She held the landing craft, but Tucker had better cover, and of course Whitfield was a wild card.

She might just have to reconsider taking Tucker alive.

Patricia fired her laser to keep his head down and pushed off left, skimming over the metal hull, careful to keep her body straight so she didn't go off after Yu. She clenched her teeth and grabbed for a handhold, pulling herself down behind a large puncture in the hull.

It was a dangerous maneuver jumping in space, but now she had better cover and a clear shot at anyone approaching the landing craft. And maybe, *maybe* Tucker didn't know exactly where she was.

"So where's your knight, Tuck? Is she there? Can I say hi? Hi, Sandra or Alexi or whatever your name is. Thanks for looking after my little brother."

"Shut up," Tucker snarled. She was getting to him.

Something moved to her left. Patricia turned in time to see Whitfield jumping for her. She jerked her laser up and fired, hitting her dead center. But the woman kept coming.

Is she wearing armor? Patricia wondered, and then Whitfield hit her. For a moment she struggled with the knight, finally managing to push her away.

The other space suit slowly drifted away, arms and legs spread out like a starfish, slowly spinning against the stars. Sunlight flashed against her facemask.

And what Patricia saw wasn't the dangerous ROM traitor, but a mummified horror, staring at her with long-dead eyes.

She stood and glanced back toward the Mark VII, just in time to see it turn gracefully away from the station and fall toward the planet below.

"What took you so long?" demanded Tucker as he strapped himself into the landing craft's copilot seat.

"I had to get a prop," said Alexi.

"A prop?"

She shook her head. "You don't want to know." She tossed him a data cube and Tucker snatched it out of the air. "Also, I figured you might want this."

"Clarion Note," Tucker whispered. He turned to look at her. "Patricia said—"

"Haven't you learned by now you shouldn't listen to anything Patricia says?"

Tucker looked down. "So what's the plan now?"

"We'll broadcast your virus from the landing craft." Her eyes found the khaki and green world growing in their canopy. "And then we go to ground."

CHAPTER 11

LCAF SUPPLY DEPOT
TRUXTON, VORZEL
COVENTRY MILITARY PROVINCE
LYRAN COMMONWEALTH
20 DECEMBER 3140

Senior Warrant Officer Malcolm Craig stood in a warehouse stuffed to capacity and beyond. The racks were full, and materiel overflowed into offices and aisles and bathrooms.

And still the forklifts and the big yellow IndustrialMechs brought more.

From where he stood, Craig saw Condor lift fans, a *Salamander* knee actuator, bundles of myomer, and grease for an Ultra-class 120mm autocannon. There were kilometers of wire, piles of fasteners, oceans of lube oil, mountains of armor plating, blizzards of paper.

Everything a growing army needed.

He even had a hundred gross of red tape.

Unfortunately, *Hauptmann* Weiss didn't want to hear any of it. "Send it back," he shouted, turning red. The *hauptmann* didn't seem to do anything but shout these days. "Send it all back!"

Craig tapped the screen of his 'puter impatiently with a slim stylus. "*Hauptmann* Weiss, sir, we just got it."

The angry officer waved a 'puter of his own. "This is an order from *the Archon*. Do you hear me, Craig? *The Archon*." His voice dropped to a fierce whisper. "She wants everything here shipped *back* to Bolan Province *immediately,* and if you don't do that *right now,* so help me God, I'm going to break out a coil of rope from that box over there—" The officer actually *pointed.* "—and *string you up myself."*

"I would love to accommodate you, *sir,"* said Craig tightly, "but all our lift capacity is busy sending this stuff coreward to the Melissia Theater. What am I supposed to do? I can't *crap JumpShips."*

If looks could kill, Craig would have been burned to a small pile of fine carbon ash. As it was, the *hauptmann* turned on his heel and stalked off.

Which was very good, because just then an IndustrialMech came by and set a pallet of gyroscope parts down on the deck in the exact spot where he'd been standing.

CAMPBELL PLANETARY PARK
ARCADIA
BOLAN MILITARY PROVINCE
LYRAN COMMONWEALTH
22 DECEMBER 3140

For a moment, just a moment, Colonel Roderick Steiner of the First Steiner Strikers saw the end to the Wolf invasion of Arcadia.

He watched from the shadows, his cockpit bathed in darkness except for the soft gleam of his console, the nuclear fire at the heart of his *Rifleman IIC* carefully banked.

Watched as a Cluster of Clan Wolf's Gamma Galaxy tore into the light, fast elements of his Strikers.

Roderick shook his head. The Wolf Hussars were a proud unit. He was going to use that pride against them.

He had lured the Wolves into a classic trap, dangling his light, fast vehicles in front of them. The fast machines had "blundered" into the Wolves as they moved along a low ridge that paralleled a thick, deciduous forest. The ridge was a jagged spine of granite too sharp for the fast machines to traverse and the press of thick-trunked redwoods would take away the Strikers' lone advantage—speed.

Unable to head north or south, the mix of hovercraft and light 'Mechs did the only thing they could—they bolted, running east along the ridge.

And the Wolves did what wolves do.

They ran down their prey.

Unable to lose their pursuers over the uneven ground, the Strikers picked a spot and drew partway up the ridge, grabbing what high ground they could. They drew partway up the ridge, and set a line.

And waited for their deaths to come.

At first, the Strikers almost held their own. The first of the Wolves to hit the Lyran line were themselves fast machines, so mostly a match for Roderick's people.

A pair of Demon medium tanks painted tan on top and dark gray on the bottom hit a Condor painted in green forest camo, the blue Steiner fist marking its slanted nose.

The Demons traded off their miniguns and medium lasers against the Condor's miniguns, a Valiant Arbalest LRM fifteen-pack, and its LB-X autocannon. The hovercraft picked one of the Demons and pushed it back with a sustained pull from its Mydron Excel autocannon before turning on the second.

It was a good move, but Roderick found he was sweating, hoping the Condor's commander was being careful with his loadouts. The Strikers had been plagued with supply problems, and Roderick had held his unit together for the last two months with duct tape and baling wire. There wasn't a single plate of armor or one round of ammunition he could afford to waste.

That's why this plan *had* to work.

And it looked like his boys and girls were in the fight.

Until the Wolf heavies lumbered up, joining the battle. They trickled in at first. Pain lanced through Roderick's jaws as he gritted his teeth. Watching the heavies hit his people was like watching a car accident. Had to let the Wolves get into position.

The moment of victory *was* coming. But it was not yet here.

He watched his people buckle under the fierce assault. Somehow he made himself hold his fire. A massive *Tundra Wolf* stalked forward, splitting its shot, peppering a Condor with its Longbow LRMs, smashing a VV1 with ATMs, and worrying a *Stinger* with its Series 7K ER large laser.

That was all Roderick could stand.

"Striker Heavies, this is Striker One. *Forward.*"

Roderick stalked his *Rifleman IIC* out of the trees, joined by a lance of heavy and assault 'Mechs, a pair of JES tactical missile carriers, and a Behemoth.

Roderick tore into the *Tundra Wolf*'s vulnerable rear armor with his pulse lasers, followed by long pulls on his autocannons, a stream of shells shattering armor in the *Tundra*'s back.

The *Tundra* started to turn to face Roderick, but a Striker SM1 Destroyer from his fast line slid forward and tore into the Clan heavy with its Ultra autocannon, hammering the *Tundra Wolf*'s forward armor with twenty millimeter shells.

So the *Tundra* turned *sideways*, extending its arms right and left, trying to target both opponents at the same time. It was a gutsy move.

Unfortunately, Roderick had seen it coming.

He was already moving right. His *Rifleman* wasn't any faster than the *Tundra*, but the SM1's attack had given him the jump on the Clanner.

He melted armor on the *Tundra*'s left arm with stitches of emerald fire. Then he cleared the Clanner's back and raised his arms, dropping his reticle over the *Tundra*'s wounded back, anticipating a gyro kill.

He pulled into his primary triggers and his autocannons roared, tearing into the Clanner's dilapidated armor, his machine shaking with the vibration of all that lethal power pouring into the Wolf machine.

Until his right autocannon guttered out.

Followed ten seconds later by his left.

He'd drawn down to the bottom of his ammunition bins.

The SM1 surged forward to save him, slamming the *Tundra* with its massive autocannon. Until its gun, too, fell silent.

Suddenly, Roderick understood just how desperately close to the line they were. They might have enough ammunition to fight their way free of this battle, though that was a stretch.

But there was no way they could press their assault.

"All Strikers, this is Striker One." Roderick's throat closed painfully around the words. "Fighting withdrawal, *fighting withdrawal.* Form up on me."

For a moment—just a moment—Colonel Roderick Steiner of the First Steiner Strikers saw the end to the Wolf invasion of Arcadia.

And then it all went to hell.

THE WASTELAND
LUYTEN 68-28 (EXACT COORDINATES UNKNOWN)
PREFECTURE X
14 SEPTEMBER 3140

Tucker fought his way through a stinging, pelting storm, his face sandblasted by the blistering winds. He staggered forward, driven by nothing more than the desperate hatred of sand, sand, everywhere *sand.* He tasted it on his tongue, it worked its ways between his toes, chafed beneath his goggles, irritated his eyes.

When the blazing sun roused the wind to a howling fury, it even flayed skin.

There had been a time when the wasteland had been covered by rich, dark soil, growing soil, *living* soil.

And then the Jihad had come to Luyten.

The first nuclear strike had vaporized all the soil to a radius of forty kilometers. The rest it had lifted into the world's sky and dumped it upon the trickster wind.

But what really killed the wasteland was radiation. Heartless gamma burned plants and animals alive, not their bodies, but their *cells,* sending cancers spiraling through the flesh of living things.

The animals died first, their bloated bodies rotting in the sun. Then the plants, no longer nourished by the soil or pollinated by the insects. And when the last twisted, sickened shoots were gone, the rains came, pounding an earth that could no longer slake its thirst. Flash floods washed away the last of the soils.

Leaving only wind—and sand.

"Over here," Alexi croaked.

Tucker turned toward the sound of her voice. Saw the dark shape of her body through the swirling sand. Staggered toward her.

"Shelter," she said.

Tucker moved faster. He saw nothing, nothing but her. And then— His heart skipped a beat. Suddenly, there was *something.*

A desperate smile came to his cracked lips and he found a way to hobble faster. And then there was a *door* which meant there was an *inside.* He hurled himself inside and found himself on *tile.*

Alexi struggled to close the door against a growing pile of sand. "A Blakist outpost," she grunted. "It must've been missed when the main base was hit."

Tucker spied a rack bearing olive drab cans labeled *Emergency Water.* He staggered over and grabbed a can, pulled the pop tab, drank it down. It was tepid, but it was *wet.* He upended the can, drinking as much as he could and letting the rest run down his face, cutting rivulets through the dust that caked his skin.

He finished the first one and threw the empty can aside. Grabbed another.

"*Tucker, no.*" She knocked the can from his hand. "We have to check for radiation first."

"I don't care about radiation," he snarled. He bent down and picked up the can. Popped the tab.

Alexi watched him drink, her mouth hanging open. She shook her head. "I'm sorry," she whispered.

He stopped drinking and looked at her.

"This is supposed to be a rescue." She shook her head. "But it isn't. It's a desperate flight, moving across the desert, trying to stay ahead of your sister. Trying to carve survival out a wicked, poisonous land."

She picked up a can and smashed it against the wall in an angry overhand throw. Tucker jumped.

Then she sank to the floor, sitting cross-legged, her face buried in her hands.

Tucker slowly put down his water and settled on the floor next to her.

"I've done the best I can."

"I know," he said gently.

She raised her head, turned to face him. She was crying, big, silent tears tracing through the dust that coated her face. "I'm sorry I hurt you, Tucker."

He said nothing, he just sat there watching her.

"Do you remember when I gave you the noteputer?" She swallowed. "You were angry with me. You asked who was watching me. Don't you see? They *were* watching me. Buhl didn't trust anyone. I had to—"

She raised a trembling hand to touch his face, but stopped, her fingers millimeters from his cheek. "But it doesn't matter, does it? Maybe you can understand why I had to do it. The logic of it. But it was still wrong. That's the terrible thing about war, Tucker. Sometimes you have to do things you *know* are wrong. Everyone knows soldiers pay with their lives. But sometimes, sometimes we pay with our *souls.*"

She looked at him, her eyes—her *hazel* eyes—searching his face.

Tucker stared back at her, unsure of what to say. What to feel. He felt hollow inside.

Alexi swallowed. Then she bent her head and began to sob softly.

After a moment, Tucker reached out and, taking her chin in his hand, gently raised her face to his. She looked at him, those hazel eyes rimmed with red, misery written in every line of her face. Something broke in Tucker, some final bulwark.

And he leaned over to taste her lips.

In the morning, thunder roused Tucker. For a moment he savored the feeling of Alexi's body curled against his, the warmth of her, the softness of her.

But the thunder did not stop.

Tucker leaped to his feet and dashed outside without bothering to dress. What he saw was a DropShip, an immense ovoid falling out of a clear blue sky. Painted on the vessel's hull was an emblem, ten meters tall, proudly proclaiming the DropShip's origin.

The emblem was blue and green Terra ringed by ten golden stars and backed by a knotwork banner, beneath the motto *Ad Securitas Per Unitas*. There was no question where this vessel was from.

The Republic of the Sphere.

THE ROYAL PALACE
THARKAD CITY, THARKAD
DONEGAL MILITARY PROVINCE
LYRAN COMMONWEALTH
22 FEBRUARY 3141

Melissa Steiner sat upon her throne and watched Duke Stanislav Zdenekova stride across the long, blue carpet, her cold eyes tracking him like one of the BattleMechs at her side might track an enemy machine before unleashing their terrible weapons.

It was a most apt comparison.

Ordinarily, this was the kind of meeting she would have taken in a conference room over a nice glass of plum brandy. But not today. Today was going to be a lesson.

An *example.*

Although, and her eyes flickered to the galleries that dominated the throne room's wings, it did seem as if attendance had fallen off at court. No matter—and her gaze turned back to Duke Stan—what would happen today would get around.

The small, round man stopped before the foot of the dais and offered her a shallow bow that was not *quite* disrespectful.

No bright smile lighted Duke Stanislav's cinnamon face. *So it's going to be that kind of meeting,* thought Melissa. *Good. It will just make a better example.*

She glanced at the pair of BattleMechs stood on either side of her, the blue-and-white checkerboard *Fafnir* and the blue *Defiance* with gold accents. Let him challenge her here, in the very seat of her power.

"You summoned me, Archon?" said Duke Stanislav stiffly.

"You don't seem happy to see me, Duke Zdenekova," she said, daring him to admit it.

"I mean no disrespect, Archon," the duke said coldly, "but my world is under assault. I should be standing with my people against Clan Wolf."

That stung. She heard the murmurs ripple through the galleries. *No, you are not the selfless patriot,* thought Melissa. *That is not the story we will write today.*

"Because your years of military experience would be such a great asset to your people in this troubling time," she shot back.

"I have no military experience, as I believe the Archon knows," said Duke Stanislav. "Nevertheless, I would be with my people on Gienah, and suffer whatever dangers they suffer. Sometimes leadership is not merely an exercise in power, Archon, but also an exercise in *conscience.*"

The murmurs grew a little louder.

Melissa studied Zdenekova like she might study a bug. So he had come to fight? Very well. She would crush him. She had to.

Vedet was already conducting a guerrilla public opinion campaign against her. The master of Hesperus II had a habit of living on that little patch of land *just* on the safe side of the line that separated disagreement from treason.

The tape of his speech on Hesperus had been right on the line. Standing in front of a pair of BattleMechs as if *he* were Archon. Like a Brewer would ever sit on *this* throne. (An *Atlas* and a *Zeus,* no less. What was that man compensating for?)

Well, Vedet was no longer a political problem. Melissa had turned that problem over to Gunter Duiven. Just as soon as Loki located Vedet, he would be dealt with. She suppressed a grim smile. Let him try to use his smooth political tactics against her secret police.

And she would act just as harshly against Zdenekova if need be. She could not allow the grievances of these two men to ignite a firestorm of revolt among her nobles.

"Very well, Duke Zdenekova, let's discuss this war you seem so concerned about. Do you believe that trafficking in dissent, in criticism, in *treason,* is helpful to the war effort?"

Zdenekova drew himself up to all of his limited height. "I engage in no treason, Archon. But neither did I whistle for the wolves to come."

"If you truly supported the prosecution of this war—"

"*This war?*" roared Zdenekova, cutting her off. "The war against Clan Wolf? The war *you* assured me six months ago *we would never have to fight?*" His voice dropped to an arctic whisper. "Is *that* the war you speak of, Highness?"

Melissa realized the murmurs had disappeared. The people in the galleries were leaning forward. There was absolutely no sound in the chamber except the distant *clank* of machinery.

"You tread dangerous ground, Duke Zdenekova."

"So what? You will offer me my life for my silence? *What will you offer the people of Gienah, Highness?*" He shook his head. "I fear that soon my people will have no appeal except to Alaric Wolf."

A gasp rippled through the throne room.

Melissa bolted to her feet. "I will not be spoken to in that—"

Someone hit her, tackling her, riding her to the ground. She smashed into the dais, the man on top of her.

And then everything happened at once.

A terrible shriek shattered the room's calm and Melissa saw a flash of ruby light.

She looked to the throne room's entrance and flashed on an armored shape, a soldier in power armor, its right arm ending in a laser, its left in a nasty three-fingered claw.

A missile rack built into the suit's carapace located over the soldier's helmet.

Hauberk battle armor.

As she watched, a second soldier appeared.

The *Defiance* was already moving, taking a half-step right. It leaned over, placing its right-arm PPC on the ground directly in front of her, using its armor and the PPC's flared shape as an impromptu shield.

Then it raised its left arm and horrible lightning lashed out and caught the first Hauberk dead center.

Melissa felt static discharge raise the hair on the back of her neck. Her ears rang with the terrible whip-crack of the particle projection cannon.

The shield in front of her vibrated with each missile hit, each splash of ruby light.

The *Defiance* let loose with its LB 10-X, the autocannon's deep rattle filling the room, joined by the 'Mechs two lasers and its Trellshire Minigun.

Melissa felt like someone had stabbed her in the ears with an ice pick.

And then, just like that, it was over. The little Hauberks never really stood a chance against a monster that massed nearly forty times what they did. Their only hope was surprise, and when they failed—

(to kill her)

—their battle was lost.

The Diplomatic Guard agent who'd saved her life got off her and jerked her to her feet. He was shouting something, but she couldn't hear him, couldn't hear anything at all.

She tasted smoke on her tongue, smelled the sweet, sharp odor of expended explosives. The iron tang of blood

Two more guards ran up to her, each grabbing an arm, bodily carrying her out of the throne room, moving her quickly to safety. She caught images: her gilded throne melted down to golden slag, priceless murals scoured from the walls by stray lasers, two columns crushed, the roof above them sagging dangerously.

Duke Zdenekova's body lay across the ribbon of blue carpet, smashed and bleeding.

Well, I was right, she thought unsteadily, *what happened here today will definitely get around.*

It wasn't until they cleared the throne room and put her in an armored limousine that sped away from the palace escorted by a pair of SM1 Destroyers that she realized the *Fafnir* had not stepped forward to defend her.

Not at all.

THE WASTELAND
LUYTEN 68-28 (EXACT COORDINATES UNKNOWN)
PREFECTURE X
17 SEPTEMBER 3140

They walked out of the desert, using the twisted black column of smoke on the horizon as their pole star. After half a century, war had come again to Luyten. Tucker knew there was a chance the Republic forces had been defeated by the Com Guards, but he no longer cared.

He just wanted to be free of the desert.

Alexi guided on the column of smoke, and Tucker guided on her. The hunger and the sand and the blistering heat had taken their toll. She'd dropped five or six kilos, and every gram of body fat she'd ever owned. She was a slim creature built of long ropes of muscle and pure determination. She stalked forward, back straight, daring the desert to stop her.

Tucker staggered after her, every step a wracking, lurching agony. But following, always following.

On the morning of the third day, they spotted something on the horizon. It started as a speck of black, nearly lost in the horizon's heat blur. They just stood there, watching it. Even Alexi was too tired to speak.

And really what was there to say?

The speck grew into a hoverjeep painted khaki. Tucker coughed as he watched the jeep race toward them, a deep phlegmy cough from deep in his chest. He put his left hand to his mouth as he hacked. He'd caught something in the last few days. Just his luck. All the plants and animals were dead, but somehow he'd caught a virus.

Alexi screamed. "Tucker, *Tucker*! It's a Republic jeep. I can see the insignia." Suddenly she was running, sprinting, *capering*.

Tucker stared at her for a moment and then, resigned, he shuffled after her.

The jeep pulled to a stop next to Alexi. "I am Knight-Errant Alexi Holt on an undercover mission for Paladin Sorenson. Recognition Code Alpha Forty-Seven Tango Eight."

"Confirmed," said one of the soldiers in the jeep.

She turned and pointed at Tucker. "This is Tucker Harwell. He needs help."

Alexi ran back to him and took his arm, a dazzling smile on her tanned face. "We made it, Tucker," she whispered. "We *made* it."

One of the soldiers looked at him, and for an unguarded moment shock stole across her face, eyes wide, mouth hanging slackly open, before she quickly locked it down again.

"You have taken the ComStar base?" Tucker's voice was cracked and thick and swollen. "You have prisoners?" He paused. "Casualties?"

"That's right," said the female officer, staring at him.

"My sister is Com Guards," he croaked. "Want to see her."

"Tucker," said Alexi gently.

"Sir," said the officer, "I think we should get you checked out first. Then—"

"Sister *first*," Tucker barked. He sat down on the sand. "Sister first. Or *won't go*."

"Tucker, I'm responsible for your safety," insisted Alexi.

He looked straight ahead.

"Sure, buddy, we'll take you wherever you want to go," said the female officer.

Like he was so far gone he wouldn't know what a lie sounded like. He looked up at Alexi.

She sighed. "All right, Tucker. I promise." Alexi nodded to one of the soldiers. "Help me get him into the jeep."

They got him settled, and then they were skimming across the desert sand.

Tucker coughed again, spraying phlegm over his hand. One of the soldiers leaned back and handed him a rag. Tucker opened his hand to wipe it clean, but instead of phlegm, he saw a bright scarlet smear of blood.

The Republic forces had not quartered themselves in the Omega One's captured buildings, avoiding the former ComStar base almost as if it were unclean. Instead they'd set up a little tent city, utilitarian structures of steel scaffolding and khaki canvass encircling their *Overlord*-class DropShip.

It was a jumble of sounds and smells: the sharp odor of grease and the mechanical clank of troops in battle armor. The ominous rumble of BattleMechs working through his bones like a wicked base line. The shouts and laughs and curses of people, the sizzle of grill-cooked meat, the *clink* of bottles, the smell of BO.

All of it rolled together in a tumultuous whole.

They took him to a corner of the camp that contained several dozen black bags laid out on the sand, good sturdy bags fashioned from double-ply plastic, each with their own white tag.

The jeep pulled to a stop and Tucker climbed out. A soldier rushed up in khaki fatigues.

"He's looking for his sister," said Alexi Holt. "Patricia Harwell."

"Yeah, I think she's—" began the soldier, and then he glanced at Tucker's face. "I mean, hold on. Let me check."

There's no sentimentality here, thought Tucker. *This is just a job.*

Alexi took his hand in hers.

The soldier went through the columns and rows of black bags until he found what he was looking for. He bent down to check the tag.

Alexi squeezed his hand.

The soldier unzipped the bag to reveal—

Patricia. She just looked like she was sleeping.

"All right, that's enough," Tucker croaked.

"I'm sorry," Alexi whispered.

"Are you?" he asked. "Are you really?"

"Aren't you?" She looked up at him, those hazel eyes searching his face.

"I just wanted to make sure... Really gone."

"*Tucker,*" she said softly, a touch of shock in her voice. "She was your sister."

My sister, Tucker thought dully.

He cast back to a moment when he had tried to tell Patricia something, something he thought meant everything. "You are my sister. I love you. I *love* you. Whatever you do to me. I want you to know. I want you to *remember.* I forgive you."

Tucker no longer remembered the young man who could think such a thing.

"My sister," whispered Tucker. "Was a *monster.*"

"She was fighting for what she thought was right," said Alexi. "Who would not consent to be a monster in service to God?"

He turned to look at her, trying to understand exactly what she was saying. But it was at that moment that his time ran out. Darkness swept over him.

THE ROYAL PALACE
THARKAD CITY, THARKAD
DONEGAL MILITARY PROVINCE
LYRAN COMMONWEALTH
17 MARCH 3141

The long, wide hallway was paneled on one side in dark cherry, polished to bring out the lustrous maroon highlights in the dark wood. Life-size oil portraits lined the wall: Katrina, Hanse's wife Melissa, Victor, Peter, Adam, Adam's son Andrew. And yes, Katrina Steiner-Davion was there, too, next to her *verdammt* brother. Why *shouldn't* she be there? Katrina had been strong. She had always acted to secure her realm first. What else was an archon supposed to do?

Opposite the paintings were ferroglass windows inlaid with delicate veins of wrought iron. The peaked windows started at waist level and reached up to the hall's high ceiling. Sunlight slanted through the windows, splashing gold across a forest green carpet that swallowed the sound of her footsteps as she walked beside *Leutnant-General* Maurer, her security detail trailing discreetly behind.

The Hall of Archons was a peaceful place. But Melissa was not at peace. She hadn't been since her own subjects—*her own soldiers*—had tried to kill her.

"Certainly, Highness, the young woman deserves to be cashiered," said Maurer, "but to turn her over to Loki—"

Melissa stopped, turned on him. "She didn't get off a *single shot*. The *Defiance* pilot managed to save my life *and* single-handedly smash the Hauberk squad."

"She froze," said Maurer softly. His gray eyes locked on her face, his iron brows furrowed. He was a young general, in his fifties, but his face was already careworn. "That happens sometimes in combat."

"Or she had a conflict in loyalty," said Melissa coldly. "*That* happens sometimes in politics."

"There was no connection between her and the conspirators," said Maurer pressing, "no indication of subversive—"

Melissa slashed her hand down, simultaneously cutting off Maurer and sealing the MechWarrior's fate. "This is not a court-martial, and you are not a defense attorney. You are a general. So, *Herr* General, why don't you develop a plan to win this war?"

"In fact," said Maurer stiffly, "I *have* developed a plan to win this war. A plan to deal with the one factor that, up until now, has guaranteed our defeat."

"Alaric Wolf," said Melissa as they reached the end of the long hallway.

Maurer sighed. "No, Highness, not Alaric Wolf."

They stepped through the arch that led to another hallway, and a pair of soldiers in standard armor stepped forward and pulled Melissa and the general into an alcove.

A platoon of armored soldiers stepped into the Hall of Archons, assault rifles leveled.

Melissa heard a deep voice call out: "Surrender now, and you will not be harmed."

They were going to take her security team.

She struggled against the soldier who pinned her arms behind her back. The first *crack* froze her in place. And then: *crack, crack, crack.*

"Hallway secure," called out a woman's voice. "Two prisoners."

Two—out of six Diplomatic Guard agents.

The soldier holding Maurer let go of him and stepped back. It took a moment for Melissa to process what she was seeing. "*You.*"

He nodded equably. "Me."

Acid dripped from Melissa's tongue. "I never would have believed you would betray the Commonwealth."

Maurer didn't rise to the bait. He simply shook his head. "I have not betrayed the Commonwealth, Archon. Only you."

"You ordered the attack by the Hauberks."

"No, Highness. But the assassination attempt did convince me that you were losing your grip on power, that something would have to be done. We should be fighting the Wolves, Highness. Not each other."

"Why?" she whispered.

"Everything you've done, Highness—your invasion of the Marik realms, your overture to Clan Wolf, your vendetta against Duke Vedet—*everything* has been a disaster."

An officer stepped up to her, a *hauptmann*. "We're going to take a little walk, Archon. If you so much cry out or run, my people will put you down, is that clear?"

Melissa favored him with a bitter laugh. "And if I follow all your little rules, *then* you'll let me live."

The soldier stared at her for a moment with cold, flat eyes. Killer's eyes. Melissa never saw his armored fist. One second she was standing there looking into those scary eyes, the next she was on the floor, tasting blood.

Not a flicker of emotion troubled Maurer's impassive countenance.

"*Is that clear?*" repeated the soldier.

"*Ja,*" Melissa mumbled. She spit out a tooth. The soldier helped her up.

Maurer held a hand and they began walking again, this time with a very different security team trailing behind.

"We *will* kill you if we have to, Archon," said Maurer, "but that's not our aim. We will announce that you are suffering from nervous exhaustion and appoint an acting archon."

Melissa snickered. "You think the people won't see through that?"

"How many will want to?" said Maurer blandly. "Do you really think the people are crying out for *your* leadership, Melissa? All we have to give them is the veneer of legality, and they'll accept it."

Light fear fluttered in Melissa's stomach. Maurer's words had the ring of truth. "And then?" she said trying to keep a handle on the situation.

"Our candidate will win the war, and the people will flock to him. Then you will abdicate in his favor. Cooperate, and there will be no reason to kill you."

Melissa snorted. "And who is your 'candidate,' Maurer? You? Whatever you think of me, the Lyran people will never stand for a military dictatorship."

Maurer stopped before a door and pushed it open. "I quite agree, Highness."

A man sat in the room at a teak conference table inlaid with black glass. He wore a charcoal suit, a royal blue tie, and a bright yellow shirt that set off his dark complexion beautifully.

Duke Vedet Brewer.

"No..." she whispered.

The soldier with the flat eyes shoved her into the conference room. Maurer followed and closed the door behind him.

"Hello, Melissa," said Vedet, smiling broadly. "I don't know how Zdenekova felt before he died, but rest assured *I* am glad to see you."

Melissa turned on Maurer. "But you *hate* Duke Vedet."

Vedet chuckled. "But not as much as they hate being destroyed by the Wolves."

"Just so," said Maurer.

Melissa looked from Maurer to Vedet, and then she laughed.

Maurer started.

"I think there is one thing you are forgetting, *Herr* General. In order for your plan to work, Duke Vedet has to win the war." She shook his head. "There is no magic bullet. He won't make any more progress than I did, not until you find someone who can take down Alaric Wolf."

Maurer look startled, but when Melissa looked over at Vedet, he looked smug. He lifted a communicator to his mouth. "Nathan."

Melissa frowned. Nathan Hawkins was Vedet's personal assistant. What was he—

The door opened behind them, and Melissa turned to see a beautiful woman with dark red hair and sharp, green eyes. A black leather jacket over a black tank top hugged a curvaceous figure. Black leather trousers outlined slim legs. A symbol graced the black tank top.

A red hourglass.

"Melissa Steiner," said Vedet happily, "please allow me to introduce you to the only person to ever defeat Alaric Wolf on the field of battle.

"Anastasia Kerensky."

CHAPTER 12

HÔPITAUX UNIVERSITAIRES DE GENÈVE
GENÈVE
TERRA
FORTRESS REPUBLIC
7 DECEMBER 3140

Tucker almost couldn't believe the nightmare really was over. He'd read newspapers, watched local news, even checked the steel asset plate riveted to the medical monitor in his room for the hospital's name. At night he went to his window and searched the dark sky for Luna's gleaming face.

Anything to prove to himself that he really was on Terra.

And now they were finally letting them go. He found a pair of jeans and a red polo shirt in the oak wardrobe in the corner and slipped them on. Exhaustion, dehydration, radiation poisoning—these could all be treated. But there was nothing the doctors could do to heal his damaged mind.

The thought left him cold. A part of him had been stolen away by his sister's madness and no force in the universe could make him whole again.

He drew a deep, shuddery breath. So. The new Tucker Harwell would begin a new life, a *joyous* life, free of intrigue and secrets of universe-shattering import.

He checked the wardrobe one last time, wanting to make sure he left nothing behind. Once he left the hospital he wasn't coming back. Nothing there.

He frowned at the empty space. Something felt vaguely wrong. *Well, what did you expect to find?* he asked himself. His uniform had been filthy and irradiated, probably destroyed. And the slug thrower. They'd never let him keep a weapon in a hospital. And Alexi's rank pip. Whitfield had destroyed Alexi's pip, or *Alexi* had destroyed Alexi's pip. He shook his head, it was hard to keep it all straight some times.

But wasn't there something...

A knock at the door interrupted his train of thought. Alexi stepped into the room, followed by a man.

Plastic surgery had accomplished what Patricia had never been able to do: kill Sandra Whitfield. The knight looked like herself again, her face more angular than Whitfield's, the long auburn hair replaced by a short, spiky blond look. Alexi wore a pale green sundress that picked up the color in her eyes.

Tucker smiled. *This* was the Alexi Holt he remembered from Wyatt.

She smiled shyly back. Then she leaned forward and touched his arm. "Tuck, I want you to meet Paladin Kelson Sorenson."

The paladin's face was weathered by age, his forehead marked by deep furrows. He had dark hair, cut short, but there was a touch of silver mixed in with the black. He wore it shaved on the sides, no doubt to facilitate better neurohelmet contact. He flashed a polished, disarming smile.

But his gray eyes were flat and calculating.

Tucker shook hands with the paladin. "Thank you, Paladin. For rescuing me."

Sorenson shook his head. "You don't need to thank me, Tucker. Seeing to your safety is my duty."

Tucker noted the word *is.*

Alexi squeezed his arm. "The paladin has an exciting opportunity for you, Tuck."

Sorenson nodded. "We'd like you to take over a special project to end the blackout, to undo the damage caused by the Blakists."

"The same work I was doing for ComStar," said Tucker slowly.

"No, not the same," said Sorenson. "Because here your work will benefit all of humanity—not just a single twisted faction."

There was a time when Tucker would have accepted that statement at face value. But his ordeal had changed him. Now it occurred to him that whoever engineered the end to the blackout would command immense power. Whether it was Buhl—or Sorenson.

He felt a little flutter of unease in his gut.

"Why not do it yourself?"

"We don't know what an SHPG looks like," said Sorenson, "or how to undo its influence."

That's what was missing—*the cube.* They'd taken the data cube from him. It made sense really, that kind of information couldn't just be left lying around a hospital room, it had to be safeguarded.

Still, it left a bad taste in his mouth.

"Tucker," said Alexi softly, "the blackout has to be ended. War stalks us in the darkness. The Wolves slash through Lyran space. Malvina Hazen gathers her terrible strength. Terra hides behind a wall while her children are devoured by the great houses."

She shook her head. "All my adult life I have fought for civilization. But everything I've done will count as nothing next to what you could do if you ended the blackout."

He looked into those green eyes and saw the passion there, the desperate need to make things right. He knew he could never say no to this woman.

"All right, Paladin Sorenson," he said, still looking at Alexi. "I'll help you."

BLAUHIMMEL DROP PORT
HOLLABRUNN
BOLAN MILITARY PROVINCE
LYRAN COMMONWEALTH
24 MAY 3141

Ian Murchison stood on the tarmac, feeling Hollabrunn's hot, summer sun bake the life right out of him. All around him, great clanking avatars of war debarked from their DropShips, carrying with them the sharp smell of metal and heat, the stink of grease and diesel, lift fans stirring up swirling clouds of dust, BattleMechs shaking the earth.

It would have been easy for Ian to be killed. All it would take would be a single BattleMech, maybe that little *Puma* over there, to step one foot out of place and bring its massive weight down on his fragile frame. No one would even notice—certainly not the *Puma*'s pilot. He wouldn't be missed, not until it was time to lift.

Maybe not even then.

He turned, saw Anastasia Kerensky walking toward him, and felt a twinge of guilt. It was true he didn't understand the reason for half the things she did, but he *did* think she'd miss her *coregn*.

She wore MechWarrior togs, combat boots, a utility belt over shorts, and a cooling vest over a thin, cotton tee. She stood next to him, not looking at him, not speaking. For a few moments they watched the debarkation in silence.

After awhile, and without turning to look at him, she said, "You look troubled."

"Confused."

She waited.

"I was surprised that you accepted Duke Vedet's offer."

"Is not the proper term Archon Vedet?"

Murchison snorted. "Not in my universe. Vedet is a dishonorable leader, *quiaff*?"

Anastasia nodded. "*Aff*, and his rival Melissa is a fool. This is what makes it the ideal situation. The Lyran Commonwealth teeters on the brink of disaster. When we save it, it will be the greatest accomplishment in the Inner Sphere."

Murchison raised an eyebrow. "And what will you win? Fame, fortune? More contracts?"

"*Aff*. All of those things."

"I really hate to tell you this, but you sound more like a Spheroid every day."

"To accumulate power in the Inner Sphere, one must understand how Spheroids think."

Murchison turned to look at her. As a freebirth and a physician, he was about as different from Anastasia as he could be. And yet sometimes he thought he understood her better than anyone else in the Wolf Hunters. "That's a funny point of view for a Clanner."

"I *am* Clan," said Anastasia. "But that is not all I am. If the universe will teach me, I will learn."

"And what will you learn today?" he asked, curious how she would answer.

A tight, dangerous smile flashed across Anastasia's pretty face. "I will impart a lesson to our former brothers and sisters in Clan Wolf. Today I am not here to learn. Today I am here to *teach*."

DIE EISENBERGEN
HOLLABRUNN
BOLAN MILITARY PROVINCE
LYRAN COMMONWEALTH
25 MAY 3141

Die Eisenbergen stabbed into a blue sky, their flanks cleared of vegetation by a local mining interest, their peaks free of snow. The gray color of the granite *Eisenbergen* gave them their name: the Iron Mountains.

Star Colonel Bart Radick of Gamma Galaxy's Seventh Battle Cluster cared nothing for the poetry of the majestic landscape. He only cared how it would affect his grasp on victory. As soon as he crested the foothill and saw the shape of the land beyond, he stopped worrying.

He saw it would be his privilege to cleanse Anastasia Kerensky's *chalcas* from Clan Wolf.

He watched a gunmetal gray *Vulture* backstep as it fired its half-dozen extended-range medium lasers. Its cockpit was painted blood red, a matching paw print painted on its chest. *Wolf Hunters,* he thought with disgust.

Well, we shall soon see who is hunting whom.

The mercenaries were falling back, the *stravag* Anastasia conducting a well-ordered fighting withdrawal.

He gave the filthy money-soldiers credit for their discipline, but immediately took it away for the stupidity of their commander.

He picked out her *Savage Wolf,* painted like the *Vulture* except for the addition of a red alpha on its left leg and an omega on its right.

She had backed her command into a trap.

The Wolf Hunters held a small plateau that necked down into a narrow mountain pass. On their left, the mercenaries were up against a sheer rock wall, and they had a steep drop-off carved out by an ancient glacier on their right. With the Wolf Hussars coming down out of the foothills, the mercenaries would be driven back into the pass.

Radick did not have to beat Anastasia Kerensky.

The land was going to do it for him.

The pass narrowed as it twisted back into the mountains. It would funnel the Wolf Hunters into a smaller and smaller area, bunching them up, making them easier to target, making it impossible for them to concentrate their fire.

Making it impossible for them to run.

"All Hussars," said Radick, calling to his Wolves, "Long line abreast. Form up on me as we come down out of the hills. Flanks, keep the *surats* from escaping."

A series of "*Affs*" tumbled out of his radio as his people acknowledged their orders.

The Wolf Hussars fell into a long line as they descended from the hills, pushing Anastasia's force back into the pass that would be their destruction. Radick glanced left and saw that the plateau descended into a natural ramp that led into the valley beyond the drop-off. His line was about a quarter-klick from the spot where the land broke into two parts, valley and pass. That two hundred fifty meters was an escape hatch for the Wolf Hunters, if Anastasia realized the danger.

It was a hatch he was going to close.

"Striker Trinary, hold your right side and swing your left forward. Anchor the left end of the pass. Assault Trinary, anchor the right flank. All units guide on the Command Trinary. Hussar One, moving left."

Radick stalked his *Ryoken II* forward of the Wolf line and left, pushing his machine close to its eighty-six kph max speed to get there. If the Wolf Hunters tried to break out, the pressure would come on his left side, and he would be there to support the light, fast units of Striker.

He targeted an enemy *Koshi* and punched a pair of Gauss slugs into the light machine's chest from long range. He glanced down and saw a yellow bloom of heat flare over the *Koshi*'s heart. So he had smashed through reactor shielding. The next shot ought to kill the little machine.

He glanced right and noticed one of his SM1s swinging forward, chasing a Condor caught too far in front of the mercenary line, but also screening out a Wolf *Thor.*

"*Neg!*" shouted Radick. "Hussar One Three, this is Hussar One. Hold your position. *Hold your position!*"

"As ordered, Star Colonel," answered Star Captain Melanie. The SM1 whipped around and swung back into line.

If he could keep his people in a long line while Anastasia's people bunched up, he would be able to catch the mercenaries in a brutal cross fire at the same time they were screening their rear units from the fight.

Radick dropped his reticle over the *Koshi* again, waited for the pair of Gauss rifles to recharge. Then he slammed another pair of ferrous-nickel slugs into the light 'Mech at hypersonic speed, following it with a flight of missiles that shattered armor all across the light machine's chest.

The *Koshi* blossomed white on his thermal scan.

Then it immediately started to drop in temperature. *Reactor shutdown.* The 25-ton *Koshi* had pushed its heat curve too hard, and its reactor had shut down in response. The light 'Mech was no longer a war machine.

It was a statue.

Radick dropped his reticle over the *Koshi*'s "head" and fired. With one shot he cored the cockpit, killing the *Koshi*'s pilot and taking the light 'Mech out of the fight.

He saw movement in his peripheral vision and looked right. Anastasia Kerensky's *Savage Wolf* was stalking toward him, trying to save her MechWarrior.

Too late.

And as he watched, his left flank reached the place where the earth fell away, his trap swinging shut on the Wolf Hunters. He was about to do what even Alaric had been unable to do.

Defeat Anastasia Kerensky.

Radick triggered a common frequency. "Anastasia," he said, deliberately dropping her Bloodname, "you abandoned the ways of the Wolf and dishonored the Kerensky name. Now you shall learn the price of *chalcas*."

He dropped his reticle over the *Savage Wolf*'s cockpit, tying in both Gausses and all his LRMs.

And then the skies opened.

He heard the powerful *boom* of artillery even through his sound-deadened cockpit. Looked up. Gun emplacements, high wall above the above the pass. Saw a JES III painted gray to match the mountains launching a flight of sixty missiles.

And because he was looking up, he saw a pair of Yellow Jacket gunships diving out of a clear blue sky. One of the VTOLs targeted Radick, smashing its own Gauss slug into his chest, raining shards of Forging ZK20 all over the plateau.

"Really?" said Anastasia, shouting over the common channel so he could hear her over the thunder of destruction raining down on his line. "I dishonored the Kerensky name? And you are doing so well for Radick."

In a moment, Radick saw a Demon smashed by artillery shells. Saw LRMs gut a Bellona tank. The fire was concentrated at the point where Striker married up to the Command Trinary. Had to get clear of the kill zone. But the mercenaries were pounding the way forward. Only one way to go.

"Striker Trinary, shift left."

His fast units darted down the natural ramp that led into the valley. Radick stalked after them, effectively dividing his unit. Disaster loomed unless he acted fast.

"Assault and Command Trinaries, drive forward and engage the enemy at close range." That would prevent Anastasia's artillery from retargeting and taking out the rest of his unit.

He looked up. His Strikers were bunched below a wall about fifteen meters high. "Hussar Five, leap up onto that wall." The *Ocelot* had jump jets. "Throw yourself into the enemy flank."

The mercenaries would not expect *that.*

If he could sow enough disorder in their ranks, he could reform his unit. His Strikers were fast enough to get around the corner and smash into the mercenary lines.

The day could still be won.

"*Aff,* Star Colonel," snapped MechWarrior Kenneth. He crouched and jumped, rising on golden plumes of plasma. The *Ocelot* arced over the wall's edge, lost from sight for a handful of seconds.

And then it plunged back over the side again, spinning down in gravity's cruel grip, shattering against the valley's rocky floor.

Radick looked up. And saw the *Savage Wolf* perched on the edge of the pass, leaning over, looking at *him.* Aiming those paired particle projector cannons right at his cockpit.

It was the last thing he ever saw.

THE ROYAL PALACE
THARKAD CITY, THARKAD
DONEGAL MILITARY PROVINCE
LYRAN COMMONWEALTH
8 NOVEMBER 3141

Archon Vedet hated everything about Melissa's office. He hated the dour colors, the forest greens and the dark woods. He hated the plum brandy on the credenza. He hated the vase of flowers—yellow tulips, fresh cut daisies—that the staff left on the desk every day, lending the room a floral scent.

But he *loved* being here.

He loved sitting in her chair, loved reading her correspondence, loved putting his feet up on her ironwood monstrosity of a desk. He toyed with the idea of taking a picture of himself drinking her plum brandy and having it sent to her in the undisclosed location where Maurer was holding her.

With his luck, Maurer probably wouldn't deliver the picture. The man had no sense of whimsy.

"This is not appropriate," said Maurer, almost as if to prove Vedet's point. "You cannot appoint a *mercenary* operational commander of the Bolan Military Province."

Vedet stared at the man. He was sorely tempted to let this issue go, but he didn't for two reasons. First, Melissa had been right that he *had* to win this war. And second, he'd come to power in a military coup. He couldn't let the High Command think they owned him.

"Kerensky's winning," said Vedet placidly.

"Of course, Archon, but—"

Vedet held up his hands. "Let's not rush past that point. When she landed on Hollabrunn, the Wolves were sweeping through Bolan Province. She smashed the Seventh Battle Cluster on a world that was the central thrust of their offensive. Then she hit Senftenberg and won there, too. Dar-es-Salaam. Mariefred." Vedet shook his head. "She stopped their advance. *Now* she's actually pushing them *back*."

"She's not a Lyran citizen—"

Vedet raised an eyebrow. "That's what you're concerned about? What it says on her *passport*? Should we tell the worlds she's liberated: 'Sorry, we're going to turn your planet back over to the Wolves because Anastasia Kerensky's not *Lyran*'?"

Maurer turned red. "If she loses—"

"*Bitte, Herr* General. You are not worried about what you will do if she loses. You are worried about what you will do if she *wins*."

Maurer looked at him for a long moment, cold fury written across his face. "We shall have to consider this," he said darkly.

"Consider it as long as you like," said Vedet amiably. "But the order stands. Anastasia Kerensky has operational command in Bolan until I say she doesn't."

Maurer turned and stalked out, slamming the door behind him.

Vedet studied the door for a long moment, thinking. As long as he kept winning, he was safe. It was not like the military could replace *another* archon.

Which was good, because he *really* liked being in this office.

OUTPOST-CLASS DROPSHIP *COEUR DU LOUP*
HIGH ORBIT
WOLF-OCCUPIED HYDE
BOLAN MILITARY PROVINCE
LYRAN COMMONWEALTH
24 NOVEMBER 3141

Clan *batchall*s were often filled with bluster and bravado, what Ian insisted on calling "smack talk." One of the things Anastasia had learned in her life as a warrior was that people were unnerved by things that disrupted a normal pattern. So she chose to be courteous, even friendly during her *batchall*s, knowing most Clanners would either be infuriated—or concerned.

Furious that she had treated them with disrespect, or concerned she knew something they did not, and so she had no reason to fear them. Fury unbalanced her opponents. And concern led to doubt. Either way she gained an edge.

Just by using Spheroid good manners.

Which is why she smiled at the two warriors on the viewscreen of her large DropShip. "Alaric—" She tilted her head. "Is it still just Alaric, *quineg*?"

"*Aff*," said Alaric, and if he was offended by her allusion to his failure to win a Bloodname, he did not show it. Apparently he had learned something about manners in the Inner Sphere, too.

"Well, either way, it is gratifying to see you again. And you as well, Verena," she said glancing at the woman standing at Alaric's right hand. Verena had served under Anastasia in the Steel Wolves. When she had formed the Wolf Hunters, she had dismissed Verena, and the woman had harbored doubt and resentment about it ever since.

She did not have the same emotional control as Alaric. Her face was totally blank. *Well, if you cannot say something nice...*

"It is most gratifying to see *you* again," said Alaric. "Our last meeting was most instructive. Though I must confess I did not enjoy the torture."

She heard Ian shift behind her. He had never liked the idea of torture.

"Well, it would hardly be torture if you enjoyed it," said Anastasia. "But I did it for a reason."

"And what was that?" said Alaric.

"I did it to strengthen you. To show you your limits. To give you a perspective Clanners often lack. So you would rise to leadership within Clan Wolf." She held her hands out, palm up, as if to say: *"And here you are."*

Alaric smiled, a cold smile. Well, so much for manners. "And why did you do this *favor* for me?"

"Because I know I can beat you, Alaric," she said softly. "Absolutely every time."

"Shall we put your supposition to the test?" asked Alaric.

"As many times as is required," answered Anastasia.

"I will defend Hyde with everything I have," said Alaric.

"That works out well," said Anastasia, "for that is how I plan to attack it."

The image of the two warriors winked out as the connection was broken, an image of the planet Hyde turning slowly in the blackness of space, its small green continents sprinkled across an immense expanse of pelagic blue.

Ian drifted to her side and said in a low voice, "Do you really believe you can beat him?"

"Archon Vedet did not hire me to lose," she said.

Ian grunted at the meaningless answer—another technique she had learned from Spheroids—and waited. Usually the doctor was a patient man, but after a few minutes of watching her watch the planet he drifted away, knowing he did not have Anastasia's patience.

Did she really believe she could beat Alaric Wolf?

No. She did not believe she could stop Alaric. She *knew* she could. Alaric was intelligent, cunning, and savage—the perfect Clan warrior. But that was all he was.

Anastasia was something more.

She had long ago learned that Clan society's focus on martial prowess made the Clan warrior the best, most determined fighter in human space. But the Clans' rigid code of honor made them inflexible. Their single-minded devotion to war made other aspects of human behavior a mystery to them. Love, greed, tenderness, family—all were virtually unknown among the Clans. And all those emotions motivated people, they were all levers that could change behavior.

There were times when even treachery had its uses.

And so, ironically, the Clans' very devotion to war had made them inferior warriors. Any who might dispute that conclusion only had to look at ComStar's defeat of the Clans on Tukayyid, the annihilation of Clan Smoke Jaguar, or the failure of even a single Clan to take Terra.

It was an uncomfortable truth, but Anastasia was not one to hide from truths, no matter how uncomfortable. If one worshipped war, if one were determined to be a warrior worthy of the name Kerensky, one had to look beyond the Clans. One had to truly understand what it meant to be human.

And that was why she was certain of beating Alaric. Because like him, she was Clan.

But *unlike* him, she was so much more.

OUTSIDE CALIFAR
WOLF-OCCUPIED HYDE
BOLAN MILITARY PROVINCE
LYRAN COMMONWEALTH
24 NOVEMBER 3141

Alaric Wolf stood on the edge of a precipice, looking out at the sea. He was reminded of another time, another day. Another sea.

This ocean was different than the one he remembered from that day with Verena on Autumn Wind. This ocean was not gentled by a sloping beach, colored green by curls of sand and the interplay of light and shallows.

This ocean was *rage.*

The water below the cliff was deep, and so here the sea was cobalt blue and governed by oceanic swells. The sea smashed against the shear rock face with undeniable fury, breaking itself into white foam against the towering wall.

But always coming back for more.

Somehow the land won all the battles. But the sea would win the war. *This is me and Anastasia,* Alaric thought. *But which of us is the land?*

And which the sea?

Alaric had fought Clanners. Mercenaries. He had battled Republic troops. Soldiers of the Marik-Stewart Commonwealth and the Free Worlds League. Now he fought the Lyran Commonwealth. In all those battles he had lost only once.

To Anastasia Kerensky.

Alaric was a savage warrior, a fierce competitor with no give in him at all. He was a tactical genius, a magician in the cockpit of a BattleMech, an exacting commander with the gift of getting the best out of Clan troops. He had been coached in Spheroid politics by a woman who was maybe the most devious and ruthless ruler in the Inner Sphere's history. He laughed at pain, brushed aside fear. He was single-minded. Nothing dwelled in his heart but the call to glory.

None of this was why he won.

He won because he understood the expectations of the men and women he faced in battle, and developed plans that subverted those expectations.

But for the first time since Anastasia Kerensky had defeated him on Yed Posterior, he faced an opponent he could not read, could not *know.* When last they met, Anastasia had outthought him at every turn. Alaric knew he had grown since then, but he would not fool himself into thinking he knew her mind.

If he did not know her mind, all he could do was rely on his other strengths.

And hope they would be enough.

"You are thinking of the Trial of Possession, *quiaff*?"

He turned to find Verena standing behind him. He smiled just a little bit, just a little curl at the corners of his mouth, but on Alaric it might have been a broad grin.

"*Aff,*" said Alaric softly, and found something dwelled in his heart beyond the call to glory, after all. He touched her face.

She smiled as his fingertips ran down the line of her jaw. Then she looked away. "Do you really think we can beat her?" she asked the sea.

Even after all these years, Verena's dismissal from the Wolf Hunters still ruled her mind. She hated Anastasia Kerensky, but deep beneath the hatred, she nursed a little seed of doubt and self-loathing.

Verena was a dedicated, and sometimes brilliant commander. But until she cast away her doubt, she would never be great.

"Anastasia Kerensky was born Wolf," said Alaric. "But she has sold her heritage to serve corrupt masters. The Lyrans—" He shook his head. "The *Lyrans,* Verena. They attacked their neighbors and then, when it suited them, they turned on us. Now they face a grave threat and what do they do? They betray each other. What kind of warrior fights for such people?"

"She is using them," Verena whispered, still talking to the sea. "The clever Lyran money-changers think they are using *her,* but they are wrong. Do not think that Lyran weakness is proof of *her* weakness. It is a sign of her *strength.*"

"Perhaps you are right," Alaric allowed. "But anyone who examines her career objectively must admit that she has made at least one critical error."

Verena snorted, her eyes still marking the ocean. "Really? What was that?"

Alaric reached out and took her chin in his hand, pulled her face towards his, gazed into those incredible cerulean eyes. "She cast you aside."

Alaric pumped a double flight of advanced tactical missiles into a ZetMet MiningMech, shaking the mining mod and shattering armor all across the machine's chest. But the mod kept coming, rolling forward on its dual treads, spanging machine gun bullets off Alaric's canopy.

The mod's paired machine guns could do little damage to the *Savage Wolf,* but they were the only weapons the miner had, since Alaric had just cut apart his missile launcher with his lasers.

Alaric recognized the machine gun fire for what it was—a distraction. The miner was trying to buy time to bring his real weapon to bear: the massive, whirring drill that made up its right arm.

But Alaric was not about to be distracted.

He stepped his machine right and sighted in on the miner's centerline, slicing through damaged armor with his lasers. An explosion rocked the miner as emerald fire tore apart the mod's Conlee 105 internal combustion engine.

The mining mod glided to a smooth stop, its whirring drill only meters from Alaric's cockpit. He turned his back on the machine and left it. It was no longer a threat.

Still, the mining mod disturbed Alaric on another level. The chief executive officer of Zettle Metals had assured Alaric she had turned over all war material to their new masters. But as soon as mercenaries in Lyran employ turned up, ZetMet MiningMechs somehow found their way into the Lyran lines. Alaric wondered what other hidden advantages Anastasia Kerensky might possess.

Even a small advantage might be enough to tip the balance.

The two armies had met on the sweeping coastal plain south of the city of Califar, where the land itself admitted little opportunity for artifice.

The trees had been clear cut long ago by the mining interests to build homes for their workers, and make roads for mining traffic. Alaric was certain the decision made perfect economic sense. This was a Lyran world, after all.

But what it meant for him was there was little cover. By mutual agreement, Califar to the north-northeast was off limits to fighting. Neither he nor Anastasia Kerensky wanted a bloodbath. There were low mountains to the east and the ocean to the west. Behind Alaric's line was one of the Zettle mines, abandoned on the eve of battle.

They fought on an empty plain, surrounded on all sides by obstacles. It was very much like fighting within a Circle of Equals.

Alaric's flanks were holding, but his center, commanded by Verena's *Jupiter*, was falling back under a sustained attack led personally by Anastasia Kerensky. His line was a shallow bowl, and if he was not careful, the dish was going to shatter.

The Wolf Hunters had numbers on him. The Wolves held more than thirty Lyran worlds, all of which had to be garrisoned, not to mention their Marik holdings. When Anastasia took a world, she was greeted by throngs of cheering Lyrans grateful to be "liberated." She did not have to leave troops behind to hold the planets she conquered.

Alaric faced a brilliant commander and a superior force on land that would allow no tactical deception. Only one weapon remained to him.

Savagery.

The fighting along the front lines had grown brutal. *Cruel.* It was the Wolves' only hope.

A dark brown Condor flashed by, its lift fans screeching as it probed for weakness in the mercenary line. The hovertank nearly brushed up against a hundred kph as it darted toward Hauberk infantry, tearing into the power-armor troops with its LB-X autocannon, then arcing into a tight turn that would have been beautiful.

If the tank had not suddenly found a Wolf Hunter *Vulture* standing in its path.

Alaric bared his teeth and pushed his *Savage Wolf* into a lumbering run, kicking his great machine up to its maximum speed of eighty-six kph, knowing the Condor was about to die.

Even if the Condor did not know it yet.

The hovertank's commander threw his rudder over, sending the Condor into a sideways slide that threw off the medium 'Mech's firing solution for a second.

But only for a second.

The Condor commander hit the accelerator, but no matter how fast he was, he was not going to outrun the *Vulture's* weapons. The mercenary pilot bit into the tank's right quarter, melting Starslab armor until it ran like water, burning the Condor's scarred brown hide, and setting fire to the grass as it dripped down.

But the real blows came from the missiles.

The *Vulture* had launched a flight of twenty Great Bow long-range missiles that rippled across the Condor, finding the Valiant Arbalest LRM fifteen-pack and igniting a sympathetic explosion.

Alaric charged forward.

Just as the tank went up in a ten-meter column of molten fire.

Careless of his heat curve, Alaric plunged into the inferno, dancing yellow-orange flames sheeting off his ferroglass canopy. Heat spiked in his cockpit in response to his act of self-immolation. The fire provided him only a second of cover.

But it was going to be enough.

Star Captain Merrick of the Wolf Hunters had turned away from the Wolf Condor he had just destroyed when he glanced down at his rear-view strip. For a moment he did not understand what he was seeing.

Something was emerging from the fire. For just a second he thought the Condor had the powers of the phoenix, that it had been reborn in flame. If so, it had taken on a new, more deadly form.

He flashed on a sleek cockpit limned in fire, the pilot a shadow behind his canopy, arms reaching forward out of the inferno. Reaching for *him*.

Green beams of death lanced out from the *Savage Wolf,* slicing into Merrick's right knee where it was most vulnerable—in the back. He glanced at his wireframe in time to watch the knee flicker red, telling him he had lost most of his armor there.

Merrick was being attacked by a myth, but *not* the myth of the phoenix.

This was the myth of Alaric Wolf.

For a startled second, Merrick did not turn.

The *Savage Wolf* hit him again.

Alaric's heat load soared, turning his cockpit into an oven. As he came out of the fire he dropped his reticle over the gunmetal *Vulture*, which was already turning away. Completely dialed into its prey, the medium 'Mech had not noticed the approaching *Savage Wolf.*

His targeting pip drifted from the *Vulture*'s back down to its right knee

Alaric panted, his overheated body desperately trying to pull oxygen out of the cockpit's brutal atmosphere. He did not slide his covers away from his missile racks—there was a slight chance that a stray flame would ignite the warheads.

So he went to his lasers, melting the thin armor over the *Vulture*'s knee joint.

Heat spiked and Alaric started to gray out, knowing he was on the edge of heat stroke. From somewhere far, far away he heard the shrill call of an alarm. *Heat alarm.* Without thinking about it, he slapped the override button.

Then he took another step forward.

And fired his lasers again.

Instantly the heat alarm was back. Alaric overrode it *again* and looked up in time to see the *Vulture* topple forward, its right leg severed at its backward-bent knee. The Wolf Hunter machine hit the ground with a terrific crash.

Alaric felt the earth *move.*

He staggered forward, his *Wolf* sluggish with heat, unable to return fire without risking a reactor shut down. By moving forward instead of returning to the safety of his own line, Alaric had bared his neck to the Wolf Hunters.

But it seemed no one wanted to confront the monster that had come charging out of the fire.

Slowly, his heat levels began to drop. It took only seconds, but a handful of seconds could be a lifetime on a live battlefield.

He reached the *Vulture*, struggling to prop itself up on one leg and continue fighting. Alaric reached forward with his right arm, setting the barrel of his large laser against the enemy pilot's canopy, the ferroglass outlined in crimson paint.

The Wolf Hunter pilot froze, staring into the barrel of the massive weapon.

Truly this one possesses a Wolf's spirit, Alaric thought. He felt regret. If this had been a different point in the battle, he might have claimed the *Vulture* pilot as *isorla*. But there was no time for the taking of bondsman now.

Now there was only time to clear the enemy from the field.

He pulled his trigger, and the *Vulture* pilot died in green fire.

Anastasia glanced right in time to see Alaric execute the *Vulture* pilot. Just like that, she had lost the BattleMech anchoring her right flank. If the Wolves led a determined assault against the flank, the line would buckle and split. So she had to pull Alaric's attention away from her right side.

And to *his* center.

The *Jupiter* holding the center was a monster, 100 tons of pure mean. The blocky assault 'Mech sported a pair of fifteen-missile box launchers over its shoulders and four Ultra-5 autocannons, two over each hand. But its real offensive power was the pair of Type XX extended range PPCs the machine held in its armpits.

It outgunned Anastasia's *Savage Wolf* and outmassed her by a good 25 tons. But Anastasia did have one advantage.

The *Jupiter* was piloted by Verena Wolf.

For the better part of an hour she had been working Verena back, launching fast, probing attacks, keeping her off-balance, bending the Wolf line.

Now it was time to *shatter* it.

"Command Star," she called out over her Command Trinary circuit, "*to me.*"

She stalked forward, leading out an SM1 and a pair of Condors. All vehicles fast enough to run if this went bad.

Anastasia moved directly toward the *Jupiter.*

She selected a common frequency. "It is time to end this, Verena. You have fought well, but it will soon be over. I offer you your life. Power down your weapons and I will take you as a bondsman."

"What a kind offer," Verena sneered. "Here is my answer."

The assault machine fired its PPCs. One missed clean right, but the other slagged armor across Anastasia's right leg

Anastasia answered with her own particle projection cannons, but she was a better shot. Azure lightning wreathed the *Jupiter*'s cockpit.

She half-expected Verena to break right there. But she did not. Probably because she would give no quarter to her former commander.

It was a mistake.

Anastasia's *Savage Wolf* was a virtual twin of Alaric's except for the extended range PPCs she favored over the large lasers. It was no match for the *Jupiter* in a stand-up fight, but it was not exactly a pushover either. And the Ultra-20, two LB-Xs, and the two LRM fifteen-packs of the surviving members of her Star more than made up for the firepower she gave up to the *Jupiter.*

If Verena had her own Condors, she could have thrown them at the Anastasia's hovertanks, drawing them off with glancing attacks before they reached her line.

But Anastasia had burned the Wolf Condors into slag twenty minutes earlier.

If Verena had Demon tanks she might have brought them up, using them to run interference while her *Jupiter* provided covering fire.

But Anastasia's SM1 had torn the Demons into scrap a half-hour before.

Verena Wolf was out of options.

Anastasia's Star let loose.

Verena staggered backward, her wireframe checked with reds and yellows. She launched a double flight of LRMs, sending missiles corkscrewing toward Anastasia's cockpit. But she

was off-balance, and one flight missed clean left, the other scattered shots across the *Savage Wolf*'s right missile pod.

She recycled her PPCs and traded lightning with the *Wolf.*

The Destroyer pivoted on its cushion of air, reacquired, and walked a line of death from its brutal autocannon right up Verena's left side, scouring armor until reds and yellows flickered to reds and *blacks.*

Verena realized she had been so focused on Anastasia Kerensky that she had lost track of the hovercraft. She turned, laying into one of the Condors with parallel streams of autocannon fire while chasing the Destroyer with a flight of missiles.

Her Ultra-5s tore apart the Condor's lift skirt, spilling air, and sending the 50-ton tank into a terrible end-over-end tumble that scattered debris in a long line that cut right through the battlefield.

But the damage had already been done.

Her *Jupiter* was badly wounded, and she no longer had the support units to guard her sides while she hammered the *Savage Wolf.*

Verena's throat tightened painfully. Alaric had *given* her the center of the line, had given her the first shot at Anastasia. She had been confident she would be able to crush the woman's *Wolf* and split the mercenary line. Instead she had been defeated, confirming Anastasia's opinion of her, and undercutting Alaric's faith.

She selected the all-unit frequency. "Shadow Wolves, this is Shadow Two. Left and right flanks shift in to reinforce the center."

She had just condemned the Wolf right and left to a desperate fight to keep from being flanked. All because she could not hold.

She took little consolation in the fact that the Wolves might still win the day. However the day ended, Verena had been defeated.

The next words were tough to push out through her painfully constricted throat, but Verena was a warrior, so she said them anyway. "All Wolves. Reform at Grid Two Six Four One."

And then: "Fighting Withdrawal."

Anastasia saw the Wolves falling back, and a grim smile came to her face. She felt nothing either way for Verena Wolf, the woman who had once served beside her. It was enough that she *understood* Verena, and knew how to use that understanding in battle.

The Wolves were falling back through a ZetMet mining camp. The camp was filled with industrial obstacles that would break up the Wolf line, forcing them into unfavorable match-ups. By the time they withdrew from the camp, the Wolves would be severely battered, and Anastasia could take them.

But why wait even that long?

Anastasia saw the disorder in the Wolf middle, Alaric's right and left pulling in to try and protect the center. So while Alaric's concentration was on his center, and he personally tried to hold his flank on Anastasia's right against her probing attacks, maybe it was time for a little surprise.

She selected a very special frequency and said, "Task Force Zephyr. Sinister. Execute."

As she stalked forward, Anastasia Kerensky allowed herself the luxury of glancing left, where her line faced off against a vulnerable Wolf flank.

Sinister was a word from ancient Latin.

Meaning "on the *left*."

"Shadow One, moving right!" Alaric shouted, ducking behind his line and throwing his *Savage Wolf* into what passed for a sprint. The Wolf center was falling apart faster than planned. If the day was to be saved, MechWarrior Timothy and his *Cougar* were going to have to hold the left side.

Alaric had business on the right.

He pushed through a broken landscape, feeling the uncertainty of crushed rock beneath his feet. The mining camp was dotted with tailing piles. There was equipment everywhere: abandoned MiningMechs, rock crushers, a processing plant, conveyor belts.

And a settling pond filled with murky gray water.

Alaric took careful aim at the pond, dialed down the power of his right laser, and fired. For a second the pond flashed emerald green as the light refracted through the water.

Then he turned and stalked toward the center of his line, knowing his appearance would signal Anastasia to hit his left flank with everything she had, and also knowing that his left could not take that kind of punishment.

Alaric just hoped he had timed it right.

Task Force Zephyr Commander Candy shoved her Destroyer into a brutal turn, lifting the inside edge of the hovercraft up as she banked hard. Candy was not worried. She knew her vehicle could make the turn.

Had to make the turn.

The SM1 straightened, dropping to level, and then shot forward, running flat out for the gray scar in the land that was the ZetMet mining facility. Candy was leading in two Condors and two Demons. Their job was to slip around Anastasia's left and smash into the rear of the Wolf right

It was working, too, until Candy saw BattleMechs rising out of a pool of fetid, gray water.

For a moment—only a moment—she was startled.

The pilot of the *Sun Cobra* coming out of the water was not quite so slow. Candy saw the *Cobra* execute a half-turn, bringing the two Gauss rifles in its arms to bear.

At her.

Then she saw a flash of silver.

Alaric glanced right and saw his little surprise, a Star of light 'Mechs, slamming fire into a collection of gunmetal gray fast-movers.

She tried to flank me on the *right*.

At once, Alaric knew the battle was lost. His 'Mechs had stopped the flank, punishing the Hunters horribly for even trying, but *his* surprise was blown, too. Alaric would not be able to slip his Star behind Anastasia's lines to wreak havoc. And with her superior numbers and better position, there was no way to win.

His jaw clenched, he reached forward to toggled his all-unit frequency.

"All Wolves, this is Shadow One. Fighting Withdrawal, prepare to execute emergency extraction."

He had *lost*. The Lyrans would have Hyde back.

Courtesy of Anastasia Kerensky.

HARWELL HOUSEHOLD
GENÈVE
TERRA
FORTRESS REPUBLIC
24 NOVEMBER 3141

Tucker turned off the living room lights, sank into the leather armchair, buried his face in his hands. Bright, sharp pain radiated from his eyes, stabbing into the top of his skull. It throbbed in time with his pulse. It would not go away.

But the pain was not the worst part.

The worst part was not being able to do the things he used to do. Not being able to *know* the things he used to know.

This should have been the happiest time of his life. During the day, he worked on the most important problem in the field that had fascinated him since he was a child, and at night, he came home to the woman he loved.

But the work was so much harder. He would reach for something he *should* know, a theory, an equation, sometimes just a *word*, and it would be gone. Absent. Like reaching for the peanut butter on a shelf, only to find it was suddenly missing.

Oh, and being told you would never, *never* be allowed to buy any peanut butter to replace the missing jar.

Tucker's team still was making progress. He still saw things others didn't, still had flashes of insight, but it was like a blind man working through a maze. He spent most of his day bumping into walls.

When he found his way to freedom, it was an accident.

There were days he wanted to quit, just give it all up. Tucker the bright young genius could have solved the problem. But not Tucker the brutalized prisoner.

Partly he kept at it because he didn't know what else to do, but mostly he didn't quit because he couldn't bear to see the disappointment in Alexi's eyes.

Strong hands reached down and kneaded his shoulders, expertly working out the knots in his muscles. He felt her breath on the back of his neck. Smelled lavender—and vanilla. "Rough day?" she whispered huskily.

"Some days it seems futile."

"It isn't, Tucker. I know it isn't. *I* believe in you."

"I just—"

"*Shhh.* Just lean back. No, don't open your eyes."

She laid something shockingly cold across his face.

"The frozen wash cloth should help with the headache. Just lay there and rest for a minute. I'll get you a drink. And then later we'll have a nice dinner. Lasagna, maybe? I picked up some fresh-baked bread at the market."

She stood, he heard her stand. She touched his forehead, smoothing his hair back. "I know it's hard sometimes. But it'll be fine, Tucker. I promise."

Then he heard her step out of the living room and pad across the kitchen floor.

Tucker took a deep shuddery breath. It was so damn hard sometimes.

Thank God for Alexi. What would he ever do without her?

**OUTPOST-CLASS DROPSHIP *COEUR DU LOUP*
IN TRANSIT TO DAR-ES-SALAAM
BOLAN MILITARY PROVINCE
LYRAN COMMONWEALTH
7 JANUARY 3142**

During space travel the human body often endured too little acceleration—or too much. Over time, zero-g weakened bones and muscles. Combat acceleration, on the other hand, could kill the careless spacer in an instant by snapping a neck or sending a weak heart into arrest.

Anastasia had ordered *Coeur du Loup*'s captain to maintain a steady one-gee burn. Her task was hard enough as it was.

Two men had joined her in the DropShip's wardroom to discuss the defense of Bolan Province. Both were named Steiner. *(By the founder, is there anyone in this region of space not named Steiner? And would they all start calling themselves Brewer now?)* These men were her best commanders—but they also presented her biggest political problems.

Landgrave Jasek Kelswa-Steiner leaned across the blue tablecloth draped over the wardroom table, body hunched over a noteputer, eyes scanning the intel summary she would present to the assembled commanders of Bolan province in three days.

He looked up. "So the Wolves have *retaken* Hyde?"

Anastasia nodded.

"And we're not going to take it back?"

She shook her head. "I hate to think what it cost to take that world the first time. Besides, keep reading."

Colonel Roderick Steiner said nothing. He just stood at the wardroom's ferroglass bulkhead, looking out at the stars—Steiner, or *Frost*, as he was calling himself again—did not have Jasek's holostar good looks, but he was not a bad-looking man, shorter than she liked, with close-cropped blond hair, and green eyes that were unusual for a Steiner.

Maybe it was the eyes that would allow him to survive.

"Alaric's declaring victory." said Jasek. "He's saying he will remain on his side of a border that runs from Hyde through Arcadia and Loric to Bella I unless he's attacked. So the war is over? Is this— Do you think it's a trick?"

Anastasia shook her head. "*Neg.* The Wolves have just moved most of their population halfway across the Inner Sphere, fought three major wars, and conquered nearly sixty worlds that must now be integrated into Clan Wolf. A cessation of hostilities is the smart thing to do."

"You sound doubtful," said Jasek.

"Not doubtful, but I am...*surprised* that the Wolves realized this was the wisest course of action."

Surprised and unsettled, she admitted to herself. Alaric Wolf was showing more insight than she would have expected. And that could only be dangerous.

"Vedet's being handed a de facto truce," said Jasek, looking at Anastasia. "Will he take it?"

"Of course he will," snapped Roderick. "This way he can pretend he stopped the Wolves."

"Vedet *did* stop the Wolves, *quiaff*?" said Anastasia gently.

"No," snapped Roderick, "that was *you,* Alpha Kerensky. All *he's* done is play politics to steal Melissa's throne."

There was a moment of uncomfortable silence. And here was the question Anastasia needed answered. She needed both these men to hold Bolan against the Wolves. Roderick was cousin to the former Archon, and understandably hated Vedet. Jasek was a former soldier of the Republic who Vedet had helped in his desperate attempt to save Skye from the Jade Falcons.

Could these two men work together?

Anastasia opened her mouth to say something, but Jasek beat her to it. "And do you believe the three of us here have the means to address that issue, Colonel Frost?" His voice was hard.

Roderick wheeled on him, his hands balled into fists, green eyes flashing. Then he dipped his head. "*Nein,* Landgrave," he said softly.

"Then let it go," said Jasek firmly. He turned to look at Anastasia. "So what happens to Colonel Steiner here?"

Roderick straightened, his chin thrust up defiantly.

Anastasia studied him for a moment. "No one thinks the Wolves are done with us. The unit once known as the First Steiner Strikers is to be folded into the Stormhammers. Colonel, as long as you continue to call yourself Frost and you renounce the throne, you can retain your command."

It was the very example of a Spheroid deal. Everyone knew Colonel Roderick was a Steiner—but by merely calling himself Frost, he could get them to ignore this uncomfortable fact. Willful ignorance. She was not sure if it was madness or brilliant flexibility. Perhaps it was a little bit of both.

The two men looked at each other.

"It's not a bad offer," said Jasek gently.

"It's only because Vedet can't get Loki to kill me. But...I never wanted the throne anyway. I would've been perfectly happy to be Roderick Frost if Trillian never—" He shook his head, drew a deep breath. Then he came around the table and shook Jasek's hand.

Anastasia nodded. "Good. Take the noteputer. Read the strategic outline of our defensive plan. I want your opinions by tomorrow. I have a bad feeling round two is going to begin before any of us are ready."

Both men nodded and stepped out of the room.

Anastasia sighed. One problem solved. But another loomed. She turned to look back out at the stars.

"Who are you, Alaric Wolf?" she whispered to the empty room. "And more importantly, what are you becoming?"

OUTSIDE CALIFAR
HYDE
WOLF EMPIRE

Alaric Wolf followed Khan Ward as they walked across the battlefield. The sun was setting in the west, colored blood red by the coming dusk and scattering bronze light across the ocean. Above them, the bowl of the sky was starting to purple, the brighter of the stars coming out, managing to escape the sun's hegemony.

The battle had been short, but violent. It had spilled over the plains and onto the white beach beyond. Khan Ward started inland, where the battle had begun, and followed its progress west to the water.

Seth Ward said nothing, but his dark eyes marked the remnants of the savage fighting: the stink of burning diesel mixed with the smell of burning grass, strips of metal scorched black and twisted into unrecognizable shapes, pools of brass shell casings, the sweet taste of explosives on the wind.

Khan Ward stepped onto the beach, careful to avoid a patch of smoky glass where stray laser fire had melted the sand. There were no BattleMechs or vehicles anywhere. Alaric had seen to it that all salvage had been removed from the field before the Khan arrived.

He had been scrupulously accurate in his after action report. Still, it was one thing to *read* about something and quite another to *see* it—a point hammered home to him by his mother.

Finally, the Khan turned to Alaric. "Why did you retake this world?"

"I desired it," said Alaric simply. "I am Clan."

Seth Ward shook his head. "So arrogant. We are not Jade Falcons."

Alaric bowed his head. "I request *surkai,* my Khan," he said, naming the Clan Rite of Forgiveness. "I meant no disrespect." He hesitated. "And I am not Malvina Hazen."

Khan Ward studied him for a long moment. "Desire is a sufficient reason to compel a warrior to action. But if you are to one day win a Bloodname and become saKhan, you must learn to think more rigorously, *quiaff?*"

SaKhan. It is not the position of the junior Khan I aspire to, thought Alaric. But all he said was, "*Aff.*"

"Good," said Khan Ward. "A Khan cannot always afford a warrior's vanity."

"After the Wolf Hunters took this world, it was garrisoned by planetary militia," said Alaric reasonably. "I knew there would be little risk. And it has some strategic value. Our new Wolf Empire needs the metal production to support our weapons factories."

"You knew we planned to call a truce with the Lyrans." Khan Ward shook his head. "It was *your* idea."

"All the better reason to take it now—before the truce. So we would not have to take it later when the Lyrans are stronger."

Khan Ward studied him for a long moment. "As atonement for your arrogance, I order you to present me with a plan to integrate our new holdings into Clan Wolf. From this task may you learn humility."

Alaric bowed his head. "As ordered, my Khan."

With that, Khan Ward turned and walked away. For a moment, Alaric watched him go. The task the Khan had set for him had been intended as a punishment, since it was something not normally assigned to a warrior. But he would learn much from this exercise. And when the Wolf Empire was ready to resume its invasion of the Lyran Commonwealth, he would know it.

He had lied to his Khan. He had not retaken Hyde for its limited strategic value. He took it to erase the stain on his honor handed to him on this world.

But when he had arrived, he had discovered his second conquest of Hyde had not changed anything. It did not change the fact he had been defeated by Anastasia Kerensky.

Twice.

He had won glory and power, and maybe even love. But Alaric looked up into the purple heavens, at the Lyran stars sprinkled across Hyde's sky.

And found he wanted *more*.

PART THREE

The Effects of Predation

"Predation is an essential part of the natural world. The winnowing of the weak by the strong is necessary to the survival of both predator and prey species. Such is true in the affairs of humanity, too, the strong must take from the weak for the good of all. Of course, with humans it is not always clear which is which."

—Khan Seth Ward of Clan Wolf,
Announcing the Formation of the Wolf Empire,
1 January 3142

CHAPTER 13

OVERLORD-CLASS DROPSHIP *BEC DE CORBIN*
ZENITH JUMP POINT, ARCTURUS
DONEGAL MILITARY PROVINCE
LYRAN COMMONWEALTH
12 JUNE 3142

Beckett Malthus did not believe in Christ or Allah or Jehovah or Shiva. He did not worship any Spheroid God. Like most Clanners, he believed Spheroids clung to religion out of weakness and fear.

But as he watched Malvina Hazen sit in a web chair, holding Cynthy in her lap and brushing the girl's long blond hair, he could not help thinking that if there *was* a God, he was certainly going to Hell.

Malthus had once served Khan Jana Pryde, but when she found it expedient to cast him aside, he had allied himself with Malvina Hazen, using the young *ristar* as a blade to cut Jana for her betrayal. By the time he realized just how dangerous that blade was, it was too late.

Now the blade wielded *him.*

Which was how he had ended up midwifing the rule of the most monstrous bloodfoul in Clan history. If that had not earned Malthus a trip to Hell, he did not know what would.

And with his luck, he and Malvina would have adjoining cells.

The woman leaned forward and whispered something in the girl's ear. Cynthy giggled. They sat facing the ferroglass port that made up the wardroom's outer bulkhead.

Malthus had positioned himself as far from them as he could without obscuring his view. He stood behind the table where the ship's officers took their meals, his boot anchored in a steel loop, watching as his ship hovered near the Olympus-class charging station that commanded the system's zenith jump point. A cloud of JumpShips and DropShips surrounded the station, most having arrived with agricultural equipment or readying to depart with food.

By Malvina's explicit order, their departures were cancelled.

She had ordered all jumpers and DropShips to power down and surrender to the Jade Falcon armada.

As Malthus watched, a DropShip, a *Mule,* drifted *away* from the station.

Ten seconds later a light chime sounded and a voice over the intercom circuit reported: "One of the DropShips is running, Chingis Khan."

"Launch fighters," ordered Malvina, "but do *not* destroy her. Fire on her engines only. The *Mule* is to be captured whole, her crew taken alive. As soon as she is disabled, board her and bring her back to the charging station."

"As ordered, Chingis Khan," answered the bridge officer.

Malthus let out a breath he had not realized he had been holding. Malvina's orders were uncharacteristically generous. Normally she did not tolerate disobedience of any kind. The *Mule*'s crew was quite lucky Malvina did not decide to just blow them out of the sky, which would have been a decision more typical of her usual problem solving approach.

"I do not understand," said Malthus.

"What is it you do not understand?" Malvina asked, not looking up from the girl's silken blond hair. "My orders regarding the war—or the DropShip?"

"Let us start with the war," said Malthus. "If the true objective is to reach Terra before the Wolves, why waste time and energy attacking the Lyran Commonwealth? Why not use the *desant* as a base to drive toward Prefecture Ten?"

Desant was the name for the Jade Falcon incursion into the region of Skye. It was an ancient Russian word that meant descent, an allusion to a paratroop assault.

"The Mule is secured, Chingis Khan. Elementals boarding her now."

"Very well," said Malvina. This time she did turn to look at Malthus. "The *desant* is an orphan, cut off from our Occupation Zone and subject to harassment from the Lyrans and the Republic." She shook her head. "We must join the *desant* to our territory. But that means taking a swath of worlds in the Donegal Military Province, something the Lyrans will never stand for unless—"

"Unless we first cut off their heads."

Malvina smiled broadly. "A most apt metaphor, Khan Malthus." She turned back to the little girl's hair.

"Chingis Khan, a message from the boarding party," said the bridge officer.

"Go ahead," said Malvina.

Now another voice emerged from the intercom. "Chingis Khan, this is Star Captain Roy. We have secured the DropShip as ordered. The count is thirty-four, nineteen crew, and fifteen passengers."

"Proceed, Star Captain."

"As ordered, Chingis Khan."

Proceed? Malthus felt a chill wriggle down his spine. What did *that* mean? It could not be good. He watched the *Mule* slowly drift back to its original station, using a single working engine.

"We still suffer from the after-effects of the rending," said Malthus trying another approach.

"Which is why I enlisted the help of Clan Hell's Horses."

"But would it not make more sense to delay until—"

"Until when?" Malvina raised one white-blond eyebrow. "Until the Wolves take Terra?" She shook her head. "Throughout the history of the Clans, two have always stood above all others: Wolf and Jade Falcon, competing for the right to lead the Clans into the future. Now the Wolves stand on the edge of taking Terra, and *we must stop them.*"

Malthus opened his mouth. And then closed it again.

Whatever Malvina might say, her attack on the Lyrans was motivated by one simple reality: she *wanted* to fight. There was no aspect of Malvina's life not governed by violence, including sex. She coupled with her warriors to bind them more tightly to her. She coupled as an act of conquest. there was no tenderness in Malvina's touch.

Only war.

Malthus believed she would fight the whole universe single-handed if she could.

This need for blood was where Malvina's horrific Mongol Doctrine had come from, the use of ostentatious violence to quickly bend her enemies to her will. He might as well argue against a hurricane as argue for restraint.

It was one of the reasons he found the relationship between Malvina and the girl so unsettling. There was no obvious sign of violence between them. Malthus did not understand.

He glanced out the viewport and thought he saw a hatch opening on the retrieved *Mule.* "What is happening?"

Malvina just smiled.

Malthus frowned. He stepped forward and tapped the ferroglass surface, bringing up a touch screen. A few more taps, and the raw view through the port was replaced with feed from a telescope trained on the *Mule.*

He watched a pair of armored Elementals step to the edge of an open airlock. Between them they carried a person in coveralls.

No spacesuit.

The Elementals gently pushed the doomed man at the station. The man thrashed for a little while, his arms and legs pumping furiously. After a minute or two, they stopped.

The new corpse gently drifted toward the charging station.

By the time Malthus looked back at the *Mule*, the Elementals were back with another struggling crewman.

The count is thirty-four. Malthus's mouth tasted dry.

Once on a pretty spring day on Skye, Malthus had seen Spheroid children folding newspapers into the shape of boats and launching them across a pond, laughing as their silly makeshift toys drifted slowly across the blue water. That was what the Elementals looked like to Malthus, sending their silly makeshift toys drifting slowly across the black of space.

He turned around to look at Malvina, still brushing the girl's hair. "It occurs to me that only the captain of the *Mule* disobeyed you. The crew, certainly the passengers, should not be held responsible for the action of their commander, *quiaff?*"

Malvina shrugged. "Thirty-four makes a far better demonstration than one."

"Of course," Malthus whispered, trying to keep the horror out of his voice.

Malvina pushed Cynthy out of her lap. "If you will excuse me, Bec."

"Yes, Chingis Khan," Malthus croaked.

The little girl had not said a single thing during the entire conversation, but just before she turned to leave, she flashed Malthus an insouciant smile and *winked at him.*

Malthus's breath caught. He watched the two monsters drift out of the wardroom.

And then he turned to watch the Elementals hurl another struggling victim out of the airlock. Malthus watched all thirty-four people die.

Certain the whole time that he was going to Hell.

THE ROYAL PALACE
THARKAD CITY, THARKAD
DONEGAL MILITARY PROVINCE
LYRAN COMMONWEALTH
22 JUNE 3142

Trillian felt the shock like a blow to her gut. For a moment she could not speak, could not even think. She thought she had been ready for it, but to step into Melissa's office and see that *traitor* sitting behind her cousin's desk—

She felt the mask slipping from her face, felt her lips curl, her jaw *lock*, cold rage washing over her. She had always been such an accomplished politician. To lose her control now, *here*—

Vedet smiled at her. "Trillian Steiner. I am so glad to see you. Do you have everything you need? I am sorry I haven't had the chance to visit you. Tell me of your accommodations. Are they adequate?"

Something stilled her tongue. *The only reason Melissa and I aren't already dead is he doesn't know exactly where the military's holding us. He's fishing for information.* The thought sent a chill wriggling down her spine. This was the most dangerous meeting of her political career. She would have to be very careful.

She drew a deep breath. "You're new at this, *Duke* Vedet, so I'll give you a pointer. Concern for prisoners' accommodations is well below the station of an archon."

Vedet sighed. "You don't trust me. How disappointing."

"But not, I trust, surprising."

"I could have called this meeting with Melissa, but I had hoped you would be more...reasonable."

"I have always found the Archon to be perfectly reasonable," said Trillian tightly.

He leaned forward across the desk. "All right," he said coldly, "we'll do this the hard way. *I* am the Archon. I have just saved the Commonwealth from Melissa's disastrous alliance with the Wolves. The people see me as a hero, the merchants are back to business, and the military is willing to deal with me."

"Loki is still loyal to Melissa," Trillian shot back.

"Perhaps," admitted Vedet, "but the rest of the Lyran Intelligence Corps isn't. She always dealt with Loki directly, rather than going through the LIC proper, and that ruffled feathers. I gather there's some kind of shadow war going on now. When it's over, the most partisan members of the intelligence services will be dead, and those left will support whoever's left standing. *That will be me.*"

Trillian stared at him, unable to punch a hole in his arguments, and hating herself for it. "What do you want?" she finally said.

Vedet sat back and folded his hands on Melissa's beautiful desk. "I want to consolidate my rule. I ask you to publicly pledge your loyalty to me."

Suddenly it occurred to her what this was really about. Melissa's Wolf policy had cut deeply into her support, but that didn't automatically translate into love for Vedet—a lot of people might like to see some *other* Steiner on the throne.

Like her?

"I'll release you and I'll guarantee Melissa's life," said Vedet

"But not her freedom."

Vedet shrugged. "You're a politician, Trillian. Skilled in making the best deal you can get, *nein*?"

"And if I won't agree?"

"Then I'll have Melissa killed." He said it matter-of-factly, like he was talking about shutting off the light before he left the room. How had this *Hurensohn* become Archon?

"You can't," said Trillian, "the LCAF won't let you."

Vedet smiled. "I didn't say *today*." He shook his head. "I won't be on probation forever. I beat the Wolves. Soon, the Commonwealth will return to prosperity. Perhaps we will even reclaim some of our lost planets from Alaric Wolf. The people will accept me as the true Archon for all these reasons. But my biggest advantage is *time*. After a while, people will simply get used to me."

He stood and came around the desk, towering over her, crowding her. She took a step back.

"When that day comes, Trillian," he whispered, "I *will* kill Melissa. Unless you help me now."

Trillian stared up at Vedet. Could she trade Melissa's life for her throne? And what right did *she* have to make this decision for her cousin? For the whole Steiner line?

But he'll kill Melissa.

Trillian opened her mouth—

—Just as there was a rap at the door.

Irritation flashed across Vedet's dark face. He turned and leaned back, touching an intercom button on the desk. "Not now."

But the door opened anyway. *Leutnant-General* Maurer stepped into the room, his face chalk white.

"General," said Vedet, his voice cold, "I told you—"

Maurer cut him off. "Clan Jade Falcon and Clan Hell's Horses are attacking in force. They've launched three major axes of attack: Melissia; towards Coventry, through Sargasso, Santana, and Zanderij; and a third prong through Donegal Province to link the JFOZ to their Skye holdings."

Vedet's face went slack with shock, his mouth hanging open, his eyes wide and staring.

Trillian let a broad smile stretch across her face. "I am afraid I'm going to have to say no to your kind offer, *Duke* Vedet." Her smile widened a notch. "But please *do* give Malvina Hazen our warmest regards."

THE GREAT DESERT
JADE FALCON-OCCUPIED APOSTICA
DONEGAL MILITARY PROVINCE
LYRAN COMMONWEALTH
23 JUNE 3142

Malvina Hazen looked up into the lavender sky as a shooting star traced a diamond white trail in the sky, falling *up*. Another DropShip shaping orbit as it rendezvoused with a fleeing JumpShip. She watched the shooting star hurtle towards the sky's zenith.

Cynthy had told her it was an Inner Sphere custom to make a wish upon a falling star, so Malvina did. She wished the DropShip's crew Godspeed. She wished that they would escape and herald her coming, spreading her message far and wide.

Such was the way of the Mongol Doctrine.

Sweat stung her eyes. Malvina wiped her forehead with the back of her arm. It was hot on Apostica, pushing thirty Celsius even at twenty hundred hours. Despite the way the sweat burned her eyes, dried her mouth, and irritated her stumps of flesh where they met her artificial limbs, she was still glad of it.

The absence of sweat was one of the signs of heat stroke.

She had lost five warriors to heat stroke in the last week, Jade Falcons too hard-headed to admit they were in trouble, men and women who had died in their cockpits as the planet's heat burned the life right out of them.

A dozen more had lived, but were under intensive medical care. They were just as lost to her as their brothers and sisters—at least for now.

Malvina would not make that same mistake, which was why *Black Rose* stood behind her, the *Shrike* a still sentinel in the warm night, a chain-link ladder lowered from its cockpit.

She would make the terrorist come to her.

And just like that, he did. She saw the blinking running lights of a captured Hasek Mechanized Combat Vehicle. The Hasek arced toward her, finally grinding to a stop some twenty meters away, halogen-bright headlights trained on her.

Bec Malthus climbed out first, his bearded face set into its normal dour expression. Malthus was followed by a point of Elementals in full armor, two dragging a man between them. Malthus turned and said something to the Elementals and they released the man.

Good.

The party walked toward her, Malthus and the terrorist side by side, the Elementals a few paces behind, at least three lasers trained on the Apostican's body.

Malvina was glad to see her soldiers were not being complacent, though she would kill the first Elemental who fired on the prisoner.

The terrorist was tall and slender-built, though she could see his arms rippled with muscles. His wild black hair was sprinkled with silver, and he wore a matching beard. His bronze skin was obviously well acquainted with the sun. He wore a loose-fitting white tunic, brown denim work pants, and, khaki combat boots. He carried his body relaxed, as if he were waiting only for the right moment to spring in any direction. If she gave him even the slightest opening, he would kill her.

Malvina smiled. She felt a stirring deep within herself. *Ah, if only there were time.*

When he was four meters away, an Elemental stepped forward and grabbed the man's shoulder, jerking him to a stop.

The man glanced back and then turned to look at her. "Malvina Hazen."

Malvina took a step forward. "Nicholas Spanner."

"I do not expect mercy from you," said the man. "I am ready to die. Even my wife and children are ready for my death. But before you kill me, let me just say that I'm a freedom fighter. You will never conquer Apostica."

"You are a terrorist," said Malvina. "And I have already conquered Apostica."

An insolent smile flashed across Spanner's face, his teeth very white against his deep tan. "Then why are we talking?"

"I legally conquered Apostica the moment the Lyran garrison surrendered to my forces. Partisan warfare will not be tolerated."

"We are not bound by Clan laws," said Spanner. "And we are not *asking* for your tolerance."

Malthus looked worried, but Malvina had no intention of killing the terrorist, however much Spanner baited her.

"Well, we shall see," said Malvina. "Normally when Clans face terrorists on conquered worlds, a village or city is selected near the site of the terrorist attack. Some percentage of the population is slaughtered to send the message that terrorism will not be tolerated. But here on Apostica—"

"Here on Apostica there are very few villages and cities, and none near the location of partisan activity. Most people live hidden in caves or underground buildings, very difficult for an army on the move to find and dig out."

"True," admitted Malvina.

"Have we finally found a flaw in your Mongol Doctrine? Terror only works when you can find a population to terrorize."

Malvina laughed out loud. "You are amusing, Nicholas. Truly I will miss you." She leaned towards him. "I have a thermonuclear device. Several actually."

Malthus frowned, surprised. *Confused.*

"That's great," Spanner sneered. "Should work real well against a dispersed population already living in what amounts to underground bomb shelters."

"So there's nothing we can do," she whispered.

He shrugged. "You can kill me. And you can attack the next world on your list. But you will never subdue Apostica. You will always have an enemy at your back. We will bleed you in the desert. Pour all of Jade Falcon into this world if you like. We will never surrender."

Malvina nodded. "You know, I believe you." She pulled a canteen from her hip, unscrewed the cap, and took a long pull. She gasped when she was done, wiping her mouth with the back of her hand. "Oh, that is good. It occurs to me that Apostica is a thirsty world, Nicholas Spanner. Most of your water is mined from comet nuclei. Since I control the approaches to your world, that water is gone, of course. But there is ground water, too, located in eighty-three principal aquifers across the face of the world."

The terrorist said nothing. Malvina was gratified to see he looked worried.

"I had engineers from my scientist caste disassemble a score of nuclear devices," she said softly. "The atomic trigger is a material called plutonium-239. It is extremely toxic *and* extremely persistent." She glanced at Malthus. "What is the half-life of plutonium-239, Beckett?"

He frowned. "I believe it is twenty-four thousand years, Chingis Khan."

"And what are the symptoms of radiation poisoning?"

Malthus drew a deep breath. "Fatigue, loss of appetite, hair loss, vomiting, loose skin, weight loss, loose teeth, vomiting blood." He paused. "Death."

Nicholas Spanner was pale under his deep tan. "You wouldn't," he whispered.

"Really?" she said. *"That* is what you are pinning your hopes on."

"I-I surrender. The partisan attacks will stop. I'll give you whatever—"

"It is too late for that," said Malvina. "We have already poisoned every aquifer on the planet. We will tell the people what is in the water, of course. But after awhile they will drink anyway, even knowing about the plutonium, because they will be *so* thirsty." She turned and winged her canteen out into the desert night. "And nothing is worse than being *thirsty.*"

She turned back to Nicholas Spanner. "You said your wife and children were ready for your death. Are you ready for theirs?"

He lunged at her, but the Elementals were ready. They knocked him to the ground before he could take a second step. He struggled against their hold, though he might as well have fought against a mountain. "You *monster*!"

"*Neg,* Nicholas Spanner. I am not the monster. *You* did this when you resisted me. This is the lesson of the Mongol Doctrine."

The Elementals jerked him to his feet.

"But I do have some good news for you. My forces have caught a DropShip trying to escape this world. We have informed the captain he is free to leave—*if* he takes you with him. So go. You are free. And please. Tell the Commonwealth what transpired here."

She jerked her head and the Elementals dragged the sobbing man off to the Hasek.

Malthus lingered for a moment.

"You have something to say, *quiaff*?"

"Malvina," he whispered. "An *entire* world?"

She smiled. She always knew her object lessons were particularly effective when she managed to shock Malthus. "If this entire planet dies, Khan Malthus, I can be certain I leave no enemy at my back."

ATLANTICA MOUNTAIN PARK
SARGASSO
COVENTRY MILITARY PROVINCE
LYRAN COMMONWEALTH
8 JULY 3142

Star Colonel Yaroslav, commanding officer of Gamma Galaxy's Ninth Talon Cluster, stalked his *Turkina* up a slim ribbon of ferrocrete that climbed into the sky. On his left was a steep rock wall, shale cracked by time and wind and rain, shattered rock strewn across the narrow road by a careless god.

On his right, the land sloped away beneath the shade of Douglas fir and Scotch pine and silver spruce. Yaroslav saw a stream twisting through the forest, cutting across earth too shaded to grow grass, bubbling into white froth when it punched past a rock. Once he came around a corner and saw a jerk of motion to his right. He swiveled his torso and almost let go with his LB 5-X autocannons and his PPCs—before he saw the deer.

He was engaged in a dangerous—some would say reckless—maneuver. His Cluster moved up, strung out behind him in a long column on a road that could barely support the weight of his assault 'Mech. His beloved *Turkina* left talon-shaped footprints in the ferrocrete. If his Cluster were flanked, they would have a difficult time fighting from their current position, and they would have an even more difficult time forming up into something better.

But what others might call reckless, Yaroslav chose to see as efficient. He was facing *stravag* planetary militia, mewling freebirths little better than bandits. He did not expect them to flank his column.

He expected them to run for their lives.

The light clatter of muffled helo blades won his attention. He glanced right and saw a Warrior H8 painted in forest camo with blue trim skimming along the treetops aimed at his column's right quarter. Working hard not to be seen.

Yaroslav felt his pulse to quicken. He had ordered his VTOLs to remain hidden unless they had something to report.

"Aero Six, Jade One."

"Go ahead, Aero Six."

"I am getting magscan contacts in the next valley."

Yaroslav nodded. *Finally.* BattleMechs were huge hunks of steel massing anywhere from 20 to 100 tons. Whenever that much ferrous material crossed a magnetic line of force, it generated an electrical current.

One that could be detected by MAD gear.

"This is the militia, *quiaff*?"

"I do not know, Star Colonel. I have negative visual."

"Very well, fall back behind the column so your presence does not spook the *surats*."

"As ordered, Star Colonel."

And that was why Star Commander Tristan would never rise above his current station. *Of course* it was the militia. Yaroslav did not need a visual to tell him that.

Who else could it be?

Sargasso was a little world of no significance other than its location on the road to Coventry. Lyran troops, so badly beaten by the Wolves the year before, were now spread out all across Commonwealth's coreward border desperately trying to stem three separate Falcon thrusts. The Dragoons had been drawn into the murky politics of the Draconis Reach, Malvina Hazen raced to Timkovichi to smash the heart of the Kell Hounds, and the cowardly Wolf Exiles hid on Arc-Royal. Unwilling to face their own brothers in last-year's conflict, Yaroslav knew they would never dare stand up to his Jade Falcons. This little world could bleat all it wanted for reinforcement, but no one would come.

There was no one left.

Yaroslav glanced at the Park Service map he had uploaded to his *Turkina's* tactical computer before following the militia into the mountains. He overlaid it with a topo map. Five or six klicks away, the road flattened at its highest point and then dipped, following the valley's rim. The park map showed the symbol for a scenic lookout, which was the Spheroid way of identifying a good place to recon the valley below.

In less than ten minutes he would confirm Aero Six's report. No doubt that would be the beginning of the end for this world. Yaroslav had already conquered two Lyran worlds, and he was eagerly looking forward to taking a third.

During the Rending that had smashed Clan Jade Falcon, Yaroslav had sided with Jana Pryde over Khan Malvina Hazen. He had done so because he had been ashamed of the Mongol Doctrine. It was beneath a Clanner to use tactics of terror.

But now Yaroslav had to admit the Mongol Doctrine quickly convinced Spheroids to lay down their arms. It reduced the size of garrisons needed to hold Lyran worlds, leaving more troops for fighting.

Yaroslav looked into his future and saw more conquests to be added to his Codex, the chance to earn a Bloodname, and perhaps a Galaxy of his own to command. Who would not follow the banner of a leader whose tactics promised such victories?

He turned a corner and saw the road flattening out before him.

"All Jade Falcons, Jade One. Stand by your weapons. On my order we will execute a right oblique and charge down into the valley, fanning out into a line abreast as we reach the bottom of the slope."

His trinary commanders acknowledged his orders.

Yaroslav reached the top of the road and turned to look down into the valley. A long, gently sloping hill opened into a plain of emerald grass ringed by heavy forest. His trained eye picked out gashes in the grass, earthen scars that suggested the passage of heavy machines. And he saw movement in the trees. There was something down there.

And it was no deer.

He had found the Sargasso Planetary Militia. He could not pick out individual machines, but they should not be hard to find. The fools had fled so fast they had not had time to paint over their gaudy parade colors: pale yellow with royal blue trim.

Soon those ridiculous colors would be scoured from their machines.

Yaroslav triggered his all-unit channel and issued a shrill Falcon's cry. Then he charged down the hill, his troops following him like a wave.

Halfway down the hill he saw a *Wolfhound* stalk out of the forest. Yaroslav was startled to see that the 'Mech was not painted in militia colors. It was reddish-brown with slate highlights. Beneath the cockpit was an emblem: a red Wolf head backed by an eight-point star.

The symbol of Clan-Wolf-in-Exile.

A *Warhammer* stalked out from the trees next, followed by an *Atlas* and a *Defiance.* Machines boiled out of the forest.

Star Colonel Yaroslav's gut suddenly tightened.

Maybe this would not be quite so easy as he had thought.

SUMMER VELDT
TIMKOVICHI
COVENTRY MILITARY PROVINCE
LYRAN COMMONWEALTH
15 AUGUST 3142

From the top of the Summer Mountain, Malvina Hazen looked out on the troublesome world of Timkovichi. Two forces met on a wide flat plain, the tropical grasses high enough to brush a BattleMech's knee.

She pressed a pair of binoculars to her face and settled on a red *Awesome* with black trim. The great machine surged forward and lashed into a Clan Hell's Horses Demon wheeled tank painted gray with black trim.

The *Awesome*'s particle projection cannon flayed armor from the Demon, opening huge rents in the tank's protection that the BattleMech exploited with its lasers. A gout of orange fire ballooned from the tank as the laser fire ignited a secondary explosion.

The *Awesome* stalked forward to find more prey.

Freebirth! What circle of hell had spat out the Kell Hounds?

Timkovichi was supposed to be an easy world, a *nothing* world. And yet, the Kell Hounds would *not* give it up. Their stubbornness had thrown her entire invasion plan into delay. Incukalns waited for her assault, but as long as the Hounds kept the Horses' Beta Galaxy tied up, she dared not begin.

The Kell Hounds boxed her up on Timkovichi. The Wolves-in-Exile surged out of Arc-Royal, throwing themselves in the path of her invasion. Perhaps worst of all, Clan Wolf crouched in their newly formed empire, ready to pounce. If they struck across the Lyrans' lightly defended rimward border they would race toward Tharkad. And in this race there was no prize for second place. On every side she was beset by dogs, baying packs of curs that yelped and tore at their betters.

The communicator at her belt crackled. She lifted it to her lips. "This is Anglico."

Anglico. Air and Naval Gun Liaison Controller. An ancient phrase from a long-dead Terran nation known for projecting naval power ashore.

"Anglico, this is Red Talon. Holding station, awaiting NGFS directions."

Malvina raised her binoculars and found the *Awesome* again. She centered it in her viewfinder and pressed a red button, bouncing a needle-thin laser off her target, the binoculars measuring the beam's return. Emerald numbers flashed in her view.

"Depression: four six point two. Bearing two five four true. Range to target: one four point three three thousand." And then using another ancient phrase: "*Red Talon*, you are weapons free."

Somewhere high overhead the *Aegis*-class heavy cruiser was rolling in space, bringing its starboard batteries to bear. *Talon*'s Tactical Action Officer was working through a trigonometric problem, joining the spherical coordinates she had just given him to her constantly updated GPS position to develop a firing solution.

She dropped her binoculars and slipped on dark goggles.

The Exiles and the Wolves would still need to be dealt with, of course, as well as the balance of the Kell Hounds, but the force down on that plain represented the bulk of the mercenary unit's command staff.

It was a very good beginning.

Malvina felt a twinge of guilt for what was about to happen to the Horses' Beta Galaxy, but then they had failed her. They had not pushed the Kell Hounds off the planet. Such failure deserved punishment.

Besides, they called themselves The Apocalypse.

Her operation would simply give them a first-hand understanding of what that word really meant.

"Anglico, Talon. Take cover. Weapons release in five."

Malvina did not move.

A column of emerald fire split the sky, burning her eyes even through the dark goggles. Even from more than fourteen klicks away, the lasers' shriek stabbed into her ears like ice picks. Designed to punch through the tough hide of a WarShip, naval-grade lasers were among the most powerful weapons man had ever created.

The *Awesome* took a direct hit and just *melted away.*

Green fire swept across the field like a savage wind, killing friend and enemy alike, burning vehicles and BattleMechs down to nothing. It did not look like a naval attack.

It looked like the wrath of God.

Tears streamed down Malvina's face as she watched. Whether their source was her glorious emotions or the injury done to her eyes, she did not know. *Such power.* She suddenly felt an electric thrill of desire crackle through her body.

She reached out a hand, wanting to touch the carnage.

And hold it inside her.

GIENAH WELTRAT
ALLIAGO CITY, GIENAH
WOLF EMPIRE
24 NOVEMBER 3142

Before Alaric Wolf had come to Gienah, the planet's capitol had been a magnificent structure. In English, the word *weltrat* meant literally "world council." Gienah's Weltrat had been the planet's legislative seat. Its facade was faced in white marble, its grand, neoclassical roof supported by Doric columns, its two wings separated by a large rotunda set beneath a golden dome.

But war is never kind to treasures.

A Lyran *Spider* stationed at the Weltrat to defend the legislature had jumped away from a *Tundra Wolf* stalking toward it. The Wolf pilot had hit the retreating light 'Mech with a flight of LRMs, taking out the *Spider*'s jump jets and cutting its flight drastically short.

The BattleMech assigned to defend the capitol had instead smashed into the building's west wing. Alaric had seen to it that the *Spider* was repaired and pressed into service, this time under Wolf colors.

The building he had not bothered to fix.

So as Alaric Wolf sat in one of the twenty-three seats that ringed the rotunda, he heard the distant sound of dripping water, the wind's moan as it played through smashed halls, the sudden crack of lightning as the storm outside lashed the crippled building.

It was here that Clan Wolf met to decide the fate of the Inner Sphere.

Someday these decisions would be taken in the Court of the Great Father, the future capital of the Wolf Empire, to be built on the very spot where the weltrat stood today. The Court would be majestic, a sprawling building of steel and green marble and silvered ferroglass, a living monument to Nicholas Kerensky, the father of the Clans.

Alaric had used every trick he knew to delay its construction.

As part of his *surkai*, he had been given the task of approving all major construction projects throughout the Wolf Empire. Clan Wolf had prosecuted three costly wars. Much *isorla* had been taken—but much equipment had been destroyed, and many stores consumed.

To make matters worse, the Wolves had lost nearly a half-million civilian workers when they attacked the Lyrans— and the populations of the conquered worlds were not yet acclimated to the Clan way.

All of which was to say the Wolves desperately needed war material, and their factories were ill-equipped to provide it. So resources that might have gone to civilian building projects were funneled instead into the Wolf war machine.

Alaric was certain that the Great Father, if forced to choose, would have preferred a savage monument built of myomer and ferroglass and blood to a monument of cold stone.

"And so we turn to the matter of Malvina Hazen," intoned Liam Ward. The Wolf Loremaster wore black clan leathers, with a short cape of wolf fur over his shoulders. His face was hidden by a black wolf mask inlaid with gold.

SaKhan Garner Kerensky, whose responsibilities included the oversight of Clan Wolf's intelligence service, leaned forward and said, "The Watch reports Malvina Hazen does not reserve her Mongol Doctrine for Spheroids. She has used her war of terror to force the Hell's Horses to her side."

An angry murmur rustled through the circle of Wolves.

Alaric noticed that neither Khan Seth Ward nor Loremaster Liam Ward spoke. Katrina Steiner sat next to Liam, her face hidden by her own Wolf mask. *What do you see, mother?* he wondered. *More than me?*

Or less?

Alaric held his tongue. He allowed those who might be allies to press forward, fanning out before him like a striker trinary, so he might assess the strength of the enemy line before he struck.

"The *stravag* Malvina Hazen shreds the Lyran Commonwealth with her talons," said Galaxy Commander Elise Ward, her voice rising in anger. "She flies toward Tharkad, and only the valiant stand of the Exiles keeps her from swallowing the coreward half of the Commonwealth whole."

"Let her swallow it then," said Khan Seth Ward mildly. "Let her choke on it. It is no concern of ours."

Behind his own mask, Alaric smiled. *An early declaration by the enemy.*

The angry murmur in the room dropped away to nothing as the assembled Wolves weighed their Khan's words.

Alaric let the words hang in the silence for a moment, and then leaned forward. "Is it not our concern, my Khan? Malvina is *Clan.* Her brutality reflects on us."

"Malvina is Jade Falcon, and we are Wolf," said Liam Ward, his face hidden behind his mask. And then smoothly: "One would think you would not need to be reminded of the difference, Galaxy Commander Alaric."

"Oh, *I* understand the difference, Loremaster. Do *you?*"

Liam Ward leapt to his feet and slammed the bottom of his staff against the marble floor with a sharp *crack.* "*I* hold true the traditions of Clan Wolf. None may challenge me."

Across the room, Katrina Steiner turned her gray wolf mask slightly so that its ruby eyes settled on Alaric. It was doubtful anyone else caught that small flicker of motion, but Alaric read her meaning clearly: *Careful.*

But instead of taking his mother's advice, he slumped back in his chair, his left arm draped around the chair next to his, his posture relaxed. Insouciant. He removed his own mask, so all might read his face.

The Loremaster was the one person in the room whose position was unassailable except by a vote of the Wolf Council. He was subject to neither a Trial of Refusal or a Trial of Position.

But that did not mean he could not be attacked. "If I have given *personal* offense, Liam Ward," said Alaric, making it clear his contempt was for the man, not the position, "I stand ready to meet you in a Trial of Grievance."

Alaric could not call a trial against the Loremaster, but he *could* invite the Loremaster to call one against *him*. If Liam did not, he looked weak.

Liam dropped his own mask to reveal the expression of cold rage that tightened his features. He opened his mouth, and Alaric cut him off. "Or if you fear to fight me personally, I will fight any champion you care to name."

Deadly silence fell over the chamber. Liam Ward's face was chalk-white, his eyes livid with hatred. Despite the man's superior position, Alaric had backed the Loremaster into a corner. If he did not fight Alaric or if he had another warrior fight for him, he would look cowardly. If he *did* fight, Alaric would certainly kill him.

"You are out of order, Galaxy Commander Alaric," snapped Khan Ward. "A Loremaster may not be challenged to a trial."

"I did *not* challenge him to a trial," said Alaric, "I believe *he* challenged me." It was not quite true, but it *felt* true—a distinction that fully a quarter of the warriors sitting around the circle would miss.

Katrina lowered her own mask. She watched Alaric quite closely, her mouth a tight, thin line.

"By tradition, Loremasters do not fight trials," said Khan Ward. "I forbid this entire discussion on that basis."

"Excuse me, my Khan, but I do not believe you *can* forbid it. Did our Loremaster not just say: '*I* hold true the traditions of Clan Wolf. None may challenge me.' If he wishes a trial, by his own word, none may interfere."

He looked from Seth to Liam and back to Seth.

The Khan dropped his own mask, his features so hard they might have been carved from stone. "Do you wish to fight *me* in a Trial of Grievance, *quineg*?" Seth Ward's voice was low and deadly, a clear warning that Alaric had pushed his point much further than was wise.

Seth was a slim man, but he was strong and dangerous. And clever. He hadn't risen to the Khanship by accident. Alaric gave himself sixty-forty odds.

"My intention, Khan Ward, was to discuss the threat to Clan Wolf posed by Malvina Hazen." Alaric leaned forward, offering a smile full of teeth to match the cold rage washing across Seth's face. "But if my Khan wishes to fight a Trial of Grievance..." Alaric's voice rang out: *"I stand ready to meet him in a Circle of Equals."*

Contrasting his strength and courage with Liam's fear.

Khan Ward waved his words away. "Then have your say and let us move on to matters of true importance."

Thus Seth Ward was forced to *ask* Alaric to make the case he had been using Liam Ward to suppress.

Liam sank back into his chair, roses blooming on his pale cheeks, his dark eyes never leaving Alaric's face.

Katrina wrapped her right fist in her left hand and put it to her mouth, leaning forward to listen.

"Malvina Hazen sullies us all," said Alaric.

"She is a monster," said Khan Ward, "we all know this."

Alaric shook his head. "She is worse than a monster, my Khan. She is *bloodfoul.*"

The term referred to a story about an inherited bloodborne virus that could degrade an individual's very genetic code. In a culture where an individual's worth was measured by the value of his or her genes, there was no greater obscenity.

"Nicholas Kerensky's wisdom was great, my brothers and sisters. His father had seen the fall of the Star League and the beginning of the Succession Wars. Nicholas himself lived through the Pentagon Wars. He engineered Clan society to *prevent* such bloody conflicts. When warriors—or Clans— fight trials to settle their differences, the lives of civilians are spared, the infrastructure of civilization protected."

"We know this, *quiaff*?" said Seth Ward coldly.

"*Aff,*" said Alaric, "*you* do, but Malvina Hazen does *not.* She perverts Kerensky's vision, turning the idea of limited war into an instrument of terror, a scalpel that cuts at the very fabric of human civilization."

There was silence in the rotunda except for the distant sound of rain.

"We are not engaged in a public relations battle with Malvina Hazen," said Katrina Steiner dryly.

"We are not," agreed Alaric. "The threat is much more dire. Malvina Hazen builds a base from which she will attack Terra. When she holds humankind's first world in her talons, she will be *ilKhan,* the Jade Falcons *ilClan.* We noble Wolves will be forced to swallow her madness, and the Great Founder's vision will have been finally destroyed by his own children."

"Terra lies safe behind Exarch Levin's wall," said Khan Ward softly.

"Has any wall ever stopped a Clanner, *quineg*?" asked Alaric. "We must thrust deep into the Lyran Commonwealth to be in a position to stop Malvina's madness."

Khan Ward stared long at Alaric, his dark eyes marking the Galaxy Commander's face. There were two reasons Seth Ward could not allow the renewed invasion of the Lyran Commonwealth.

Only one of which he could say aloud.

"I believe Fortress Republic will withstand Malvina's assaults for a good time," said Khan Ward, "and we *need* that time. Our own military forces have been devastated by war. It would be foolish for us to rush forward, only to throw ourselves into the Falcon's talons. For the past months, Alaric, you have busied yourself with the construction of our Wolf Empire. Can you say this is not true, *quineg*?"

And there it was. The argument Seth Ward could publicly speak. And the real reason he had assigned Alaric the *surkai* of reconstruction, so Alaric would be forced to kill his own request for a renewed invasion.

Alaric smiled. "*Aff,* my Khan. I can say it is not true."

And it *was* untrue. For Alaric had plundered every possible resource (if he were a Spheroid, the word would be *embezzled*) buying supplies from the Free Worlds League, converting IndustrialMechs, robbing sibkos of young warriors with which to garrison worlds, so he could send older soldiers to the front-lines.

Alaric rose from his seat, held a noteputer above his head. "I can provide three additional Galaxies."

A gasp arose from the assembled Wolves.

He tossed the noteputer at Seth Ward, who caught it with a sharp *slap.*

Alaric stalked into the center of the circle, turned to face each man and woman, in turn. "My Wolves, the time is *now.*" He settled finally on the rigid face of Seth Ward. "My Khan," he said softly.

Khan Ward was strong enough that he did not look down at the noteputer, did not break eye contact with Alaric. But neither did he say that he could not afford to let Alaric lead yet *another* invasion, because the young *ristar* had already grown too powerful.

"I will bid to lead this invasion personally," said Seth Ward.

A slow, feral smile stretched across Alaric's face. It was the answer he expected. The only answer Seth Ward *could* give. Alaric knew he would lose the bid. Khan Ward would lead the renewed invasion of the Lyran Commonwealth.

But Alaric would win his own invasion corridor. And perhaps there were greater prizes to be had than the world of Tharkad.

He returned to his seat and as he sat down he caught a glimpse of his mother. For a second, Katrina Steiner's careful control of her emotions slipped, and Alaric saw what lay beneath. Their eyes met, and he saw she was impressed.

And maybe...just a little frightened.

CHAPTER 14

The heart of the Smolnik Defense Bunker was a space no bigger than a couple hundred square meters. Militia techs were crowded along the walls, studying tactical displays that had been outdated when Exarch Levin had erected his fortress. An entire wall had been given over to a viewscreen.

Right then, the screen showed Alaric Wolf. He wore a simple gray jumpsuit, arms folded across his chest, *literally* larger than life.

"It appears that we are to meet in combat once more," said the Wolf officer. His intense blue eyes were the size of Anastasia's fist.

"That is exactly right," said Anastasia, "*just* once more."

"I thought you were willing to meet me as many times as it took."

Anastasia flashed him a cold, hard smile. "I am. I have simply determined that one more time is all it will take."

Alaric snorted, the hint of an amused smile playing at the corners of his lips. "Very well, one more time."

"My forces will wait for you *here*." Anastasia leaned forward and touched a button, transmitting a map. "The

Marinov Plains. Nice open grounds." She smiled. "No room for tricks."

Ian shifted from one foot to the other. It took all of Anastasia's self-control not to knock him down right there with a fist to the throat. The Smolnik Militia's commanding officer was more circumspect. He stood watching the screen as if he were made of stone.

Alaric apparently had missed Ian's fidgeting. He looked to the side, studying his own maps, thinking. His blue eyes snapped back to front. "This location is near the city of Nowy Gdansk. Your intention is to make the city off-limits to fighting, *quiaff*?"

Anastasia nodded. "*Aff.*"

"Bargained well and done." The giant image of Alaric disappeared, replaced by a black screen.

Ian barely held his temper even *that* long. "What are you thinking? By choosing to fight on the Marinov Plains you give up all hope of tactical deception."

"Are you a military expert now, Doctor?" Anastasia asked coldly.

"This is not Hyde, Anastasia. This time the Wolves outnumber us. If we are going to win, we need—" He suddenly stopped talking, his mouth a round "oh," his eyes bulging out of their sockets.

Because Anastasia had reached down and bent back the middle finger of his left hand, breaking it cleanly.

"You are mistaken," she said in a voice that did not deviate one millimeter from perfect calm. Then she let go of his hand and turned to face the militia commander, Colonel Michael Devane. He was a stocky man, square face, iron gray hair tamed by a regulation buzz cut. Stolid. "We have preparations to make, Colonel."

The militia officer glanced around the room at the technicians hunched over their consoles. "I believe you are correct, Alpha Kerensky."

He and Anastasia stepped out of the command center, Ian following behind, cradling his left hand in his right.

They stepped into a small, empty office, just the three of them.

"Ian. Your never-ending need to express yourself risks shattering morale and alerting the Wolves of our plan."

"You could have just told me to be quiet," Ian said angrily.

"I did," said Anastasia coolly. "You were not listening." She shut the door. "And speaking of not listening, has this room been swept?"

The Colonel nodded. "Twenty minutes ago. We're sweeping the entire facility every one to two hours on a random schedule."

"Very good," said Anastasia. What of the people of Nowy Gdansk? An operation of this size—"

"We can keep the secret," he said gruffly. "At least for a week or two. Should be more than we need. The planetary government has persuaded several theme parks to open their gates for free. That'll draw the children. Word-of-mouth evac will start at t-minus fifteen mikes along designated routes."

"That will get a lot of people clear," said Anastasia, "but not everyone."

The colonel said nothing.

She nodded. "Plans?"

He handed her a noteputer. "It's all there." Then he turned to leave.

Anastasia stopped him with a hand on his shoulder. "Colonel. If we cannot maintain operational security, this will not work."

He rounded on her, hands clenched into fists. "Smolnik is not a pawn on a board to me, Alpha. Smolnik is my home." He jerked his head at the noteputer he'd given her. "You'll find my sister's name on that list." His face twisted into that something that was part horrified and part proud. "No one is going to talk."

Anastasia studied that face for a long moment, and then finally nodded.

The Colonel stepped out of the office, closing the door gently behind him.

Ian watched him go, then turned on her. "What the hell is going on?"

Anastasia picked up a piece of paper from the table and turned it over. She quickly sketched a map. "Nowy Gdansk," she said pointing at the city. "The plains south of the city. The drop port *north* of the city." Her finger traced a line between them. "The autobahn joining the two."

Ian stared at the makeshift map for a long moment. "You...plan to fall back through the city, *quiaff*?"

"*Aff.*"

"But you told Alaric..." His voice trailed off. He glanced down, absorbing the map and what it meant. He looked up. *"What have you done?"* he whispered fiercely.

"We will defeat Alaric Wolf here on Smolnik, and this time there will be no fighting withdrawal. His death will blunt the Wolf invasion. We will then siphon off troops and send them coreward to take out Malvina Hazen. Neither invasion can survive without its leader."

"But the city—" said Ian, his voice filled with horror.

"You just heard our plans for evacuation. But many civilian volunteers will remain behind."

"Not just volunteers, it sounds like."

Anastasia continued as if he had not spoken. "They will hide in the buildings, armed with lasers and SRMs. There are mines beneath the street. Paint bombs and thermal flares to obscure the Wolves' vision. Napalm. When the Wolves enter the city, I will order the guerrillas to strike. For a moment, the Wolves will be pinned."

"And then?" Ian whispered.

"My artillery and aerospace forces will finish them."

"Not just the Wolves," Ian snarled. "The city, too. The *people.*"

"Yes," said Anastasia. "The people, too."

"T-that's monstrous."

She nodded. "*Aff.*"

Ian stared at the back wall for a long moment. Anastasia knew he was trying to marshal an argument that would force her to change her mind. "What if—" He shook his head. "What if you pay this terrible price and it doesn't matter? What if Alaric sees through your little trick." He turned to look at her, his eyes burning into hers.

"But he will not," said Anastasia. "Alaric will not see the danger because he does not burn with hatred like the people of the Commonwealth. He does not have a family to sacrifice himself for. He knows not love or desperation or hope."

Her voice dropped to an intense whisper. "He does not know the value of treachery."

UNION-CLASS JUMPSHIP *TERROR'S EMISSARY*
IMPROVISED LZ, GRÜNBERG AGRICULTURAL DISTRICT, HORNEBURG
COVENTRY MILITARY PROVINCE
LYRAN COMMONWEALTH

They sat in silence and darkness, only the two of them, surveying the star map projected on *Emissary*'s wardroom bulkhead. Beckett observed that Malvina's small body was perfectly still, her white-blond hair pulled back in a ponytail, her eyes locked on the spill of blue stars.

Do you see it now, Chingis Khan? thought Beckett. *Do you see the failure of all your plans?*

The diagram was the latest intelligence summary brought to them by JumpShip. Without widespread HPG transmission, interstellar travel was the only way to communicate what was going on in the outside universe. And so Beckett had set up command circuits with the other Jade Falcon commanders driving through Lyran space so Malvina could track the progress of her war.

The map showed three separate Jade Falcon offensives: the Melissia Thrust, designed to pin the Lyrans' anti-spinward forces in place; the Arcturus-Apostica Thrust, intended to join the Falcon holdings in Skye to the rest of the Occupation Zone; and the Sargasso-Zanderij Thrust, a feint toward Coventry to draw Lyran forces away from the true target.

Tharkad.

And all of it had worked just as Malvina had planned.

The map showed the panicked movement of Lyran forces as blue arrows. At the beginning of the war, the map was a forest of blue arrows stabbing coreward from the

Commonwealth's rimward border, racing toward the defense of Melissia and Arcturus and, most importantly, Coventry.

Now that Coventry had been bypassed, the blue arrows were suddenly all pointing at Tharkad as the Archon pulled his troops in to protect his capital.

The LCAF was spending more time leaping from system to system than fighting.

Malvina's war plan was a brilliant strategy, cleverly conceived and flawlessly executed.

Except for one thing.

The misdirection had created a power vacuum along the Lyrans' rimward border, a vacuum that Clan Wolf was vigorously exploiting. Three brown arrows stabbed across the border.

"It is as I foresaw," said Malvina softly. "In the end, the battle for humanity's future must come down to Wolf and Jade Falcon."

Beckett said nothing.

Malvina turned to look at him. "What? No opinion, Beckett? No comment? No long, rambling discourse on why the path I have placed us on is mad and inevitably disastrous."

Beckett drew a deep, steadying breath. "I am certain Chingis Khan sees the danger as clearly as I."

"*Aff*," said Malvina bitterly. She turned her face back to the map. "The Wolves may very well reach Tharkad before we do. Every moment we are stalled on Horneburg and Westerstede is a moment we draw closer to defeat."

Malvina was right, of course. The Lyrans were fighting desperately to hold the pair of worlds that served as gateways to Tharkad, giving the Archon time to reinforce his capital. Horneburg and Westerstede were selling themselves dearly so Tharkad might survive.

Beckett had never before seen such courage and sacrifice on a planetary scale.

And while the Falcons were bogged down within sight of their final objective, the Wolves were racing coreward. Beckett's gaze focused on the two brown arrows stabbing toward Tharkad, one labeled: Khan Seth Ward, Alpha Galaxy, the other: Galaxy Commander Alaric, Beta Galaxy.

(Alaric, not Alaric *Wolf.* Malvina was not one to invent a last name for a Clan warrior who had failed to earn a Bloodname. In this, Beckett agreed with her.)

The map validated everything Malvina had just said. If the Lyrans continued to hold out on Horneburg and Westerstede, the Wolves *might* reach Tharkad first.

But she was still wrong.

"I am sorry, Chingis Khan, but that is *not* the greatest threat."

She turned toward him again, her eyes wide with fury. *Will you kill me, my Khan?* Beckett wondered. Perhaps that would be better than serving as handmaiden to a *bloodfoul.*

"Really, Beckett?"

The big man shrugged and pointed at the third brown arrow, the one labeled saKhan Garner Kerensky, Three Reserve Galaxies. He steepled his hands before his face and leaned forward. "The Wolves have launched simultaneous assaults on New Kyoto, Algorab, and Zaniah, isolating Solaris and bypassing heavily-defended Hesperus II. Do you believe even for a moment, Chingis Khan, that the Wolves will stop at the Lyran border?"

She turned again to look at the map.

Unless Beckett was very much mistaken, the Wolf saKhan would push into the abandoned worlds of Prefecture VIII, most likely taking Phecda and Wyatt—with its working HPG—and finally Zosma, only stopping at the gates of Exarch Levin's impenetrable wall.

Earning for Clan Wolf a spot in the race for Terra once Fortress Republic fell.

Malvina licked her lips.

Beckett leaned forward. "You and I took Skye, Malvina. When you join our territory to the *desant,* when you make it a contiguous part of the Jade Falcon Occupation Zone, we will have a perch on the doorstep of Prefecture X. But if the Wolves complete their spinward thrust, that will no longer be a unique advantage."

Malvina shook her head. "Our intelligence indicates Garner Kerensky is weaker than either Seth or Alaric. And he leads troops not yet blooded. The Wolves' two most dangerous warriors race toward Tharkad.

"How much power do you think it will take to capture these Republic worlds now that they have been cut off? Do you imagine their best soldiers have any hope of standing up to a Wolf Khan leading three Galaxies of Clan warriors?"

Malvina sat a little straighter in the darkness, peering at the map. "What do you propose we do about this new danger, Beckett Malthus?"

Beckett said nothing. There was a limit to how far he dared push her, and he was already perilously close to the line.

For a long moment, pregnant silence hung unbroken in the darkness.

And then Malvina finally saw it for herself. "*Neg!*" she roared.

"*Think*, Malvina," said Beckett in a low, earnest voice. "Think upon why you decided to take Tharkad in the first place. You intended to break the Lyran spirit by ravaging their capital. To make certain they did not dare challenge our conquest of their spinward holdings. Would not the Wolf conquest of Tharkad accomplish this goal just as well? If we shifted our forces, reinforcing the *desant* and taking vulnerable Republic worlds, we could—"

"You are saying we should give way to the *Wolves*? Is that the counsel I am hearing from a Khan of Clan Jade Falcon?"

Beckett closed his mouth. He knew the next word he spoke might very well mean his life. So he said nothing.

"Tharkad is *mine*," Malvina hissed. "I will not retreat before victory."

She stood and swept out of the wardroom.

Beckett watched her go, knowing he had been foolish to suggest abandoning the Tharkad campaign. She would never agree to such a course of action, *could* never agree.

It was not that she failed to understand the strategic implications of her actions.

It was just that she could never bring herself to turn away from a fight.

AUTOBAHN, NOWY GDANSK
SMOLNIK
BUENA MILITARY PROVINCE
LYRAN COMMONWEALTH
17 FEBRUARY 3143

Anastasia Kerensky backstepped her *Savage Wolf* along the autobahn, hitting the Wolf *Thor* with her PPCs, but holding off on her missiles. Emerald and ruby lines sliced past her, some coming from the enemy—others from her own line. The angry rumble of autocannon fire penetrated her cockpit. An azure flash of lightning shattered the armor over her left ankle.

She was not even sure where the PPC fire had come from.

Anastasia moved her machine through a desperate, angry maelstrom of fire, both sides fighting with a savagery rarely seen. The Hunters were pushing through the northern part of the city's center, lines shifting and reforming, desperately trying to hold on, *hold on* just a little bit longer.

The city was silent around her. Anastasia had allowed the authorities to clear the autobahn. There would still be people *inside* the city, people who had not received the word to evacuate or who had not made it out in time. But the autobahn had been blocked off. It was completely empty.

Save for the guerrillas hidden in the buildings that lined the street.

Alaric's assault had been brutal, pressing her line mercilessly, pushing her back. It occurred to her that the last two times she had beaten him, she had numbers on her side.

Not this time.

This time she was going to have to beat him like a Spheroid, using every advantage within her grasp—whether or not it was honorable.

The *Thor* pilot hit back with his LB-X autocannon and his PPC, shattering armor all along her right side, but easing off his trigger early, careful not to drag a line of shells across the ferrocrete parking garage on her left.

Apparently Alaric had not given up on the idea of *Zellbrigen*, even though Anastasia was retreating through the city.

Anastasia hit back with man-made lightening, worrying the *Thor*'s delicate right knee. She could tell by its limp that the heavy had already taken some damage there. If she could just lock up that knee—

But she did not hit it with a flight of advanced tactical missiles—she did not have any to spare.

Good thing this battle was almost over.

She backstepped her machine over a crude "X" painted over the black ferrocrete roadbed in construction yellow. It was not subtle, but it *was* clear, and the Wolves would not understand what it meant.

Not until it was too late.

Suddenly her mouth tasted dry. She was going to throw away the lives of civilians, throw them into a meat grinder, to save herself and her unit. All at once it did not matter that it was the only way or that it was their choice. *She was going to throw away the lives of civilians.*

And she was not Malvina Hazen.

Across the eight-lane front, she watched Alaric's *Savage Wolf* cut into the bubble cockpit of one of her Demon tanks. And that was where she found the will to do what had to be done.

She reached forward and toggled a special frequency. "Nowy Gdansk, this is Alpha. Wolf Trap. *Execute.* Wolf Hunters, throw yourselves *forward.* Close the door on Clan Wolf."

Her people suddenly stopped running and *surged,* pushing right into the Wolves' terrible fire. Anastasia stalked her 'Mech forward, pushing through the *Thor*'s assault and watching yellows flicker all across her wireframe but paying the pilot back with a PPC strike to his cockpit that dropped the BattleMech like an unstrung puppet.

They were paying a butcher's bill, but they had stopped the Wolf advance. Anastasia stood in there smashing her precious missiles into a *Uller,* chasing an SM1 with the ugly crackle of a PPC strike.

Five seconds. Ten. *Fifteen.*

Something is wrong.

No mine explosions. No ruby beams or corkscrewing missiles slanting down from skyscraper windows. No blue paint splattered across ferroglass canopies. No jellied gasoline clinging to armor, burning with its terrible, ferocious stink.

Nothing.

"Nowy Gdansk. Nowy *Gdansk.* Wolf Trap, Wolf Trap. Execute. *Execute.*"

Nothing.

"Commander, Nowy Gdansk, report. Report. *Colonel Devane. Report.*"

Nothing nothing nothing.

It is too late. She did not know why or how the plan had failed, but one thing was certain. It was too late.

She closed her eyes for a second, feeling the weight of it, knowing the opportunity to kill Alaric Wolf and save the Lyran Commonwealth was lost. Now all she could do was try to save her command.

And that was a long shot at best.

"All Wolf Hunters," she snarled into her voice-activated mic, "this is Alpha. Broken play. I say again, *broken play.*"

She stopped the *Uller* with a brutal one-two PPC punch to its centerline, poured missiles into a Condor coming up on the outside.

"Quarterback scramble. Ground units, break off, *break off.* Fighting withdrawal on Striker One. Rear Guard on me. Assault trinary stop and lock. We are going to hold the road open."

Her striker machines were darting back behind her protective fire—those that were not already burning piles of scrap at the side of the road.

"Aerospace, I need covering fire *now.* Artillery break and reform. Target the autobahn at kilometer—" She glanced down at her map as she poured more of her fury into the helpless *Uller,* "—kilometer one two four. We will bring them to you. Stand by to spike your guns. After the first barrage, there will not be time to withdraw. We will send a Hasek for you."

The *Uller* fell back. Every instinct in Anastasia's body told her to stalk forward and finish it, but a *Vulture* with fresh armor stepped forward to take its spot.

She sent missiles corkscrewing into the Clan machine's cockpit.

"DropShips, we are coming in hot."

The *Vulture* slashed at her with a half-dozen medium lasers and ripple fired all four Great Bow launchers, spreading eighty long-range missiles across her broken line.

Right then, Anastasia knew it was not going to be enough. She had given all the right orders, had used every last resource she had, but it just was *not* going to be enough.

Alaric was bringing forces up along her right. He was going to flank her, cut off their escape route. She just did not have the tools to stop him.

Her Wolf Hunters were going to die right here.

Her radio crackled and a voice, a *man's* voice, one she did not recognize, earnest and deep, said, "Wolf Hunters, proceed along vector two eight four."

"Who is this?" she snarled.

She looked up and saw the blue sky crisscrossed with wounds of golden fire. DropShips coming down hard and fast. BattleMechs dropping from the sky, their jump packs flaring.

BattleMechs painted red, white, and blue.

"Wolf Hunter Actual, this is First Davion Actual."

She just had time to think: *Julian Davion?*

And then the voice said, "We're here to help."

Julian Davion dropped his *Templar's* reticle over the left leg of a Wolf *Vulture* pounding a gunmetal gray VV1 Ranger. His targeting pip burned gold and he tore into the *Vulture's* left hip with his PPCs, burning deep wounds in the Wolf's armor. Julian tied in his TharHes four-pack and—

An autocannon hammered his cockpit from the left. Julian stepped right and pivoted. A captured *Bushwacker* painted Wolf-brown stalked toward him, trading off its autocannon with its large laser.

Until a pair of Kinnol main battle tanks in Davion red, white, and blue tore into the medium 'Mech with a mix of PPCs and missiles, joined late by a gunmetal Joust adding its ruby laser to the fight.

The wash of brilliant green light across Julian's cockpit told him the *Vulture* was back.

The Wolf and Wolf Hunter lines had completely dissolved, the battle falling into a grand melee.

It was madness.

Julian had waded into the fight to bloody the Wolves' noses, to give them something to think about. But now it was time to bring order out of chaos.

"Guards," Julian roared. "*On me!*"

One of the Kinnols dropped back to hold Julian's left, followed thirty seconds later by the Wolf Hunter Joust. The *Bushwacker* had smashed the second Kinnol. A Davion *Centurion* staggered forward to hold Julian's right.

He toggled the private channel he shared with Callandre Kell. "Take your Destroyer, pick up a couple Condors and the Wolf Hunter VTOLs, and chase away anything behind our lines."

"I have an idea," she snapped. "Why don't we kill them instead? Or does that violate Lord Davion's code of honor?"

"We're here to save the lives of Lyran mercenaries," he snapped back. "I would have thought—"

—*that would have meant something to you.* He stopped abruptly, not wanting to say the rest of it. Sorry for the part of it he *did* say. "Just do it, Callandre. *Now.*"

But she already was doing it. Whatever differences had grown up between them, Callandre was still a brilliant battlefield commander. He flashed on her little task force chewing up a pair of Wolf Condors, destroying one and sending the other fleeing, before turning their attention to a Clan IndustrialMech mod.

Julian turned back to the *Vulture,* pounding it with a quartet of SRMs followed by the whip-crack of his two arm-mounted PPCs.

Slowly the Wolf Hunters were untangling themselves from the melee, the stronger machines joining Julian, the weaker sheltering behind his line or running west toward the *Markeson Pride* and safety within the circle of the DropShip's guns.

Julian managed to lash the *Vulture*'s left hip, hobbling the 60-ton 'Mech.

And paying for it with a wash of emerald fire across his canopy and flickering yellows on his wireframe.

Suddenly a red-and-black Destroyer darted in, but Callandre didn't aim at the wounded hip, instead she smashed a long stream of Ultra-20 shells into the *Vulture*'s cockpit.

And then just as quickly as her SM1 had appeared, it was *gone.*

He toggled their personal channel. "*Hip,* Callandre. His left hip is nearly locked up. You could've taken him down."

"I don't shoot at Clanner's *hips,*" she snarled, "I shoot at their *heads.*"

Julian scowled. She had not been the same ever since she'd learned about the Kell Hounds' destruction. Somehow, she blamed herself. It was ludicrous, but she didn't want to hear it. So she was mad as only Calamity Kell could be mad. Mad at herself for not saving her unit, and mad at Julian for picking her to be his Lyran liaison, and thus saving her life.

But nowhere near as mad as she was at Clanners.

Taking too many chances, the SM1 raced in again, this time punching through the *Vulture*'s cockpit and taking the pilot *out.*

And then her Destroyer raced off, to find another enemy to destroy.

Anastasia stood in the center of the terrible storm, fighting to give her people time to extricate themselves from this disaster of her making. Fighting to take the best possible advantage of the slender hope held out by Julian Davion and his First Davion Guards.

She stood in, her armor a desperate checkerboard of yellows and reds, her left missile-launcher blown to hell, and her right down to the last few flights of advanced tactical missiles.

She stood *in.*

Anastasia fought so ferociously, dispatching opponents one after the other, that she did not notice she was alone until it was too late. She looked up and found that her Wolf Hunters had all fled.

Or had been destroyed.

That was when she saw the *Jupiter* stalking toward her. The 100-ton beast was painted dark brown, with savage orange highlights that looked like fire.

Verena Wolf.

Her radio crackled. "It is time to end this, Anastasia. You have fought well, but it will soon be over. I offer you your life. Power down your weapons, and I will take you as a bondsman." The triumph rang in Verena's voice.

And she had every reason to be triumphant. The *Jupiter* had 25 tons on Anastasia's *Wolf* and the *Wolf* had seen heavier use. There was no way for her to stand up to the pair of extended range-PPCs, the two missile launchers, and the quartet of Ultra-5 autocannons.

Anastasia set her machine as the *Jupiter* bore down on her, closed her eyes, drew a deep breath of superheated air into her chest. She would lose a slugfest in minutes.

This had to be ended quickly.

"No answer, Anastasia," sneered Verena. "Has your terror gotten the better of you?"

Anastasia opened her eyes, marked the shadow of Verena's body in the *Jupiter*'s cockpit. She reached forward—

—And powered down her targeting system.

Verena laughed. "Who would have believed it? The great Anastasia Kerensky humbled by—"

Anastasia pulled into her trigger, her missiles flashing out in a purely manual shot, running straight and true, smashing into the *Jupiter*'s ferroglass canopy. Starring it. *Cracking* it.

Anastasia threw her machine right, bringing her *Wolf*'s arms up and firing manually and on the move, but two shards of azure lightning still somehow following the missiles right in, smashing through the cracked ferroglass.

For a moment the *Jupiter* just stood there. And then slowly, horribly, it toppled over.

Anastasia's radio was filled with a scream of incoherent rage. She glanced left and saw another *Savage Wolf* stalking toward her.

Alaric Wolf.

Julian Davion understood that a battle was like the confluence of two mighty rivers. Powerful currents collided, roiling the water, sometimes pushing flotsam and jetsam downstream.

Sometimes catching debris in swirling eddies.

Julian's line was moving steadily west, Julian's *Templar* anchoring the rear-guard as his forces covered the Wolf Hunters running for the cover of the First Davion's *Fortress*-class DropShip.

And then Julian looked up and saw Anastasia Kerensky caught in one of those eddies.

She was three, four kilometers distant. Far out of range.

Julian saw two *Mad Cat IV*s facing off, one painted dark brown with molten orange accents, the other painted gunmetal gray, its canopy limned in red the color of bright arterial blood.

There was no doubt how this confrontation would turn out. Alaric's *Mad Cat* was scarred. Anastasia's was *battered.*

It was impossible. There wasn't time. He'd have to fight through the Wolf line and by then— It was *impossible.*

Still, Julian stalked his machine forward.

Callandre's red Destroyer slid up in front of him, blocking his path. "Callandre, *get out of the way.* Anastasia needs our help."

"Look again, *Lord Davion.*" Her voice was heavy with contempt. "Aside from Alaric's *Mad Cat*, there's seven, eight vehicles surrounding her. That's a Circle of Equals. If you violate the circle, they'll tear you apart. You can't save her."

He stepped right to go around her, but Callandre jogged her SM1 forward, still blocking his path.

"Damn it, Callandre, this is *not a game.*"

"No," she said coldly, "it's not."

"I'm going," he said tightly.

"Then so am I."

"*No, you're not.*"

"What? *You're* the only one who can die a stupid, pointless death for no good reason? Where is *that* written?"

Julian drew a deep breath. "Calamity—"

"Please, Jules," she said softly. Something caught in her voice. "It's not—I know it's hard, but— You know I'm right."

And he did. But that didn't stop him from hating it.

Julian took one last look at the gray *Mad Cat* awash in a sea of brown.

And then he turned and looked away.

Alaric's *Savage Wolf* stalked toward her, but did not fire. Anastasia saw the Wolves closing around her in a ring, in a *circle,* the pack surrounding its wounded prey. Preventing escape.

The dark brown *Wolf* stopped, facing her. Alaric's extended-range large lasers did not have the same punch as her PPCs, but that was her only advantage. Alaric still had both launchers and doubtless superior missile loadouts. But the biggest disparity was in armor. Alaric's *Wolf* had taken damage around the cockpit and across the left leg. But Anastasia's *Wolf* was showing reds and yellows all across her front.

Against an average MechWarrior, hell, even a *good* MechWarrior, she might have had a chance.

But this was Alaric Wolf.

She looked at his magnificent *Savage Wolf* and knew she was looking at the instrument of her death.

Her only possible victory was to take him with her.

She keyed her radio to a common channel. "Well, I was right," she said dryly. "It looks as if we only require one more meeting."

She did not get the cold chuckle she expected from Alaric.

Instead he keyed his own transmitter and made an announcement to all the assembled warriors: "I am Galaxy Commander Alaric of Clan Wolf. I command the Shadow Wolves of Beta Galaxy and I pilot a *Savage Wolf.* I invoke the ritual of *Zellbrigen,* and challenge Anastasia Kerensky to a duel of warriors. In this solemn matter, let no one interfere."

"*Seyla,*" called out the assembled Wolves.

And then he triggered an alpha strike, missiles streaking toward Anastasia, emerald fire slicing towards her.

Anastasia had been ready for the attack, she stepped right just before he let go, so his right laser missed her close left, but the other laser melted already weak composite on her left side and the missiles rippled across her cockpit.

She fired her own missiles, a double shot, one flight after the other, then lashed out at Alaric's cockpit with her PPCs.

"That trick will not work on me," he snarled.

"It worked well enough on your girlfriend," she snapped.

"You killed Verena, and all you can do is *joke*." He ripped into her with his lasers, launching another double flight of missiles.

"Why should you care?" asked Kerensky, aiming at his cockpit, but missing high. "I am sure you will find another female warrior to pass your 'Trial of Position.'"

Alaric's voice was ice. "You never appreciated her value."

And then he stepped forward and smashed into her left leg with flight after flight of missiles, lasers carving deep into the leg's myomer muscles, reaching for the ferro-titanium bones beneath.

Anastasia punched out before her machine toppled over.

She rose high in the sky on jets of flame and then her chute popped, jerking her upward. She looked up.

In time to see a DropShip rising into the blue, blue sky. Her mouth tastes dry. *I am finally abandoned.*

Wind swirled around her, moving her parachute across the sky. A sudden gust smashed her into a building. Crimson pain exploded in her left leg, and for a moment darkness took her.

She awoke on the ground, looking up at the traitorous sky, the sky into which all her most desperate hopes had just fled. Her leg throbbed with such agony she could scarcely breathe.

The ground shook with the deep rumble of near thunder, the vibrations sending shooting flares of pain up her injured leg. Incandescent supernovas exploded in Anastasia's head. She gritted her teeth against the pain.

And looked up.

Darkness fell over her, and she shivered with the cold. It was the shadow of Alaric's *Savage Wolf.* He stood over her, blocking out the sun.

Blocking out the sky.

She looked up at his cockpit and set her face into a mask of calm, determined to show him no pain, no fear. A tiny victory, but it was all she had left. She stared stoically up at the *Savage Wolf* prepared to meet her death.

Alaric raised his 'Mech's right arm and aimed it at her, the massive barrel a scant meter from her head. Anastasia did not flinch, did not even look at the weapon that was going to vaporize her down her constituent atoms, so there would not be even a *molecule* of Anastasia Kerensky left. She looked up at Alaric in his cockpit.

And waited.

Then, for the second time that day, he shocked her.

His voice boomed from his BattleMech's external speakers: "Yield."

Anastasia Kerensky lay on a stretcher her leg immobilized, no longer feeling any pain.

No longer feeling anything at all.

All her life she had understood the universe around her, looked at it with a cold, dispassionate eye. And because she *did* understand it, she was able to bend it to her will.

Not anymore.

She did not understand any of this.

Alaric walked toward her, still wearing MechWarrior togs, his blond hair lank with sweat, his blue eyes burning with an intense fire she had never seen when he was her captive.

She did not understand why Alaric had spared her, why his medtechs were working so hard to heal her? Unless—

Of course. She would not have a quick, simple death. When Anastasia had captured Alaric, she tortured him, she *broke* him. Could she expect any less now that the tables were turned?

She swallowed, readying herself for what would come next.

So he had no words when he knelt beside her and slipped three bond cords around her wrist. The three white loops indicated that she was his servant, little more than his *property*, but they also held the promise that one day he would cut the cords, making her a full-fledged warrior of Clan Wolf.

"I will never forgive you for killing Verena," he said, his voice tight with emotion, "but you were born to serve Clan Wolf. I *will* see to that."

"No..." She shook her head. "No t-torture?" She hated herself for the weakness in her voice.

"I am *not* Malvina Hazen," he said. "Or," he added bitterly, "Anastasia Kerensky." He looked down at her, his eyes holding hers. "We Wolves are strong. In battle, we are ruthless. But we are *not* monsters."

She looked up at him for a long moment. He did not turn away.

"Tell me one thing," she whispered. "How did you neutralize the guerrilla assault in the city?"

"I will not tell you." Alaric smiled. His smile was proud, but it was not cold or cruel. "I will show you."

They loaded her in the passenger's side of a hoverjeep, careful, oh so careful not to jam her injured leg. Alaric slid into the driver's side. The jeep slowly lifted.

And turned toward the city.

Alaric did not look at her. The jeep moved slowly, drifting down the autobahn at no more than fifteen kph. After a minute, Anastasia gathered she was supposed to be watching. There was little to see beyond the wreckage of battle—actually the wreckage of her Wolf Hunters, not to put too fine a point on it. Thank the Great Father there were no civilian casualties. She was glad she had cleared the autobahn before the battle.

They turned down a street. It looked like any street in any city. A green street sign hanging from a light pole proclaimed that it was *Frederickstrasse.* There were cars parked along the side of the street. Buildings pushing into the sky.

And then she saw the first body.

A woman in a light blue summer dress sprawled across the sidewalk, blond hair fanned over her face like a veil. Who had murdered her? Wolf infantry? Elementals? Anastasia looked for the pool of blood, the charring from a laser.

But there was nothing.

She turned and looked a question at Alaric. He did not look at her, did not say anything.

He just turned down the next street.

Here a metallic red Durandel-British "Blue Nova" had swerved from the road, its sleek bumper crumpled against a parked truck. The driver was slumped over his steering wheel, but the glass was not starred. In fact, other than the damage caused by the crash there was nothing wrong with the car at all.

She glanced right and saw another body, a man—only this time a Wolf medtech crouched over the prone form, administering a drug and checking the man's pulse.

They're not dead.

Anastasia turned to Alaric. "You gassed them." Her voice was hushed with wonder. "You put them to *sleep.*"

Alaric only smiled.

She shook her head, startled that Alaric Wolf would show mercy to a dishonorable guerrilla force. But there was something even more surprising. That he would have the insight to understand the city would be used against him.

Anastasia suddenly saw how she had been defeated. This was not the same Alaric Wolf she had beaten before.

He was something more.

Much more.

CHAPTER 15

PROJECT SUNLIGHT
GENÉVE
TERRA
FORTRESS REPUBLIC
18 MARCH 3143

A single desk light gleamed in Tucker's office, splashing soft buttery light across the chaos of his desk. In his heart, he believed the answer was here *somewhere,* buried in the clutter, if only he could find it.

He felt the same way about his mind.

The broad windows that made up two walls of his corner office looked out on darkness through which he could barely make out a sleeping Geneva. The gloom had crept into his office when he'd turned off the lights.

Not that he had a choice.

Tucker's head rang with pain, and light only made it worse. The headaches had grown steadily more agonizing in recent weeks, so bad that he could barely stand them even with best pain drugs legally available. Tucker got the distinct impression that Sorenson would get him pain drugs that were *not* legally available if he wanted. All he had to do was ask.

And Tucker *would* have asked—if he thought there was a chance in hell there was anything out there that would work.

He shoved aside some papers and touched the black glass inlaid into his teak desk, bringing up the time in blue phosphorescent numbers: *02:14.*

He rubbed his eyes with the heels of his hands. Two o'clock in the morning. No wonder he was so tired. Maybe... maybe he should just go home.

His team was making progress, but it was slow, *too damn slow.* The project was called Sunlight, because they were supposed to chase away the darkness. But as much good as they'd done so far, Sunlight was too grandiose a name. Hell, *candle* was too grandiose a name.

And there were consequences for their failures.

Alexi's position allowed her access to The Republic's best intelligence. What was happening outside Prefecture Ten's walls was terrifying. The Jade Falcons and the Wolves were tearing through the Lyran Commonwealth, no doubt readying themselves for an assault on Terra.

Would Exarch Levin's wall really stand up to a Clan's fury?

People are dying, Tucker, because you *haven't found the answer.*

He drew a deep shuddery breath and sat up straight.

"I will work until we find an answer," he said to the empty office, the deserted facility. Tucker stared, his mind fogged with fatigue, not knowing what to do next.

When stumped, return to first principles.

He leaned forward and called up the document he'd found on the derelict space station, the only piece of evidence they had regarding Clarion Note. Unfortunately, it wasn't really a technical document so much as a strategic directive discussing the use of the SHPG as a tool to cause a blackout. A weapon.

What he wouldn't have given for a set of simple schematics.

But it was all they had. So he read it again, projecting it up onto the wall screen to save his tired eyes.

He was half-asleep as he read until a little section of text jerked him to full consciousness: "*A blackout is a devastating weapon, but like any WMD, its use cuts both ways. A total blackout cannot help but lead to unforeseen consequences.*"

Tucker's heart was pounding in his chest. *What the hell?* He put a hand to his forehead. Why had he reacted so strongly to those two sentences? He shook his head. *You are cracking up, Tucker.*

Then he thought, *No. I've seen that before.*

He leaned forward and typed the phrase "*like any WMD, its use cuts both ways*" into a search engine and selected The Republic's collection of interstellar communications documents.

He let it run, turning to look out at the darkness. After five minutes he glanced back at his desk screen. Still running. He shook his head. "You are a fool, Tucker." He reached forward to interrupt the search—

The computer beeped.

It found something. The document was a communications overview from the early days of The Republic, back when Devlin Stone was Exarch. Tucker remembered it now. It had been a study of the consequences of a communications blackout.

He opened the file and looked from his desk screen to the wall screen and back again. He reread both passages three times.

They were identical.

He blinked. How could that be? When he'd first read the study, he thought it was a strategic assessment of a ComStar interdiction. During the Succession Wars, ComStar had maintained a monopoly in interstellar communications. Sometimes, to punish the great houses, they would turn the flow of messages off, until the targeted house acquiesced.

But an interdiction was a policy, not a WMD. So the passage really didn't make sense if one were discussing an interdiction.

And more importantly, how had Blakist language come to be repeated in a Republic document?

THARKAD CITY
THARKAD
DONEGAL MILITARY PROVINCE
LYRAN COMMONWEALTH
2 JULY 3143

The armored Avanti limousine slowly worked its way through the crowded streets of the capital city. Julian Davion sat in the back in a comfortable brown synthleather seat beside Callandre Kell.

Silence stretched between the two of them, a silence born of the terrible things that had happened on Smolnik, and the terrible things that had happened on Timkovichi. A silence born of the terrible things happening on Tharkad right now.

And Julian's refusal to help earlier, when it might have made a difference.

He turned and tapped his window button. The darkened window lowered with a smooth electric hum. It was a pretty spring day on Tharkad, unseasonably warm for the cold world, so Julian expected to smell sunlight and cherry blossoms from the trees lining the road. He expected to see young couples pushing strollers down sidewalks, old women talking on stoops, old men playing chess in the park.

That was not what he saw.

Instead he saw the shattered glass of a broken storefront, heard the wail of a distant siren. The streets were crowded with traffic, but the sidewalks were deserted. He smelled smoke and tasted wild-eyed panic on the wind. He looked up and saw a blue sky filled with black specks, DropShips darting away from the world like flies scattered from a disturbed corpse.

For there were two monsters coming, Malvina Hazen on one side, and Alaric Wolf on the other.

And billions would be left to their tender mercies.

Julian understood why Caleb had finally sent his First Davion Guards to the Commonwealth, to stain Julian with the terrible defeat about to happen here. He understood the political calculations behind his cousin's actions.

But the people. What of the cost to the people? What kind of prince could act without considering the cost to the people?

Tharkad's terror was like broken glass in Julian's gut. He reached forward and touched the button, hiding the sorrow and the terror behind the darkened window.

He looked straight ahead, his body somehow both too hot and too cold at the same time. How could this happen? *How?* He felt a wave of helplessness wash over him. There had to be a way to stop it—*there just had to be a way.*

He had not felt this helpless since Harrison had died.

Julian glanced at Callandre. *What must she be feeling?*

Callandre wore a Kell Hounds uniform, the uniform of a unit that no longer existed. There was no color in her hazelnut hair—as if the color had been washed out of her. She stared straight ahead, her doe-brown eyes locked on the limousine's forward windshield, her skin pale, her eyes ringed with dark circles as if she hadn't been sleeping. Her hands were gathered in her lap.

There was nothing Julian could do for the people of Tharkad.

But there was something he could do for his friend.

He reached over and gently took her hand and held it between his. She did not turn to look at him. But after a few seconds she closed her eyes and rested her head on his shoulder.

Which was how they rode the rest of the way to the VTOL that would take them to the palace.

THE ROYAL PALACE
THARKAD CITY

There were no courtiers in the throne room, Trillian noted, the galleries were empty. At this time of disaster, the nobility was no longer posturing. Or if they were, they were doing it somewhere else.

Aside from the guards, only a handful of people stood at the foot of the Archon's throne in the shadows of the two BattleMechs (now an *Atlas* and a *Zeus* painted in the colors of the First Hesperus Guards.) There was Vedet himself, of course, Maurer, Melissa, and rounding out the little group,

Julian Davion of the Federated Suns and the last of the Kell Hounds, Callandre Kell.

A truly motley group to determine the fate of a Great House.

"The Wolves have just jumped in-system," said Maurer. "They didn't bother with a pirate point, they came in through the zenith point. It's Alaric Wolf. We've received a communication from him. He plans to present his *batchall* in person." He looked down and drew a heavy breath. "LIC estimates that Malvina Hazen is a single jump away. Khan Seth Ward, about the same."

"Well," said Trillian, "good thing you changed archons. Imagine how bad it would have been if you *hadn't*."

Maurer met her eyes. "The high command has come to believe we may have made a mistake."

"Well, that is of great comfort," said Melissa dryly.

"*I am Archon*!" Vedet roared.

Nobody looked at him.

"We must decide what to do next," said Maurer.

"This has been the capital of the Lyran Commonwealth for seven hundred years," said Melissa stiffly. "We will not abandon Tharkad in her hour of need."

Silence filled the throne room. Trillian was not a military expert, but she *was* an accomplished politician adept at reading faces. On Vedet's face she read terror, on Maurer's, shame and resignation. The young Davion lord was angry.

And Callandre Kell's face was naked with pain.

From these expressions, Trillian pieced together the answer.

It was the young Kell Hound who stepped forward to say the words. "The Kell Hounds have been annihilated," said Callandre Kell in a low, flat voice. "The Exiles have spent their power in delaying the Falcon advance as much as they could. Anastasia Kerensky is lost to us, two-thirds of her Wolf Hunters captured or killed. Jasek Kelswa-Steiner and Roderick Steiner fight desperate battles to hold back the other Wolf assaults. I'm sorry, Highness, but—" Her voice broke on the word and she looked down.

"Mercenaries!" said Vedet desperately. "We could contract mercenaries."

Trillian looked over at Melissa. The Archon looked away.

Suddenly, Trillian understood.

For months, *years,* Melissa had been pouring kroner into ComStar, propping up the communications giant in some mad scheme to bolster her power. Trillian would not say it in front of Melissa's enemies, but like all her schemes, this one had backfired. Now, when the money could have been used in Tharkad's defense, it was gone.

"There is no time," said Melissa.

Trillian thought only she knew the Archon was lying.

"We've stripped the outlying worlds," said Vedet. "Concentrated our forces here on Tharkad. C-could it be enough?"

"*Nein,*" said Maurer softly. "Many of those forces are no better than militia. Even with the remnants of the Wolf Hunters and the First Davion Guards." He shook his head. "It would be a desperate fight against one Clan force. Against three..." His voice trailed off.

"Could we hold until—" Melissa looked over at Julian Davion. "Until help came from the Federated Suns?

Julian was tall and strong in a dress-green AFFS uniform, short red-blond hair framing a handsome face. *He looks like a young general,* Trillian thought. *Or a young prince.*

He drew a deep breath, shook his head. "I am sorry, Archon. Caleb sees me as a political rival. He sent me here to—" He stopped.

"To hang the Commonwealth's defeat around your neck," said Trillian coldly.

Julian nodded. "There will be no more reinforcements from the Suns. You have the swords of the First Davion Guards, Highness." He bowed his head. "But that is all. I *am* sorry."

"You are all *fools,*" snarled Vedet. "If we can't win, then we must salvage what we can and *flee.*"

A disgusted silence hung in the room. If Trillian had been standing next to the Duke, she would have slapped him.

"*I* will not abandon Tharkad," said Melissa coldly.

Trillian recognized that tone of voice and realized the discussion was over. So she was surprised when Julian Davion spoke.

"The battle for Tharkad is lost," he said gently. "The battle for civilization is not. Please, Highness. Save your armies for another day."

The Archon glared at him. "If this were New Avalon, would you abandon it?"

It was a tough question, but the young Davion did not shrink from the challenge. "If it meant saving the rest of the Federated Suns, then yes."

Melissa shook her head. "You may be a fine general, Lord Davion, but you don't have what it takes to rule a Great House."

Julian Davion stiffened, but he did not answer the Archon's barb.

Maurer frowned. "Highness, I really don't think—"

"What?" Melissa snapped. "What is it you really don't think? Do you not think I should be Archon? Who here do you plan to appoint in my stead? Please feel free to try." Her voice was acid. "You're bound to get it right sooner or later."

Melissa glanced over at the young woman standing beside Julian Davion. "Callandre Kell, I charge you with the defense of Tharkad." She looked back at Vedet, and then to the Lyran general, her eyes blue fire. "You'll forgive me, General Maurer, if I give this task to a soldier I can trust."

Callandre Kell and Julian Davion stood in silence on a third-story stone balcony watching Tharkad's gold sun fall into the arctic horizon, coloring Mount Wotan's snow pack with yellows, reds, and pinks. It was cold, as only Tharkad could be cold, but Callandre didn't wear a jacket over her uniform, didn't hug herself, or rub her hands together. She needed the chill.

Needed something to wake her up.

Callandre Kell, I charge you with the defense of Tharkad.

How had the universe come to *that?*

"May I join you?"

She turned back and saw Lady Trillian Steiner dressed in a dark green tunic and a long, black skirt that looked lovely against her fair skin.

"Of course, Lady Steiner."

For a minute they all stood together, watching the sunset.

Callandre wondered what the other woman was thinking. Trillian and Melissa had only been released from captivity that morning. Rage boiled up within her. "Duke Vedet—" she spat the name out, "—is a coward."

Lady Steiner nodded without turning to look at her.

Callandre pounded a fist into her hand. "And Melissa is truly brave."

"Melissa," said Lady Steiner, "is a fool."

Callandre's breath caught.

"She is the true Archon," said Lady Steiner, "and I will follow her to the end of my life. But she *is* wrong."

"How can you say that?" Callandre asked.

Julian shook his head. "Vedet *is* a coward, Callandre. But now is the time for cowardice. You understand the military match-up as well as I. There is no possible way to hold Tharkad."

Callandre turned to look at Julian. He had changed since Caleb had sent him into exile. Jules seemed more dour. No, that wasn't right exactly. He seemed more *burdened,* as if he were weighed down by a heavy duty.

One he would not—or *could* not—explain to her.

She was willing to give Julian the space he needed to keep his secrets, but she missed being able to talk about anything with her friend.

"No possible way to hold Tharkad, huh?" she said. "Well, you don't mind if I try anyway, do you?"

Julian's smile was a flash of white against his tanned skin. "Only if you let me help."

Callandre put her hand on his arm and turned to look at the Archon's cousin. "Will you answer a political question for me, Lady Steiner?"

She laughed. "Only if you call me Trillian."

"Very well, Trillian." Callandre's voice grew grave. "Why did the military return Melissa to power?"

"Well, it helped that Duke Vedet was a failure *and* a coward. But I think it was more than that. I think they know we're facing the last days of Tharkad—" She paused. "Maybe even the last days of the Commonwealth." She shook her head. "I think that here, at the end of things, they wanted to do the right thing."

Callandre absorbed that in silence. Then she bowed her head. "If you will excuse me, Lady Steiner, I have preparations to attend to."

Trillian nodded. She watched the young woman turn and disappear inside the palace. Without turning to look at Julian Davion, she asked, "Is she up to the task?"

The Davion lord's voice was firm. "Here, at the end of all things, there could be no one better."

INVADER-CLASS JUMPSHIP *LOPE*
ZENITH JUMP POINT
THARKAD
DONEGAL MILITARY PROVINCE
LYRAN COMMONWEALTH

Anastasia Kerensky stood on *Lope*'s small observation deck and looked out on the world of Tharkad. The planet was distant, but the JumpShip had good telescopes, good enough to resolve the dot of light into a disc, a cold swirl of blue and white no bigger than a ten-pfennig coin.

Such a small thing to carry with it the rage of emotions she felt within her.

Suddenly, Anastasia realized she was not alone. She tasted the intruder's presence, felt the movement of air, heard the soft intake of breath. His image was not reflected in the ferroglass of the viewport, but he was there nonetheless.

She shifted her weight slightly, bending her knees a few millimeters, tensing her legs, readying herself to spin and kick.

"You prepare to fight me," said Alaric. "That is unworthy of a bondsman."

Anastasia exhaled. At once the tension fled her body. "If I am unworthy, Alaric, why do not you kill me?"

"Perhaps I shall," said the Wolf officer easily.

"Perhaps you shall *try.*"

"It would be a most interesting contest. But then we have already had that contest, *quiaff*? Why should you believe it would be any different this time?"

His words were like a blow to her gut. She reached a hand out to the flat surface of the viewport to steady herself. "I wish you would brutalize me," she whispered. "I wish you would torture me, as I did you. I wish you would kill me."

He stepped forward so he was standing directly behind her. She felt the heat of his breath on her neck. "I will *not*," he whispered.

She closed her eyes.

After a moment Alaric said, "You know, it is not the world that makes you feel this way. You do not truly care about Tharkad. If you did, you *would* strike me down now, or you would try, even if you knew it would cost your life. No it is not the world. It is the *defeat.*"

Anastasia swallowed, remembering her last visit to Tharkad. "Duke Vedet thought I would defeat you and save the Commonwealth," she said softly.

"Duke Vedet is a *stravag* fool," said Alaric coldly.

"It would seem so," Anastasia whispered. She turned to face him. "Will you tell me one thing, Galaxy Commander Alaric?"

He snorted. "Before we are done, I suspect I will tell you many things. But we may begin with one if you like."

Anastasia swallowed. "Did you... Did you really love Verena?"

Alaric broke her gaze, looked out the viewport. For a long moment he was silent. "It is hard to say," he finally said. "I am Clan. We Clanners do not understand what love truly is, *quiaff*? All I know is that there were times I acted against my best interest because I feared hurting her."

His voice dropped so low that Anastasia could barely hear it. "There were times...I would have rather been with her than fight."

Anastasia felt her breath catch. It was a startling admission from a warrior of Alaric's accomplishment.

"There is something we Clanners lack," he said slowly. "Something that is present in the warriors that have beaten us: Anastasius Focht, Victor Steiner-Davion, Devlin Stone. Surely you understand this, Anastasia Kerensky. Is that not why you challenged the ways of Clan Wolf and formed the Wolf Hunters?"

Anastasia found herself nodding.

Alaric caught her gaze, turned the full power of those blue eyes on her. "Did you ever consider, Anastasia, that maybe the thing we are missing is love?"

She looked up, seeing the fierce pain that tightened the muscles of his handsome face. Her life as a Clanner gave her no words to express what she was feeling, so she searched her memory for the words of Spheroids.

"I am sorry," she finally said, "for Verena's death."

THE ROYAL PALACE
THARKAD CITY, THARKAD
DONEGAL MILITARY PROVINCE
LYRAN COMMONWEALTH
9 JULY 3143

Melissa Steiner sat on her throne, waiting for Alaric Wolf to come. She sat with her back straight against the padded chair, her head held high, her eyes clear.

The throne room was mostly empty, save for Callandre Kell, Julian Davion, and Trillian, all of whom stood by her throne, a pair of holorecorder crews, and a scattering of agents from the Diplomatic Guard. A grim smile flitted across her face. Not that the bodyguards were likely to do any good if Alaric arrived in his *Mad Cat*.

The room was quiet and a little forlorn. The traditional BattleMechs had been removed, sent to serve with the forces defending the city. The murals had not been repaired since the assassination attempt. The damaged columns had been fixed, but they had been painted a color of cream that didn't quite match their neighbors.

And, of course, the galleries were empty.

But Melissa had restored the carpet, the beautiful ribbon of Steiner blue that led to the dais. If nothing else, she had that beautiful color blue.

Her courage was bolstered by the memory of Gunter Duiven's words. Before the meeting with Alaric, the former head of Loki had approached her and whispered, "Highness, if the Wolves betray your trust, you will be avenged. This I swear."

And Melissa *did* take comfort from Gunter's words. The Wolves were strong, *ja,* but no Clanner could hope to be half as duplicitous as a Steiner.

Alaric arrived at precisely twelve noon, as they had agreed. He wore brown Wolf leathers and a dark brown wolf mask enameled with copper highlights, its eyes gleaming emeralds.

Trailing two meters behind him and to his right was a woman.

Melissa was startled to see it was Anastasia Kerensky. The woman stared straight ahead, her face blank. She wore no red hourglass, and she had traded her black riding leathers for drab, gray coveralls, but there was no mistaking that dark red hair and those features, somehow both beautiful and threatening at once.

Julian Davion's sharp intake of breath told the Archon that he, too, recognized the former Wolf Hunter.

Disgust filled Melissa. *This* was the woman who was supposed to be the Commonwealth's savior.

Alaric strode into the room as if he owned the place. The very thought gave Melissa a twinge. He stopped five paces from the throne, the camera crews following him all the way in.

Alaric reached up and removed his mask, so she might see his face. He was a handsome man, his blond hair longer than she last remembered and tied back, his face strong, his blue eyes mesmerizing, the orbital scar accentuating rather than detracting from his beauty.

How much easier it would be to kill him right here and now, Melissa thought. *How strong would the Wolves really be without Alaric?* Unfortunately, the answer probably was, strong enough. And there was no telling how the Wolves would react if she violated their bizarre sense of honor. Maybe they'd do nothing.

Or maybe they'd bombard Tharkad from space.

"Archon Melissa Steiner," Alaric said. "You and I have business to conclude."

"We do indeed, Galaxy Commander," said Melissa in a firm, steady voice. "But before we do, I would like an accounting of Clan Wolf's actions. My fondest hope was that the Wolves and the Lyrans would learn to work together. We extended the hand of friendship to you, and you betrayed us."

Melissa braced herself. If he was going to kill her, this would be the moment. Trillian edged forward, as if readying herself to dive in front of the Archon.

But Alaric just smiled and shook his head. "We had no allegiance to betray, Archon. We were, are, and always will be only loyal to the way of the wolf. I believe our confederates made that very clear when we entered into our arrangement. You," he said softly, "did not listen."

"Tell me, Alaric. When was the moment you decided to turn against us?"

"The very first moment you tried to manipulate us, Archon. A wolf will bite when you try to slip a collar around its neck." He shook his head. "And we *are* wolves. Not *dogs.*"

Their civilians, she thought. *It all started with their civilians.*

"But do not fear, Archon, you may not live to see it, but your vision of Clan Wolf and the Lyran Commonwealth working together *will* come to pass—if," he raised an eyebrow, "not precisely in the way you envisioned it."

You may not live to see it.

Trillian put a hand on her shoulder.

Callandre stepped forward. She shook with fury. "You shall pay for your insolence, Alaric."

Anastasia looked up, a look of curiosity on her face.

A sharp smile flashed across the Clanner's face. "Search your feelings carefully, Callandre *Kell.* You do not hate *me.* If I were you, I would save your rage for Malvina Hazen. I am sure she will be along shortly."

Melissa felt a chill at his words, but she managed to stand and say: "What do you bid to take the world of Tharkad?"

Alaric chuckled. "Why, everything I have, of course. And Alpha Galaxy, as well, when my Khan arrives. But we do not need all of Tharkad, Archon. We fight only for Tharkad City and the continent of Bremen."

Melissa's jaw sagged open, and for a moment she could not speak. Finally, she said: "W-what do you suggest we do with the *rest* of the planet?"

"Well, that is up to you, Archon," and Alaric flashed her one of his beautiful, infuriating smiles. "But if I were you, I would discuss the matter with the Jade Falcons."

Julian Davion watched Alaric turn and walk out of the throne room, Anastasia following behind him like a dog on a lead.

He made himself remain still, standing at attention as they left. Then they were lost from view, and suddenly Julian found himself striding down the long, blue carpet.

"Jules?" Callandre called after him, but he ignored her.

He pushed out into the outer hallway. "*Alaric Wolf,*" he called.

Alaric turned, his face calm, implacable. "Julian Davion. Do we have a matter to discuss?"

Julian shook his head. "I will not let you take her."

Alaric glanced at Anastasia, whose face was perfectly blank. "She is *isorla,* legally won. You may not stop me from taking her."

Julian looked at the Lyran soldiers lining the long highway and raised an eyebrow. "Oh?"

"It would be a violation of our customs."

"But not *ours.*"

"You will not do this."

"Why not? Will you fight us any harder if I violate this rule? You're already all in, Alaric. That leaves you with no additional leverage."

"You are an honorable man, Julian Davion," said Alaric. "You may pretend otherwise, but I do not believe you."

"All right. Then I challenge you to a Trial of Possession for Anastasia Kerensky, just you and me."

Alaric raised an eyebrow. "Augmented or unaugmented?"

Julian stepped toward the Clanner so he was only centimeters away from him. "Whatever you like," he said slowly, drawing out the words.

Alaric nodded to himself, obviously considering. "You are honorable *and* courageous. You would have made a fine Wolf, Julian Davion. Of course, depending on how things go, you still might. But for now, I am afraid I must say *neg*."

Alaric started to turn away, but Julian took a step toward Anastasia and held out his hand. "Come with me."

Only then did she look at him. "*Neg*," she said.

"Anastasia." Julian shook his head. "It's okay. He won't— He *can't*—"

"*Neg*," she said again, this time with a little more force.

Julian stared at her, not understanding. "I tried to save you," he said. "On Smolnik, I tried to save you."

"But you failed," she said.

"And that is why you cannot take her," Alaric said. Julian looked over at the Clanner. A tight smile stretched across his face. "Because she knows I hold the key to understanding the true nature of war."

"No, you don't," said Julian.

Alaric turned and strode away. "We shall see soon enough," he called without turning.

Anastasia followed him without another word.

OVERLORD-CLASS DROPSHIP *BEC DE CORBIN*
LOW ORBIT, THARKAD
DONEGAL MILITARY PROVINCE
LYRAN COMMONWEALTH
15 JULY 3143

Beckett Malthus stood on the bridge of his ship, awaiting Malvina Hazen's explosion. She stood with a boot tucked into a steel loop, her hands on her hips, glaring at the face on the viewscreen.

He was a young man, blond with blue eyes—Galaxy Commander Alaric of the Wolves. *Alaric! Freebirth!* He did not even have a Bloodname, and yet this young whelp had reached Tharkad before either Malvina *or* the Wolf Khan.

"If this is the Wolf idea of a joke, it is a very poor one indeed," Malvina hissed. "And if this is not a joke, it is even worse."

Alaric shrugged as if he were arguing with a fellow warrior over the outcome of a football match, rather than with the most dangerous person in all human space. "We have already bid on Bremen. But we have not challenged the Lyrans for possession of the continents of Franz, Grolsch, Heidelberg, and Sutherland. Whether you choose to take them is up to you. It has nothing to do with we Wolves."

"You filthy *surat*. *You* lay claim to Tharkad City, and then seek to *mollify* us with the rest of the world."

Alaric answered her insult with a thin, dangerous smile. "We Wolves take what we want," he said easily. "As to why we do not want the rest of Tharkad—well, we have never felt the need to explain ourselves to Jade Falcons. I shall not start now, Khan Hazen."

"*Chingis* Khan," she snarled.

Alaric shook his head. "Not today, Khan Hazen. Someday you may be the Emperor of all Mankind. But you are not today."

She stared at him, her blue eyes blazing. "I think we should see who truly deserves Tharkad City."

Malthus noted she did not phrase it as a formal challenge. From that alone, he knew how this would turn out.

Alaric nodded. Suddenly Malthus realized the boy had seen the same thing. *This young Wolf possesses a remarkable political mind.*

"To fight for what we want, that is the way of the Clans, *quiaff*? But if you challenge me to a Trial of Possession, you should know that I have my entire Beta Galaxy here. And Khan Seth Ward has just jumped into the system with Alpha Galaxy, three pocket WarShips, and a *Congress*-class frigate. And I think you will find that the Lyrans fear your Mongol Doctrine so much that many of them will fight by my side."

Here, finally, was a flaw in Malvina's tactics. The Mongol Doctrine did not work against enemies who refused to yield to terror.

Beckett watched Malvina stare at the young Wolf on the screen, her face glacial, thinking. A battle with the Wolves would be apocalyptic, costing enough men and machines that the Lyrans might well regain all they had lost in a wave of counterattacks.

But if she bid on the rest of the world, the Lyran forces would be divided between two dangerous foes. She could claim she had conquered Tharkad—and the Jade Falcons would have time to rebuild.

A cruel smile spread across Malvina's rosebud lips. "I see wisdom in your words, little Wolf cub." Her blue eyes marked Alaric's young face. "But I say now, there will come a day when Tharkad is governed under a single flag."

If Alaric was intimidated, he did not show it. "We are Clan," he said. "Is there any other way?"

The screen flickered to black.

Enraged, Malvina Hazen turned and pushed herself across the bridge, slamming the hatch behind her.

Malthus did not even watch her go. He stared at the dark screen. His greatest sin was that he had brought the *bloodfoul* Malvina to power. Now, for the first time since she had plunged the Warship *Emerald Talon* into the heart of Sudeten, he felt a glimmer of hope.

For it occurred to Khan Beckett Malthus of Clan Jade Falcon that Alaric Wolf might just be the one man in the whole of the universe who could undo his sin.

NORTHWEST OF THARKAD CITY
THARKAD
DONEGAL MILITARY PROVINCE
LYRAN COMMONWEALTH
17 JULY 3143

Tharkad's defenders faced the Shadow Wolves across a featureless, snow-covered battlefield. This was farmland, flat and irrigated. The foothills didn't take over the landscape until one traveled further south, toward the mountains. As machines moved across the field, they scraped the snow clean, leaving dark spots mixed in with the white.

The battlefield looked like some kind of crazy, crooked chessboard.

Only this wasn't a game.

Julian dropped his reticle over a brown *Thor* dusted with white. The snow had come the night before, and the Wolf 'Mechs must have gone without shelter. Alaric obviously didn't want his machines caught in their DropShip berths in the event of a surprise Lyran attack.

Julian pulled into his triggers, and twin shards of lightning scoured snow, paint, and armor from the *Thor*'s chest.

Alaric was right to be wary, but that wasn't the surprise he should've been looking for.

"Jack-in-the-box," he called out.

Before the *Thor* could answer, Leftenant Theresa Sparks darted forward in her *Legionnaire* and tore into the Clanner with her RAC-5. For a moment the deadly rattle of the rotary autocannon filled the battlefield, massive brass casings falling like rain, depleted uranium shells hammering armor from the *Thor*'s chest, the Davion machine's targeting computer making every shot count.

The *Thor* pilot locked up, caught between two dangerous opponents and not knowing which to hit.

So he hit neither.

Julian chose that moment to step forward and fire his TharHes four-pack. The missiles corkscrewed in, rippling across the *Thor*'s chest. Julian saw a dirty cloud of abraded armor. In a second the debris settled out of the air.

And he saw the titanium sheen of the *Thor*'s bones.

Overmatched and off-balance, the Wolf pilot backstepped out of range, replaced by a *Vulture* moving up to take its place, the great machine leaving immense tracks in the snow.

At once, the *Legionnaire* fell back, released from its jack-in-the-box attack. Julian ripped into the *Vulture* with his paired PPCs to cover Theresa's retreat.

The First Davion Guards had two vital duties. The first was to hold the center of the Lyran line. The two sides were arranged in a long-line abreast that started a couple klicks from the northern edge of Tharkad City and stretched almost due northwest.

If the Wolves managed to punch through the line, their fast-movers would swing south and race toward the Triad, eight klicks south of the city.

Julian was not going to let that happen.

Fortunately, he had the tools to hold his ground. Callandre had given him the bulk of her reserves. The center of the Lyran line was a thick knot of military power, power Julian was using sparingly.

So far.

Every once in a while he would hit the Wolves with a jack-in-the-box attack, throwing them back whenever it looked like they might be gaining a toehold, but otherwise he held back his reserves.

Because protecting the middle wasn't his only duty.

The Guards' second task involved the unit of fast machines at Julian's back. There were two *Legionnaire*s, one Lyran and one his, fast little machines with a deadly little punch. There were Condors and Demons.

There was Callandre in her SM1.

Waiting for Julian to open the door for her.

Julian looked anxiously up into the gunmetal sky.

Before it was too late.

Alaric stalked his *Savage Wolf* left, toward the center of the line. His Wolves were holding the line well. Rather than trying to swing around the Lyran left flank or punch through a weak spot in the line, Alaric had held his reserves back.

He did not want a race to the Triad.

He wanted to end this with one swift blow.

His command channel crackled, and he heard the *whoop* of crypto synching up. "Shadow One, this is Wolf Actual. Report situation."

The *Snarling Leap*'s massive engines punched the signal right through Tharkad's atmospheric interference.

"All is in accordance with our plans, my Khan." He looked over at the Lyran line and saw the garish red, white, and blue of the First Davion Guards, picked out Julian Davion's *Templar*. "I expect the opening phase of Lock Down to begin in one zero minutes."

"Very well, Shadow One. We expect drop in four five minutes."

Alaric watched a wounded *Thor* fall back from his line. He smiled. This was exactly the opportunity he had been waiting for.

He stepped forward and dropped his reticle over the *Templar*'s chest.

"Good hunting, my Khan," said Alaric. And then he pulled into his triggers. "Shadow One, out."

Julian looked across the line and saw Alaric Wolf's *Mad Cat IV* just as the Galaxy Commander lowered his lasers and tore into his *Templar*'s chest armor.

He had never been so happy to be attacked. "*Guards, to me!*" he shouted. "*Doorman, Doorman, Doorman!*"

And they came, ignoring their heat loads, ignoring their wireframe schematics and their weapon loadouts.

Ignoring their very survival.

They *came*.

All at once, Alaric saw the First Davion Guards *surge* forward, in a desperate, ferocious attack that was joined by their Lyran reserves. A pair of Kinnol main battle tanks tore into a Wolf *Vulture*, joined by a Davion *Centurion*.

A JES missile carrier fired wave after wave of SRMs in a fierce attack on the Wolf line to the *Wolf*'s right, pinning Alaric's people so they could not come to the *Vulture*'s aid. The JES was supported by Hauberk battlesuit infantry, hoverbikes, and VV1 Rangers.

Julian's *Templar* put a flight of missiles into Alaric's cockpit, then stalked right, cutting into a *Koshi* with his PPCs. Thumper artillery tied down that side of Alaric's line, joined by the brutal fire of a Behemoth II and a *Packhunter.*

All of it appearing at once.

Like a massive offensive line overpowering their undersized opponents, the Guards opened up a huge hole in Alaric's line.

And Julian Davion's offensive backfield punched right through.

This was the point of maximum danger. All might be lost.

"All units, Shadow One," Alaric called, "Segment. Right, hold position. Reserves, close and kill. Left, *with me.*"

As the commander of Tharkad's defense, Callandre Kell should have been back behind the lines, well away from the action.

But that just wasn't her style.

So when Jules opened the door, she was the first one through. She led out Condors and Demons and a pair of *Legionnaires.*

All of them looking for Alaric Wolf.

Jules was right. There was little hope of chasing the Wolves off Tharkad. But that wasn't the same as *no* hope. If they could kill Alaric Wolf, they might rattle Beta Galaxy, might roll them up. Then, when Alpha got down, they might have a chance.

But *only* if they killed Alaric Wolf.

It was the only card Callandre had to play.

"Hold on Guns, this may be a little rough."

The Sergeant Major riding in the Destroyer's left cockpit just grunted. Brad Zimmer had never ridden with Calamity Kell before, so he didn't know what "a little rough" meant.

He was about to find out.

The hovertank skimmed over the flat snow-covered fields like a skater racing over rink ice. Callandre punched it, and the Destroyer flashed forward at nearly 130 kph.

She marked the position of Alaric's *Mad Cat* and jerked her control stick over, putting her vehicle into a brutal sideways slide that only ended when she punched it *again,* sending the Destroyer careening in an entirely new direction.

This time Zimmer's grunt was much more appreciative.

The massive roar of the Destroyer's Ultra AC/20 filled her cockpit as they punished Alaric's 'Mech.

Until something smashed into her.

She looked right and saw a *Thor* pounding toward her while it smashed her armor with its LB-X. For a moment, she held her shot on Alaric.

But then the *Thor* ripped into her side with its actinic-bright PPC.

Gritting her teeth, Callandre slid her machine around, bringing her own autocannon to bear on the new threat.

She ripped into the *Thor*'s already damaged chest, but the Clan heavy kept coming. The last hundred meters, it was shedding armor at a fearsome pace and it had the herky-jerky motion that indicated a failing gyroscope.

It staggered right—Callandre thought to get clear of her gun—but then *fell,* suddenly toppling toward her.

She saw it coming and slid left, but the *Thor* pilot managed to deliver a glancing blow, hard enough to rattle Callandre in her cockpit and damage her lift skirt, reducing her speed and maneuverability.

She looked up and realized the *Thor*'s kamikaze attack hadn't been an accident. All her fast-movers were engaged in brutal, close-range fights.

And Alaric and three Stars of Clan machines had pulled out of the fight and were running.

But *not* west and south toward the Triad. Instead, they were heading south and east.

Callandre swallowed.

Toward the city.

THARKAD CITY

Alaric stalked his *Savage Wolf* down Seth Marsden Avenue, sowing panic as he followed the six-lane ferrocrete road through the elegant business district. He stepped into the intersection of Seth Marsden and Fourth, using the long barrels of his lasers to rip down the suspended street lights. He crushed an abandoned green minivan parked along the right side of the street, smashing it with one downward thrust of his massive foot. He came across an overturned tanker truck, its tank glinting silver in the early morning light as gasoline spilled out into the street.

He tied his lasers into his primary triggers and dropped his reticle over the prone truck. The pip flashed gold and Alaric pulled into his triggers.

For an instant the world was filled with the shriek of his lasers and then they were drowned out by the roar of a brutal explosion. Windows shattered all along the street, raining jagged shards. A column of orange fire shot fifteen meters into the sky. The detonation was powerful enough to toss the truck up and flip it over so that it landed on its *other* side.

Even through his sound-deadened cockpit, he heard the song of war: the tinkle of breaking glass, the groan of overloaded structural beams, the ragged cry of rended metal.

The screams of desperate people.

Alaric tied in his external speaker and his amplified voice boomed across the burning street. "I warn you, citizens of Tharkad City, do *not* flee."

Of course that just made them run all the harder.

Alaric's loud and destructive march through the city had produced plenty of damage.

But not many casualties.

Which was his goal. Alaric had no desire to kill civilians. But he *did* want to move them out of the way. So ruthlessly, relentlessly, he herded them south.

Toward the Triad.

Julian Davion lumbered down First Street in his *Templar* and stopped at the place where the east-west street intersected

Seth Marsden. First was deserted. Except for a pick-up truck that had careened into a fire hydrant, sending a fountain of water into the air, there wasn't a single vehicle on the street.

Marsden, on the other hand, was a parking lot.

Civilian vehicles trying to flee the city jammed the north-south road. The street was a six-lane road and the three northbound lanes had quickly been appropriated by people moving south. Motorcycles and bicycles streamed down the sidewalks, joined by the occasional impatient car.

Despite all their effort, people were moving no faster than a couple car-lengths an hour. Accidents caused by speed and panic clogged the city's southbound roads. As frustrated people abandoned their vehicles, things just got worse.

Tharkad City's millions were locked in the middle of a battle, and there was no way for them to get out.

Julian leaned into the intersection, looking north and emerald fire washed over his canopy.

He flashed on the brown shape of a Wolf *Mad Cat*, and then it disappeared behind the bank on the corner of Second and Marsden, screening out Julian's shot.

Julian cursed savagely in English, French, and German.

Alaric Wolf.

When it was clear the Wolves were heading for the city, Callandre had detached Julian and the Guards to pursue. The whole carefully crafted plan had devolved into a disorganized melee, with units scattered throughout the city.

Somehow Julian had managed to stumble across Alaric and *he couldn't get a shot.*

The Clanner was a block north of him, but Julian couldn't move north without crushing trapped civilians. Both ends of First were closed off by a street full of human shields.

Frustrated, he toggled a private channel. "Callandre, Julian."

"Hey, Jules. Was that you swearing all over my common frequency a minute ago? I don't think you would have tolerated that when you were in command."

"I have Alaric cornered at Second and Marsden."

"Nice form, though, I have to give you that. Three languages is impressive. Learn to swear in Mandarin, and you'll be a force to be reckoned with."

"*Callandre.* Listen. If you can work your Destroyer around—"

"I heard you the first time, Jules!" Callandre snapped. "No, I can't work my Destroyer around. I'm bottled up just like you. All my troops are."

Julian heard the frustration in her voice. Not only was the defense of Tharkad City her responsibility, but Callandre Kell was used to a more freewheeling version of warfare. She liked to use her SM1's speed to dash in and pound BattleMechs with her Ultra-20 Autocannon, and then dash out before her victims could return the favor. Now she couldn't move at all.

"Don't worry, Callandre," said Julian gently. "We can't move north, but they can't move south either. That means they can't punch through the city and reach the Triad. The Royal Palace is safe as long as—"

Something flickered in Julian's field of vision, something falling out of a gray sky.

DropShips. Landing Craft. 'Mechs with jump packs.

Julian's mouth suddenly tasted dry. Alaric Wolf had trapped Bremen's defenders in Tharkad City, and now Khan Ward and the Wolves' Alpha Galaxy were falling out of a cloud-bedecked sky.

There would be no one to stop them as they marched on the Royal Palace.

JUST OFF THE COAST OF THE TATYANA ISLANDS

Malvina Hazen's *Shrike* put a clawed-foot down on the sea bottom, sending a cloud of white sand rising up to obscure the crystalline blue water. She took another step forward. She heard the deep rumble of her 'Mech's own footfalls like the promise of distant thunder, at once more diffuse and more powerful than what she would have heard conveyed to her by air.

A shimmering school of metallic-red and green fish darted out of her way. Even the beasts and fowl of this world were smart enough to avoid Malvina Hazen's wrath.

The Lyrans, however, were not quite so wise.

Well, they would learn their lesson soon enough. She glanced right and saw Star Commander Branch's *Turkina*, colored blue by the sea. Just beyond the *Turkina* was the shadowy silhouette of an *Eyrie*. The rest of her Command Trinary was hidden from her by the camouflage of the sea.

Somewhere overhead, Beckett Malthus was leading an attack against the Star League-era base the Lyrans called Sommerposten. She had not left him quite enough power to take the facility, but she expected him to make a good showing nevertheless. The Lyran forces were divided and the bulk had remained on Bremen to fend off the Wolves. What remained was drawn from a dozen different worlds, many units little better than militia, and none of them properly integrated into a single fighting force.

Against these defenders she sent a slightly smaller force of Clan warriors, Jade Falcons tested by battle and hardship, hardened veterans commanded by one of the most devious minds to ever come out of an iron womb.

Aff, she expected Beckett to hold his own.

There was now a slope to the sandy bottom. Her beloved *Black Rose* was no longer strolling along the bottom. She was *climbing.* Malvina glanced up. The sea was no longer an unbroken expanse of deep blue. Overhead it glowed with quicksilver brightness, the sun calling to her.

She needed Beckett to do no better than engage the Lyran defenders in a brutal assault. She did not need him to win, did not *want* him to win. For when her Command Trinary appeared suddenly in the Lyran rear, the defender's line would shatter like hammer-struck glass.

And Malvina Hazen lived for such moments.

Her *Shrike*'s head broke the ocean's surface at last, and Malvina was born into victory.

THE ROYAL PALACE
THARKAD CITY

Leutnant-General Maurer's high boots echoed loudly in the empty throne room as he strode across the marble floor. The general officer wasn't quite running, but he was moving rapidly and his face was pinched with concern.

Trillian guessed it wasn't good news.

He reached the foot of Melissa's throne and executed a sharp bow. "Highness, I regret to inform you that a large Wolf force has broken through our lines and is approaching the Royal Palace. We must evacuate at once."

"How is this possible?" Melissa asked coldly.

"With respect, Highness, I believe—"

"You have not answered my question," Melissa snapped. "You have come and told me that the LCAF is about to surrender my capital. Is it too much to ask how this came to happen?"

"Archon," Trillian said softly.

Melissa did not even turn to look at her.

Maurer licked his lips. "Alaric Wolf's Beta Galaxy struck deep in the city. When our frontline forces responded, they were trapped by a flood of refugees, leaving no one to oppose Alpha Galaxy other than our reserves. Now, Highness. We must go."

A soft smile touched the Archon's lips. "No," she said softly.

Trillian gasped. "*What*?" She took a step toward Melissa. "*No?*"

"There are only minutes, Highness," said Maurer urgently. "The Wolf Striker Trinary approaches, carrying toads. Even if we get you into a Destroyer now, they will pursue."

Melissa looked over at Trillian. "Evacuate my cousin. I invest her with my proxy. She shall act in the name of the Archon until I decree otherwise."

"No..." whispered Trillian, unable to keep the horror out of her voice. "*No.* Come with us, Melissa. Nothing is to be gained from this."

Melissa met her gaze. "Weren't you listening, Trillian? General Maurer just told us what is to be gained. If the Wolves capture me here, they will have little reason to pursue a fleeing Destroyer. They can have one of us or both of us. You tell me, which better serves the Commonwealth?"

Trillian stared at her cousin, open-mouthed. Then she understood. She threw her shoulders back, straightened her back. "Leave me behind, then. I look enough like you to fool the Wolves for ten, twenty minutes. Maybe more." She looked to Maurer for help. Her gaze took in the four Diplomatic Guard agents.

"It might work," said Maurer.

"*Nein*!" Melissa roared.

Trillian turned to the lead agent. "*You*. You have sworn to protect the life of the Archon!" she shouted.

The agent looked straight ahead, not looking at Trillian. He held his rifle at port arms, his knuckles white on the weapon's barrel. "I have my orders, Lady Steiner," he said stiffly.

"You see," said Melissa. "This is the way it will be. I am still Archon. I still have the power to arrange things to my liking."

Trillian shook her head. "But why? *Why?*"

Melissa reached out and gently touched Trillian's face. "As Duke Vedet is so fond of saying, these are *my* Wolves. Now it is time for a reckoning between them and I."

"*No,*" Trillian whispered. "This is madness. You must come with us."

Melissa dropped her hand. "There have been failures during my rule," she said. "But perhaps when our people think of House Steiner, they will remember my courage at the end."

"I'll stay by your side," said Trillian.

"*Nein,* Trillian."

"*But—*"

"*No.*" Melissa shook her head. "You really were loyal to me all along, weren't you?"

"*Always,*" said Trillian fiercely.

"How things might have been different if I had realized that sooner," Melissa whispered. "You must go, for you shall be the political arm of House Steiner in exile. I need your genius."

Melissa nodded and the Diplomatic Guard grabbed her by the arms.

Trillian's eyes blurred, her throat constricting painfully. "My Archon." She reached out to her cousin.

But Melissa had already turned away.

Melissa sat on her throne, back straight, hands resting on the chair's armrests, staring straight ahead. A laser pistol rested in her lap. The throne room was absolutely empty. She would place no more of her subjects in danger.

She waited.

Tharkad was about to fall, and there was nothing she could do about it. She might have made a stand against the Wolves *or* the Jade Falcons. Or perhaps she could have beaten both clans—if Vedet and her generals hadn't turned against her.

But in the end, there was no point in blaming others. *She* was Archon. Responsibility rested with her.

And Tharkad was about to fall.

World of her birth, of her ancestors. Capital of the Commonwealth since 2407. And now, it was finally going to fall.

She did not want to live to see the end of this day.

Melissa heard sounds coming from the outer corridors, the metal *clank* of troops in power armor. She swallowed, but otherwise she gave no outer sign of distress. She was surprised how calm she was.

An Elemental burst in the throne room. He was *huge,* pushing three meters, and clad in armor. He cradled a rifle in his arms, the barrel exactly centered on Melissa's chest. He moved forward, never taking his eye off the target.

"Archon Melissa Steiner," shouted the man. "Do not move. You are a prisoner of the Wolf Empire."

Melissa reached for the laser pistol in her lap.

The Elemental cleared the forest of columns. There were three more at the door.

Melissa stood.

"*Do not move!*" the Elemental roared. "Put your hands above your head. If you move, I *will* fire!"

Melissa raised her pistol and squeezed the trigger.

Ruby fire washed over the Elemental's faceplate.

The giant screamed and dove right.

Melissa heard the staccato roar of automatic gunfire.

Then she heard nothing at all.

THE ROYAL PALACE
THARKAD CITY
THARKAD
WOLF EMPIRE AND JADE FALCON OCCUPATION ZONE
18 JULY 3143

Their footsteps echoed through the empty halls of the Lyran throne room. Alaric had ordered the room's lights secured, save for the small lamps that illuminated the murals, the throne, and the absent BattleMechs. The Royal Palace had been closed; the Lyrans sent home.

He and Seth Ward walked alone through the great throne room.

"Is it not satisfying to know that we Wolves brought down House Steiner, *quiaff*?"

"*Aff*," said Khan Ward, stopping before the dais. The word was a rumble from deep within his chest. "But this does not excuse your actions... Your *arrogance*."

"I performed my *surkai* as you instructed, my Khan."

"You never embraced your *surkai*," growled Khan Ward. "You attacked Tharkad, though that target was to be mine."

"You had the central invasion corridor," said Alaric, "and yet I reached Tharkad first. Should the wolf fail to bring down the prey because his packmates lag behind?"

"*You gave Tharkad to the Jade Falcons!*" the Khan roared.

"To prevent a war that would have brought ruin to both Clans."

"I have indulged you, Galaxy Commander Alaric."

"Have you?" said Alaric softly, "because I do not believe—"

A figure leaped out of the lower gallery and lunged toward Seth Ward. Alaric flashed on a big man with ebony skin, a rictus of hate twisted across his face, his powerful body clothed in black, a knife clutched in his right hand.

Alaric threw himself at the assassin, delivering a brutal punch to the killer's throat, followed by a knee to the gut. The man doubled over and Alaric twisted his neck, snapping it in an instant.

The assassin's blade clattered to the ground.

The Khan had his sidearm out, his laser trained on the assassin. Alaric allowed the man's body to fall to the floor, and Khan Ward slowly lowered his weapon.

Alaric knelt and picked up the knife. Its tip was stained maroon. "Poison," he snarled. "If he had even scratched you—" He shook his head. "This stinks of Loki, Melissa's secret police."

A shape, no more than a silhouette, appeared at the distant door to the throne room. "My Khan, I heard a disturbance."

Ward turned his attention to the door.

Alaric felt the weight of the blade in his hand.

In a flash, he raised the poisoned knife and *threw it.* It caught Khan Ward in the throat, slicing right into his windpipe.

The Khan turned to him, his eyes wide with shock, hands going to his throat. He made a terrible, gurgling sound.

"Hurry!" called Alaric. "The Khan needs help!"

The poison was already working. The Khan had sunk to his knees, his face purple.

The Khan's guard charged into the room and found Alaric standing over the dead Loki agent's body, Seth Ward collapsed on the floor.

At that moment, Alaric realized that he was Vlad *and* Katherine *and* Victor. He was all three at once. And he could present any of those faces to the world without losing the use of the other two.

All three of those mighty leaders had their strengths and weaknesses, but not Alaric. He would harvest only their strengths—leaving their weaknesses to rot. Guided by no value other than expedience, he would wear whichever mask was demanded by the occasion. And so he would be the most flexible warrior in the galaxy.

And the most dangerous.

"What happened?" asked the panicked guard.

Seth Ward lay on his back, bleeding from his mouth, his tongue swollen, staring up at Alaric with accusing, dying eyes.

"He was murdered," said Alaric, "by an assassin."

ASGARD, MOUNT WOTAN
THARKAD
DONEGAL MILITARY PROVINCE
LYRAN COMMONWEALTH
20 JULY 3143

Snow floated through the leaden sky as Trillian looked up, watching the Warrior VTOL fight the treacherous mountain wind. She stood on the edge of a square landing pad ringed with flashing lights and marked with a white "*X*." Behind her was the massive Asgard facility, the headquarters of the vast Lyran military.

This day, it was just one more citadel waiting to fall.

The *throp-throp-throp* of the helicopter's rotors battled the wind's howl for supremacy. The Warrior was painted dark brown with molten orange highlights and it carried within it a emissary from the new masters of Tharkad.

Clan Wolf.

Trillian's mouth tasted dry. She felt hollow inside. Melissa was dead, and Tharkad was about to fall. The Jade Falcons controlled the Tatyana Islands, and the Wolf Khan sat on the Steiner throne.

There was nothing left.

Trillian knew she wasn't permitted to fire on an ambassador under a flag of truce, but would it be her fault if the helo crashed? Maybe she could fire on it and *pretend* it crashed.

Maybe it would crash on its own.

Unfortunately, the Wolf pilot knew his business. He hovered the Warrior over the landing pad, like it was a clear summer day.

Callandre Kell strode up to her, followed by Julian Davion.

"How is the loading going?" Trillian shouted over the roar of the descending bird.

Callandre looked terrible. She was pale and there were dark circle under her doe-brown eyes. "Eight hours, Lady Steiner. Our surviving forces will be ready for lift in eight hours." She swallowed and shook her head. "For the first time, I think I understand why disgraced Combine warriors commit *seppuku.*"

Julian squeezed her hand.

Trillian shook her head. "You were dealt a losing hand, and you did the best you could."

Callandre's voice was bitter. "A warrior must learn to lose battles. But this was *Tharkad.*"

"You didn't lose it, Callandre," said Julian.

"He's right," said Trillian. "In fact, if you want to wait around for five minutes, you can watch *me* give it away."

The Warrior finally set down, bouncing slightly on her rubber tires. Ground crew raced out to chock and chain the VTOL. A hatch slid open and a figure emerged, running crouched to clear the *whirring* gray death promised by the helo's rotors. The man's long blond hair blew back in the wind.

It was Alaric Wolf.

Trillian Steiner almost ordered him shot down right there. It took all her will to keep her mouth firmly shut.

When he reached them, Trillian bobbed her head in a little nod that was as much courtesy as she could bear to extend. "Here to gloat?" she snapped.

A small smile twitched at the corner of the Clanner's lips. "Not at all, Trillian Steiner."

Trillian drew a deep breath. It was a bitter moment, undoubtedly the most bitter moment a Steiner had ever faced, but she *would* face it, if for no other reason than she owed it to the people of Melissa's realm.

She gestured at the Asgard facility, where even now, aides were frantically shredding classified documents and wiping hard drives. "Would you care to come inside?"

Alaric shook his head. "*Neg.* I will not be here long enough for that to be necessary. I am here to request *hegira,* honorable withdrawal from the field of battle."

Trillian just stared at him.

Julian's face was slack with shock. "You're— You're *leaving*?"

Alaric nodded. "We Wolves have no need for Tharkad. So we will leave. If you permit us."

"Yes," said Trillian. "I mean *aff.* I mean *go.* Please *go.*"

"Farewell, cousin," said Alaric. "I am sure we will meet again."

And then Alaric turned and raced back to the helicopter, its rotors still turning. He climbed in, the hatch shut behind him, and the VTOL fell up into the gray sky.

"The Wolves," said Callandre slowly. "They... They *never* intended to hold Tharkad."

"It was a feint," said Julian. "But what...?"

There was a moment of silence.

"*Terra,*" all three said at once.

Trillian shook her head. "They distracted us and the Jade Falcons. Their real aim must have been to lay claim to an invasion corridor on the border of Fortress Republic."

"Speaking of the Jade Falcons..." said Callandre.

"I will offer Malvina Hazen *hegira,* too," said Trillian. "Now that the Wolves are gone, we don't have to divide our forces. Even the mad Malvina Hazen will see she needs to retreat."

"And if she doesn't?" asked Julian.

Trillian turned to look at Calamity. "Then kick that damn bitch off my planet."

Callandre snapped off a salute. "Yes, ma'am!"

Trillian swallowed. She, Callandre Kell, Julian Davion, even Maurer and Vedet. They'd all been wrong. Only Melissa had dared to hope that Tharkad could be saved.

She drew a deep shuddery breath and looked over at Julian Davion. The young noble wore a perplexed frown on his handsome face. "What is it?"

He shook his head. "It's probably not important."

"But?" Trillian pressed.

"Did Alaric just call you '*cousin*'?"

OVERLORD-CLASS DROPSHIP *BEC DE CORBIN*
LOW ORBIT, THARKAD
DONEGAL MILITARY PROVINCE
LYRAN COMMONWEALTH

Beckett sat in the back of the room, keeping very, very quiet. He gave himself even odds of surviving this meeting. And maybe *that* was optimistic.

"You *withdrew*?" Malvina screeched. "How *dare* you!"

The image of Alaric Wolf on the wall screen shrugged. "I really do not understand you, Malvina Hazen. First you are angry because I am here. Then you are angry because I leave."

"This is *not* what we agreed. Your actions forced—"

Forced me to withdraw, she almost said before she stopped herself. It was a measure of how furious Malvina was that she almost admitted such weakness to Alaric Wolf.

"*We* did not *agree* on anything," said Alaric pointedly. "I serve only the ways of Clan Wolf. I made no promises to Clan Jade Falcon. But—" He held his hands up, "You will recall that you indicated your desire that Tharkad be ruled under a single flag." He smiled broadly. "And now it will be."

"Not a *Lyran* flag," Malvina snarled.

Alaric shrugged. "Such are the fortunes of war."

Malvina slammed her fist on the comm board, breaking the connection, and the screen went black. Without a backward glance, she stormed out of the space.

Leaving Beckett Malthus to contemplate the perversity of a universe where the instrument of salvation for Clan Jade Falcon's soul was a young whelp from Clan Wolf.

ZDENEKOVA SQUARE
ALLIAGO CITY
GIENAH
WOLF EMPIRE
24 AUGUST 3143

Bright sunlight splashed across the wide expanse of flagstone the Lyrans had called Zdenekova Square. The square abutted the royal quarters so Gienah's Duke might address crowds from a balcony or preside over troops passing in review.

It was also a fine place for a fight.

Alaric's eyes picked out the holorecorders in their various locations. An especially fine place for a *broadcast* fight.

Alaric stood next to Star Colonel Thomas, a hulking Elemental. Both men faced Liam Ward. Beside the Loremaster was a device that had an inverted cone at its center. His eyes sought out both warriors.

"What transpires here will bind us until we all shall fall. As this is your fifth battle, you know well the honor for which you fight." He nodded towards Alaric. "You, Alaric, have seen thirty-one years. Why are you worthy?"

"I have conquered worlds in The Republic, the Free Worlds League, and the Lyran Commonwealth. I killed Thaddeus Marik and defeated Landgrave Jasek Kelswa-Steiner. I defeated Anastasia Kerensky in single combat and took her as my bondsman. And I conquered Tharkad City, the heart of the Lyran Commonwealth."

"And you, Thomas, who have seen twenty-six years. Why are you worthy?"

Star Colonel Thomas began reciting his qualifications, great battles won, worlds conquered.

The Loremaster clapped his hands together. "The heroism and courage displayed by both of you has been verified. Your claims are not without substance. No matter what fate you meet in battle, the brightness of your light will not be diminished." He waved both men forward. "Present the tokens of your legitimate right to participate here."

Both men handed their coins to the Loremaster, silver disks with Clan Wolf emblems on the obverse, and on the reverse, a scroll with the Bloodname *WARD* written on it above their names.

"The horrible chaos of war is reflected in this Trial of Bloodright. When one coin has successfully stalked the other and they complete their transit through this cone, the hunting coin will be superior. That warrior is given the choice of style for the fight. The owner of the inferior coin then decides the venue for the fight. In this way, each will fight on a battlefield not wholly of his choosing. Do you both understand this?"

"*Seyla*," answered both warriors.

The Loremaster inserted each coin in its respective slot. The two coins dropped through lengths of transparent pipe until they hit the inverted black cone with a hole at its apex, spinning round and round as gravity chose their fates.

The winner of the Bloodname would almost certainly be determined by the play of the coins. If Alaric was allowed to choose an augmented fight, his *Savage Wolf* would easily crush a lone Elemental in power armor.

But in a hand-to-hand fight, the Elemental would kill him.

No doubt the commentators were explaining this all to the population of Gienah as they watched from their homes.

Round and round flashed the coins.

Until they clattered down to the well's bottom. Liam withdrew the coins and looked up. "Alaric is hunter."

Is that a note of disappointment in his voice?

Star Colonel Thomas took the news of his death bravely. He stood at attention, waiting for Alaric to pronounce sentence.

"I choose to fight augmented."

Thomas swallowed. Liam started to turn away.

"But not with a BattleMech against power armor."

Both Loremaster and Elemental turned back to look at him.

Alaric smiled. "With *knives.*"

Both men had stripped to the waist. For a moment, they stood facing each other.

Then Thomas lunged at Alaric, seeking to end it quickly.

Alaric danced away from the attack. He was faster than the Elemental, but not as much as he had hoped.

He swung his body around, hitting Thomas with a flying kick to the jaw.

The blow landed, *hard.* But not hard enough. The Elemental did not fall, did not even take a knee. Thomas spit out a shattered tooth and then *grinned,* revealing a film of blood on the teeth he had left.

"Perhaps you should have taken the BattleMech, Alaric *Wolf.*"

"The battle is not over yet, Thomas."

The Elemental lunged again, this time swinging his knife in a long, slashing attack.

Alaric dove right, but not quite fast enough. The blade sliced through his chest from nipple to side in a blow that only *just* glanced off his ribs.

A little closer and Thomas would have punched the knife *through* his ribs.

Alaric hit the ground and rolled, not *right,* away from the Elemental, but left, toward him. He came up *under* the man and behind him. With a precise cut, he severed the Elemental's left Achilles tendon and leaped backward.

A good thing, because Thomas turned his fall into a mad lunge.

That missed Alaric by millimeters.

This time Thomas *did* sink to a single knee. With his Achilles cut, he could not put any weight on his left leg. Now he was as slow as Alaric had originally hoped.

"It is over, Thomas. Yield."

"It is over?" asked the Elemental, flashing a bloody smile at him. "Well, then come here and finish it, little man."

Alaric set himself, studying the wounded Elemental. Thomas's chest gleamed with sweat. Alaric studied those powerful muscles.

"You taste fear," sneered the Elemental. And he began to laugh.

Alaric drew a deep breath—and then his arm flashed forward. A cruel *thud* stilled Thomas's laughter, Alaric's blade protruding from the Elemental's chest, just below the heart.

"Your left lung is punctured, Thomas. Shall we wait for you to drown in your own blood? Or will you yield?"

Alaric saw the surrender in the man's eyes as he fell.

Alaric was glad Thomas had lived.

There had been a time when he would have killed Thomas as a matter of course, simply because he dared to challenge him. But now he saw that Thomas would one day serve him, as would all Wolves.

And Alaric would not willingly throw away any weapon.

Alaric stepped over to the dais where Loremaster Liam Ward stood beside Katrina Steiner. Liam found he was bitterly disappointed that Thomas had failed to kill Alaric. That had been an extraordinary throw of the knife.

Almost as extraordinary as the throw that had killed Seth.

For a moment, just a moment, he toyed with the idea of pointing out this coincidence.

But Seth's guards swore the Khan had been murdered by a Loki agent. And Liam would not subject his Clan to a civil war. He was not Malvina Hazen.

Which meant he would have to perform the perverted Bloodname ceremony dreamed up by Alaric and his mother. It was a dark day indeed when a Steiner-Davion would be allowed to take the name *Ward.*

But that would not be the end to the day's perversions. Normally the Bloodname ceremony was an occasion of great gravity and dignity, attended only by Bloodnamed warriors. Not this time. Alaric had plans for this particular ceremony. The young warrior would reveal his *chalcas.*

But there was nothing Liam could do. He was adept at seeing several moves ahead in the game. So he knew he could delay Alaric's ascendancy.

But he could not stop it.

Bloodnamed Wolves in gray leathers gathered around Liam and Alaric in a circle. A golden lamp in the shape of a wolf had been placed between them on a stand.

Liam raised his voice. "*Trothkin,* seen and unseen, near and far, living and dead, be of brave heart. Another of your number has been blooded." Holorecorders trained on the Loremaster caught his words and sent them to the people of Gienah. Eventually they would be carried to all the conquered worlds of the Commonwealth.

"Five battles he has fought, defeating a Star of his peers, and he is victorious. We have all witnessed his contest, and none may deny the rede of it."

"*Seyla*," cried out the assembled Wolves.

"Alaric, your Bloodname exalts you above the mere warriors with and against whom you have fought. Ten and ten and five are the number who bear the same surname as you. With it, you become a member of the Clan Council, and are eligible for election to even greater office and responsibility."

Liam looked down at him. "Give me your dagger."

Alaric handed the Loremaster his silver dagger, presenting it pommel first.

Liam reached forward and took Alaric's left hand, slicing deeply into his palm. Alaric smiled tightly at the pain, but did not complain. He closed his fist around the cut and reached for the lamp. He squeezed out a drop of blood and the lamp's flame hissed.

Liam returned the blade to Alaric. "You are now and for all time known among the Clans as Alaric Ward. All are to abide by the rede given here. Thus it shall stand, until we all shall fall."

"*Thus it shall stand, until we all shall fall*," echoed the assembled Wolves.

"And now to the business of the pack," called out Liam. "I call for the election of a new Khan to replace Seth Ward."

Galaxy Commander Elise Ward's voice rose above the murmur of Wolves. "I nominate Alaric Ward."

And as the voices of the Wolves rose in acclamation, Liam knew his beloved Clan had truly lost its way.

Alaric stepped through the gathered Wolves to a waiting microphone positioned before a trio of holorecorders. *This* was what the whole thing had been about: the knife fight with Thomas, the public Bloodname ceremony, his quick election as Khan.

"Brothers and sisters of the Lyran Commonwealth. What you have just witnessed is a sacred ceremony of Clan Wolf.

You have seen the winning of a Bloodname, the elevation of a simple warrior to high rank.

"But there is more here than you may know. I regret to inform you that Archon Melissa Steiner is dead. At the end of her life, she acted to save the people of Tharkad from terror and destruction."

His blue eyes gazed steadily into the holorecorders. "The Lyran Commonwealth is without an Archon."

"Brothers and sisters, please allow me to remind you of your history. At the end of the Jihad, Peter Steiner died without leaving a viable heir. Adam Steiner stepped forward to steer the Commonwealth in trust for the *true* Steiner line."

Alaric shook his head. "But Adam made a mistake. For there *was* an heir from the original Steiner line. At the end of the conflict known as the FedCom Civil War, Victor Steiner-Davion sent his sister Katrina into exile with the Wolves.

"Katrina Steiner is *my* mother." He raised his voice. "I am her *heir.*"

"I do not expect those listening to believe my word." He pressed his hand to the bleeding flap of skin Thomas had cut into his chest and held his bloody right hand out to the cameras. "So I offer my blood as proof that I carry Katrina Steiner's genetic legacy within me."

"Brothers and sisters of the Lyran Commonwealth, within the Wolf Empire I shall always be known as Khan Alaric Ward. But to you I will be known by another name."

He raised his voice into a triumphant shout. "*Archon Alaric Steiner!*"

THE ROYAL PALACE, THARKAD CITY
THARKAD
DONEGAL MILITARY PROVINCE
LYRAN COMMONWEALTH
31 AUGUST 3143

Trillian Steiner reached a trembling hand forward to pause the recording. Alaric Wolf, Alaric *Ward* (or was it Alaric Steiner?) was framed in the shot, a jagged slash of blood running diagonally across his bare chest, his blond hair matted to his head by sweat.

The composition had been arranged so that a pair of banners hung behind him, one blood red and bearing a wolf's head, the other a mailed fist centered on a field of Steiner blue.

Just like the banners Melissa arranged before the conference with the Wolves, she thought. *My God, that was a lifetime ago.*

Melissa's lifetime.

"He's crazy," said Julian softly. "No Lyran will follow him."

Trillian shifted in her chair and said nothing.

"He's lying," said Callandre. "He's got to be."

"Look at that those eyes," Trillian whispered, "those blue eyes. The golden hair, the bone structure. *Gott im Himmel.* Why didn't I see it before?"

"Still," said Callandre, "we could *say* he's lying."

Trillian shook her head. "First rule of politics. If you know an uncomfortable truth is going to come out, don't bother lying about it—that only makes it work."

"He's Trueborn," said Julian. "The fact they scraped a few cells from the inside of Katrina's mouth doesn't make him Archon. Ask yourself: what if the Free World's League had cloned a Steiner? Genetic code alone wouldn't make him or her an heir to the throne."

"The difference is that Katrina presumably consented to the birth of this child. This wasn't some half-baked plot. Ask *yourself,* how is this different from finding that Katrina had given birth to a son naturally?"

Julian frowned. Callandre looked deeply troubled.

"Don't get me wrong," said Trillian. "I'll use every gram of anti-Clan prejudice against him. I'll intimate that he's a genetic freak, a monster. I don't believe he's the rightful heir to the throne. But he *does* have a case."

Julian shook his head. "The Lyran people will never accept a Clanner as their leader."

"Been to Rasalhague lately?" Trillian snapped. "How about the Raven Alliance?" She drew a grave breath. "Don't underestimate Alaric, either of you. If he *is* Katrina's son, and if she's been tutoring him, he might understand Lyran politics better than anyone alive. He'll win the people's gratitude for standing against Malvina Hazen."

She reached out and touched the screen, her fingertips brushing across Alaric's image.

"And he's a Steiner."

PROJECT SUNLIGHT
GENÈVE
TERRA
FORTRESS REPUBLIC

Tucker Harwell held a little drive in his hand. Its casing was translucent green plastic, and it was no bigger than a man's thumbnail.

Such a small thing to destroy a man's dreams.

It contained answers, no, *the answer:* who triggered Gray Monday and why. Oh, it hadn't been written down in a single, convenient place, but Tucker had used Alexi's access code to access the records of The Republic's security directorate, to read through the information that Republic agents and knights and paladins had collected.

Enough information to put it all together.

An amber light blinked on his screen, and then disappeared. *They're monitoring me.*

Tucker drew a deep breath and stood, suddenly understanding what had to be done with a clarity he'd rarely experienced in his life. He closed his hand into a fist around the little drive, protecting the terrible secret.

And then he walked out of his office—out of his *life*—and disappeared into the crowds of people that haunted Geneva's streets.

THE HALL OF ARCHONS, THE COURT OF THE GREAT FATHER
ALLIAGO CITY
GIENAH
WOLF EMPIRE

Alaric and Katrina strolled down the replica of Tharkad's Hall of Archons, sunlight slanting through the great peaked windows, painting bright white squares on the dark green carpet. The hallway smelled like rich, lustrous wood and citrus polish.

His mother had been furious when Alaric returned Tharkad to Trillian Steiner. He had originally decided to build this replica of her beloved hall as a peace offering.

But he found he liked it, too.

Katrina's eyes settled on each portrait as they walked along the long hallway. The *portraits* were not replicas. Alaric had brought *those* from Tharkad. As she studied the paintings, he studied her. She was dressed like the princess she once was: in a flowing white silk dress, her waist belted in gold, her hair tied back with white ribbons, its straw color hinting at the bright yellow it had once been.

For once her face was unguarded. She was illuminated by joy's brilliant light. But if her joy shined out brightly, it cast a dark shadow.

Her lip curled when she saw Victor's portrait. "This will come down," she snarled.

Alaric said nothing. He loved his mother and wished for her happiness.

But he would not take down his father's portrait.

He had made his own adjustments to the line of paintings, taking down Vedet's portrait and replacing it with Melissa's. Alaric had fought alongside Vedet during the campaign against the Marik-Stewart Commonwealth. He knew Vedet to be a fool and a deeply dishonorable man.

Melissa's rule had also been disastrous, but in the end she had stayed behind to stand for her people when she could have easily run. Alaric would honor her spirit, if not her actual accomplishments.

And soon, his own portrait would be added to the long line.

Katrina stopped to stare up at her own portrait, her eyes shining, her mouth drawn into a thin, tight line. "What might have been," she whispered. "If only—"

Alaric stood by her side for a long moment, allowing her to savor the moment. After a long time she turned, reached up and touched his face. "My son. I thank you for this gesture, though—" her voice grew cold, "—it would have made far more sense to keep Tharkad itself."

Alaric bowed his head. "I am glad of your pleasure. And...I wish to ask for your counsel."

She smiled. "Of course."

They walked down the hallway, drawing near its end.

"I am trying to decide what to do with Anastasia Kerensky. She is a Trueborn Wolf, the only person within our Clan with the skill and the determination to challenge me as I challenged Seth. If I send her away, might she not grow into a threat to my power as Malvina Hazen did to Jana Pryde? But if I keep her close, will she not gain allies among the ruling council?"

Katrina nodded. "You already know the answer, my son. You must kill her and kill her now. While she is still a bondsman. *Before* she has the opportunity to gain support."

At that moment, Anastasia Kerensky stepped into the hallway, her dark red hair pulled back into a pony tail, wearing a simple gray jumpsuit without rank or insignia as befitted a bondsman, the three white cords still looped around her wrist.

Alaric drew the silver blade at his hip. Anastasia *froze*. Their eyes met.

Then he pivoted and plunged the knife deep into Katrina's chest.

His mother's eyes widened in shock. Alaric took her in his arms, his stomach twisted inside him, his throat suddenly tight. He felt moisture leaking from his eyes. *Tears.*

This is what it means to cry.

"I am so sorry, mother," he whispered. "But Anastasia is no threat to me. She will be my strong right arm. I think she is a threat to *you*. By telling me to kill her, you put your position above mine. And you are too dangerous for me to allow that. By telling me to kill her, you really told me to kill *you.*"

A tear of dark blood trickled from Katrina's mouth. Her blue, blue eyes locked on Alaric's. "I...am...*great.*"

"*Aff,*" said Alaric. "You *are* great—and that is why you had to die."

Anastasia Kerensky stood over Alaric as he held his dying mother, her heart pounding in her chest. For an instant, she had believed that Alaric meant to kill her.

But now she saw she had been wrong—in so many ways.

She saw that Alaric had acted with the ruthless necessity of Vlad Ward and the cunning insight of Katherine Steiner-Davion.

But it was his tears that had truly won her over. There was a touch of nobility in this man. Ironically, it was compassion that would make him the most dangerous warrior in all human space.

Anastasia knelt and bowed her head. "My Khan," she whispered.

Alaric turned to look at her, his blue eyes locked on her face. Then he stepped toward her.

Without a word, he took the knife still stained with Katrina's blood and cut the bond cords from Anastasia's wrist.

GENÈVE
TERRA
FORTRESS REPUBLIC
14 SEPTEMBER 3143

Tucker carried a copy of *La Tribune de Genève* under his arm, and stopped at a flower cart to buy a bunch of lovely yellow daffodils. Trying to look like a tourist.

He glanced behind him.

Caught a flicker of movement as the man looked away. He was tall and slim, his well-tanned arms cabled with muscles.

He wore expensive sunglasses, silvered, so Tucker couldn't see his eyes, a tasteful white-gold chain necklace over a dark blue polo and white cotton slacks. His raven hair was slicked back and arranged in a two hundred-stone haircut. He could have been a rich tourist—no doubt that was exactly what he was supposed to look like.

But Tucker had seen the man before as he had purchased some oranges and a trout in the market.

The man said something to a jewelry vendor. The vendor pointed in the direction opposite Tucker and the sleek man walked off. Which meant the man *was* a tourist after all.

Or he had just passed off his target to another Republic agent.

The hairs rose all along the back of Tucker's neck.

Tucker bowed his head to the flower vendor and said "Thank you," in halting French. He picked a direction at random and walked off quickly, brisk enough to cover some ground, but not quite fast enough to attract attention. His shoes clicked against the cobblestone road.

At first, Tucker believed he was being too paranoid. Now he was beginning to believe he couldn't be paranoid enough.

A warning rumble of thunder rolled across the iron sky. Rain? Was it supposed to rain today?

He had acted quickly, using a public terminal to hack his bank, transferring the balance of his account into *another* account, and then withdrawing it from an ATM before anyone could trace the transaction. So he had money.

For as long as it would last.

The question was what to do next? He couldn't risk showing his face in a maglev station or a drop port. He couldn't buy or rent a car. They'd be looking for him. So he had rented a room in a dirty little hotel where roaches darted into the corners every time he snapped on a light and prostitutes plied their trade noisily in the next room.

He couldn't go back there now.

No loss.

The rain started as a drizzle, spreading great wet splotches across his *Tribune.*

He wanted to call his family, wanted to talk to his father. But of course they'd be waiting for that. What did you do when the authorities knew every move you might make?

It rained harder now, pelting him, gluing his clothes to his body, turning his paper into a soggy mess. He dropped it in the street and ducked down an alley, sheltering beneath a fire escape that kept most of the rain off.

What should he do now? Where could he possibly go?

A sudden actinic flash of blue-white light ignited the world, followed almost instantly by the sharp *crack* of near thunder.

Tucker shivered. *That was right on top of me.*

Another flash, followed by thunder's deep, angry voice.

Only this time the incandescent light revealed a shape in the mouth of the alleyway. Tucker's right hand closed around his—

(slug thrower)

—flowers. He looked down. Daffodils. All he held were cheerful yellow daffodils.

"W-who's there?" Tucker asked.

And then she walked out of the shadow. He could barely see her in the storm's half-light, but it was enough. He recognized the planes of her face, the spiky-short hair, the eyes. And one more thing.

The weapon in her hand.

"Oh, Tuck," Alexi whispered, "why couldn't you just leave it alone?"

"It's not my job to keep your secrets," he said bitterly.

"It's just history," she said. "It doesn't have anything to do with us, or solving the blackout. "It's just *history.*"

"You lied to me, Alexi. You never really cared for me. All this, our apartment, our *love*—" he choked on the last word, swallowed and shook his head. "All of it was just a way to keep me from learning the truth."

Alexi swallowed. He could see the tension in the lines of her face. The grief. "No, Tuck," she said in a strangled voice. "I loved you—*love* you. But Paladin Sorenson asked me to—"

"Don't *talk* to me about paladins and knights!" he roared. "Don't rest your argument on the broken integrity of your grand Republic!"

"Tucker, please listen—"

But Tucker was done listening. He rushed at her.

She hesitated, her uncertainty probably saving his life.

The weapon went off with a huge concussion, echoing painfully in the narrow alley. Fire flashed through Tucker's left arm, but then he was on top of her, the gun in his hands.

He stepped back, the gun in his shaking right hand, the slug thrower's barrel doing a little dance, the daffodils somehow, ridiculously, still in his left hand.

He dropped the flowers and leveled the weapon at her, steadying it with both hands. "You've lied, you've done nothing but lie. *Everything.* Everything a *lie.*"

"Tucker, *please*—" She held her hands out. It was almost a sob.

"Why didn't you tell me, Alexi?" he said between clenched teeth. "Why didn't you tell me that *the blackout was Devlin Stone's plan?*"

And then he plunged into the storm, leaving nothing behind but a bunch of cheerful, yellow daffodils scattered across the rain-slicked cobblestones of a lonely alley.

ACKNOWLEDGMENTS

Thanks first and foremost to Loren Coleman for introducing me to *BattleTech* and giving me the opportunity to write this book. I will always be grateful for the chance to play in this wonderful universe.

To Kris Rusch and Dean Smith, brilliant writers and the best teachers I have ever known. I would not have come this far without their mentoring, patience, and generosity.

I appreciate Randall Bills, who is always gracious in sharing his immense *BattleTech* knowledge. Herb Beas, who let me bang on House Steiner and Clan Hell's Horses with nary a complaint. Thanks to John Helfers—this book benefited tremendously from his editorial insight. To Øystein Tvedten and Patrick Wynne for their many contributions to this story. To Jason Schmetzer, a brilliant writer and editor. To David and Troy Stansel-Garner, good friends and the people who make everything work.

To all the folks at Catalyst Game Labs who have done amazing things in a short time. To the authors of the preceding *MechWarrior: Dark Age* novels—thank you for all your wonderful stories. To the artists of the Oregon Writers Network—it is an honor to be in your company.

To all the *BattleTech* fans spread throughout the Inner Sphere—thanks for keeping the dream alive!

And finally, to my sister Elissa Hattemer who has always believed in me. My children, Steven, Katie, and Andrew, who are joy incarnate. And, most of all, my thanks and love to my entertaining wife, Jo Anne, who fills the world with laughter.

ABOUT THE AUTHOR

Steven Mohan, Jr. was born in Washington state—and then promptly moved away. An Air Force brat, he visited many different parts of the world as a child, a habit he continued after he was commissioned as an officer in the United States Navy. Unlike Johnny Cash he hasn't been everywhere—but he's made a pretty good start. Currently he lives in Pueblo, Colorado (one more place marked off the list) with his wife and three children. He works as a senior quality engineer.

Steve began writing gaming fiction in 2004 with his first BattleCorps short story. Since then he's sold more than a half million words of fiction set in the *BattleTech* and *MechWarrior* universes, as well as writing for *Shadowrun*, *Leviathans*, *Eclipse Phase*, and *Arcane Legions*.

He's also sold original fiction to markets as diverse as *Interzone*, *Polyphony*, *On Spec*, and several original DAW anthologies. His stories have won honorable mention in *The Year's Best Science Fiction* and *The Year's Best Fantasy and Horror* and he is a former Pushcart Prize nominee.

A Bonfire of Worlds is his first novel.

BATTLETECH GLOSSARY

AUTOCANNON

A rapid-fire, auto-loading weapon. Light autocannons range from 30 to 90 millimeter (mm), and heavy autocannons may be from 80 to 120mm or more. They fire high-speed streams of high-explosive, armor-piercing shells.

BATTLEMECH

BattleMechs are the most powerful war machines ever built. First developed by Terran scientists and engineers, these huge vehicles are faster, more mobile, better-armored and more heavily armed than any twentieth-century tank. Ten to twelve meters tall and equipped with particle projection cannons, lasers, rapid-fire autocannon and missiles, they pack enough firepower to flatten anything but another BattleMech. A small fusion reactor provides virtually unlimited power, and BattleMechs can be adapted to fight in environments ranging from sun-baked deserts to subzero arctic icefields.

DROPSHIPS

Because interstellar JumpShips must avoid entering the heart of a solar system, they must "dock" in space at a considerable distance from a system's inhabited worlds. DropShips were developed for interplanetary travel. As the name implies, a DropShip is attached to hardpoints on the JumpShip's drive core, later to be dropped from the parent vessel after in-system entry. Though incapable of FTL travel, DropShips are highly maneuverable, well-armed and sufficiently aerodynamic to take off from and land on a planetary surface. The journey from the jump point to the inhabited worlds of a system usually requires a normal-space journey of several days or weeks, depending on the type of star.

FLAMER

Flamethrowers are a small but time-honored anti-infantry weapon in vehicular arsenals. Whether fusion-based or fuel-based, flamers spew fire in a tight beam that "splashes" against a target, igniting almost anything it touches.

GAUSS RIFLE

This weapon uses magnetic coils to accelerate a solid nickel-ferrous slug about the size of a football at an enemy target, inflicting massive damage through sheer kinetic impact at long range and with little heat. However, the accelerator coils and the slug's supersonic speed mean that while the Gauss rifle is smokeless and lacks the flash of an autocannon, it has a much more potent report that can shatter glass.

INDUSTRIALMECH

Also known as WorkMechs or UtilityMechs, they are large, bipedal or quadrupedal machines used for industrial purposes (hence the name). They are similar in shape to BattleMechs, which they predate, and feature many of the same technologies, but are built for non-combat tasks such as construction, farming, and policing.

JUMPSHIPS

Interstellar travel is accomplished via JumpShips, first developed in the twenty-second century. These somewhat ungainly vessels consist of a long, thin drive core and a sail resembling an enormous parasol, which can extend up to a kilometer in width. The ship is named for its ability to "jump" instantaneously across vast distances of space. After making its jump, the ship cannot travel until it has recharged by gathering up more solar energy.

The JumpShip's enormous sail is constructed from a special metal that absorbs vast quantities of electromagnetic energy from the nearest star. When it has soaked up enough energy, the sail transfers it to the drive core, which converts it into a space-twisting field. An instant later, the ship arrives at the next jump point, a distance of up to thirty light-years. This field is known as hyperspace, and its discovery opened to mankind the gateway to the stars.

JumpShips never land on planets. Interplanetary travel is carried out by DropShips, vessels that are attached to the JumpShip until arrival at the jump point.

LASER

An acronym for "Light Amplification through Stimulated Emission of Radiation." When used as a weapon, the laser damages the target by concentrating extreme heat onto a small area. BattleMech lasers are designated as small, medium or large. Lasers are also available as shoulder-fired weapons operating from a portable backpack power unit. Certain range-finders and targeting equipment also employ low-level lasers.

LRM

Abbreviation for "Long-Range Missile," an indirect-fire missile with a high-explosive warhead.

MACHINE GUN

A small autocannon intended for anti-personnel assaults. Typically non-armor-penetrating, machine guns are often best used against infantry, as they can spray a large area with relatively inexpensive fire.

PARTICLE PROJECTION CANNON (PPC)

One of the most powerful and long-range energy weapons on the battlefield, a PPC fires a stream of charged particles that outwardly functions as a bright blue laser, but also throws off enough static discharge to resemble a bolt of manmade lightning. The kinetic and heat impact of a PPC is enough to cause the vaporization of armor and structure alike, and most PPCs have the power to kill a pilot in his machine through an armor-penetrating headshot.

SRM

The abbreviation for "Short-Range Missile," a direct-trajectory missile with high-explosive or armor-piercing explosive warheads. They have a range of less than one kilometer and are only reliably accurate at ranges of less than 300 meters. They are more powerful, however, than LRMs.

SUCCESSOR LORDS

After the fall of the first Star League, the remaining members of the High Council each asserted his or her right to become First Lord. Their star empires became known as the Successor States and the rulers as Successor Lords. The Clan Invasion temporarily interrupted centuries of warfare known as the Succession Wars, which first began in 2786.

BATTLETECH ERAS

The *BattleTech* universe is a living, vibrant entity that grows each year as more sourcebooks and fiction are published. A dynamic universe, its setting and characters evolve over time within a highly detailed continuity framework, bringing everything to life in a way a static game universe cannot match.

To help quickly and easily convey the timeline of the universe—and to allow a player to easily "plug in" a given novel or sourcebook—we've divided *BattleTech* into six major eras.

STAR LEAGUE
(Present–2780)

Ian Cameron, ruler of the Terran Hegemony, concludes decades of tireless effort with the creation of the Star League, a political and military alliance between all Great Houses and the Hegemony. Star League armed forces immediately launch the Reunification War, forcing the Periphery realms to join. For the next two centuries, humanity experiences a golden age across the thousand light-years of human-occupied space known as the Inner Sphere. It also sees the creation of the most powerful military in human history.

(This era also covers the centuries before the founding of the Star League in 2571, most notably the Age of War.)

SUCCESSION WARS
(2781–3049)

Every last member of First Lord Richard Cameron's family is killed during a coup launched by Stefan Amaris. Following the thirteen-year war to unseat him, the rulers of each of the five Great Houses disband the Star League. General Aleksandr Kerensky departs with eighty percent of the Star League Defense Force beyond known space and the Inner Sphere collapses into centuries of warfare known as the Succession Wars that will eventually result in a massive loss of technology across most worlds.

CLAN INVASION
(3050–3061)

A mysterious invading force strikes the coreward region of the Inner Sphere. The invaders, called the Clans, are descendants of Kerensky's SLDF troops, forged into a society dedicated to becoming the greatest fighting force in history. With vastly superior technology and warriors, the Clans conquer world after world. Eventually this outside threat will forge a new Star League, something hundreds of years of warfare failed to accomplish. In addition, the Clans will act as a catalyst for a technological renaissance.

CIVIL WAR
(3062–3067)

The Clan threat is eventually lessened with the complete destruction of a Clan. With that massive external threat apparently neutralized, internal conflicts explode around the Inner Sphere. House Liao conquers its former Commonality, the St. Ives Compact; a rebellion of military units belonging to House Kurita sparks a war with their powerful border enemy, Clan Ghost Bear; the fabulously powerful Federated Commonwealth of House Steiner and House Davion collapses into five long years of bitter civil war.

JIHAD
(3067–3080)

Following the Federated Commonwealth Civil War, the leaders of the Great Houses meet and disband the new Star League, declaring it a sham. The pseudo-religious Word of Blake—a splinter group of ComStar, the protectors and controllers of interstellar communication—launch the Jihad: an interstellar war that pits every faction against each other and even against themselves, as weapons of mass destruction are used for the first time in centuries while new and frightening technologies are also unleashed.

DARK AGE
(3081-3150)

Under the guidance of Devlin Stone, the Republic of the Sphere is born at the heart of the Inner Sphere following the Jihad. One of the more extensive periods of peace begins to break out as the 32nd century dawns. The factions, to one degree or another, embrace disarmament, and the massive armies of the Succession Wars begin to fade. However, in 3132 eighty percent of interstellar communications collapses, throwing the universe into chaos. Wars erupt almost immediately, and the factions begin rebuilding their armies.

ILCLAN
(3151-present)

The once-invulnerable Republic of the Sphere lies in ruins, torn apart by the Great Houses and the Clans as they wage war against each other on a scale not seen in nearly a century. Mercenaries flourish once more, selling their might to the highest bidder. As Fortress Republic collapses, the Clans race toward Terra to claim their long-denied birthright and create a supreme authority that will fulfill the dream of Aleksandr Kerensky and rule the Inner Sphere by any means necessary: The ilClan.

LOOKING FOR MORE HARD HITTING BATTLETECH FICTION?

WE'LL GET YOU RIGHT BACK INTO THE BATTLE!

Catalyst Game Labs brings you the very best in *BattleTech* fiction, available at most ebook retailers, including Amazon, Apple Books, Kobo, Barnes & Noble, and more!

NOVELS

1. *Decision at Thunder Rift* by William H. Keith Jr.
2. *Mercenary's Star* by William H. Keith Jr.
3. *The Price of Glory* by William H. Keith, Jr.
4. *Warrior: En Garde* by Michael A. Stackpole
5. *Warrior: Riposte* by Michael A. Stackpole
6. *Warrior: Coupé* by Michael A. Stackpole
7. Wolves on the Border by Robert N. Charrette
8. *Heir to the Dragon* by Robert N. Charrette
9. *Lethal Heritage* (The Blood of Kerensky, Volume 1) by Michael A. Stackpole
10. *Blood Legacy* (The Blood of Kerensky, Volume 2) by Michael A. Stackpole
11. *Lost Destiny* (The Blood of Kerensky, Volume 3) by Michael A. Stackpole
12. *Way of the Clans* (Legend of the Jade Phoenix, Volume 1) by Robert Thurston
13. *Bloodname* (Legend of the Jade Phoenix, Volume 2) by Robert Thurston
14. *Falcon Guard* (Legend of the Jade Phoenix, Volume 3) by Robert Thurston
15. *Wolf Pack* by Robert N. Charrette
16. *Main Event* by James D. Long
17. *Natural Selection* by Michael A. Stackpole
18. *Assumption of Risk* by Michael A. Stackpole
19. *Blood of Heroes* by Andrew Keith
20. *Close Quarters* by Victor Milán
21. *Far Country* by Peter L. Rice
22. *D.R.T.* by James D. Long
23. *Tactics of Duty* by William H. Keith
24. *Bred for War* by Michael A. Stackpole
25. *I Am Jade Falcon* by Robert Thurston
26. *Highlander Gambit* by Blaine Lee Pardoe
27. *Hearts of Chaos* by Victor Milán
28. *Operation Excalibur* by William H. Keith
29. *Malicious Intent* by Michael A. Stackpole
30. *Black Dragon* by Victor Milán
31. *Impetus of War* by Blaine Lee Pardoe
32. *Double-Blind* by Loren L. Coleman
33. *Binding Force* by Loren L. Coleman
34. *Exodus Road* (Twilight of the Clans, Volume 1) by Blaine Lee Pardoe
35. *Grave Covenant* ((Twilight of the Clans, Volume 2) by Michael A. Stackpole
36. *The Hunters* (Twilight of the Clans, Volume 3) by Thomas S. Gressman
37. *Freebirth* (Twilight of the Clans, Volume 4) by Robert Thurston

YOUNG ADULT NOVELS

OMNIBUSES

NOVELLAS/SHORT STORIES

1. *Lion's Roar* by Steven Mohan, Jr.
2. *Sniper* by Jason Schmetzer
3. *Eclipse* by Jason Schmetzer
4. *Hector* by Jason Schmetzer
5. *The Frost Advances (Operation Ice Storm, Part 1)* by Jason Schmetzer
6. *The Winds of Spring (Operation Ice Storm, Part 2)* by Jason Schmetzer
7. *Instrument of Destruction (Ghost Bear's Lament, Part 1)* by Steven Mohan, Jr.
8. *The Fading Call of Glory (Ghost Bear's Lament, Part 2)* by Steven Mohan, Jr.
9. *Vengeance* by Jason Schmetzer
10. *A Splinter of Hope* by Philip A. Lee
11. *The Anvil* by Blaine Lee Pardoe
12. *A Splinter of Hope/The Anvil* (omnibus)
13. *Not the Way the Smart Money Bets (Kell Hounds Ascendant #1)* by Michael A. Stackpole
14. *A Tiny Spot of Rebellion (Kell Hounds Ascendant #2)* by Michael A. Stackpole
15. *A Clever Bit of Fiction (Kell Hounds Ascendant #3)* by Michael A. Stackpole
16. *Break-Away (Proliferation Cycle #1)* by Ilsa J. Bick
17. *Prometheus Unbound (Proliferation Cycle #2)* by Herbert A. Beas II
18. *Nothing Ventured (Proliferation Cycle #3)* by Christoffer Trossen
19. *Fall Down Seven Times, Get Up Eight (Proliferation Cycle #4)* by Randall N. Bills
20. *A Dish Served Cold (Proliferation Cycle #5)* by Chris Hartford and Jason M. Hardy
21. *The Spider Dances (Proliferation Cycle #6)* by Jason Schmetzer
22. *Shell Games* by Jason Schmetzer
23. *Divided We Fall* by Blaine Lee Pardoe
24. *The Hunt for Jardine (Forgotten Worlds, Part One)* by Herbert A. Beas II
25. *Rock of the Republic* by Blaine Lee Pardoe
26. *Finding Jardine (Forgotten Worlds, Part Two)* by Herbert A. Beas II

ANTHOLOGIES

1. *The Corps (BattleCorps Anthology, Volume 1)* edited by Loren. L. Coleman
2. *First Strike (BattleCorps Anthology, Volume 2)* edited by Loren L. Coleman
3. *Weapons Free (BattleCorps Anthology, Volume 3)* edited by Jason Schmetzer
4. *Onslaught: Tales from the Clan Invasion* edited by Jason Schmetzer
5. *Edge of the Storm* by Jason Schmetzer
6. *Fire for Effect (BattleCorps Anthology, Volume 4)* edited by Jason Schmetzer
7. *Chaos Born (Chaos Irregulars, Book 1)* by Kevin Killiany
8. *Chaos Formed (Chaos Irregulars, Book 2)* by Kevin Killiany
9. *Counterattack (BattleCorps Anthology, Volume 5)* edited by Jason Schmetzer
10. *Front Lines (BattleCorps Anthology Volume 6)* edited by Jason Schmetzer and Philip A. Lee
11. *Legacy* edited by John Helfers and Philip A. Lee
12. *Kill Zone (BattleCorps Anthology Volume 7)* edited by Philip A. Lee
13. *Gray Markets (A BattleCorps Anthology)*, edited by Jason Schmetzer and Philip A. Lee
14. *Slack Tide (A BattleCorps Anthology)*, edited by Jason Schmetzer and Philip A. Lee
15. *The Battle of Tukayyid* edited by John Helfers
16. *The Mercenary Life* by Randall N. Bills
17. *The Proliferation Cycle* edited by John Helfers and Philip A. Lee

MAGAZINES

1. *Shrapnel Issues #01–#05*